DANGERS

AND

DIFFICULTIES

DANGERS

AND

DIFFICULTIES

A Novel of World War II

JOHN

RHODES

ROUNDEL HOUSE

Published by Roundel House, Wilmington, North Carolina
johnrhodesbooks.com

Edited and designed by Girl Friday Productions
www.girlfridayproductions.com

Cover design: Anna Curtis
Project management: Sara Addicott
Editorial production: Kylee Hayes
Image credits: cover © Shutterstock/Laborant;
Shutterstock/Verina Marina Valerevna

ISBN (paperback): 978-1-7353736-7-6
ISBN (ebook): 978-1-7353736-8-3

Library of Congress Control Number: 2024920858

First edition

For Kimmie, RIP

For all who gave their lives for our freedom in 1944

I have been at the centers where the latest information is received, and I can state to the House that this operation is proceeding in a thoroughly satisfactory manner. Many **dangers and difficulties** which at this time last night appeared extremely formidable are behind us.

—Winston Churchill

Address to the House of Commons, 6 June 1944

PART ONE

Overlord

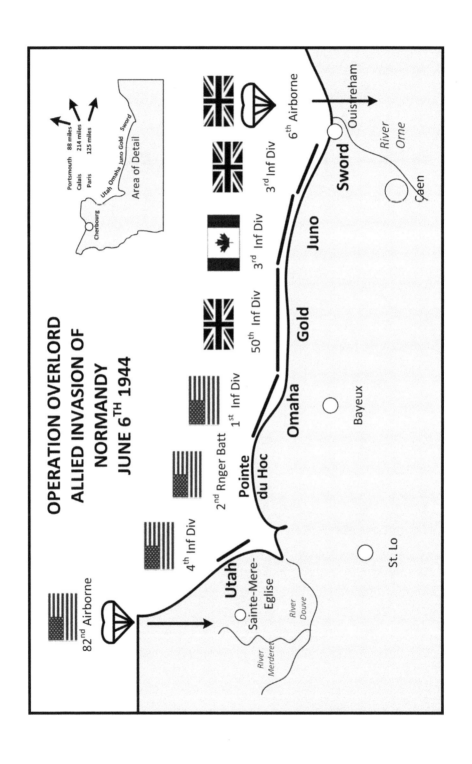

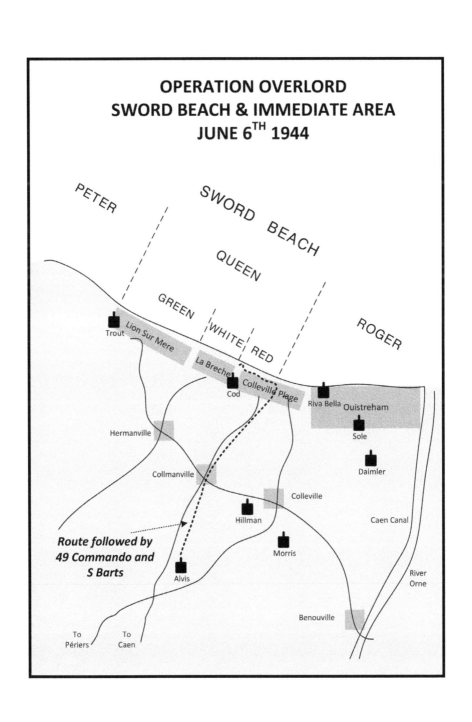

OPERATION OVERLORD
SWORD BEACH & IMMEDIATE AREA
JUNE 6TH 1944

PETER

SWORD BEACH

QUEEN

GREEN

WHITE RED

ROGER

Trout

Lion Sur Mere

La Breche

Colleville Plage

Cod

Riva Bella Ouistreham

Hermanville

Collmanville

Colleville

Sole

Daimler

Hillman

Caen Canal

Route followed by 49 Commando and S Barts

Morris

Alvis

River Orne

To Périers

To Caen

Benouville

ONE

LCA 1654, 524 LCA Flotilla (SS *Empire Arquebus*), Force S, Eastern Task Force, Baie de Seine
6 June 1944, 0630 Hours

Johnnie Shaux was cold, wet, and acutely uncomfortable, huddled on the deck of a landing craft in the company of thirty other cold, wet, and acutely uncomfortable men. The night seemed preternaturally black. The malevolent wind was making everyone as miserable as it could, whipping the English Channel into an uneven, lumpy chop.

The assault landing craft—officially known, in the Byzantine bureaucratic language of British armed forces, as a landing craft assault (LCA)—was chugging through the waves at its torpid top speed of 7 miles per hour. The LCA was rectangular in shape, forty feet long and ten feet wide, a shallow wooden barge with a closed ramp instead of a bow. Every so often, a wave would smack into the ramp at just the right angle to spray a deluge of cold seawater over the men aboard. The landing craft was crewed by four Royal Navy hostilities-only sailors whose average age, it seemed to Shaux, was about fifteen, and they were commanded by a pimpled RNVR sublieutenant who looked somewhat younger.

There were thirty soldiers around him, kernels of darkness in the night, mostly members of 49 Royal Marine Commando—Four-Niner Commando, as it was known. They were, like Shaux, huddled down below the gunwales in a vain attempt to escape the worst of the weather, loaded down by their big backpacks and their weapons; they were crammed together shoulder-to-shoulder along the sides, each alone with his thoughts. Flight Sergeant Cranmer crouched beside Shaux, weighed down not only by his rucksack and equipment but also by the bulk of a portable Wireless Set No. 62 radio with all its accoutrements.

Soon dawn would break, and LCA 1654 would reach the coast of Normandy. Shaux reflected that he had often gone into battle but always in the comparative comfort of a nice and dry aircraft cockpit far above the earth and at speeds approaching 400 miles per hour. It seemed a bit ironic, a bit of a step backward, that this time he should find himself wallowing along in the swell all the way down here.

* * *

SHAEF (Supreme Headquarters Allied Expeditionary Force) Forward, Southwick House, Hampshire, England
6 June 1944, 0630 Hours

Eleanor Shaux stared at the huge map of the English Channel on the wall in Southwick House, General Eisenhower's tactical headquarters just north of Portsmouth. At the top of the map was the south coast of England, with all the ports and harbors and estuaries from which the invasion fleet was being launched. The middle of the map was the English Channel, with red ribbons designating mine-swept lanes representing the planned courses of the Operation Neptune invasion fleet.

At the bottom of the map stretched the coast of Normandy, marked with the five beaches that constituted the main Allied landing zones. From west to east—from left to right as she looked at the map—lay the American landing beaches code-named Utah and Omaha, and then the British and Canadian beaches: Gold, Juno, and Sword.

The three British and Canadian beaches had originally been given code names standing for fish—goldfish, jellyfish, and swordfish—but

Winston Churchill had objected to the notion that men would be asked to die on a beach named Jelly and had peremptorily changed it to Juno.

Her eyes were drawn to the rightmost eastern beach, Sword, the landing target for the British 2nd Army's 3rd Infantry Division. The three-mile-long beach was divided into sectors—Oboe, Peter, Queen, and Roger—and each sector was itself divided, so that Queen was subdivided into Queen Green, White, and Red. There, just to the right—to the east—of the center of the village of Lion-sur-Mer was Queen Red, and somewhere to the north of Queen Red, somewhere in the predawn darkness, the LCA carrying Johnnie would be butting through the Channel chop.

For the past nine months, she had devoted every waking hour to planning for this moment, and it was very hard to realize that it was finally here. It was all supposed to have happened yesterday, but the Channel had been too rough for small landing craft and amphibious vehicles, and General Eisenhower, the Supreme Allied Commander, had called for an agonizingly suspenseful twenty-four-hour delay. The weather still wasn't much better today, but Ike had decided it was just good enough and had given the order to proceed. It must have been an excruciating decision, she thought; if Ike played safe and delayed, the next windows for the right tides and phases of the moon were weeks away. If he took the chance and went ahead, the weather could worsen suddenly, and catastrophe might strike the invasion forces.

She glanced up at the big time and date display on the wall: 6 June 1944, 0630. This was a moment that would go down in history, one way or the other, she thought: this was H-hour on D-Day at last.

* * *

LCA 1654
6 June 1944, 0645 Hours

The skies were noticeably brighter, and Shaux, peering over the gunwale, could see that LCA 1654 was just one in a line of LCAs that had been launched from the big freighter SS *Empire Arquebus*. It had been lowered down the side dangling from steel cables and then dumped unceremoniously the last three feet into the lumpy waves. The coast of

Normandy was an indistinct smudge ahead of them to the south. Off to the left, he could see the cruiser HMS *Scylla*, the Eastern Task Force flagship, and beyond that he could see long muzzle flashes as an elderly cruiser fired her 6-inch guns at the coastal village of Ouistreham. Beyond *Scylla* there were many other flashes stabbing the gloom as half a dozen more ships pounded the coastline to suppress German defensive fire.

Altogether, dozens of destroyers, cruisers, and battleships were battering this part of Hitler's Atlantic Wall, his long chain of defensive gun batteries, beach obstructions, minefields, machine-gun nests, pillboxes, antiaircraft flak batteries, anti-tank devices, strongpoints, and endless miles of barbed wire. Eleanor had told Shaux that Erwin Rommel, the Desert Fox, Germany's best general, was in charge of the fortifications. Inland, waiting for any Allied troops that could penetrate the wall and advance off the beaches, were tens of thousands of German troops with their thousands of artillery pieces and Panzer tanks.

Shaux glanced at his watch and saw it was 0645. Another three miles—perhaps thirty minutes—to the beach.

He sat back down against the bulwark and fumbled with his waterproof cigarette case. He lit two cigarettes with his prized American Zippo lighter—a gift from his friend Bob O'Neill, a USAAF B17 pilot—and handed one to Cranmer.

"Half an hour to the beach, Flight," he said.

"Can't 'ardly wait, sir," Cranmer said.

Shaux drew on his cigarette. He didn't like the sea. He'd almost drowned in it twice, once escaping Dunkirk back in 1940 and once in the Mediterranean in 1942, and he didn't want to attempt a hat trick. Yet here he was—voluntarily—in a small boat in rising seas, sailing towards an enemy coastline from which dozens of guns were firing back.

No, he thought, upon reflection, it wasn't ironic he was here. It seemed strangely inevitable, the logical result of a logical sequence of events.

Last year, he'd been flying de Havilland Mosquitos. The last mission involved bombing a U-boat pen in the far north of Norway. The attack had been successful in putting the pen out of service, but he'd lost every other aircraft in the squadron and landed with his navigator dead beside him. No one else in the history of the RAF had ever managed to lose an entire squadron in a single op, but the Air Ministry propaganda machine had smoothly reframed the mission from what Shaux considered a disaster into a triumph, with Shaux cast in the role of an intrepid, invincible hero. An RAF photographer had instructed him to look not at the camera but off into the sky above the photographer's right shoulder as he took Shaux's picture. The resulting image, as it appeared in several newspapers, left it up to the viewer to decide whether Shaux was searching the skies for enemy aircraft, or mournfully recalling his lost squadron, or contemplating eternity with appropriately heroic equanimity.

He'd been "rested"—RAF parlance for being taken out of active operational duties—and assigned to the loathsome job of touring factories and dockyards as an officially designated war hero: "And now, ladies and gentlemen, let's welcome the man who bombed Hitler's U-boat pens . . . *Johnnie Shaux!*" Then Eleanor had asked him a casual question about the best way to target tactical fighter sweeps against moving enemy armor, pinpoint attacks in a fast-moving battle space. That had led to the notion of Air Ground Support Control (AGSC), already successfully pioneered in North Africa and the invasion of Italy, which had led to the notion that ground forces invading Normandy should have among them experienced RAF officers who could radio in Mustang and Typhoon aircraft to strafe enemy positions and vehicles, which had led—inevitably, with twenty-twenty hindsight—to Shaux sitting in a LCA, chugging towards the coast of Normandy in one of the first waves of the great Allied assault, with Flight Sergeant Cranmer and his radio beside him.

When the concept of AGSC had been adopted, Shaux had been attached temporarily to an RAF Servicing Commando unit—Shaux had previously had no idea that the RAF, like the Army and the Marines, had its own commandos—and had been sent to Achnacarry in the Scottish Highlands for commando training.

It had been an interesting experience. He and a contingent of other trainees had travelled by train to Spean Bridge railway station, where they were met by Color Sergeant Johnston of the Royal Marines.

"These here rucksacks are Pattern 42 Bergens," Johnston said. "Each Bergen contains your necessary clothing and supplies, your first aid kit, and your rations, enough for forty-eight hours. These webbing straps are your 1937 Pattern Web Equipment that carry your M1911 sidearm in its holster, your Fairbairn-Sykes fighting knife in its sheath, your water bottles, your grenades, and your ammunition pouches. Put the webbing straps on first, and then your Bergen."

Shaux struggled his way into his webbing, festooned with canvas pouches containing absurdly heavy objects.

Johnston inspected him and shook his head.

"Posture, sir, posture! If you stand up straight"—he stepped behind Shaux and jerked his shoulders back—"and keep your straps nice and snug, like this"—he tugged sharply on several straps—"then you might look less like a Glasgow drunk on a Saturday night and more like a member of His Majesty's fighting forces.

"Sir," he added. "Now that's sorted, this here's your Bergen."

Just as the webbing and its pouches weighed down his chest, the Bergen knapsack now weighed down his back. Perhaps it would balance his drunk-like posture.

"Now, all trainees will take a M28M1 Thompson submachine gun from them racks there and form up on the road outside the station in columns of three."

The trainees organized themselves into the semblance of a military platoon.

"Your tommy guns are fully loaded and lightly triggered, so you may want to check that the safety is on. They have a tendency to fire if dropped."

Shaux stared at his gun as if it was a cobra coiled and ready to strike, and gingerly felt for the safety catch just behind the trigger guard. It was in the back-facing On position, thank God.

"Never, ever handle a weapon without verifying it's safe," Johnston said, as Shaux inwardly berated himself for such a stupid error. "You're supposed to kill the enemy, not each other."

It occurred to Shaux that Johnston had made sure everyone's safety catch was on before they touched the weapons, and perhaps the guns were not really loaded, but that didn't detract from the sharpness of the lesson.

Johnston stood back and inspected the untidy column of trainees, shaking his head, perhaps in sorrow but more probably in pity.

"Achnacarry Castle is eight miles up the road, just a nice walk to stretch your legs. Any trainee who fails to keep up will be RTU'd."

It began to drizzle. Johnston drew himself up like a drill sergeant on parade.

"Squad will advance: QUICK . . . march!"

The next month convinced Shaux that he was immortal, that he could survive any hardship. The trainees slept under canvas and cooked their own food. They marched—in full equipment—at least ten miles every day. They often went through an assault course, a series of muddy obstacles to crawl under or climb over, interspersed with rope bridges and cables over marshes and gullies.. They did gymnastics twice a day. They waded chest-deep along the chill shoreline of Loch Arkaig to simulate wading ashore in a beach landing.

Occasionally Johnston or one of his assistant torturers would toss a live grenade in the recruits' general direction or fire a Sten subma-chine gun just over their heads.

"Just a reminder to keep your bloody heads down," Johnston would explain.

Every exercise was preceded by the threat of being RTU'd—returned to unit, sent back in disgrace for not being tough enough to survive. Color Sergeant Johnston seemed certain that he'd have to RTU Shaux—the officer who looks like a Glasgow drunk on a Saturday night, as he always referred to him—but Shaux discovered in himself an inner stubbornness, a sheer bloody-mindedness, to keep going, to prove Johnston wrong. Each night he'd collapse onto his sleeping bag on the rock-hard ground with every muscle aching. At least there were no insects in his bedding—it was far too cold for them to survive. Each morning, as dawn was breaking, he'd be woken by the harsh sound of bagpipes played badly, and scramble from his tent to face another day's trials and tribulations.

Shaux had never thought of himself as unfit or weak, but as he pulled himself hand-over-hand along a rope across a rushing stream, he realized just how weak and feeble he really was. If he let go, he knew, he would not only fall ten feet and break an ankle or worse but also be RTU'd promptly, and doubtless Johnston would chuckle as he pronounced his fate. Best not to fall.

Nor had Shaux thought of himself as squeamish or pacifistic—after all, he had spent the last four years shooting down more enemy aircraft than he cared to remember—but at first, he had found it very hard to punch another trainee in the face or knock him over and wrestle him into submission in hand-to-hand combat.

"Not bad, sir," Johnston had said when Shaux finally grappled another trainee into surrender, half buried in mud. "But next time just kick 'im in the nuts—it's much less effort. Plan ahead for it; look for the opportunity and then seize it. Carpe diem, as they say."

He had been horrified when Johnston had explained how to knife a man—"upwards, under 'is ribs, all the way up to the handle, as hard as you can, and give it a good wiggle when you're all the way in"—and he had been even more appalled when Johnston made them practice on a freshly killed deer: "A stirring motion, sir, round and round, like you're stirring a big pot of stew, to make sure you hit its 'eart."

One evening they had marched twelve miles away from the camp and finally halted just as night was falling. A single jeep was waiting, and Johnston climbed into it.

"Any trainee arriving back at camp without all 'is equipment gets RTU'd," Johnston announced. "And the last man back gets RTU'd regardless."

The jeep had departed just as the moon rose above the glen.

Somehow, a month after that first march up from Spean Bridge, Shaux was still standing, and he and the other surviving trainees paraded before Achnacarry Castle to receive their black-and-red Combined Operations badges from the presiding colonel.

"I knew you'd do it, sir," Johnston told Shaux. "The stringy-looking weak ones always seem to, begging your pardon."

And now, by coincidence, Color Sergeant Johnston was sitting two places along from Shaux as the LCA pushed towards Normandy in the growing daylight. Doubtless Johnston was planning ahead for the opportunity to kick a member of the German Wehrmacht in the nuts.

* * *

SHAEF Forward, Southwick House
6 June 1944, 0645 Hours

Eleanor stood in the map room, listening to reports filtering back from the landing areas. She knew the tide rose from west to east—from left to right as she looked at the map—as it flooded up the Channel from the Bay of Biscay, so the landings were already beginning on the western American beaches, Omaha and Utah. The first two infantry waves had landed, and she heard the tactical intelligence officer (TIO) reporting that thirty-two tanks had already come ashore on Utah Beach.

The TIO also announced that the inshore squadron of the Royal Navy Bombardment Force D off the eastern British beaches—HMS *Arathusa*, HMS *Frobisher*, and all the rest—had opened fire with their 6- and 8-inch guns. They would be pounding the beaches and the beach paths leading inland through the dunes and all the known and suspected German strongpoints. They'd fire for the next forty-five minutes and cease firing just before the first landing craft, Johnnie's among them, reached the surf.

So far, she thought, there had been no major disasters. So far, the timetable seemed to be holding. There were reports that many of the overnight paratroop and glider units, both British and American, had been blown off course, but they wouldn't really know until full daylight.

She looked around the room. Eisenhower had just walked in; they said he'd been sleeping through the early hours. He seemed calm, she thought, for a man who was taking the biggest risk in the recorded history of the world. Someone gave him a cup of coffee, and he lit a cigarette.

"How are we doing, Eleanor?" he asked as he passed her.

"So far, so good, sir."

He paused to ruffle the hair on Charlie's head. Charlie was her big black Bouviers de Flandres, the only dog with unlimited access to Southwick House.

"Paws crossed, Charlie," Eisenhower said. "We need all the luck we can get."

He moved on to consult with his staff, and Eleanor secretly crossed her own fingers, an absurdly childish gesture for a woman who was widely known to be the most ruthlessly objective person in the whole of SHAEF, known for the coldly scientific precision of her analyses, notorious for her watchword: "There is no room for luck in mathematics."

And yet, she thought, luck was everything. Luck had given her an intuitive understanding of mathematics when there was nothing in her background to explain it. Luck had given her the insight to see the war as a mathematical construct, a zero-sum function building on Princeton mathematician John von Neumann's new theory of games. Luck had brought her resulting mathematical model to the attention of Winston Churchill, who had catapulted her into the highest circles of Allied war planning. And luck had brought her Johnnie, in the form of a casual meeting in a library in Oxford, when they had both needed the same textbook at the same time.

They had married late in 1940, as the London blitz reached its crescendo. Well, they hadn't really married; they'd legalized an affair. He was a fighter pilot, flying into acute danger every day. She was working sixteen hours a day developing her model, nicknamed Red Tape by Churchill. They spent the nights in each other's arms and then went their separate ways; he was her lover rather than her husband, and she was his mistress rather than his wife.

They had lived that way for two years. The more he flew, the greater the chance that he'd be shot down and killed. It had gone on and on until the tension of waiting for him to die had finally become too much to bear. Well, that wasn't really true either, she admitted to herself. At that time, they'd been stationed in Malta in the Mediterranean, and she'd missed the high-pressure challenge of working for Churchill, the thrill of telephoning his private office in 10 Downing Street and saying, "I'd like ten minutes of the PM's time, if that's possible," knowing that the ten minutes would be arranged expeditiously.

This combination of reasons—the screaming uncertainty of whether this was the day Johnnie would die and the frustration of not sitting at the conference tables when the big decisions were made—had finally caused her to abandon Johnnie in Malta in the autumn of 1942. She'd tried to bury herself in her work, but to no avail. During the following year, she'd realized she couldn't live without him. She was fiercely independent, a woman at the top of her profession carving out a new form of applied mathematics—the kind of person Eisenhower would ask, "How are we doing, Eleanor?" on the morning of D-Day, for

God's sake!—and yet her happiness, her self-respect, were entirely and absurdly dependent on one specific man out of the two billion men on earth.

She'd gone to him, not literally crawling on her hands and knees but certainly sobbing uncontrollably, and he had taken her back. She was an addict, she had concluded. She was incapable of moderation. She was addicted to cigarettes and coffee, addicted to the intellectual challenge of her model, addicted to the absolute discipline—the austere beauty—of mathematics, addicted to moving in the innermost circles of power, addicted to being a powerful woman moving among powerful men, and addicted to Johnnie—even more than ever since he had returned from Scotland with a newly and delightfully chiseled body.

She glanced at the clock; it was now 0648. In approximately 42 minutes, he'd be under machine-gun fire. She lit a cigarette.

TWO

LCA 1654
6 June 1944, 0710 Hours

Shaux stared ahead towards the beach, now a gray-green line beyond the steel-gray breakers. He guessed it was ten minutes away at this speed, fifteen at the most. He had often anticipated this moment but never how deafening it would be. Big naval shells were screaming over his head and exploding like thunderclaps on the beach and the dunes behind them, throwing up clouds of dirt and sand. The LCA's two Ford V8 engines were yammering unsilenced, so that every word had to be shouted into the next man's ear. Waves smacked against the sides of the landing craft, and the wind shrieked and snatched at everything that was not tied down.

A salvo of 3-inch rockets howled overhead, long columns of orange flame that lit up the surface of the sea as if it was a brilliant sunset. They were fired from a big LCT(R) far behind Shaux's LCA. Shaux was not a fan of rockets. They were far inferior to guns in his opinion, very hard to aim, and even when you aimed correctly, had a strong tendency to wander off course. Still, he acknowledged that they looked very dramatic in newsreel films, and no doubt many war reporters back in the fleet were taking lots of photographs and making newsreels.

Ahead, close to the beach, he could see the hard-to-believe shapes of DD Shermans swimming ashore. These waterproof amphibious tanks weighed thirty tons and were wrapped in tall canvas screens. They were wallowing through the breakers, pushed by boat propellers driven off their rear track idlers. They looked clumsy and vulnerable as well as ridiculous, Shaux thought. He sent an urgent prayer for their survival, although he did not believe in God. If he and the other occupants of LCA 1654 were going to get off the beach alive, it would be because the DDs had landed first and cleared the way.

A loud flat thud, like the loudest clap of thunder imaginable, overwhelmed all other sounds. To his right, off Juno Beach, Shaux saw a large Canadian landing craft lift itself from the sea in two separate hundred-foot-long pieces, spilling tanks and troops into the water before crashing back down in two enormous splashes. The minesweepers had done the best they could, he was certain, but this must have been a mine too many.

It often struck Shaux that the people doing the actual fighting on the front line have almost no idea whether they are winning or losing. All they know is what they can see. On the other hand, the people away from the front lines, like Eleanor back in SHAEF, have a much clearer idea. Was everyone in the invasion fleet on course, or was this wretched wind blowing everyone astray? Was LCA 1654 even approaching the right beach? How were the Americans doing away to the west? Or the Canadians on Juno Beach? Were German Panzer columns forming up to launch counterattacks as soon as LCA 1654 reached the shallows? Eleanor would know; all he knew was that it was very cold and very wet.

He could hear a couple of Australian accents among the commandos as they sorted out their gear and checked their weapons and lit their last cigarettes. Shaux had really liked Australia when he'd been down there in 1942; perhaps he and Eleanor should consider emigrating when the war was over. Someone had once asked him to describe Australia in a single word, and he had answered, "Clean." Unlike the Normandy beaches, there were no tank traps or rolls of barbed wire on Bondi Beach, no machine-gun emplacements in the dunes overlooking it, and no mines in the warm waters of the Pacific Ocean. It was something to discuss. Eleanor had predicted that the war would end less than a year after an invasion, and now the invasion was finally happening. The phrase "after the war" was acquiring a sense of realism.

Of course, he reflected, it might be a hair premature to be planning his long-term future while approaching a heavily fortified enemy beach.

Flight Sergeant Cranmer hauled himself to his feet beside Shaux and began to assemble his load. He was a big man, and he needed to be. Shaux estimated that his Bergen weighed forty pounds, his radio another thirty pounds, and all his other bits and pieces probably another thirty pounds. As if all this was not enough, he picked up a PIAT handheld anti-tank gun and slung it over his shoulder.

Shaux picked up his Thompson submachine gun—his "tommy gun," as it was universally named—and checked the safety catch. He did not like this type of gun. It was very popular among American gangsters, so they said, and it made him feel as if he was Bugsy Capone, or whatever that racketeer chap in Chicago was named. At least Shaux's tommy gun was fitted with a straight magazine rather than one of those weird circular things.

Back in Scotland, he'd asked Color Sergeant Johnston how accurate a tommy gun was.

"It's all right at short ranges, sir."

"How short?"

"Well, it's really good within two feet," he had said.

The RNVR sublieutenant shouted into a loud-hailer. "Ten minutes, gentlemen, prepare for landing. Ten minutes." His voice cracked on the last syllable.

"Ready, Flight?" Shaux yelled into Cranmer's ear.

"Can't 'ardly wait, sir," Cranmer said again.

* * *

SHAEF Forward, Southwick House
6 June 1944, 0710 Hours

In the past year, the Americans had emerged as the dominant partners in the Anglo-American alliance. Eleanor had emerged as one of the Brits the Americans accepted—well, tolerated—in their counsels, in part because she did not resent American leadership or consider it insulting and humiliating, as many in the British government and military circles did. In part they accepted her because she had something—her model—they found useful and had not yet duplicated or surpassed. In part they accepted her because she could bridge the gap between diplomatic and military policy as well as the gap across the Atlantic. And in part—she often thought in large part—they accepted her because she was only a woman, and she was therefore, in the last analysis, no professional threat. When the war was finally won and the spoils were distributed among the winners, she—and all the other women contributing to the war effort—would be dismissed to return from whence they came, and the balance of the sexes would revert to its rightfully patriarchal status quo ante.

The amphibious attack on Normandy, and everything that went into it, was code-named Operation Neptune, the first phase of the much larger overall invasion plan that was named Operation Overlord. For the last nine months, Eleanor had worked closely with Walter "Beetle" Smith, Eisenhower's chief of staff, and his British deputy Frederick Morgan, as they and their staffs developed the plans for this morning in exquisite detail. She had loved it. Everything demanded exactitude, every contingency had to be anticipated and a counter developed, and everything had to fit together seamlessly. The plan required thousands of ships, thousands of aircraft, and tens of thousands of men to work as one. Neptune was an intricately designed machine, like a perfect timepiece crafted by Swiss watchmakers but on a vast scale.

One thing that could not be planned, however, was the weather. She glanced across the room to where Jim Stagg, SHAEF's chief meteorological officer, was gathered with other senior Met people staring at their weather maps. Eisenhower had made the decision to delay the invasion from yesterday until this morning but only because Stagg had convinced him that the weather would be too bad yesterday and just about tolerable today.

The invasion required the correct tide at dawn—rising but not fully risen so that underwater obstacles would be visible and landing craft could get close to the beaches but avoid getting stuck aground. It required no worse than moderate winds so that airborne troops would not get blown off-course, and it required the moon to be full with no low clouds so that the pilots could find their targets in the hours of darkness before the invasion. The window of opportunity for these conditions was from the fourth to the sixth of June; the next opportunity would be at least two weeks away and perhaps much longer.

Poor Jim! The Met map showed a low-pressure area south of Greenland and another north of Scotland. Between them stretched a weather front like a giant curlicue arcing gracefully southeastward across the Atlantic from Greenland to Bordeaux in southern France, and then curling upwards across France, the Low Countries, and Norway before turning again and wrapping itself around the Orkneys in a final flourish.

The weather would be bad for days and even weeks. But would it be too bad? Jim had persuaded Ike to delay a day, from Monday 5 June to Tuesday 6 June, and Ike had decided to go ahead today rather than face a delay of weeks or even months. Now the question was whether the winds and tides would let the landing craft come ashore safely and whether the two thousand Allied ships in the Channel would be able to hold their stations and keep their timetables.

She and Jim often joked about the differences in their disciplines, her watchword that there is "no luck in mathematics" in sharp contrast to the wild vagaries of the weather that made forecasting so difficult.

"Don't worry, Jim," she had told him. "Meteorology is an exact science, and it's not your fault that it hasn't been discovered yet."

She recalled that another invasion fleet had sailed these waters in 1588 when King Philip II of Spain sent his armada to conquer England. It had been the greatest naval force ever assembled, before which the English navy was greatly outnumbered and outgunned. But the winds had arisen—these same winds—and blown the Spanish fleet right through the Channel, up the North Sea, around Scotland, and down the coast of Ireland, and half the mighty galleons and half their crews perished beneath the waves.

Now an even greater armada had been assembled and stood to sea: How would the winds decide its fate?

* * *

LCA 1654
6 June 1944, 0720 Hours
Sword Beach seemed much narrower than Shaux thought it should be, and darker. He guessed the wind must be pushing the tide higher up the sand than forecast, and the pall of thick, oily smoke above the beach was turning everything into a gloomy gray. Neither the high tide nor the pall of smoke were good: the high tide would leave little room on the beach for landing, and the smoke would make it difficult for aircraft to find their targets.

The navy was still firing salvo after salvo against the enemy but was now aiming two or three hundred yards inland, so their shells were exploding in rumbling thuds rather than sharp cracks. Shaux knew the naval bombardment was designed to "walk" ahead of the troops landing on the beaches and pushing their way into the dunes.

Above the dunes, he could see a line of holiday houses. Built so that families could enjoy the innocent pleasures of the golden sands on sunny summer days, they were now fortified machine-gun nests.

Shaux could see men lying on the beach—either dead or taking cover from enemy gunfire—and men wading ashore through the shallows from an LCA ahead of Shaux's. A Cromwell tank with a massive flail in front of it was pushing up the beach towards the dunes, sending up a spray of sand as it cleared a mine-free pathway. Two Sherman tanks followed closely in its tracks, while two more Shermans were smoldering at the water's edge.

An explosion shook one of the holiday houses overlooking the dunes, and most of the men on the beach—those who were alive, Shaux realized—jumped up and ran forward. Shaux guessed the explosion had been caused by a mortar fired by the soldiers on the beach, and the house was a German machine-gun strongpoint. But there were still plenty of other strongpoints; a large-caliber machine gun began to stammer, and the running men threw themselves down again—or perhaps were thrown down.

"Two minutes!" the sublieutenant shouted into his loud-hailer.

Shaux checked his equipment one last time and rolled his shoulders to adjust the weight of his Bergen. The shallows and the beach were just like Loch Arkaig and the assault course back in Scotland, he thought—he'd survived those, and this was just another exercise. The only difference was that if he failed here, he'd be RTU'd to a French cemetery.

Two sailors climbed precariously onto the forward bulkheads, ready to release the ramp. Another machine gun began to chatter, and Shaux heard rounds buzzing over his head. One of the sailors in the bow toppled forward into the waves. Another scrambled up to take his place.

The LCA directly ahead of 1654 lowered its ramp with a mighty splash. The commandos aboard began to jump down into the sea and wade ashore. The water was waist-high, Shaux saw. Thank God! He'd been afraid that he might have to disembark in deeper water and swim ashore—try to swim ashore—weighed down by all his gear.

The chattering machine gun turned its attention to the men in the water around the LCA ahead. One commando, then another and yet another, spun round with their arms uplifted in similar gestures and then collapsed into the water as one, as if they had been rehearsing together in a chorus line and agreed on the appropriate posture for being shot dead before even reaching dry land.

LCA 1645 caught an unusually strong wave and surged forward, barely missing the landing craft and the men ahead of it. The sublieutenant yelled, and the sailors on the bulkheads released the ramp. LCA 1645 jerked to a sudden halt—they must have hit an underwater obstacle—and everyone pitched forward onto their hands and knees. It was as well they did, as more machine-gun rounds snarled just over their heads.

"Come on, lads!" Color Sergeant Johnston shouted.

The men clambered to their feet and began jumping down into the water. Shaux followed, stumbling down the ramp and almost falling into the water. Beside him, Cranmer missed his footing and slid forward, grabbing at Shaux as he did so. Shaux tried to stay upright, but the combined weight of Cranmer and his equipment pulled him off the ramp and under the water. They came up coughing and spluttering, chest-deep in the swells. The sublieutenant shouted at them through his loud-hailer to get moving.

Shaux began to wade towards the beach. He had seen newsreels of the Allied landings in Sicily and Italy, with the troops disembarking methodically and wading forward manfully, ready to do battle with the enemy. Any illusions that Shaux might have had that he would land like that were gone forever; he was splashing ignominiously through the shallows like a half-drowned rat and being yelled at by a teenager for being too slow and holding up traffic.

He stumbled on something squishy in the shallows and saw it was a dead marine. Looking along the water's edge, he saw a whole line of bodies gently moving with the waves.

A machine gun chattered in his direction yet again. Shaux threw himself down, half in and half out of the water. He was still clutching his tommy gun, but, alas, the enemy was more than two feet away. A dead man floated beside him.

This is all going really well, he thought, as machine guns played along the water's edge. The theoretically waterproof radio had been drowned and might not work. The heavy smoke over the beaches probably meant that precision air operations wouldn't be possible, so he had nothing to do, even if the radio was working after all. And he still hadn't reached the beach.

* * *

SHAEF Forward, Southwick House
6 June 1944, 0720 Hours

The TIO announced that landing craft of the 524 LCA Flotilla, Johnnie's flotilla, were now at the beachhead and unloading, and an officer on a ladder placed a smaller wooden marker with 524 painted on it against Sword Beach. Eleanor was surprised that on this of all occasions, having spent almost four years waiting to be informed that Johnnie was dead, she found she was convinced he would not die. The notion of Johnnie going into battle by storming an enemy-held beach wearing a steel helmet rather than a leather pilot's helmet was so unexpected, so unlikely, that the threat to his life seemed unlikely too.

Bramble, her senior deputy, came into the map room. He was, she considered, the least military man in the British Isles, if not the whole of Europe. He headed the growing team of mathematicians and analysts who ran the Red Tape mathematical model. He had been with her since the Battle of Britain, profoundly irritating and irreplaceable.

When Beetle Smith had become COSSAC—chief of staff to the supreme allied commander—the name of Eleanor's group of analysts and mathematicians had reverted to its previous name of MI6-3b, with an (S) added to it for bureaucratic reasons she had never known. Eleanor had been promoted to the WAAF rank of air commandant, making her the equivalent of a brigadier. Bramble was now an improbable lieutenant colonel.

Eleanor's rank was a great source of amusement to her and Johnnie because he was a mere group captain and therefore obligated under the Emergency Powers (Defence) Act of 1939 to obey her slightest whim or face charges of insubordination or worse—whims she took great pleasure in indulging.

Her principal responsibility in the Overlord plan was Enemy Intentions Assessment, the job of predicting German reactions to a broad variety of Allied strategies and tactics. EIA, as it was known, caused her to become a sort of devil's advocate, finding and pointing out weaknesses in other people's plans, often—usually—to their great annoyance.

The Allies had to have, and had achieved, air superiority over northwestern France. The invasion fleet and the men on the beaches would have no chance of survival if they were open to enemy bombing and strafing. It was exactly the same situation—in reverse—as the Battle of Britain in 1940, when the German Luftwaffe was trying to drive the RAF out of the south of England and the Channel so that the Wehrmacht could invade. The RAF had not been driven away, the Luftwaffe had not achieved control of the air above England, and therefore Hitler had not been able to invade. Now, in 1944, the combined forces of the American Eighth Air Force and the RAF had been able to so wound the Luftwaffe that the Allies controlled the airspace above the beachheads and the invasion could take place.

This was now the fourth Allied amphibious attack in Europe in eighteen months—preceded by Operations Torch into Morocco, Husky into Sicily, and Avalanche into Italy—and the Allies had learned a great deal. One particularly important lesson had been the need for very close air support for units fighting their way inland from the beaches. Troops fighting ditch-to-ditch or house-to-house needed to be able to call in fighter-bombers to destroy particular tanks or particular enemy pillboxes or bomb particular roads. That role had traditionally been supplied by artillery, and still was, but the ability to bomb or strafe the enemy from above added a very powerful capability, particularly against moving tanks, trucks, and columns of men.

Johnnie had often conducted fighter sweeps across enemy territory, operations known in the RAF as "rhubarbs." He had therefore been a natural choice to coordinate these operations from the ground. He had spent the past few months working with infantry platoon and company commanders and tank squadron commanders, developing and practicing the air strike request process and the necessary signals protocols, and working with the British and American air forces to streamline their responsiveness—to be able to have a rocket-armed Typhoon, or a B-25 Mitchell carrying 500-pound bombs, above a target within two or three minutes. His friend Bob O'Neill, now a one-star general in the Eighth Air Force posted to SHAEF, had jokingly referred to him as Lord Rhubarb, and the name had stuck.

There was very little friction between the American and British air forces, perhaps because their skills and resources were complementary rather than competitive. The US Eighth Air Force bombed by day, for example, while the RAF's Bomber Command bombed at night, and comparisons were not drawn easily. In addition, each respected the other's tenacity and sacrifice: both RAF and USAAF aircrews suffered appallingly high casualty rates—50 percent or more—and yet kept fighting.

Unfortunately, the same mutual regard could not be said of the armies, perhaps because the two most successful generals, the American George Patton and the British "Monty" Montgomery, were bitter rivals. Montgomery was now in command of 21st Army Group, which included all the British, American, Free French, and Canadian armies, while Patton, to his fury, was temporarily sidelined in command of the nonexistent FUSAG, the First United States Army Group, a massive deception designed to fool the Germans into thinking that the invasion would take place across the Straits of Dover and that Normandy was just a sideshow.

Monty was aboard a cruiser in the Channel, waiting for the beaches to be taken so that he could land, probably tomorrow. Patton was sulking in Dover, doubtless hoping Montgomery would encounter difficulties and he would be asked to take over.

Eleanor thought they were both odious, but perhaps it took arrogance and egotism to succeed on the battlefield. Generals like the American Omar Bradley and the British Alan Brooke were far more pleasant, but perhaps they lacked the necessary killer instinct. She thought of them as organizers rather than warriors, just as she thought of Ike as more a diplomat than a soldier.

THREE

Sword Beach
6 June 1944, 0730 Hours
New explosions shook the houses overlooking Sword Beach, and again the enemy machine guns ceased firing. Someone ahead of Shaux—perhaps it was Johnston—yelled a command into the sudden silence, and dozens of prone figures rose and started moving up the beach. Shaux picked himself up from the water's edge and lumbered forward, hampered by his equipment and finding it unexpectedly difficult to find traction in the wet sand. Cranmer grunted at his side.

They worked their way through a band of so-called Czech hedgehog anti-tank barriers, six-foot-high contraptions made of steel I-beams welded together at wide angles like giant knucklebones. A few yards further up the beach, they encountered a thicket of barbed wire. The twisted corpses of entangled marines hung within it. Machine guns abruptly reopened fire, and Shaux threw himself down behind one of the bodies. Cranmer fell with him, one arm over Shaux to protect him. Shaux had not thought the phlegmatic Cranmer capable of emotion or generosity but found it oddly touching. Perhaps Cranmer was just as nervous, just as wound up, as he was.

Shaux glanced back. Shells from the distant shapes of cruisers and destroyers off the coast were still howling overhead. More LCAs were approaching the beach, and more Shermans were wallowing in the breakers. There were whitecaps on the waves, and the steel-gray sea seemed rougher. A DUKW—an American-made amphibious truck universally known as a Duck—emerged from the sea and burst into flames. Two soldiers, their uniforms on fire, leapt back into the water.

The beach was beginning to get crowded as more men and equipment waded ashore, but it seemed to Shaux that there was no point to any of it if the marines here in the advanced guard couldn't get off the beach and silence the enemy guns. There were dozens of ships waiting beyond the shallows, a vast armada that should be pressing forward but that was, until the beach was cleared, on the point of stalling.

This was warfare cast back to the primitive slaughter of the last war, he thought. In that conflict, men had risen from their trenches and advanced across a mine-strewn, barbed-wire-festooned no-man's-land in the teeth of enemy machine-gun fire. Now, in this conflict, men were wading ashore onto a mine-strewn, barbed-wire-festooned beach in the teeth of enemy machine-gun fire. Nothing really changes, he thought; all warfare, since the dawn of time, had always come down to sharp weapons and vulnerable flesh.

Shaux assumed it was only a question of time—not much time— before he and Cranmer were killed if they remained here, halfway up the open beach, directly in the fields of fire of what seemed to be a half dozen well-fortified heavy-caliber machine-gun emplacements, with only the bodies of fallen marines for cover. He very much doubted he and Cranmer could find a way forward through the wire, which stretched in each direction as far as he could see. He cringed away from imagining himself caught up in it like a human scarecrow.

A DD Sherman appeared off to his left, climbing through the dunes towards the houses, with a plume of dark exhaust fumes rising from its snarling engine. If the tank had climbed that far, it must have found or forced a way through the wire somewhere in that direction.

"We've got to move, Cranmer. We can't stay here," Shaux said. "We'll crawl along this side of the wire until we find the gap that Sherman made."

Cranmer did not respond—it was incredibly noisy again—and Shaux turned to repeat his plan.

Blood dripped from Cranmer's helmet. His eyes were wide open, staring sightlessly. He looked resentful, as if he had not expected to be killed so soon, less than twenty yards from the water's edge, and frustrated that all his months of preparation and training for D-Day had been wasted for so little—he'd dragged the heavy radio around for nothing. "Can't 'ardly wait" had been his last words.

Shaux removed Cranmer's arm from his own shoulders as delicately as he could. Cranmer lay beneath the weight of the radio set and its bits and pieces. Somehow Shaux would have to carry the radio himself: his sole reason for being in France was to communicate by radio, and if he didn't bring it, he might as well get back on the LCA and go back to England an abject failure. He started to struggle with the straps securing the radio to Cranmer's back.

Color Sergeant Johnston appeared beside him, followed by several marines crawling purposefully on their knees and elbows.

"Leave that radio; it's full of holes," Johnston said.

Shaux berated himself. The fusillade that struck down Cranmer had also drilled several holes through the radio on his back, and Shaux had been too confused, too overwhelmed, to see the obvious. The constant hammering of the enemy's machine guns seemed to have robbed him of coherent thought. He had been under machine-gun and cannon fire dozens of times without losing his head but always inside an aircraft cockpit and almost always with the ability to maneuver and shoot back. Now, however, he was lying out here, soaking wet and shivering with cold and encrusted with gritty sand, protected only by dead bodies, armed only with a tommy gun with an effective range of two feet, helpless against far heavier weapons firing from well-protected strongpoints.

Perhaps he wasn't shivering from lying in sodden clothing on a cold, wet beach, he thought; perhaps he was shivering with fear.

Johnston pointed to Cranmer's anti-tank gun.

"Bring that PIAT and the ammunition and follow me," Johnston said, and he and the marines crawled off along the fence line.

Johnston had a plan and seemed to know how to cope in this chaos, Shaux thought, in sharp contrast to himself. He grabbed Cranmer's PIAT and a cardboard box of shells and crawled after Johnston.

* * *

SHAEF Forward, Southwick House
6 June 1944, 0730 Hours

Eleanor glanced at the clock. With a bit of luck, Johnnie would be off the beach by now, looking for a secure position to set up his radio and make contact with the Typhoon squadrons waiting over the Channel to be called into action. Perhaps he had already found a safe spot. That part of Sword Beach was lined with holiday villas overlooking the Channel; there should be plenty of places to establish an observation post. Perhaps Flight Sergeant Cranmer, Johnnie's surly assistant, was already brewing up a cup of tea.

She shuffled through her papers and pulled out the so-called BIGOT map of Sword/Queen Red Beach, a very large-scale map showing not just roads and houses and enemy fortifications but also the estimated locations of minefields, barbed-wire barriers, Czech hedgehogs, belts of dragon's-teeth anti-tank obstructions, pathways running through the dunes, and even fields and hedgerows, all in exquisite—and possibly accurate—detail. Somewhere on that map . . . This is absurd, she thought; he is wherever he is, and guessing did absolutely no good at all. She thrust the BIGOT map back into the pile and lit a cigarette.

She listened to the TSO announcing developments as reports came in from the beaches. It seemed the Americans were encountering stiff resistance on the westernmost Omaha and Utah Beaches. Unlike the British Sword Beach, which faced relatively low-lying ground, the American beaches were overlooked by much higher ground, including the hundred-foot cliffs at Pointe du Hoc.

The American 2nd Ranger Battalion had the task of climbing the cliffs and assaulting the German strongpoints and artillery emplacements above them. It was not going well. Many of their DDs and Ducks had been driven off course by gusting winds and strong currents, and some had sunk. The surviving Rangers had landed at Pointe du Hoc an hour behind schedule and were now attempting to climb rope ladders up the cliffs in the face of withering fire from the enemy strongholds above.

God help those poor men, Eleanor thought. A little more than two hundred Rangers had set out from Portsmouth; she wondered how many would survive.

The carefully choreographed landing plan and timetable were not yet in difficulty, she thought, but they might be in danger of beginning to fray. The weather gods, probably the ultimate arbiters of who won and lost this day, appeared to be favoring the German Wehrmacht.

There was no plan B. The Allies were committed to putting more and more men onto the beaches until the German defenses broke. It was essential that the Allies establish an unbreachable lodgment—a base in Normandy from which they could not be dislodged—and then build up sufficient forces until they could then break through the Wehrmacht, east towards Paris and north towards Belgium and Holland.

The American army's primary goal was to secure the Cherbourg peninsula and the vital deep-water harbor of Cherbourg itself. The British army's primary goal was Caen, the principal town in northern Normandy and the regional hub for road and rail transportation. Cherbourg would allow the Allies to deliver the vast quantities of supplies necessary to support an army big enough to break through German resistance, and Caen would be the secure fortress behind which the Allies could build up their strength.

Cherbourg was thirty miles from Utah Beach, and Caen was twelve miles from Sword. Some SHAEF planners believed these objectives could be achieved within a couple of days, depending on the strength of the German's Atlantic Wall and the battle-readiness of the Wehrmacht units behind it. Some even thought that the British 3rd Infantry might reach Caen today. That, she knew, was Montgomery's objective.

Eleanor was not among the optimists. Last year, the British and American armies had invaded Italy with a similar landing at Salerno. Over several days of intense fighting, the Germans almost succeeded in forcing the Allies back into the sea. She feared that Normandy would be a much harder nut to crack, particularly with Erwin Rommel, the Desert Fox, in charge of the defenses.

Rommel was, in her opinion, by far the best battlefield tactician in the German army, a man who was a better general than Montgomery and at least as good as Patton. It was true that Montgomery had defeated Rommel at El Alamein, but Monty had had twice as many tanks, five times as many aircraft, and unlimited amounts of fuel. Besides, half of Rommel's army had been made up of undertrained Italian conscripts, the sweepings of Italian jails, in the desert against their will, so what would one expect?

Eleanor knew she had a reputation as a latter-day Cassandra, the Trojan princess who correctly prophesized difficulties and dangers but nobody believed her. It was said that the Greek god Apollo offered Cassandra the gift of foresight in return for the oldest of all favors. When she reneged on the agreement and rebuffed Apollo's approaches, in a fit of fury, he left her with her gift but condemned her to be disbelieved.

No god had given Eleanor foresight—nor, for that matter, offered her a similar deal—but she had been given an intuitive understanding of calculus and the principles of zero-sum game theory and a knack for expressing the clash of asymmetric forces as differential equations. She had been predicting the outcomes of campaigns and battles for four years, since first Keith Park and then Churchill had plucked her from obscurity. In addition to her refusal to let hope play any part in her calculations, she had added the principle that the key to winning is not losing—a principal that her detractors derided as a meaningless redundancy, but which had become built into Allied planning doctrine as "the Shaux Tautology."

Unfortunately, the Allies had many ways to lose in Normandy but only one way to win.

In the present situation, she believed the odds were too close to call. The Germans were defending fortified positions, and they had mobile reserves echeloned all the way back to Berlin. The Allies, on the other hand, were restricted to whatever territory they could capture—so far, just a few yards of wet sand. Allied supplies and reserves—although vast—were entirely dependent upon crossing the storm-tossed Channel. The Allies had absolute control of the sea and the sky, but the actual battle was taking place on land.

Which army was more likely to lose?

* * *

Sword Beach
6 June 1944, 0740 Hours

"Look at the white house with the tall chimneys," Johnston said, speaking slowly and clearly as if he doubted Shaux's ability to comprehend him. "Look at the left window on the upper floor, the one reinforced with sandbags. See it?"

"Yes, I see it," Shaux said.

"There's a heavy machine gun in there, a 50-caliber or bigger. When it fires you can see the muzzle flashes. Look there now! See it?"

"Yes."

"When I tell you, you will fire this PIAT through that window. Hopefully you'll knock the gun out even if you don't kill the crew. Either way they'll stop firing, at least for a moment. Got it?"

"Yes, got it."

"When you fire, the lads and I will run up that beach path over there, through the dunes and up to the houses. See where I mean?"

"Yes."

"Then we'll get to the white house and take it. That's the plan. Understand?"

"Yes, understood."

"I'll fire two pistol shots as a signal for you to fire."

"Yes."

"Any questions?"

"No, that's very clear," Shaux said.

Johnston stared at Shaux closely. "If you miss the window, we'll be killed, so don't bloody miss it." Johnston added, "Sir," as he crawled off, followed by his lads, leaving Shaux to stare at his PIAT.

The PIAT was an overgrown grenade launcher, a weapon about the size of a shotgun that lobbed a small fat bomb towards the enemy. PIAT stood for "projector, infantry, anti-tank," and the shaped charge in the bomblet could punch a hole through armor plating. When the trigger was pulled, a spring in the stock rammed a firing pin—a "spigot"—into the base of the bomb, detonating a charge that propelled the bomb forward. When the bomb struck the target, a second detonator in the nose of the bomb triggered an armor-piercing-shaped charge.

It was all a bit jury-rigged, Shaux thought, a bit crude. He took a bomb out of its cardboard container and loaded it into the PIAT. He had fired three rounds of PIAT bombs on the range up at Achnacarry Castle. The weapon had a huge recoil and tended to launch the bomb far too high.

He unwrapped a second round and laid it on the sand. If he missed with his first shot, it would take him ten or fifteen seconds to reload—seconds during which Johnston and his lads would be running up the beach path directly into the enemy's field of fire. Best not to miss, Shaux thought.

Shaux disliked self-propelled weapons. He had often fired RP3 rockets from fighter aircraft, and knew they were prone to flutter unpredictably in flight and could only be trusted at extremely short ranges. The PIAT had an advertised range of three hundred yards; fortunately, the white house was only fifty yards away. He stared along the rudimentary gunsight and into the gloom inside the sandbagged window. He was vividly aware that if he could see the enemy's position, then the enemy gunner could see him, and unlike the gunner behind his sandbagged revetment, Shaux was protected only by a few scanty stalks of dune grass; and he had lost his helmet, he suddenly realized, when he and Cranmer had fallen into the sea.

Johnston and his party were out of sight, presumably crawling as far as they could before exposing themselves to the enemy. Shaux took off the safety and aimed the PIAT at the sandbagged windowsill to allow for the jump of the recoil. The gunsights, he thought, had been added to create an encouraging impression of accuracy rather than as an actual aiming device.

There was a sudden silence; by some random fluke, the Allied naval bombardment and the enemy's guns both paused at the same moment. Now Shaux could hear the roar of the surf and the harsh cries of seabirds, as if nature was trying to restore a semblance of normality, to remind the world that this was a pleasant sandy beach where toddlers should be splashing in the waves rather than a vicious battleground with the bodies of dead soldiers washing in and out of the shallows or hung up in barbed-wire entanglements like macabre scarecrows.

But the guns fell silent only for a moment: now Shaux saw flashes inside the dark room and rounds thrummed angrily just over his head. They were far too close for coincidence—the gunner must have spotted him. Two pistol shots cracked somewhere on Shaux's left. He squeezed the PIAT's trigger. The weapon jerked backward as the bomb shot forward. The bomb marked its short flight—just half a second—with a thin trail of wispy gray smoke. Perhaps the enemy gunner could see the bomb coming, and the muzzle of the PIAT behind it, and Shaux's bare head behind the PIAT. Yellow fire lit up the darkened window as the bomb exploded in the gloom. Johnston and his marines rose from their hiding places and raced up the beach path. Shaux saw Johnston lob a grenade through the window into the blaze.

A German soldier—the first one Shaux had seen—appeared from around a corner of the house and lunged at Johnston with a bayonet. The two grappled briefly before the German sagged forward onto his knees; Shaux guessed that Johnston had seized an opportunity to kick him in the nuts.

* * *

SHAEF Forward, Southwick House
6 June 1944, 0740 Hours

A tremor swept through the map room as if a door had been blown open by an unexpected gust of wind. Everyone stopped talking. All eyes were drawn to the door. The TIO almost fell off his ladder. Turning to find the source of the commotion, Eleanor saw Churchill standing in the doorway.

"Let me not take you from your appointed tasks and duties, I pray you," he rumbled. "I am but an observer. Please carry on."

That was obviously nonsense. Eisenhower greeted him, and they chatted for a few minutes while Eisenhower pointed out developments on the big wall map. The room began to return to normal. The TIO restarted his announcements. Telephones rang and teletype machines chattered. Eleanor saw Beetle Smith, a telephone in one hand, gesticulating and beckoning to her.

"Take care of Churchill, Eleanor, for Christ's sake!" he whispered. "No disrespect, but stop him wasting Ike's time—take him away! Get him out of here! He's in the way! Got it?"

A memory of Battle of Britain Day, four years ago, leapt into her mind. On that occasion, Churchill had visited 11 Group headquarters in Uxbridge. Air Vice Marshal Keith Park, the 11 Group AOC and Eleanor's boss, had given her the task of hosting—occupying—Churchill while Park directed the crucial aerial battle over London and southern England.

"Got it, sir," she said.

Eleanor joined Eisenhower and Churchill.

"Good morning, Prime Minister," she said.

"Ah, Air Commandant, good morning," Churchill said. "I was just suggesting to Ike that we should consider, indeed I might say *seriously* consider—"

"Excuse me, General," Beetle Smith interjected, addressing Eisenhower. "You're needed immediately on this call."

Eisenhower turned away, leaving Eleanor with Churchill.

"We are dismissed, it would appear, Air Commandant," Churchill said, with the slightest shrug of his rounded shoulders.

She knew Churchill far too well to feel sorry for him. She was, frankly, surprised that he had risen before ten o'clock in the morning to be here. Of course he knew he was causing a distraction; he simply could not resist the temptation of being in the thick of things. Perhaps he was committing the scene to memory so he could write about it in his memoirs or report it to the House of Commons. She had been told he had intended to sail with the invasion fleet to see the landings at first hand, and it had taken the personal intervention of King George to stop him.

"May I offer you whatever the senior officer's mess has to offer, sir?" she asked, knowing he favored large breakfasts.

"History will record that I am the architect of this invasion," he said as she led him away. "I can be confident it will, because I intend to write the history myself. But the architects of fine buildings are seldom welcomed during the work of construction; they annoy the humble bricklayers."

Eleanor doubted that Eisenhower would care to be described as a humble bricklayer, but, then again, she would bet Eisenhower didn't care what Churchill thought of him anyway.

A steward placed a large plate of bacon and eggs before Churchill, and his mood appeared to brighten. She saw him glance towards the bar and away again, and she guessed he was wondering whether he might ask for champagne but decided against it.

"I should be on HMS *Belfast* this morning, amid the sound and fury," Churchill said, referring to the Operation Neptune flagship. "But the king forbade it and so did Clemmy."

She knew he had a deep personal respect for King George, but that would not have deterred him. She presumed the decisive influence had been his wife; Eleanor was sure that Clementine was the only person in the world he would obey without question.

"Well, doubtless it is for the best," he said, picking up his knife and fork. "Let the bricklayers proceed. Now, Air Commandant, what do we know about the immediate German response to the invasion forces?"

"These are very early stages, sir. Our first waves are just landing. It's only just H-hour plus one. It would be mere speculation to—"

"Speculate, I pray you, Air Commandant, nonetheless."

FOUR

Sword Beach
6 June 1944, 0750 Hours
Shaux crawled along a sandy path in front of the white house above the dunes. If anyone looked out a window and saw him, he thought, he would be dead for certain. He glanced towards the beach and saw more LCAs arriving in the shallows. Behind them was another row, and behind that yet another, and so on as far as he could see. Cruisers and destroyers were firing from further back in the haze, their shells howling over the beach and exploding perhaps a quarter of a mile inland.

Shaux wondered if there was an order to stop, a code word for Eisenhower to halt the flow, or if the LCAs and all the other assault craft would just keep flooding forward regardless of what might be happening on the beaches.

One of the closest LCAs opened its ramp in the shallows at the water's edge in front of Shaux, and soldiers began jumping down. A gun barrel—it looked to Shaux like an MG 131—appeared in a window directly above Shaux's head and opened fire at the disembarking soldiers. The soldiers in the landing craft had no cover and nowhere to go except forward into the hail of fire. Fully half of them, he saw, fell wading the few yards to the shore, as if the LCA was a lorry delivering cattle to a slaughterhouse. At fifty yards, the MG 131 gunner couldn't miss.

Now rounds started smacking into the wall just above Shaux's head, sending stone splinters and ricochets flying. Someone on the beach was firing back, and Shaux realized abruptly that he was as likely to be shot by his own side as by the enemy and that a splinter of stone traveling at 1,000 miles per hour was just as capable of killing him as a bullet.

The MG 131 above his head had a particularly sharp ringing sound, like a blacksmith's hammer striking steel. He could not possibly use the PIAT in this position, but he had seen Johnston toss a hand grenade through a window a couple of minutes ago, and he had better try to do the same thing before his own side shot him.

Shaux was afraid of grenades. The act of pulling out the pin seemed the exact equivalent of shooting oneself in the head. Supposing he dropped it? Supposing he hit the window frame and it bounced back down on him? He had never been particularly good at throwing a cricket ball. He had thrown three grenades at the firing range in Scotland, but not in a hurry and not under fire, and, to his secret shame, with his eyes shut. Gritting his teeth, he armed the grenade, waited for a heartbeat, stood, and lobbed it backward over his head into the window. Thank God it went in. He threw himself down again before he could be shot from the beach.

Fire erupted from the window. An enemy soldier fell out amid the flames and landed on Shaux, pinning him to the ground. His face, inches from Shaux's, was distorted by pain and shock. He clutched wildly at Shaux's throat.

The soldier was lying on top of Shaux's Colt 45 in its holster, and his tommy gun was much too long for a fight like this. The man was snarling in rage and terror as his grip around Shaux's neck tightened. Shaux managed to draw his Fairbairn-Sykes fighting knife, the only weapon he could reach. He attempted to thrust it upwards into the soldier's chest as Johnston had taught him, but he struck a webbing strap. The soldier's hands were like talons, and Shaux could not breathe. The knife was stuck in the webbing, and he couldn't wrench it free. A red mist began to form before Shaux's eyes. What would Johnston do in these circumstances?

Of course! Shaux jerked his knee upwards into the man's crutch. The soldier gasped and loosened his grip. Shaux jerked again, as hard as he could, and again, and the soldier whimpered. Shaux finally dragged his knife free and drove it into the side of the soldier's neck, remembering to twist it.

The soldier stared at Shaux in disbelief as if unwilling to believe his life was ending with so little warning. Shaux stared back, still pinned beneath him, in disbelief that he had—without thought or compunction—violently stabbed a fellow human being with a razor-sharp knife. The man's helmet had fallen off in the struggle. He seemed too old and unfit to be a soldier; his hair was gray and he was balding, his teeth were stained yellow from tobacco, and he had heavy, flabby, stubbled jowls.

His eyes lost focus at last, and Shaux struggled out from beneath him.

Shaux sat back against the wall, unwilling to acknowledge the soldier's body lying beside him. He watched the LCAs in the surf and the men advancing up the beach; they seemed far away and not quite in focus. He needed to find somewhere safer but seemed unable to move. He needed a cigarette, but that was absurd.

He had killed far too many men—pilots and aircrews in enemy aircraft, innocent civilians on the ground struck by bombs and rockets, enemy sailors in their E-boats. What about that burning pilot who had jumped without a parachute from a burning Messerschmitt 109? What about those sailors entombed in their sinking U-boat? He'd killed them all, but never had they been so close that he could touch them or look into their eyes as they died . . . The German's last sight on earth had been his killer's face.

This was ridiculous, he thought. Since he had lost Flight Sergeant Cranmer and the radio, he had no role or purpose. He was just crouching here in no-man's-land, caught between the two sides, too feeble to move. There were spare radios on a supply landing craft somewhere out there in the Channel—there was a whole boatload of RAF Servicing Commandos with all their equipment—but it would be suicidal to go back to the beach and wait for it. He couldn't stay here, but which way to go?

As a child he had been taught never to reveal his feelings. "Boys don't cry," Mrs. McKinley at the orphanage had insisted, and he never had, not even in the dark days after Eleanor had dumped him and taken his dog with her, but now sobbing seemed like a perfectly reasonable thing to do, if only to mourn the life he had just taken. Better get moving before he began.

He crawled off in the direction that didn't involve looking at the dead soldier or climbing over his body, hoping it was the way Johnston had gone before. Johnston would be impressed, Shaux thought: a kick in the nuts and even a twist to the knife! Carpe diem indeed!

* * *

SHAEF Forward, Southwick House
6 June 1944, 0750 Hours

"Well, Air Commandant?" Churchill asked. "What do we know?"

"Well, sir, let me begin by summarizing our intelligence about German positions and capabilities," Eleanor said. "As you know, Field Marshal Gerd von Rundstedt is in overall command of the German armies in Western Europe. Rommel reports to him and commands Army Group B, the German 7th and 15th Armies, occupying the immediate defenses and fortifications along the Atlantic Wall."

"Ah yes, Erwin Rommel, the Desert Fox," Churchill growled. "We meet again."

"Fortunately, sir, the German high command is split and distracted. Although there are seven Panzer divisions in France, more than enough to push us back into the sea, Rommel is in direct control of only one of them. The rest are echeloned back as far as the Maginot Line on the German border, and we believe von Rundstedt requires Hitler's personal permission to move them."

"That's a recipe for German disaster," Churchill said. "I am delighted to hear it! I have always believed it is the height of folly for politicians to interfere in military matters. They should stay in their chancelleries and leave military decisions to the generals in their headquarters."

For a moment Eleanor wondered if he was making a joke at his own expense. He, the quintessential politician, had barged into the middle of SHAEF headquarters unannounced and uninvited. But no, she decided as he popped a piece of bacon into his mouth, he seemed oblivious to the irony.

"The Germans are also distracted by Operation Fortitude, sir, our deception to keep the 15th Army tied down in the Pas-de-Calais, waiting for Patton's nonexistent FUSAG, the First United States Army Group, to attack across the Straits of Dover. They may believe Normandy is just a diversionary attack."

"Let us pray they continue to believe it, Air Commandant," Churchill said. "How would you assess our chances of success?"

"It's far too early to say, sir. We still haven't debriefed the overnight airborne operations. We don't know if they met their objectives. We're only just beginning to get photoreconnaissance flight reports, and so far, we haven't heard of any paratroopers linking up with the units landing on the beaches."

She felt like saying, "It's not even eight o'clock on D-Day morning, for Christ's sake," but managed to restrain herself.

"German indecision may be our best hope, sir," she managed. "Our worst danger is if the weather worsens and disrupts the beach landings."

Bramble entered the mess hall, stopping in awe when he saw with whom Eleanor was sitting.

"Yes, Mr. Bramble?" she asked him. In all these years, she had never been able to decide how to address him, and "Colonel" seemed an absurd title for so profoundly unmilitary a man.

"There's a new Ultra decrypt, ma'am. I thought you should see right away," he said, referring to the miraculous code-breaking operation that allowed the Allies to read encrypted German Enigma messages. The code-breaking group, known as GC&CS, was based in Bletchley Park, north of London, and run by Alan Turing. Eleanor's MI6-3b(S) and Turing's GC&CS were rivals, competing for the best and brightest young mathematicians.

"Yes, what is it?"

Bramble paused, looking uncomfortably from her to Churchill and back again.

"What's the new intelligence, Mr. Bramble? I think we can safely assume that the prime minister has the necessary Ultra security clearances."

"Rommel is away in Germany, ma'am," Bramble said. "Apparently, it's his wife's birthday."

"Really? Excellent! His second-in-command is General Dollmann, if I recall correctly?"

"Yes, ma'am, Colonel-General Friedrich Dollmann, in command of the 7th Army."

She turned to Churchill. "That may be our best news of the day so far, sir. That will make them much less decisive."

"What do we know of Dollmann, pray tell me?" Churchill asked.

"Well, sir, they say he's well past his prime. He's in his late sixties. They say he suffers from bouts of depression."

Churchill frowned, and an impish impulse carried her on.

"They say he overeats and overdrinks."

Churchill pushed away his breakfast plate as if he had suddenly lost his appetite.

"Do they indeed, by God?" he growled. "Do they indeed?"

* * *

Sword Beach
6 June 1944, 0800 Hours

Shaux crawled past another house. He had long ceased to have a plan or purpose; he was just crawling because it seemed better to be a moving target rather than a stationary one.

An arm reached out from an open doorway and seized him by the collar.

"Bloody hell, sir, what are you thinking of?" said Johnston's voice. "You'll get yourself bloody killed! Get in here!"

Shaux allowed himself to be half dragged inside. The room was filled with a dozen British soldiers, and Shaux felt a wave of relief washing over him.

"Bloody hell, sir," Johnston said again as Shaux struggled to his feet. "And I thought you had some sense in your head."

Shaux thought of telling him about the grenade and the German soldier and how he had carpéd the diem or telling him that he was simply wandering around without purpose while being shot at by both sides, but he had no words; he took out his cigarettes, lit two, and gave one to Johnston.

An officer came over to them. He had the same lightness on his feet that Johnston had, the same vigilance as a boxer, the same wary eyes and economy of movement.

"I'm Cathcart, Major," he said, in the clipped tones of the English upper class. "Who are you?"

"Shaux, RAF, Air Ground Support."

"What are you doing here?"

"My radio operator was killed and the radio was destroyed," Shaux said. "I need a new radio, preferably a Type 62."

"Do you know the frequencies?"

"Yes."

Cathcart looked at him for a moment, as if deciding if Shaux was worth bothering with in the midst of an intense door-to-door firefight, and then called over to one of the soldiers.

"Granger, you are attached to this officer," Cathcart said. "He needs your radio."

He turned away to give terse orders to his men, Shaux dealt with and already forgotten.

Granger was short and thin, the physical opposite of Flight Sergeant Cranmer, but he hefted his Type 62 as if it weighed less than a feather. They found a place to set up in the ruined kitchen, waiting while the set warmed up. Shaux pulled a list of radio frequencies from his pocket and gave it to Granger, who adjusted the tuning dials and gave a headset and a microphone to Shaux.

"It's ready now, sir," Granger said.

"Snowbird, this is Rhubarb," Shaux said. "Can you hear me, Snowbird?"

The only response was empty static.

Shaux knew that somewhere in Hillingdon House in Uxbridge, the headquarters of the Second Tactical Air Force—2TAF HQ—a dozen WAAF radio operators were listening for his call, making minute adjustments to the dials on their radios, searching the ether in the hope of piercing the pervasive veil of static.

"Snowbird, this is Rhubarb," Shaux repeated. "Can you hear me, Snowbird?"

Still only static.

"Let's try an alternative frequency, Granger," Shaux said, and Granger moved the dials a fraction.

"Snowbird, this is Rhubarb."

No response.

"Snowbird, this is Rhubarb."

It would be the height of frustration if he had managed to find a Type 62 and an operator—by pure luck—only to fail to communicate with 2TAF.

"Snowbird, this is Rhubarb."

"Rhubarb, this is Snowbird," a cool female voice replied from 2TAF HQ. "What color are your socks?"

Shaux sighed in relief. The purpose of this question was to prove to 2TAF that it really was Shaux calling and his radio had not fallen into enemy hands.

"This is Rhubarb. My socks are green."

"Thank you, Rhubarb, and good morning, sir."

Shaux knew someone would telephone Arthur Coningham, the 2TAF AOC, to let him know that Shaux was up and running, and Coningham would tell someone to telephone SHAEF to let Eleanor know.

"Rhubarb, this is Snowbird. What is your location?"

Shaux had several very large-scale BIGOT maps folded inside his jacket, and he struggled to unfold the right one.

"This is Rhubarb. My location is Sword Queen Red BIGOT Grid Delta Five."

"Sword Queen Red BIGOT Grid Delta Five," 2TAF repeated.

"Stand by, Snowbird."

"Snowbird standing by."

Shaux glanced at his watch. It was just past eight o'clock, less than thirty minutes since he had fallen from the LCA, but by far the longest thirty minutes of his life. The house shook as a shell fell nearby—who knew from which side—but Shaux didn't care; he was up and running, with infinitely reassuring British uniforms around him, no longer crawling around the Normandy coastline at random. Someone handed him a tin cup filled with hot sweet tea, and he felt as if he was home.

* * *

SHAEF Forward, Southwick House
6 June 1944, 0800 Hours

"Here is an assessment of the airborne positions in Normandy, as best we can judge," Bob O'Neill, the airborne liaison officer, said, addressing a small group in a conference room just off the main map room.

Bob O'Neill, an American one-star general, was a friend of Johnnie's; they'd first met when the RAF and the Eighth Air Force were experimenting with using Mosquitos as long-range escort fighters for B17s. He had one arm in a sling, which Eleanor knew was why he was—much to his displeasure—here at SHAEF talking about air operations over Normandy rather than flying over Normandy himself.

A sergeant spread out a large map on the table.

"As you know, the purpose of last night's airborne assaults was to establish control over the river crossings near the landing beaches," O'Neill said. He traced the courses of the rivers as he spoke. "Here in the west, near Omaha and Utah, we need to control access across the Merderet and Douve rivers to protect our left flank; and *here* in the east near Sword Beach, we need the Canal de Caen á la Mer and the Orne bridges to protect our right flank."

Eleanor had participated in the debates that led to these plans. She thought the plan to block the flanks was a good one but was worried about the center between the flanks; it was fifty miles from the Merderet to the Orne—a very big gap to leave for counterattacking Panzers. Montgomery had dismissed her concerns. He said he planned to advance so swiftly that the beachheads would not be vulnerable.

"Now, these aren't big rivers—far from it," O'Neill continued. "But they're wide enough to stop tanks and other vehicles, and slow and difficult for infantry to cross. The plan, as you know, was to blow up some of the bridges so that the Germans can't send in reinforcements as we land on the beaches. The airborne troops would also to capture and hold the remaining crossings until relieved by heavier infantry and armor coming up from the landing beaches later today, so we can use these remaining bridges to expand beyond the beachhead."

He stood back.

"That was the plan. Now, let's see what has happened. Sergeant, give us the map with our current positions."

The sergeant spread out a second map.

"The planned drop zones are marked in yellow," the ALO continued. "The positions marked in red are confirmed by radio by the units on the ground. The positions marked in blue are estimates based on incomplete information."

He pointed to the yellow areas to the west of the American beaches.

"The plan was for the US 82nd and 101st Airborne Divisions to land last night and secure positions around Sainte-Mère-Église, *here*, protecting the western flanks of the two American beaches, Omaha and Utah. The objective was to get control of the Merderet running north and south and the Doeve running west to east."

He pointed again.

"We're estimating that less than a quarter of the airborne units— gliders and parachutists alike—found their drop zones. Over here, behind Omaha, the 82nd and the 101st both missed their targets. We have no idea where many of them are, but we're afraid some landed in flooded fields around Sainte-Mère-Église and drowned."

He shook his head.

"Almost everyone who landed west of the Doeve appears to be lost or captured. They may have formed small bands to try to fight their way to the beaches, and they may be causing confusion to the enemy, but we can only account for four thousand of the thirteen thousand who landed. We have secured Sainte-Mère-Église, but we have not captured the bridge over the Merderet bridge at La Fière, which is vital to controlling the beachhead."

No one spoke. Eleanor imagined how frightening it must have been: to jump out of a C47 transport at night and descend towards a ground you couldn't see, and perhaps land safely in a field, or perhaps on a rooftop or in a tree or in a river or in a swamp, weighed down by a hundred pounds of equipment. And if you survived the landing, you would have no idea where you were or where the rest of your unit was, knowing you were lost in the midst of a massive German army . . .

"Over here on the east flank, the British flank, Operation Tonga seems to be a similar story," O'Neill continued. "The good news is that we've managed to take the bridges across the canal and the Orne. And we've captured the battery at Merville. The bad news is that many of the paratroopers and glider landings were way off their targets, just like the Americans, and we've only got about three thousand of our eight thousand men in the right places."

So, thought Eleanor, there are more than fourteen thousand para-troopers—equivalent to an entire division—scattered behind enemy lines, perhaps lost, perhaps in small groups of two or three, perhaps injured, perhaps shot, perhaps already taken prisoner

"This doesn't look good, Bob," she said.

"No, it does not," he said. "This was always going to be a high-risk operation. Let's hope the situation is better than it looks so far. It's still early days."

Launching thousands of men into the sky over enemy territory at night, she thought, in high winds, was the very definition of high risk. She crossed her fingers.

FIVE

Sword Beach
6 June 1944, 0810 Hours
Major Cathcart came into the kitchen.

"I want you to go to the end of this row of houses," he said to Shaux. "I have a message from Battalion that there's an enemy strongpoint just beyond these houses, a Tobruk that's enfilading Sword Queen Red."

A Tobruk, Shaux knew, was a tank turret on top of a concrete base, a sort of fortified stationary tank. They'd originally been invented as part of the Maginot Line. He had been briefed with photographs of them but had never seen one.

"It's too solid for us to take out. You'll have to call in air support."

"Very well," Shaux said. This, at last, was what he had come to Normandy to do.

"Johnston, take two chaps with a Bren gun," Cathcart continued. "There's Jerry[1] infantry in the area."

"Yes, sir."

---

1. British slang for Germans; the American equivalent was "Kraut," and the French was "Boche."

"You've also got this officer's PIAT. What else do you need?"

"Should be plenty, sir," Johnston said.

"Right, carry on," Cathcart said.

Johnston went first, followed by Shaux. Granger came next, loaded down with the radio and boxes of PIAT ammunition, and the two Bren gunners brought up the rear.

They crawled and scrambled through back gardens and over garden walls, past chicken coops and vegetable patches, and through gaps in fences. Everything was in disrepair. Weeds were choking the vegetables, and brambles flourished in the hedges.

It was all very unmilitary, an assault course set in a country village. Shaux had seen Home Guard units—civilian volunteers back in 1940—crawling around London in a similar fashion, practicing at being soldiers. Men and women would be going about their normal business, shopping on the High Street, waiting at the bus stop, and children would be playing; then, in the midst of prosaic daily life, a line of men in ill-fitting uniforms, carrying obsolete weapons, would solemnly crawl across the road.

A figure appeared ahead of Johnston: a woman in a dress, carrying a baby. She opened her mouth to speak, or perhaps to cry out, but Johnston put his finger to his lips, and she stepped back inside. It seemed incredible that there would still be civilians living among the fortifications on the very front line of the Atlantic Wall. It struck Shaux that the Germans really had been taken by surprise; they would have cleared the area of all civilians if they had known the invasion was coming—not for the sake of saving French lives but to make sure that there were no Résistance fighters among them.

They crawled until they reached the end of the houses. The Tobruk stood in an open area by the beach, facing west, with an unobstructed view of the shore for at least a mile, in a perfect position to sweep the beach with enfilading fire.

The Tobruk was the turret of a French Renault FT tank, an obsolescent type made in great numbers in the First World War and captured by the Germans in great numbers in 1940 when the vast but lumbering French army—then the largest in the world—collapsed before swiftly advancing columns of Panzers, some led by Rommel. The FT turret had two machine guns—Shaux guessed Reibels—that could fire in alternating bursts down the length of the beach, "enfilading" it in military jargon. Shaux knew that these twin gun arrangements permitted the gunner to maintain a high rate of fire by switching from one gun to the other so that the barrels did not overheat. He wondered if the RAF had ever used this idea, but this was no time to start daydreaming.

The Tobruk bunker itself was a squat concrete structure half buried in the ground. There were probably three or four men inside, Shaux guessed, changing the magazines as the gunner switched back and forth.

Johnston told Shaux and Granger to set up behind a firewood pile. Granger began to warm up the radio while Shaux draped an aerial in the branches of an apple tree. The Bren gunners found a spot beneath a rotting dogcart to cover a road leading away in the general direction of Caen. Shaux guessed that any reinforcements the enemy might send would come along that road. Another unexpected moment of calm fell, another moment filled with the sound of breaking waves and the harsh calls of seagulls.

The Reibels began to stammer, and Shaux, looking back along the beach, saw several DD Shermans swimming ashore.

"We're ready, sir," Granger said.

"Snowbird, this is Rhubarb."

Static.

"Snowbird, this is Rhubarb. I have trade for Harrier."

Harrier was the radio call sign for 649 Squadron, whose squadron code was HA. Harrier aircraft were P51 Mustangs, each armed with eight 65-pound RP3 rockets.

"How long will this take, sir?" Johnston asked.

"I don't know. At least three minutes after I call in Harrier."

"That's too long. These Shermans will get killed."

"Rhubarb, this is Snowbird," the radio said. "You are switched into Harrier."

Shaux could not connect directly to Harrier because of the relative weakness of mobile radio sets like the 62, but the very powerful ground-based receivers and transmitters operated by 2TAF in southern England, and perhaps by now on Sword Beach, could amplify radio signals going in both directions.

"Harrier, this is Rhubarb. I have trade for you."

"Rhubarb, this is Harrier Leader."

"Harrier designating target Sword Queen Red BIGOT Grid Delta Six."

"Sword Queen Red BIGOT Grid Delta Six."

"Target is a Tobruk tank turret at end of a road leading to the beach."

"Tobruk at end of road near beach."

"How long before they bomb it?" Johnston asked.

"Rockets rather than bombs," Shaux told him. "Two or three minutes, I would think."

"That's far too long," Johnston said. "There's another LCA landing now. We'll fire a PIAT flash-bang at the Tobruk and try to blind the gunner."

The flash-bang was a No. 69 grenade modified to be fired by the PIAT. It was filled with magnesium powder, and Shaux knew it worked like the photographic flashbulbs that newspaper reporters used. It was not designed to be lethal but exploded with a very loud bang and a brilliant flash of light that temporarily blinded anyone looking at it.

"You fire it, sir," Johnston said.

"I'm not very—"

"Just do it, sir. You didn't miss that window back there."

Shaux loaded the PIAT cautiously. This type of grenade had an all-ways fuse designed to explode on impact—any impact, such as, for example, if he dropped it.

Shaux aimed low. As long as he hit the front of the tank, or even the ground in front of it, the Tobruk gunner would be blinded for two or three minutes.

"Eyes closed!" Shaux called out.

He squeezed the trigger and shut his eyes at the same time. He heard the flash-bang explode with a loud cracking whack! The Reibels stopped firing immediately.

Shaux looked up. The Tobruk was blackened by burned magnesium, although there was no other visible damage. The Reibels had fallen silent.

"Rhubarb, this is Harrier Leader," the radio announced. "Target in one minute."

"Give me a smoke grenade, Granger," Shaux said.

"Blue smoke, sir," Granger said, handing him a modified No. 77 grenade, this one filled with phosphorus and clothing dye, producing thick blue smoke.

This time, Shaux saw the grenade hit the turret, bounce back off it, and start to emit a plume of blue smoke.

"Harrier, the target is marked by blue smoke," Shaux said into the radio.

"Blue smoke," Harrier's voice said. "Target in sight, tallyho."

Four RP3 rockets screamed above them and exploded in the dunes a hundred yards beyond the Tobruk.

A Mustang roared overhead at a hundred feet, painted brightly with its black-and-white "invasion stripes." The unmistakable sound of its Merlin engine was infinitely familiar, and Shaux felt a sudden burst of envy for Harrier One and a strong sense that he should be up there rather than down here.

Shaux had flown Mustangs, although never in combat. To his taste, a Mustang lacked the finesse of a Spitfire, a Spit's unique ability to slip through the sky as a shark slips through water, a Spit's unparalleled ability to dance with the delicacy of a ballerina. The Mustang had a more muscular, more solid feel, as if it were an industrial-strength version of a Spitfire, making it a superior gun platform, particularly when configured with six heavy 50-caliber machine guns. On a day like today, for a job like this one, he'd choose a Mustang over a Spit every time.

But the Mustang's ability to deliver ordnance was useless if the pilot delivered the ordnance to the wrong spot. In Shaux's experience, nine out of ten times, a pilot firing rockets will overshoot the target, landing fifty or a hundred yards beyond.

"Harrier, this is Rhubarb. Miss, miss, miss!" Shaux said. "Harrier Two, same target."

Shaux thought he heard Harrier One say: "Bollocks," but perhaps it was just a burst of static.

It would take Harrier One two minutes to circle round for a repeat attack with its other four rockets. In the meantime, Harrier Two should be only a minute away and was, Shaux hoped, a better shot.

* * *

SHAEF Forward, Southwick House
6 June 1944, 0810 Hours

"Well, Air Commandant, what news is there?" Churchill asked from the doorway of Eleanor's office.

Eleanor groaned inwardly. She and O'Neill were discussing the feasibility of low-level reconnaissance flights to try to locate missing paratroopers. There were by now dozens and dozens of Allied radios in Normandy, but almost none of them seemed to be working.

Perhaps they could send Lysanders, small aircraft which could fly at as little as 60 miles per hour above the treetops with the pilot and the observer literally leaning out the windows to search the paratroop and glider landing grounds. They would be able to see everything, although it would be hideously dangerous for the crews.

But how was she supposed to get any work done if Churchill was going to ask for an update every ten minutes?

"Sir, may I present Brigadier General Robert O'Neill of the USAAF?" she asked Churchill, swallowing her annoyance.

"You may," Churchill said, shaking hands with O'Neill. "Good morning, General. What's the news of the airborne troops, particularly the 82nd and 101st? I am told they have suffered grievous losses."

"It's still too early to—" O'Neill began, but Bramble burst through the open door and interrupted him. Evidently Bramble's previous awe of Churchill had dissipated.

"Ma'am, 2TAF telephoned to say Rhubarb is up and directing traffic," he announced, grinning broadly.

Eleanor had been trying not to think about Johnnie, relegating him to a nagging background dread while her foreground assessed the state of the battlefield, as Eisenhower and everyone else counted on her to do. Now she didn't know whether to feel relief that Johnnie had landed safely—he loathed the sea, having almost drowned in it twice—or fear that he was in a forward position in direct contact with the enemy.

"Thank you, Mr. Bramble," she managed.

"Rhubarb?" Churchill asked. "What, may I ask, is Rhubarb?" He seemed annoyed that this was some aspect of the operation he didn't know about, as if people were keeping secrets from him.

"Rhubarb is the code name for Group Captain Shaux, sir, Eleanor's husband," O'Neill answered for her. "He landed with the first commandos on Sword Beach as the forward AGS controller."

Churchill stared at Eleanor as if uncharacteristically at a loss for words.

"I see," he said finally. "I envy him greatly; indeed I do. Wish him Godspeed."

* * *

Sword Beach
6 June 1944, 0820 Hours
"What next?" Johnston asked. His tone was neutral, although Shaux was certain he was thinking that RP3 rocket salvos were on a par with tommy guns—completely bloody useless beyond two feet, all sound and fury, signifying nothing.

Four salvos, sixteen rockets, had failed to hit the Tobruk. The Reibels stammered briefly as if the gunner inside the Tobruk was getting his vision back and trying to see if he could aim.

Shaux was not going to criticize or defend the Harrier pilots; this display confirmed his opinion of the instability of the RP3s. Instead, he asked: "How do you take out a tank on the ground with what we've got?"

"Another flash-bang to stun the crew," Johnston answered immediately. "Then we knock the door down with a sticky bomb, and then the Bren takes the crew as they come out."

"Very well, let's do it, Johnston. How can I help?"

Johnston was as decisive as ever. "You fire the flash-bang. Then immediately load and fire another to make sure. Then I'll go forward with the sticky bomb. Meanwhile the Bren crew provides covering fire as necessary. Granger, you cover the road inland with the tommy gun in case we get visitors."

A sticky bomb was, in British military parlance, a Grenade, Hand, Anti-Tank, No. 74. It had a plastic shell that could be removed to reveal a very sticky surface made from mistletoe berries, of all things. The sticky material covered a glass bulb filled with a pound of nitroglycerine.

The idea was that someone would approach a tank at close range and throw the grenade at it, and the grenade would stick to the tank and then explode.

It was, in Shaux's opinion, a ridiculously complex and hideously dangerous weapon—to the operator, because the bomb was just as capable of sticking to the man throwing it as to the tank. Eleanor had told him that Churchill strongly believed in them—she didn't know why—and had ordered literally millions to be made. Perhaps Churchill liked tommy guns too, Shaux thought.

The Tobruk was only fifty yards away, an easy target for Shaux now that he was getting a feel for the PIAT, but it was vital that his flash-bang did not miss, because Johnston would emerge from cover and run straight towards the muzzles of those Reibels without any protection whatsoever. Johnston would be cut in two if the gunner could see him.

At some point in his years as a fighter pilot, Shaux had come to realize that he never aimed at an enemy aircraft, he just looked at it. Now he realized that the trick to firing a PIAT was to look at the target and not to aim the PIAT. He recalled a trainee pilot asking him for advice on how to aim the four cannons in a Spitfire Mark 9[2] and his advice: "Never aim, just shoot."

The novice had protested that his advice made no sense.

"Can you ride a bicycle?" Shaux had asked.

"Of course, sir."

"Every time you get on a bike, do you calculate how to balance your weight so that you don't fall over sideways, and wonder how to use the handlebars to steer, and how to use your feet to pedal, or do you just hop on and ride it?"

"I just ride it, sir."

"Exactly so."

Now it was up to Shaux to follow his own advice.

"Whenever you're ready, sir," Johnston said.

Shaux loaded a flash-bang into the PIAT. "Ready."

---

2. After much soul-searching, I have decided to use Arabic numerals instead of Roman numerals for the sake of readability, even though it is historically inaccurate. So, for example, farewell Mosquito Mk. XVIII, and hello Mosquito Mk. 18. My apologies to purists.—J.R.

Johnston glanced around to make sure everyone was in position. "Granger, watch the road, not the Tobruk."

"Right, Sergeant."

"Catesby, Ratcliff, use the Bren to kill the Jerries, not me. Got it?"

"Got it, Sergeant," they answered in unison.

"Eyes closed for the flash-bang, everyone. Fire it now, sir."

Shaux looked at the Tobruk turret, closed his eyes and fired a flash-bang, and loaded another.

"You got it," Johnston said. "No need for a second."

Shaux opened his eyes to see Johnston spring from the woodpile and sprint across the open ground to the Tobruk, holding a sticky bomb at arm's length. The Reibels remained silent—the flash-bang had done its job. Johnston reached the Tobruk, tossed the bomb at the side of the turret with the action of a nine-pin bowler, and began to run back. The bomb exploded, tearing the Tobruk's armored doors half off their hinges. A German soldier stumbled out, and another. Johnston threw himself on the ground, and the Bren gun opened fire over him.

Cannon fire came from the direction of the road.

"Jerry scout car coming up the road," Granger yelled.

The scout car was a squat, wheeled vehicle with steeply sloping sides and an open turret armed with a 20mm cannon. Shaux had been studying pictures of enemy tanks and vehicles in preparation for his AGCS role and guessed the scout car was a 222, a Leichter Panzerspähwagen, like a British Daimler Dingo.

The 222 had doubtless been sent forward to assess the situation on the beaches. Because of the Allies' absolute dominance of the skies, the enemy had no air reconnaissance and had to rely on observation on the ground.

Granger's tommy gun was useless against the 222, and the Bren was engaging the Tobruk crew.

"Close your eyes!" Shaux shouted.

He swung round, looked at the 222, closed his eyes, and fired the second flash-bang.

"Jesus Christ!" Granger screamed. Shaux guessed Granger had still been looking at the 222 when the flash-bang struck it.

The 222 kept rolling slowly forward even though its crew must have been incapacitated. If it continued, it would run over Johnston. The gunner seemed to be firing bursts at random.

Johnston was prone on the ground, pinned down by both the Bren firing over his head and by the 222's cannon. Granger was temporarily blinded.

The Bren gunners were firing at the concussed and disoriented soldiers stumbling out of the Tobruk. Being inside the Tobruk when the flash-bang hit it must have been like being inside Big Ben when the clock strikes the hour. One soldier emerged with his hands raised, but Catesby and Ratcliff ignored his gesture.

Shaux went towards the 222, stumbling as best he could along a muddy ditch beside the road, crouching to avoid the cannon. The 222 gunner had one hand covering his eyes and one hand on the stock of the cannon. It was obvious he could see nothing; he was just trying to keep his balance. Shaux pulled the pin out of a hand grenade. He didn't trust himself to toss the grenade any distance. He waited until the 222 rolled blindly past him, reached out and dropped the grenade through the open top, and threw himself down into the ditch.

The grenade exploded deep inside the 222, and the gunner—whatever was left of the gunner above his waist—began to scream.

* * *

SHAEF Forward, Southwick House
6 June 1944, 0820 Hours

Southwick House was far too small to accommodate SHAEF Forward. Most people were housed in flimsy huts on the grounds, but Eleanor had a small office inside Southwick House itself. Although it was scarcely bigger than her desk, the office was considered a mark of high prestige: one's importance and standing in SHAEF was measured by the exact distance—to the nearest inch—one's office was away from Eisenhower's. Competition for rooms was intense, and Beetle Smith personally allocated office space. Of all the hundreds of British personnel in SHAEF, only Air Chief Marshal Tedder, Ike's deputy, had an office closer to Ike's than hers.

Unfortunately, Eleanor's office was so convenient that it attracted visitors. Now, for example, Churchill settled comfortably behind her desk and lit a cigar. His secretary appeared from nowhere and took out a pencil and notepad.

Charlie glanced up at Eleanor to see if he should evict Churchill, but she shook her head. Charlie was the only dog in SHAEF Forward, again by Beetle Smith's dispensation. It was widely rumored that Ike and Omar Bradley believed that George Patton's bull terrier Willie was afraid of Charlie, and therefore Charlie was welcome in Southwick House as a way of discouraging Patton from visiting. Eleanor knew that Charlie and Patton's dog had never met, and, in any case, Charlie was far too much of a gentleman to pick a fight with a smaller dog, but she did not discourage the rumor—she also found Patton hard to take.

"Speech to the Commons: Mr. Speaker, etcetera, etcetera," Churchill began, and his secretary started to write in shorthand. "The House should, I think, take formal notice—no, formal *cognizance*—of the liberation of Rome by the Allied armies under the command of General Alexander. This is a memorable and glorious event—"

He paused and looked at Eleanor with raised eyebrows as if wondering what she was doing there. Eleanor smiled, clicked her tongue to Charlie, and went outside for a walk and a smoke. She was ninety-nine percent certain there had been a twinkle in Churchill's eye.

SIX

Sword Beach
6 June 1944, 0830 Hours

"Where have you been, Johnston?" Major Cathcart demanded, addressing Johnston rather than Shaux, who he seemed to classify as a potentially useful but strictly peripheral figure. "You're not responding on the radio, and I have reports of Panzer movements that might require AGSC."

"We were finishing off that Tobruk, and we were attacked by a Jerry scout car, sir," Johnston said.

"Is the Tobruk out of action?"

"Yes, sir. This officer took out the scout car while we dealt with the Tobruk."

"Prisoners?"

"None, sir."

"Good," Cathcart said, and turned away immediately to deal with the next issue.

Clearly the destruction of an enemy scout car was not worthy of comment. Shaux did not resent his abrupt manner in the least. Cathcart was the senior officer holding the Queen flank of Sword Beach, with

Sword Robert and the Casino stronghold still in enemy hands to their east. If the enemy could push back and turn this flank, take this little row of houses, the whole of Sword Beach might be vulnerable, and perhaps even the Canadian Juno Beach just beyond Sword.

This part of the coast was being defended by the German 716th Infantry Division, approximately eight thousand men manning the fortifications and strongpoints along the beaches. The 716th was not supposed to be tactically mobile and was manned by older men and some non-German soldiers who would rather serve here than be sent to the meat grinder of the Eastern Front. Some were men who had been given a choice of serving in the Wehrmacht or being assigned to a forced labor battalion and made the right decision. Others were Russian prisoners of war willing to fight for the enemy rather than suffer the gross inhumanity of POW camps on the Eastern Front. Shaux recalled being surprised at how old and unfit the soldier he had stabbed had seemed. But second class or not, the 716th was inflicting significant casualties on the beaches and had not been simply overrun as some had expected.

Shaux looked back along the length of the beach. It was beginning to become crowded as more and more landing craft delivered their troops, tanks, and vehicles. Big, square Churchill tanks with blades like bulldozers were pushing away the "Czech hedgehog" anti-tank barriers and barbed wire. Medical staff were attending the wounded. The dead were being laid out in neat rows under the supervision of a chaplain. A beach master stood on a wooden box directing traffic like a policeman in Piccadilly Circus.

Now that the closest machine-gun nests seemed to have been taken, the principal threat came from enemy artillery firing from further inland, and their accuracy was hampered by the enemy's loss of direct observation of the fall of shot. Perhaps, Shaux thought, this might actually work—but not if the AGCS aircraft circling patiently above could not hit their targets.

It was to some extent his own fault, he supposed. He had sunk a U-boat with RP3 rockets in the Mediterranean in 1942, and this had erroneously convinced many in Whitehall and the popular press that rockets were precision weapons. But they were no such things. Rockets—basically thin steel tubes filled with propellent with an explosive projectile stuck on the front—fluttered in flight, were easily blown off course by the wind, and suffered from ballistic droop as gravity dragged them earthward. Many pilots had a tendency to pull out of their attacking dives too early, for fear of hitting the ground, causing their rockets to overshoot their targets. Shaux did not blame the pilots: it is a fearsome thing to deliberately point one's aircraft at the ground when traveling at 300 miles per hour—and keep pointing earthward as one's speed builds up.

In the months before D-Day, Shaux had argued in vain against overreliance on rockets for ground attacks. He favored heavy-caliber weapons like the 37mm Flak 18 autocannons carried in weapon pods by Junkers 87 Stuka Gs or even the mighty 57mm Molins guns he had used in Mosquitos last year. Luftwaffe pilot Hans-Ulrich Rudel was said to have knocked out hundreds of Russian tanks with his Flak 18s.

"The problem with rockets is that you can only fire them once," Shaux had argued. "You can't correct your aim. With automated weapons you can—you observe your fall of shot and adjust, particularly against moving targets. Heavy-caliber cannon shells will go through half an inch of armor plate. Besides, you don't even have to be there to scare tank crews; they just have to know that you *might* be there. No Panzer commander is going to saunter across a cow pasture in broad daylight if he knows there might be Molins-armed Mosquitos waiting above him."

But opinions from people with practical experience carried little weight in Whitehall, he had learned. The chair-borne experts in the Air Ministry, the Ministry of Aircraft Production, the Ministry of Supply, and sundry interdepartmental committees, advisory bodies, and working groups had settled on rocket-armed Typhoons and Mustangs long ago, and therefore rocket-armed Typhoons and Mustangs it would be. Even the widely respected Sir Wilfred Freeman, Shaux's old mentor and boss, had been unable to change minds set in impermeable bureaucratic concrete.

"But what about the Stukas knocking out hundreds of Russian tanks with Flak 18s?" Shaux had asked.

"Well, Russian tanks aren't really much good," he had been told by a scientific committee chairman, contrary to almost all actual evidence. "Rockets are best. You of all people know that—you proved it in the Med."

Shaux took off his Bergen and sat down on the floor of a ruined cottage. A commando handed him hot sweet tea in a tin cup. Shaux wondered if the rations in his Bergen had been spoiled in the sea but lacked the energy to find out. Besides, he'd much rather smoke than eat. He lit a cigarette and glanced at his watch. It was 0830; he'd landed just an hour ago, but it seemed like ancient history. His uniform was still damp, and he was fairly sure his boots still had water in them. Gritty sand had found its way through various crevasses in his clothing and settled into hiding places in and around his anatomy. He tried to remember what it felt like to be warm and dry but could not.

Johnston sat down beside him.

"Nicely done with that scout car, sir," he murmured, and Shaux basked in his approval. He didn't think he had ever heard Johnston say anything complimentary to anyone before.

"Where were you before all this, Johnston?" he asked.

"The desert, sir, the LRDG."

That explained a lot, Shaux thought. The Long Range Desert Group was an almost legendary reconnaissance and sabotage unit operating behind enemy lines in the North African campaign. Many of the original members were New Zealanders. They drove patrols of three or four American Chevrolet trucks hundreds of miles across the empty desert, often at night. They were self-contained, repairing and maintaining their vehicles; carrying all their supplies, arms, fuel, water, and spare parts; navigating where few tracks and no roads existed; and carrying out their raids and operations under the harshest circumstances. Johnston must have learned his calmness and his ability to find solutions to problems—to make do with whatever was available—under desert skies.

"It was a bloody sight warmer there than here," Johnston said, and Shaux knew he would say no more.

* * *

SHAEF Forward, Southwick House
6 June 1944, 0830 Hours

"Well, Eleanor, what do you think?" Eisenhower asked.

Several of Eisenhower's senior staff, the group he called his "brains trust," were gathered in his office. Omar Bradley, Montgomery, and Admiral Sir Bertram Ramsay, all of whom were on board warships in the Channel, had joined the meeting by radio hookup, although the links were poor and contributed little more than static.

Beetle Smith and Bob O'Neill had just finished giving Eisenhower a summary of the latest intelligence from the field.

"It's extremely tight, sir." Eleanor told Eisenhower. "On the plus side, we have absolute control of the Channel and absolute air superiority. On the minus side, the weather is marginal, as you know; the airborne landings seem to have been a mess; and the enemy's 352nd Division is holding up better than expected. I'm afraid we underestimated them. Omaha, in particular, is very difficult. The Rangers at Point du Hoc are struggling."

"Those guys are really tough," Eisenhower said. "They won't give up. We'll just have to keep putting more and more reinforcements and armor on the beach, weather permitting, and eventually the 352nd will yield. We have no choice. Anything new on the weather, Jim?"

"Nothing new, sir," Jim Stagg said. "I'm afraid it's not improving, but it's still just calm enough to let the landing craft reach the beaches without turning turtle."

"What else, Eleanor?" Eisenhower asked.

"The 716th defending Sword, Juno, and Gold are soaking up our attacks, sir, but they appear weaker than the 352nd. The Canadians on Juno are doing well against them."

"Enemy intentions?"

"The two static divisions won't push us back off the beaches," she said. "That's not their job. The key strategic question now is whether the 21st Panzer Division moves or not. With Rommel in Germany and Dollmann in charge of Army Group B, we'll have to see if Feuchtinger is willing to act on his own."

"Feuchtinger is in command of the 21st Panzer, right?" Smith asked.

"Yes, sir. He has two hundred or so Panzer 4s and Panzer 5 Panthers, plus mechanized infantry, and he's only twelve miles from Sword and Juno, just south of Caen, just an hour from the beaches. We'll need constant low-level overflights in case they start to move. We need our ground forces probing inland as soon as possible. The French Résistance also is carrying out covert reconnaissance, of course, and we're in contact."

"What else?" Eisenhower asked again.

"There are two other threats, sir. One is the 12th SS Panzer at Evreux to the southeast of Sword. In many ways, they're a greater threat than the 21st, but they're not under Rommel's or Dollmann's direct control. They have to ask Hitler's permission to use them."

The 12th SS Panzer Division, commanded by Kurt Meyer, was an armored division of the Waffen-SS, the ruthless, black-uniformed military wing of the Nazi Party. It was named the Hitlerjugend Division because many of its recruits had been members of the fanatical Hitler Youth organization. The division had a reputation for extreme measures, including civilian massacres, most recently the arbitrary execution of seventy innocent French civilians dragged from their homes as a reprisal following a Résistance attack near Lille in northern France.

Both the 12th and the 21st were armed with Panzer 4 and the newer Panzer 5 Panther tanks, which were generally considered to be on a par with, or superior to, American Shermans and British Cromwells and Churchills.

"If the 21st moves, sir, they could reach the coast and split our forces," Eleanor said. "That would leave Utah and Omaha Beaches isolated. If the 12th moves, they could push through the British lines on the Orne and roll westward across Sword, Juno, and Gold."

"You said there was another threat?" Eisenhower asked.

"Yes, sir," Eleanor said. "Behind the 21st, blocking the road to Paris, is the 130th Panzer, the so-called Panzer Lehr, commanded by Fritz Bayerlein. They are reported to be the best equipped and best trained of all the Panzer divisions. They could be at the beaches in two days."

"Very well," Eisenhower said. "I want maximum overflights for reconnaissance, and I want the assault troops on the beaches moving inland on recce searches. They are to avoid combat with the 716th, if possible, and find the 21st. If a butterfly takes wing, I want to hear about it immediately, and I want a photograph of it within five minutes."

Beetle Smith picked up a telephone and started speaking. Eisenhower lit a cigarette and shook his head. Eleanor guessed at his inner turmoil.

"So, I know you don't do gut feels, Eleanor, but what's your gut feel?" he asked.

"If Rommel gets back from Germany quickly, sir, and convinces Von Rundstedt to order an all-out counterattack, *and* if he can persuade Hitler to release the 12th and the Panzer Lehr immediately, then the situation will be very difficult. However . . ."

"However, what?"

"It seems to me—to my gut—that if Hitler had wanted an immediate all-out counterattack against an Allied invasion of France, rather than a static containment strategy, he'd have put Rommel in charge. But he *didn't* put Rommel in charge."

"Good point," Eisenhower said.

* * *

Sword Beach
6 June 1944, 0840 Hours

"Battalion says that scout car you took out might have been a skirmisher for the 21st Panzer Division," Major Cathcart said. "They want forward reconnaissance patrols. I want you to go inland along that road in the direction of Collmanville. Do not engage any infantry you encounter. You're looking for armor. Is that clear?"

"Clear, sir," Johnston said.

"If you find armor, bring in air support immediately. Is that clear?"

"Clear, Major," Shaux said. Strictly speaking, Cathcart was far his junior and couldn't give him orders, and Shaux's brief was to use his own discretion on where to go and when. But he was there to support the first wave of infantry and commandos, and Cathcart clearly knew what he was doing.

"What will you need, Johnston?" Cathcart asked.

"The Bren again, sir, two scouts with tommy guns, and the PIAT . . . One man extra to carry more ammo. And Granger with the radio, if he's fit."

"Collmanville is about a mile from here. It has a church with a tall tower you should be able to see from a distance. Beyond that, there's nothing directly on this road until Biéville, a further eight miles. There are a couple of villages such as Colleville on side roads, but I'll send other patrols there. Clear?"

"Clear, sir."

"Radio in when you reach Collmanville."

"Right, sir."

"Carry on."

Shaux noted that it was not Cathcart's style to wish someone good luck when launching them into enemy territory. In fact, he had already turned back to address a new company of men who had just landed. The beach was continuing to fill up. Men and equipment were being moved into areas behind the row of houses facing the beach. He knew more than twenty-five thousand men were supposed to land here before it got dark this evening: two thousand men and their equipment every hour. The pressure to get men and supplies and tanks off the beach and inland would be intense—if the enemy 716th would permit them to do so.

Granger was rubbing his eyes and blinking constantly and looked unsteady on his feet.

"You all right, Granger?" Johnston asked.

"I'll be all right, Sergeant."

Johnston looked doubtful and glanced at Shaux.

"What do you think, sir? You decide."

"I'll be all right, sir," Granger insisted. "Of course I will."

Granger obviously had not fully recovered from the effects of the flash-bang but, on the other hand, he did understand the Type 62 radio, and he had grasped the AGSC process. If Shaux took someone else, he'd have to train him, and he might not be as reliable . . .

"I'll be all right, sir," Granger said again.

"Very well," Shaux said.

Shaux was not hungry in the least but forced himself to eat a cheese sandwich. The sandwich had seen better days; however, it contained protein and carbohydrates, and Shaux was about to launch into a potentially arduous cross-country march of unknown duration.

He rummaged in his Bergen and found an apple. It tasted of seawater, but he ate it anyway.

"Ready, sir?" Johnston asked.

"Ready."

The Johnston's patrol tramped through the back gardens of the row of houses. Half an hour ago, they had crept through it, expecting enemy soldiers at any moment. Now the gardens were filling with British soldiers and their equipment.

They reached the end of the houses. An untidy pile of enemy soldiers lay beside the ruined turret of the Tobruk, still lying where they had been cut down by the Bren. The 222 scout car was canted over in a ditch, with the body of the dead gunner sprawled across the turret. Shaux was grateful that he had stopped screaming.

"Right," Johnston said. "Fox, Morton, you take the lead. Then me, then the RAF officer with the PIAT, then Granger, then Poynings with the extra ammo, then Catesby and Ratcliff with the Bren. Keep off the road and out of sight. Keep your eyes open. This is a recce party, not a raid. Any questions?"

There were none.

"Let's get moving," Johnston said.

Fox and Morton set a steady pace, trudging through a wheat field beside the gravel road, with the rest of the party following. It would have been faster and easier to take the road, but they would have been spotted too easily by any enemy patrols that might be coming in the opposite direction. The sounds of the naval barrage and the enemy's counterbarrage began to fade. Shaux could have imagined they were hiking through a peaceful countryside. His clothes and equipment were now merely damp rather than wet, and the exercise was warming him.

The fact that the Harrier P51s had missed the target four times bothered him. If they couldn't knock out a Tobruk, an immobile tank encased in concrete, how were they going to hit Panzers moving at 20 miles per hour? It wasn't the pilots' fault; it was the inaccuracy of the RP3 weapon that was causing the problem. He'd fought that battle with the bureaucrats for three months, to no avail. Perhaps he should try again, but there was nothing he could from—

"Down," hissed Johnston, and Shaux threw himself prone.

An elderly French civilian on a bicycle pedaled slowly past them in the direction of the sea, unaware of their presence. It seemed bizarre that civilians would be wandering about in the battleground; however, Shaux reflected, this was the Frenchman's home—his gravel road, his wheat field—and the armies on both sides were the intruders. In a week or two, or a month or two, the armies would be gone, leaving nothing but the fallen, and the Frenchman would remain, free to pedal his bicycle undisturbed.

* * *

SHAEF Forward, Southwick House
6 June 1944, 0840 Hours

Eleanor leafed through the files on senior enemy commanders. MI6-3b(S) included a small group who collected and documented enemy information. They were multilingual former librarians led by a formidable elderly lady known as The Dragon, and as an inevitable and undeserved consequence, the ladies had become Dragonettes. The information came from everywhere—message intercepts, scraps gleamed from newspapers, newsreels, radio reports, intelligence agents, and from Résistance sources.

Edgar Feuchtinger, the 21st Panzer Division commander, was reported to be something of a wheeler-dealer on the fringes of the black market. He had a mistress who was an actress, reportedly of South American descent, although that tidbit might just be spice added to embellish the story. Feuchtinger was said to spend much of his time in her company in Paris—far more time than he spent in Caen. If Rommel, Dollmann, and Feuchtinger were *all* away this morning . . . who was in charge?

She opened the Army Group B Order of Battle and found the 21st Panzer. Colonel Hans von Luck—such a great name for a soldier, she thought—was in command of the 125th Panzer Grenadier Regiment, part of the 21st Panzer Division. Panzer Grenadiers were heavily armed infantry carried into battle in armored vehicles, supported by heavy self-propelled guns. Luck's regiment was stationed at Vimont, southeast of Caen. That was only a few miles from Bénouville, where the British paratroopers had captured the bridge across the Orne. Lightly armed paratroopers had no chance, none at all, against heavily armed Panzer Grenadiers.

The file said that Luck was a favorite of Rommel's, having covered the Afrika Korps' withdrawal from El Alamein in 1942. If Luck telephoned Rommel directly . . .

Who else might take action? The German chain of command was so convoluted, it was impossible to tell . . . Most of the regular ground troops in that area were under the control of 84th Army Corps that was based in Saint-Lô, directly south of the American beaches. It was under the command of Erich Marcks, a general who'd lost a leg on the Eastern Front. She thought of Marcks as a staff officer rather than a field commander—he was the author of the Marcks Plan, the first version of Hitler's plan to invade Russia in 1941.

He was probably not the sort of man to seize the initiative without approval from on high, she thought, staring at his photograph; he looked a bit mousy behind his owlish spectacles. However, with tens of thousands of Allied troops arriving on his doorstep, not to mention paratroopers dropping from the skies, he might take decisive action . . .

It was a curious coincidence that Rommel was away in Germany on the morning of D-Day. He'd also been away in Germany when Montgomery launched his attack in the battle of El Alamein back in 1942, the beginning of the end of the German occupation of North Africa. Perhaps this was an omen that today would mark the beginning of the end of German occupation of France.

She glanced at her watch. It was almost nine o'clock. Every hour the Panzers stayed in their depots was an immensely valuable hour. If the 21st held back for another hour, the British troops coming off Sword beach could be as far as . . . She pulled out a BIGOT map. Let's see: by then they could be moving towards Colleville on the way to Bénouville, to link up with the Airborne troops at the Orne bridge, or past Collmanville, probing towards Caen.

She stared at the map and wondered briefly where Johnnie was but caught herself before she could disappear down that rabbit hole again.

SEVEN

Collmanville, Normandy
6 June 1944, 0900 Hours

Shaux didn't feel at ease in France. The last time he'd been here was in 1941, when he'd been a prisoner of war. One of the engines of his Westland Whirlwind fighter had caught fire—Rolls-Royce Peregrines were notoriously unreliable—and he'd been forced to bail out. The Gendarmerie had arrested him and handed him over to the Luftwaffe. One of their pilots, Otto, had befriended him and helped him to escape rather than be transferred into the custody of the Abwehr, Germany's military intelligence service. He'd never known why the Abwehr wanted him, rather than letting him be sent to a *Stalag Luft* prison camp like all other RAF POWs, but he assumed that Eleanor might have become a person of interest in German intelligence circles.

He'd miraculously made his way to Belgium and back to England, but that feeling of being a hunted animal—a stranger in a strange land, as the bible said—had never left him. Now, back in France, he found he was constantly looking over his shoulder.

They had reached the outskirts of Collmanville, a small village dominated by a medieval church tower rising to the heavens. Johnston had them creeping up a muddy ditch that ran towards the center of the village. An old man—the same old man that they had seen earlier—stood beside the ditch, watching them approach. Shaux remembered the Home Guard soldiers he had seen crawling across a street in London and realized this patrol must look just as foolish.

"Are there any Germans here?" Johnston asked the old man.

"*Quoi?*"

"Germans?"

"*Quoi?*"

It seemed Johnston spoke no French and the old man spoke no English.

"*Où sont les Allemands?*" Shaux tried. "Where are the Germans?"

"*Les Allemands?*"

"*Où sont les Boches?*" Shaux asked, using the usual French insult for Germans.

"*Ah! Les Boches!*" the man said, finally in communication. "*Là-bas!*" he said, pointing to his left. "Over there."

Johnston and his men swung round in that direction.

"*Et là-bas!*" the old man added, pointing to his right. "And over there.

"*Partout!*" he chuckled, drawing a circle with his arms. "Everywhere."

A young woman appeared, perhaps his granddaughter, and took his hand as if he were an infant. Shaux was struck again by the incongruity of civilians in the midst of the battlefield.

"*Vous êtes Anglais?*" she asked. "You are English?"

"*Oui,*" Shaux said.

The woman did not seem excited at the prospect of being liberated. Perhaps she expected the invasion to fail, or perhaps she liked the English no better than the Germans.

"*Au centre-ville,*" she said, pointing past the church. "*Un char des Boches, un char Panzer.*" "In the center of the village, there's a German tank, a Panzer."

"*Merci,*" Shaux said.

"Kill the bastards," she told him in accented but clear English. "They are Ukrainian. Kill them all."

"Ukrainian?" Shaux asked, not certain he had understood her.

"Kill them all."

She led the old man away. Shaux wondered if the old man fully grasped what was happening—if not, what chance did he have in a war zone, riding his bicycle into God knew what? Shaux had often reflected that the cruelty of war is disproportionately cruel to the helpless.

The center of the village was a cluster of stone houses and small shops in the shadow of the church tower. Johnston signaled the patrol to take up defensive positions while he and Shaux peered round a corner into the village square. An odd-looking tank was parked close to the wall of a boulangerie, a baker's shop. Shaux saw immediately that the tank had been positioned to be protected from an aerial rocket attack by the buildings around it.

One soldier stood in the tank's open turret, staring through a pair of binoculars along the road towards the sea, while five or six others stood or sat around it in attitudes of boredom. It was reported that there were foreigners fighting in the formations that manned the Atlantic Wall defenses. Perhaps that was what the young woman had meant. He knew that some Ukrainians had sided with the Germans when they invaded Ukraine in 1941, believing that Hitler, however cruel, could not possibly be worse than the merciless Stalin. It was, after all, only ten years since Stalin had starved three million Ukrainians to death in the Holodomor famine when the bodies of dead children lay scattered in the streets of Kiev.

"What's that?" Johnston whispered, pointing at the tank.

"That's a Panzerjäger, a tank destroyer," Shaux said, recognizing it from the silhouettes he had studied. "It's called a Marder, I think. It's a German 75mm anti-tank gun mounted on an old French Lorraine armored carrier."

The gun and the turret looked far too large for the small tank body upon which it sat. The Germans had captured hundreds of Lorraine carriers when France collapsed in 1940. Shaux noted that the long gun barrel was pointing straight along the road to the beach so that the first Sherman DD or Cromwell that came up that road would be destroyed in an instant.

The Marder had an oakleaf symbol painted on it.

"That's not from the 21st Panzer," Johnston said, "That's the 716th oakleaf badge. It's part of the coastal defenses, not the Panzers."

"It can't be taken out from the air by rockets," Shaux said, glancing round the rooftops.

Cathcart's orders were to bypass the local infantry, the 716th, and search for the 21st Panzer. But if they left the Marder untouched, the troops advancing off the beach would run straight into it. On the other hand, if they attacked the Marder, they'd reveal themselves, and God alone knew how many enemy soldiers might be in or near this village. Perhaps he could call in a bombing attack, with 500-pound bombs dropped at a low level from Mustangs or Typhoons. They could knock down the buildings around the square and disable the tank. A dozen bombs would devastate the area whether or not they hit the Marder directly. That would work, although the old man and his granddaughter, and whomever else was in these buildings, would probably not survive.

"We'll have to take it out ourselves," Johnston muttered.

"A flash-bang and a PIAT mortar, Johnston?"

"You're getting the hang of it, sir!"

* * *

SHAEF Forward, Southwick House
6 June 1944, 0900 Hours

"So far, so good," David Strangeways said to Eleanor. "There's nothing to indicate they know that this is the main and the only invasion."

Colonel Strangeways was the prime mover in Operation Fortitude, a complex series of deceptions designed to convince the enemy that the main invasion would take place in the Pas-de-Calais, directly across the channel from Dover, and that Normandy was just a diversion. This was a very reasonable idea: the Strait of Dover was a much shorter and safer Channel crossing than the Portsmouth-to-Normandy crossing; Calais was much closer to Germany, so the Allies would have to fight their way across two hundred fewer miles to reach Germany; and the RAF and the Eighth Air Force had been pounding the Atlantic Wall fortifications in northern France for months. Half of Rommel's Army Group B, the 15th Army under Hans von Salmuth, was therefore deployed in the Calais area.

The secretive groups implementing Fortitude were almost as opaque and deceptive as the plan itself, with names like MI5 Section B1A, Ops(B), and R Force—they made her own MI6-3b(S) seem almost prosaic, Eleanor thought.

Strangeways—Eleanor could not imagine a better name for a man whose job was trickery—had made his reputation by developing deception tactics in the North African campaign in 1942, where he had become a favorite of Montgomery's. Strangeways had fooled Rommel in an attack on Tunis using dummy equipment and radio traffic, Eleanor recalled. She hoped he could fool Rommel again.

"I agree; so far, so good," Eleanor said. "The German 15th Army hasn't moved an inch. Hans von Salmuth appears to believe we'll invade the Pas-de-Calais at any moment."

The biggest component of Operation Fortitude was the creation of the imaginary First United States Army Group, known as FUSAG. FUSAG was supposed to consist of three imaginary armies, the US 9th and 14th and the British 4th—as big on paper as the real 21st Army Group invading Normandy. Each of these phantom armies had their own orders of battle and their own headquarters and even their own shoulder badges. FUSAG announced its presence to the world by generating large volumes of believable radio traffic transmitted from credible but illusory command centers such as Edinburgh Castle in Scotland.

Another aspect of Fortitude was the construction of rubber dummy tanks and military equipment that could be inflated to look like the real thing in order to fool enemy reconnaissance flights, although, given Allied air superiority, there were very few such flights. A much more important part of Fortitude, in Eleanor's opinion, was the XX or Double-Cross System, which turned German spies into double agents to feed false FUSAG information back to German intelligence organizations.

The icing on the cake, she thought, was putting the real George Patton in charge of the fictitious FUSAG. The Germans, it was hoped, would assume that the Allies would put their best battlefield general in charge of their most important unit. Patton was available—much to his fury—to fulfill this nonexistent role because he had slapped a soldier suffering from battle fatigue and had been removed from operational command.

"Every day Rommel keeps the 15th Army in the Pas-de-Calais waiting for George Patton is a day we can concentrate on defeating the 7th in Normandy," Strangeways said. "It's two hundred miles from Calais to Caen."

"Fingers crossed," Eleanor said.

"Eleanor! I'm surprised. I thought you don't believe in luck!"

"Touché!" She grinned. "There's no such thing as luck in mathematics, it's true. But war is not mathematics, and generals are not mathematicians."

If Fortitude works, she thought, Strangeways would deserve a knighthood. It would be one of the great deceptions in military history, on a par with the Trojan Horse.

* * *

Collmanville, Normandy
6 June 1944, 0915 Hours

Johnston listened to Cathcart's orders on the radio and relayed them to Shaux. The plan was that Johnston's patrol would destroy the Marder, and then Cathcart would immediately send Shermans and an infantry company up the road from the beach to secure Collmanville. The area between the beach and Collmanville would quickly fill with men and equipment, relieving pressure for space on the beach itself.

Johnston gestured to Fox and Morton, and the three of them entered the back door of one of the houses facing the square. A minute later, Johnston opened the door and beckoned to Shaux. The room was dark, with big wooden shutters closed across the window as if to ward off the reality of war. An elderly couple sat together in one shadowy corner. The man held a bible, and the woman's hands were busy with her rosary as her lips moved in silent prayer. Clearly they expected to die. War is so unfair, Shaux thought; their only sin was to live all their lives in a tiny faraway village in the midst of what had suddenly become a mighty battlefield.

Shaux opened the window and nudged the shutters apart a crack, opening up an excellent view of the square, with the Marder sitting at the far end and its crew still waiting listlessly. Shaux noted that the Marder driver's compartment hatch was open. If—a big if, Shaux thought—he could fire an armor-piercing AP PIAT round into the interior, it would destroy the Marder beyond salvage. A second high-explosive HE round anywhere on the outside of the Marder would kill the crew. The range was nothing—thirty yards at the most—but Shaux knew that the easiest shots were also the easiest to miss. Granger loaded the PIAT and handed it to Shaux. He poked it through the window just enough for the shell to clear the shutters.

Shaux glanced at Johnston, who nodded. Shaux peered out at the Marder and remembered his own advice to look rather than aim. There was nothing to wait for; he squeezed the trigger, and the PIAT leapt in his hands. Granger immediately took the PIAT and loaded an HE shell. Shaux looked out again and saw flames and smoke erupting from the driver's compartment. The crew seemed too shocked to move. Shaux fired again, and the HE shell exploded on the side of the Marder just above the track suspension. The blast lifted the gun turret off the Lorraine chassis and toppled it over among the crew.

Shaux pulled the PIAT back.

"Panzerjäger down. Panzerjäger down," Johnston said into the radio and received an unintelligible burst of static in response.

"Secure the approaches to the square," Johnston said to Fox and Morton, and they followed him through the back door.

Shaux heard a tommy gun open fire and the crack of a hand grenade. It seemed there were at least some enemy soldiers in the immediate vicinity. Shaux realized that he, too, had a tommy gun, and followed Fox and Morton.

There was no one in sight. Shaux crept along the wall to his left. The next corner would bring him level with the burning Marder, and it occurred to him that this was not a good idea. This kind of house-to-house fighting was best left to men who knew what they were doing. It was, however, a bit late to think of that now.

A portly enemy soldier appeared from the corner less than ten feet away. He saw Shaux and began to raise his hands.

"*Nicht schießen!*" he shouted. "*Ich ergebe mich!*" "Don't shoot! I surrender!"

This is no time for conversation, Shaux thought, regardless of whatever the soldier might be saying—the situation is far too dangerous, far too uncertain. Shaux had his tommy gun set to fire single shots and fired twice. The soldier sank to his knees and fell forward on his face.

Shaux stepped over him and peered round the corner. From here, he could see down the road to the beach, and he could see three Shermans grinding their way towards him. An infantry company was trotting behind the tanks, complete with Bren gun carriers loaded with supplies.

The other direction opened into the square, with the ruined Marder and the remains of its crew. There appeared to be no other enemies nearby, but Shaux, suddenly uncertain, returned to the old couple's room. This really wasn't a good time to be taking prisoners, he thought, not in the heat of combat—assuming the soldier had been trying to surrender, and that had not really been established.

* * *

SHAEF Forward, Southwick House
6 June 1944, 0915 Hours

The French general Marie-Pierre Kœnig approached Eleanor. She turned so that her rump was back against the tabletop and therefore inaccessible—just to save him from temptation. It was an automatic reaction ever since her first trip to Paris when she was at Oxford.

"Bonjour, Elaine," he greeted her.

"Good morning, sir."

The French relationship with the other Allies was difficult at best. In theory, France was a full-fledged ally, on an ostensible par with the United States, Britain, Russia, and China. In reality, France was on the outer fringes of the Alliance looking in.

When France had collapsed in 1940, the French government had surrendered and accepted an arrangement under which the northern and western parts of France were occupied and the southern part was nominally free under the control of a French government based in Vichy. This mishmash was known as the État Français, the French State, but more commonly as Vichy France.

Those who escaped in 1940 were known as the Free French and were recognized by Britain and the United States as the legitimate French government in exile. Unfortunately, this organization was rendered virtually useless because Generals Henri Giraud and Charles de Gaulle were archrivals and had only very limited armed forces in some of France's far-flung colonies. The situation had improved slightly in 1943: the Allies had freed North Africa, and France had therefore regained Algeria, and Giraud had wearied of de Gaulle's relentless egotism and simply given up, leaving de Gaulle unchallenged.

The problem now was that de Gaulle insisted that the Allies grant him immediate and total control over a military government in France as soon as it was freed, an absolute power Roosevelt and Churchill were not prepared to give him. So difficult had de Gaulle become that he was excluded from the SHAEF command structure. The Free French were represented by Marie-Pierre Kœnig as a delegate, effectively just an observer, and the only Free French troops scheduled to fight in Normandy, the 2nd Armoured Division under General Leclerc, were under Omar Bradley's direct command and would not land for several days. Leclerc was explicitly forbidden from taking orders from de Gaulle.

Things had come to a head three days ago, when de Gaulle had been flown to England from North Africa to be briefed on the D-Day landings. Such was his reputation that the Americans had insisted he be kept in complete ignorance until the last possible moment for fear he would leak the Overlord plan.

His meeting with Churchill had gone spectacularly badly. Churchill wanted him to broadcast a message to the French people to welcome and support the British and American forces and to follow their instructions. De Gaulle had refused to do so unless it was also announced that he was the interim, and sole, authority in France.

Churchill summoned Eleanor to his private train, where he was meeting de Gaulle.

"Ah, Air Commandant, it is time for you to earn your decoration," Churchill rumbled.

Last year Churchill had awarded Eleanor the CMG, or Companion of the Order of St Michael and St George, an honor within the complex array of British orders of chivalry, usually conferred upon senior diplomats. He had, she thought, done it out of embarrassment, after a reception at No. 10 Downing Street at which he handed out similar awards to other staff officers, diplomats, and military planners—all of whom were in less senior positions than hers but all of whom were men—but not to her.

Afterward, when drinks were served, he sought her out in the crowd.

"'They also serve, who stand and wait,'" he had said, quoting John Milton.

"So I have heard, sir," she had replied.

For once he had been at a loss for words, looking as if she had just slapped him in the face, and the CMG had followed within weeks.

Now, however, Churchill was full of words.

"Tell that French popinjay to do as he is told!" he snorted. "If he does not, I will send him back to Algiers, and there he will remain. Use all your powers of diplomatic persuasion."

She had entered de Gaulle's carriage only to be berated by him. His English was limited, so he habitually spoke French and used his British driver, Olivia Matthews, as his translator.

"I do not expect you to comprehend the situation," de Gaulle opened. "You know nothing of France. I have nothing to say to you."

"Sir, the Prime Minister has instructed me to—"

"It is necessary that I am in command in order to establish public order," he interrupted, even though he had nothing to say to her. "It is necessary to avoid the Maquis becoming an independent agency capable of causing chaos. Who knows what they might do once they have thrown off the bonds of Vichy and Berlin?"

This was a legitimate concern. The French Résistance was a loosely knit movement united by opposition to the German occupation of France rather than by an actual organization. Some Résistance groups were independent bands of guerrilla fighters known as the Maquis. Maquisards were typically young men who had fled into the metaphorical maquis or scrublands to escape compulsory conscription and forced labor, living off the land like nomads but armed with smuggled tommy guns.

In northern France, Résistance groups were somewhat networked together and coordinated by London, although secrecy and fear of betrayal tended to keep them in small and isolated units. The British supported some of these groups, who contributed invaluable intelligence and sabotage to the Allied cause, often at great personal risk.

In addition, many Résistance groups were, or were said to be, communist cells who might be waiting to stage a revolution as soon as France was liberated. Eleanor speculated that de Gaulle probably loathed communists even more than Nazis.

He had always claimed to be the leader of all Résistance groups, regardless of their style or affiliation, although Eleanor believed many Résistance groups would disagree. The Maquis, she thought, might well prefer to give their allegiance to Stalin rather than de Gaulle.

"The French need to know who is in charge and has the backing of the Allies. I, and I alone, can keep France safe."

He continued in this vein for some time, while Eleanor wondered if he realized that having his words translated for him in a flat monotone robbed them of their dramatic impact.

Eventually he paused for breath, and Eleanor attempted to reason with him.

"The French people know the Allies are their liberators and—"

"I am their—"

"In the coming weeks, thousands of young American and British and Canadian men will die in France, sir," she said, interrupting his interruption. "They are willing to sacrifice their lives to free the French people from the Nazis, but not to establish you as—"

"France is a sovereign nation, and I am—"

"The new French king?" she asked, on the edge of losing her temper. "The Allied watchword is *Vive La France*, not *Vive de Gaulle*."

"France must be governed, you foolish girl!" he shouted. "I will govern. There is no other possibility!"

"*L'État, c'est moi?*" she asked, quoting Louis XIV's famous boast, "I am the state."

"How dare—"

"If you wish to be king, sir, I suggest bring your own royal army to France instead of ours, on your own royal navy."

"That is an outrageous thing to say!" he spluttered.

"It is whatever it is, General. *C'est comme ça.*"

Oh dear, she thought, so much for my powers of diplomatic persuasion. Perhaps Churchill would take the medal back.

Now de Gaulle was back in Algeria and the Allies were landing in Normandy without, in this bizarre turn of events, the support of the French government in exile.

EIGHT

Collmanville
6 June 1944, 0930 Hours

Shaux slumped down against the wall opposite the boulangerie and lit a cigarette. There was no bread, of course, but he let himself imagine a delicious lingering aroma of baguettes baked in happier times. In actuality, smoke and a noxious odor drifted from the wreckage of the Marder anti-tank gun. The bodies of its crew were being collected by a mortuary squad from the 2nd Battalion, South Barsetshire Yeomanry. The South Barts had arrived from the beach behind a squadron of DD Shermans and cleared the few remaining enemy troops from Collmanville. It seemed that the Germans had decided that Collmanville was not easily defensible and had decided to put more resources into the nearby villages of Hermanville and Colville.

Major Cathcart appeared. He had trotted all the way from the beach in full gear but was not even breathing heavily.

"We're going to consolidate here," he said to Shaux and Johnston. "There are two batteries of Priest self-propelled guns coming up and two more companies of South Barts. We are creating as much of a lodgment area as possible between here and the beach for everything that still has to land."

He paused as shells from the naval barrage howled overhead.

"Johnston, I'm giving you a full Four-Niner Commando section, three squads—twenty-five chaps, three sergeants. Lieutenant Mills is dead, and Dawkins is wounded."

Cathcart pulled out a map and started pointing.

"You will continue to reconnoiter forward along the Caen road as far as the Alvis strongpoint, *here*. The South Barts will follow you. The South Lancs are on our right flank, and the East Yorks are on our left. Here's the Alvis strongpoint, where these roads cross. Stop just short of it and assess the situation. I'll see you there. Any questions?"

"No, sir," Johnston said.

Shaux knew the enemy had established a series of well-defended strongpoints in the farmland behind the beaches. British intelligence had code-named them for car manufacturers: Alvis, Hillman, and so on.

Cathcart turned to Shaux.

"Now, sir, I want the road swept clear of enemy traffic from Alvis all the way back southwards to Périers. Please have your chaps on continuous patrol blasting any vehicle that moves. No tanks, no lorries, no bicycles, nothing. The objective is to prevent enemy reinforcements from getting to Alvis."

"Very well," Shaux said.

"Good. You'll move out in ten minutes."

Cathcart and Johnston turned away, busy with their arrangements. Shaux returned to the wall and sat down with his back against it.

He had shot that soldier as he was surrendering. Technically, Shaux supposed, one could argue that the man had not fully raised his hands and therefore hadn't finished legally surrendering at the precise time Shaux shot him, and consequently Shaux had beaten the strictures of the Geneva Convention by a couple of seconds, allowing himself the excuse of reasonable doubt. But Shaux had seen the man's eyes and the look on his face—fear mixed with relief that it was over—and knew exactly what he was doing.

This was worse—much worse—than stabbing that soldier at the beach.

In the early days of the war, Shaux had believed that he was killing people in the service of a greater good. Since Hitler and Naziism were axiomatically bad, the war was therefore a just war by definition, and killing the enemy—and any civilians who happened to be in the way— was regrettable but necessary and legitimate. The Luftwaffe pilots he killed were almost certainly not Nazis, but somehow that didn't matter, and he was acting justly when he blew them out of the sky. Aristotle and St. Thomas Aquinas and all the other "just war" theorizers throughout history would approve.

Now he had killed a man not in some worthy cause but as a matter of personal convenience. If he had let the man surrender, Shaux would have had to disarm him, take him prisoner, find someone to take over responsibility for him, and who knew what else—all time-consuming and potentially difficult tasks. Back at commando training school, they hadn't given a class on accepting surrenders. Shooting the man was simply a pragmatic expedient to solving an issue, akin to kicking a man in the nuts.

"Your men killed my grandfather!" the young French girl's voice broke in. How could the enemy soldier possibly be her grandfather?

"What?" Shaux asked, opening his eyes and staring up at her. *"Quoi?"*

"He came to the door to greet your soldiers when they entered the village. He had a bottle of champagne he had been saving. He opened the door, and they shot him."

"I'm so—"

She spat at him and turned away.

Shaux looked at his watch. It was 0930. It was two hours since he had landed. He remembered lying in the shallows, cold, wet, still not quite on the beach and with 50-caliber machine gun rounds buzzing over his head. The difference between then and now was that the machine gunner had missed, but the girl had not.

* * *

SHAEF Forward, Southwick House
6 June 1944, 0930 Hours

Eleanor listened as the TIO announced the latest developments. Forward elements of the East Yorks, the South Lancs, and the South Barts, supported by tanks from the 79th Armoured Division, had reached the first inland villages south of Sword, creating the beginnings of a defensive wall behind which the British 3rd Division could establish a lodgment large enough to support the forward assault brigades. Self-propelled guns were coming off big LCTs—tank landing craft—and following the assault brigades inland.

Ahead of them all, probing southwards, was 49 Commando.

It was a race against time. Every hour that passed allowed the Allies to land more troops, tanks, artillery, and supplies, thus strengthening their ability to resist a counterattack; every hour the enemy failed to launch a counterattack was an hour after which they would find it more difficult to sweep the Allies back into the sea.

The lodgment area was vital for staging supplies. Eleanor had established a whole MI6-3b(S) group devoted to analyzing the exact sequence in which supplies should be landed and calculating the exact amounts. Supplies would need to be mobile; therefore, they crossed the Channel loaded on lorries and Bren gun carriers ready to be driven to where they were needed. Lorries require fuel and spare parts, otherwise they won't run, but supplies for lorries competed for priority for space against the supplies they carried.

What priority should be given to medical teams and even religious padres? Strictly speaking, medical units took up space that could otherwise be given to fighting men, thus weakening the attack force; on the other hand, morale—and basic morality—demanded that the wounded should be treated as soon as possible and not left to suffer unattended.

And what happened if one of the landing craft sank and its supplies were lost? Eleanor's team had calculated the probable loss rates and therefore the additional resources necessary to compensate. Then there was the question of what was needed when. The initial assault forces were carrying their own food, for example, but they'd need to be fed a nourishing cooked meal on D-Day-plus-one or else they wouldn't be able to fight as well as they might otherwise . . . Cigarettes were not weapons, but they must be immediately available for men fighting on the front line.

It was like writing a symphony in which every note for every instrument had to be exactly right. King Richard III, the last of the long line of Plantagenets, had lost his life and his kingdom at the Battle of Tewksbury in 1485 because he didn't have a spare horse when he needed one, where he needed one. You could argue, Eleanor supposed, that the three-hundred-year-old Plantagenet dynasty—the most powerful and successful dynasty in all medieval Europe—succumbed to a simple failure in logistics.

"A horse, a horse, my kingdom for a horse!" Richard had pled in Shakespeare's play. Well, she thought, no horse and no kingdom either.

"What news is there, Air Commandant?" Churchill asked over her shoulder. He must have grown tired of dictating speeches in her office and started prowling SHAEF headquarters.

"What news of Sword? What news of Rommel?"

"As far as we know, sir, Rommel is not yet back in Normandy. Air reconnaissance has not detected any movement of the big Panzer divisions, particularly the 21st Panzer in Caen. The Americans on Utah and the Canadians on Juno are making progress. Our advanced guard is off Sword."

"Then our progress is satisfactory?"

"We are behind schedule, sir, primarily because of the weather, but we are making some progress. Many of our airborne troops are still unaccounted for. We have gained enough ground behind Sword to establish an initial lodgment. Every hour the Panzers wait is an hour we gain."

"So much hangs in the balance," Churchill said, almost as if he was speaking to himself. "So many dangers, so many difficulties ..."

It struck Eleanor that Churchill's career, perhaps even his place in history, also hung in the balance. If the invasion became a disaster, he might not survive a vote of no confidence in the House of Commons, and he would have to resign. He would be cast out into the political wilderness, just as he had been in the 1930s, and forced to watch from the sidelines as other men made the big decisions.

When the war ended, the men in power would set out the postwar order. Clement Atlee of the Labor Party was the deputy prime minister in the National Government and had supported Churchill faithfully throughout the war, but he was his political archrival. If Churchill lost power, Atlee might take over. The thought of Atlee sitting down with Roosevelt and Stalin, instead of himself, to redraw the map of postwar Europe—indeed, the postwar world—must be infuriating to Churchill.

She recalled that he had made a speech about fate hanging by a slender thread, or something like that, although she didn't remember the details. She judged it best to offer him a ray of hope.

"Von Rundstedt ordered the Panzers to halt short of Dunkirk back in 1940, sir, if you recall. It allowed us to escape. He is still in overall command of Army Group West. Perhaps he'll make the same mistake again."

"Yes, by God, he did stop the Panzers!" Churchill exclaimed, his demeanor brightening. "Let us pray he does so once more, Air Commandant."

* * *

Collmanville
6 June 1944, 0945 Hours

Shaux watched as the square in the center of Collmanville filled with troops and equipment. When he was an RAF Boy Entrant, he had been told that the army was peopled by "brown jobs" and "squaddies" of doubtful mental capacity who were most comfortable walking on their feet and knuckles, and as a consequence he had always thought of the army as being a bit clunky in comparison to the RAF.

In the RAF, you had a squadron consisting of a dozen or so identical, sleek modern aircraft who flew a sortie in unison against a single target, even if not always successfully. In the army, on the other hand, one had dozens of different organizations with differing tasks and specialties, using wildly different equipment, usually fighting several targets simultaneously along an extended battlefront.

If one needed ammunition for one's tank, one didn't get it from a tank regiment; one got it from the Royal Army Ordnance Corps. If your tank broke down, you needed the Royal Electrical and Mechanical Engineers to repair it. You needed the Royal Corps of Signals to send a radio message, and so on. It had all seemed a bit ponderous and Byzantine, a bit nineteenth century.

But now, watching as the square filled up, he saw that all these dozens of different skills and organizations were coalescing. Four DD Sherman tanks from the 13th/18th Hussarswere followed by a Royal Army Service Corps fuel bowser and an Ordnance Corps Scammell ammunition truck. Somehow, the army's disparate groups knew how to fit together without any obvious instruction.

Four massive Royal Artillery Priest self-propelled field guns rumbled into the square. These were large 105mm howitzers installed on top of Sherman tank chassis. They had a range of ten miles, Shaux knew, which meant they could shell Caen from here, if necessary. For some reason unknown to Shaux, the RA favored ecclesiastical names like Priest and Bishop. Perhaps they wanted to reassure themselves that God was on their side.

The square had become a perfect target for an aerial attack. A Junkers 87 Stuka dive-bomber, for example, could drop a 500-pound bomb into the square and blow this part of the British advanced forces to pieces. But thanks to the Allies' absolute aerial superiority, Shaux doubted there was an airborne Stuka within a hundred miles.

Another kind of aircraft howled overhead, and Shaux knew without looking it was a rocket-armed Hawker Typhoon. The noise of its massive Napier Saber engine—twenty-four cylinders, thirty-seven liters, 2,400 horsepower—was unmistakable. This was the first of a continuous line of Typhoons that he had ordered to sweep the road to Périers, as Cathcart had requested. He had seven Tiffies flying at one-minute intervals in a seven-minute loop: in from the Channel, along the road to Périers, and then back out to the Channel. They'd do that for an hour, with each aircraft making seven sweeps before they flew back to England to refuel, and another 2TAF squadron would replace them.

Shaux had flown Tiffies a few times, although never in combat, and he didn't really like them. It was a brute-force sort of a design in his opinion: a huge engine dragging a stumpy-looking aircraft behind it, but a Tiffie was very fast at low altitudes and able to carry heavy weights—a 400-mile-per-hour fighter that could carry a ton of bombs. Shaux thought of it as a British version of a Focke-Wulf 190 or an

American P47 Thunderbolt: aircraft to be respected, in his judgment, but not loved.

Cathcart and Johnston returned.

"Here's an aerial view of the Alvis strongpoint taken at dawn this morning," Cathcart said, handing a photograph to Shaux. "I thought you might be interested."

Evidently Shaux had risen sufficiently far in Cathcart's estimation to be offered information that was not absolutely necessary. Shaux knew that the enemy had built dozens of strongpoints, or Stützpunkts, up and down the Atlantic Wall. Often these were a series of concrete bunkers for troops and dugout pits for field guns, connected by trenches and defended by sunken Tobruks.

"It's surrounded by barbed wire and dragons' teeth, as you can see," Cathcart said. "You can tell from the craters it's been bombed a couple of times so, hopefully, it will be abandoned or in poor condition."

These defensive positions were the modern equivalent of medieval castles, Shaux thought, albeit with barbed-wire entanglements instead of walls but with the same purpose of stopping an enemy from advancing past them.

Another Typhoon howled overhead.

"Time to get going," Cathcart said, glancing at his watch. "Any questions, Color Sergeant?"

"No, sir."

"Then carry on."

"Yes, sir," Johnston said.

Cathcart and Johnston were both instinctive soldiers, Shaux thought. They were completely calm—or at least they appeared to be—in the midst of chaos. He knew the ability to relax under pressure was a gift that couldn't be taught. He'd seen the same quality in a handful of pilots—Winkle Brown, for example—for whom time slows down until there is plenty of time to do whatever needs to be done without hurrying.

Johnston's section formed up on the outskirts of Collmanville. They'd be followed by four Shermans and then more South Barts infantry and the Priest howitzers. Cathcart included an anti-mine tank and an armored bulldozer. Johnston positioned Shaux and Granger with his radio in the middle of the leading commando section.

"You'll be nice and cozy here, sir."

"Thank you, Johnston. Carpe diem."

Johnston stopped, just for a second, and looked at him with the ghost of a smile. "You too, sir."

Then the moment was gone, and Johnston turned away.

"Move out," he said to the leading commandos, and the column started along the road leading to Stützpunkt Alvis.

Shaux saw the girl watching them. She did not wish them luck. He supposed she was thinking that the English were just like Germans and Ukrainians—all killers in different uniforms but without any other meaningful distinctions. Perhaps she thought the English were worse because, unlike the Germans and Ukrainians, they'd shot her grandfather as he offered them champagne.

* * *

SHAEF Forward, Southwick House
6 June 1944, 0945 Hours

Eisenhower returned to the map room, followed by Kay Summersby, his driver. She was his constant companion and widely assumed to be his mistress; if she was, neither of them seemed to care about their reputations. Patton was also assumed to have a mistress—his niece, no less—who served as an American Red Cross donut girl, but he did not take her out with him in public.

The Allied high command consisted of men of unparalleled power, she thought, many of them possessing titanic egos and accustomed to being obeyed immediately and without question. They were also middle-aged, balding men with increasingly flabby tummies who were far away from their wives. They might therefore harbor secret concerns about their inevitably declining virility and seek to reassure themselves in the arms of younger women who could be counted on for prompt and willing submission and extravagant flattery.

She wondered why she didn't like Kay Summersby. It certainly wasn't on moral grounds, God knew, and people were free to do whatever they wanted. She liked and admired Susan Travers, who was the

French general Marie-Pierre Kœnig's driver. Why should she like one woman driver and not the other?

Travers had been a Red Cross ambulance driver who had been under fire several times. She had been a driver in the 13th Demi-Brigade of the Foreign Legion, where she was known as "La Miss," before she was assigned to be Kœnig's driver.

At the Battle of Bir Hakeim in Northern Africa in 1943, a battle in which the 1st Free French Brigade proved they could stand up to Rommel's Afrika Korps, Travers had rescued her man, literally driving Kœnig to safety through a hail of enemy fire. She had thereby paid her dues in full, Eleanor thought, a person in her own right and not just some girl a French general had chosen to keep him warm at night.

Perhaps that was it, Eleanor pondered: Susan Travers had earned her right to be her lover's equal.

It was all so frustrating. She had noticed that, as Johnnie's reputation grew, she was sometimes introduced as "Johnnie Shaux's wife," rather than as "the head of Red Tape" or "SHAEF EIA." She wasn't ashamed of being his wife—to the contrary, she was very proud of him—but she was primarily herself. That was it, she thought. Society defined women as extensions of their husbands—subsets of their men—rather than as individuals in their own right.

She had fought a lifelong battle against being merged into someone else's life story—a man's life story. Her first encounter had been with Rawley, the heir to a decaying peerage, whose plan for her was to bear his children and manage his estate while he squandered her money on vapid aristocratic pursuits and expensive lovers. They had met at Oxford. She had been under extreme pressure from her mother to ensnare a "suitable" husband, and she had, in a moment of innocence and weakness, allowed Rawley to seduce her. He had subsequently treated her with humiliating noblesse oblige. Clearly she should consider herself lucky that he deigned to take her two or three times a week—if he had nothing else going on—and that she might, by extreme good fortune, one day be known as Lady Fletcher.

Johnnie was a man who wanted nothing more than to stand in her shadow, but even that seemed a fatal loss of independence.

She imagined herself many years in the future, publishing her memoir. The publisher had narrowed down the title choices to two: *A*

Fighter Pilot's Girl, or *The Creator of Asymmetric Zero-Sum Analytics,* and was recommending the one about the fighter pilot's girl.

That was her fundamental dilemma, she realized, the choice between being a successful professional and a wife. She wanted Red Tape, with all that it implied, and she wanted Johnnie, and she felt that society would not permit her to have both.

Marie Curie, with two Nobel prizes, stood in her own right . . . Catherine II of Russia . . . Amelia Earhart . . . Queen Elizabeth of England . . . Helen Keller . . . the list of women who stood alone was remarkably short. All the rest, half the world's population, were defined by their husbands and always had been.

She suspected that female praying mantises were much happier than human women; they copulated and then consumed their mates— the opposite of human social submission and an excellent premise for choice and variety. As a woman in a man's world, she had been propositioned dozens of times. In a mantis world, she could cheerfully have said yes to them all—the mantis version of the old expression must be "You *can* have your cake and eat it too!"

In her next life, if she had a choice, she would definitely be a mantis.

NINE

Collmanville
6 June 1944, 1000 Hours

A Typhoon howled overhead. They were working like clockwork, Shaux thought, with an aircraft every minute. He hoped the pilots were paying attention, because he knew from experience that this kind of repetitive patrol work quickly became excruciatingly boring. Your mind begins to drift, and you start thinking about having a pint in your local when you get back, or wondering exactly how far your girlfriend will let you go next time you see her, or realizing you really, really should have remembered to pee before taking off.

At least the pilots did not have to worry about getting jumped. In earlier years, he'd flown over France, constantly searching the skies for the little black dots that could sprout wings and turn into full-size Messerschmitts or Focke-Wolfs in a matter of seconds. Now the Allies had overwhelming numerical superiority, and almost all the Luftwaffe was back defending Germany from the relentless Allied bombing or trying to stave off the implacable advances of the Russian army on the Eastern Front. But that didn't make the skies safe; Shaux knew that far less than half of all operational aerial fatalities came from enemy action.

Someone up ahead shouted for the section to take cover, and Shaux jumped into the ditch that ran beside the road. This was the second or third time the advance guard had seen something they didn't like. Shaux was beginning to feel like a squaddie responding to that most frequent of all military commands, "Hurry up and wait," as he crouched in the ditch, coming to terms with the fact that the ditch was filled with stinging nettles while Granger produced a comprehensive catalog of sotto voce blasphemies.

Eventually one of the RM corporals—Shaux thought his name might be Poynings—appeared above the ditch.

"Sergeant Johnston wants you, sir."

Shaux scrambled out, leaving Granger to his woes. Johnston was a hundred yards ahead, crouching beside a haystack, attempting to communicate with a French civilian, a man in his thirties who was wearing overalls and the inevitable beret.

"You speak French, sir," Johnston said. "What's he saying?"

"Yes, what is it?" Shaux asked. *"Um, qu'est-ce que c'est?"*

"Attention! L'ennemi a posé des mines," the Frenchman said, jerking his thumb over his shoulder in the direction of Alvis. "Watch out—the enemy has laid mines."

"He says there's a minefield," Shaux told Johnston.

Shaux turned back to the civilian.

"Where?" *"Où?"*

"Sous la route." "Under the road."

"He says they mined the road," Shaux reported to Johnston.

"And in the fields?" *"Et dans les champs?"*

"Peut-être, je ne sais pas." The Frenchman shrugged. "Perhaps. I don't know."

"Montre-moi." Then Johnnie turned to Johnston. "I've asked him to show us exactly where the mines are, Sergeant. He doesn't know if they also mined the fields."

"Right, sir," Johnston said. "We'll take three men forward with the Bren."

He was as calm and decisive as ever, as if he'd been waiting for someone to appear and reveal an unknown minefield—and perhaps he had.

"Poynings, run back and tell the Crab to come forward. Tell them to stop here and wait for further orders."

A Crab was a Sherman tank with a rotating flail in front of it. The flail was made of lengths of steel chain. The idea was that the tank drove slowly forward with the flail spinning, and the thrashing chains set off any mines in front of the tank rather than under it—at least, that was the theory.

"Catesby, Ratcliff, you're in the lead. You, sir, and the Frog next. White, you're a runner as necessary. Move out."

"*Un kilometer,*" the Frenchman said.

"One kilometer," Shaux relayed. "A thousand yards."

Johnston led them at a brisk pace as Typhoons overflew them with monotonous regularity. The Frenchman grabbed Shaux's arm.

"*Ici, cent meters, soyez très prudent,*" he said. "Here, a hundred meters. Be very careful."

"Just ahead," Shaux called to Johnston and the party halted, kneeling on the side of the road. Johnston pulled out a pair of binoculars.

"Where, exactly?"

"*Où?*" Shaux asked the Frenchman.

"*Là-bas,*" he said, pointing forward. "*À côté des arbres.*"

Two trees stood directly ahead, one on each side of the road, as if guarding it.

"Where those trees are," Shaux reported.

"Run back and fetch the Crab, White," Johnston ordered.

They retreated to the ditch while White ran back. Another Typhoon swept over them. When issuing his orders, Shaux had stressed that the Typhoons should not attack anything north of the Alvis crossroads, and he hoped that the message had been passed on and understood.

The Crab clanked past them, emitting a plume of brown exhaust fumes and an uneven roar. Shaux knew its extraordinary Chrysler engine consisted of no less than five six-cylinder truck engines driving a common crankshaft. He guessed that two or three of its cylinders were not firing but that still left twenty-seven or so that were.

So much of the war effort was dependent on the ingenuity of engineers and civilians, he thought. Someone must have remarked that it was a pity that Chrysler's ultra-reliable six-cylinder truck engines were not powerful enough to haul a tank, and someone else had said perhaps we could fit in two engines, or three, or four, or even five, and suddenly you had a thirty-cylinder Chrysler A57 Multibank capable of pulling a thirty-five-ton tank across muddy fields at 20 miles per hour . . . The war was being fought here in Normandy, he thought, but it was being won in Detroit.

The Crab's flail started to rotate, and it advanced slowly to the trees, throwing up clouds of dust as the chains beat the road like a giant carpet sweeper. It crawled beneath the trees, and Shaux wondered if the Frenchman had been wrong or, worse, was some sort of enemy agent sent to deceive them. At that moment, a mine exploded under the flails ahead of the Crab, and then another, spraying gravel and rocks in all directions. Then a third mine exploded directly under the Crab's left track, tossing the tank sideways—all thirty-five tons of it—off the road and into the trunk of one of the trees. The tree, after a moment, toppled slowly into the field beside it.

"I'll see if the crew is all right, Sergeant," Ratcliff said, starting to climb out of the ditch.

"Wait," Johnston said.

Shaux guessed he was thinking that the enemy might have artillery trained on this spot, knowing anyone approaching along the road would have to stop to deal with the mines.

The smoke and dust from the explosions faded away.

"There, sir!" Catesby shouted.

In the far distance, a motorbike and sidecar manned by two soldiers in gray uniforms appeared at the edge of a wood.

"Les Boches!" growled the Frenchman.

A Typhoon roared overhead, and the motorbike patrol—assuming it was an enemy patrol—retreated back towards Alvis.

"We'll avoid the road," Johnston said. "Likely that's not the only place they mined."

He stood.

"Ratcliff, go back and bring up the rest of the section. Tell Granger to inform Major Cathcart we're advancing through the fields. Tell him we lost the Crab. Understood?"

"Got it, Sergeant," Ratcliff said, and departed down the road with the loping gait of a long-distance runner despite his bulky equipment.

Johnston turned to Shaux. "It'll take a few minutes for them to catch up," he said, lighting a cigarette. "It's a good job you speak French, sir. I've got no head for languages."

"Oh, I spent a few months in France," Shaux said.

"1940?"

"Exactly."

He'd been stationed in France in 1940—flying Bolton Paul Defiants, of all things—during the catastrophic defeat of the French army and the British Expeditionary Force that culminated in the miraculous evacuation of the BEF from Dunkirk.

He did not mention that he had also been a POW here in 1941, escaped, and made it back to England with the help of the Belgian Résistance and that communicating in French had made the difference between freedom and a Stalag Luft prison camp. But that was all long ago and unimportant.

* * *

SHAEF Forward, Southwick House
6 June 1944, 1000 Hours

"Cod has fallen," the TIO announced, and there was a brief smattering of applause.

"What is Cod?" Churchill demanded. "Who is Cod?" He seemed upset he didn't know, just as he had when someone mentioned Rhubarb. "Why does no one tell me these things?"

"Cod is, or was, sir, the code name for the last major enemy strongpoint on Sword Queen Red Beach," Eleanor told him. "It's on the western flank, in Colleville Plage, with two or three big guns and several machine-gun positions in casemates and Tobruks."

She pointed to the big map.

"There, sir. It was inflicting heavy casualties as the men were coming off the landing craft. Now that it has fallen, we'll be able to speed up landings significantly."

"We have subdued the Atlantic Wall?"

"I fear not, sir. We have subdued one more piece of it. Many other pieces—the Riva Bella Casino bunkers in Ouistreham, for example—remain in enemy hands and are taking a heavy toll."

"Ah, yes, I remember the casino well."

"The enemy tore it down last year, sir, and built a Stützpunkt over the cellars."

"Oh."

The Casino strongpoint, she knew, was a particularly difficult target. It was being attacked by two troops of Free French Marine commandos, the Fusiliers Marins Commandos, often called Bérets Verts, or Green Berets, which were integrated within Royal Marines No. 4 Commando. They were led by their commander, Philippe Kieffer, whose reputation for gallantry was on a par with the Special Services commander Lord Lovat. These were the only French troops landing on D-Day itself.

"The Sword Beach Assault Brigade, the first wave, has finished landing, sir," Eleanor continued. "Now the Intermediate Brigade is beginning to land. It's an hour behind schedule, which is worrisome but not outside the bounds of reasonable risk."

"Helmuth von Moltke said 'no plan survives contact with the enemy,'" Churchill said. "He was correct; in the Franco-Prussian War—"

"Excuse me, ma'am," an American officer broke in. "General Eisenhower would like to see you right away."

"Excuse me, sir," she said to Churchill. Poor man, she thought, as she followed the officer, he has no one to hear his military history lesson. He was like a fish out of water, far from the center of attention, but, she reminded herself, he should not have come to SHAEF Forward in the first place; no—he was not a fish out of water but an architect at a bricklayers' convention.

Eisenhower had gathered a small group of advisors in his office, including Jim Stagg, the meteorologist.

"We need a go or no-go on Mulberry, Eleanor," Beetle Smith said. "The weather's iffy, but Jim thinks it's still possible. Is there an EIA reason to hold off?"

Mulberry was one of the biggest and most complex of all Overlord projects: the construction of two huge floating harbors, A and B, that could support the entire invasion force. It was a miracle of engineering ingenuity: a line of massive concrete caissons called Phoenixes to act as breakwaters against storms in the Channel; inside that, closer to the beaches, another breakwater made out of sunken ships, code-named Gooseberries; inside that again a long line of floating pier heads called Spuds, where cargo could be unloaded and then driven to the shore along lengthy floating causeways known as Whales.

It would all take several days to assemble, and towing the first pieces of the puzzle across the Channel at the grand speed of 2 miles per hour required dozens of tugboats to start immediately. If the enemy could hold or recapture some Atlantic Wall strongpoints, they could shell the harbor components as they arrived.

"There are no indications of any Luftwaffe countermeasures and still no Panzer movements, sir," she said. "The enemy seems to be relying on a combination of bad weather in the Channel and its static defenses on land. They haven't made any attempt to move resources from the Pas-de-Calais, so they still believe there could be another invasion point there."

"How would you assess our progress?"

She pointed to the map on Eisenhower's wall. "Obviously Omaha is very difficult, sir. The Rangers are on top of Pointe du Hoc but under heavy attack and with no reinforcements."

Mulberry A was planned for Omaha Beach. If the enemy could hold Pointe du Hoc, they would be able to shell Mulberry A with ease.

Mulberry B was planned for Gold Beach.

"Gold, Juno, and Sword are somewhat better, but we are clearly behind schedule. The Canadians on Juno encountered heavy resistance on landing but are moving forward. In fact, they are making the best progress of all. We are clearing resistance on Gold, but, again, behind schedule, and we may not reach Bayeux today as planned. We're just approaching the first strongpoints behind Sword in the Colville area, and that will determine how far we can get today, specifically whether we can reach Caen, which looks doubtful."

"No sign the Panzers are moving?"

"Not so far, sir. Feuchtinger hasn't moved 21st Panzer out of Evreux, Meyer hasn't moved the 12th SS Panzer, and the Panzer Lehr haven't moved from the Chartres-Le Mans line."

She looked at her watch.

"It's ten. It's been twelve hours from the first airborne landings and four hours from the first men on the beach at Utah. They've had enough time to assess the severity and scale of this operation and to start moving, but I think they still haven't made any decisions. I think they're waiting for Rommel, and I assume he'll be there in the next couple of hours. The moment he arrives, he'll order 21st Panzer to move, but by then it will be too late to push us off the beaches."

"So, in your view, is it safe to proceed with Mulberry?" Eisenhower asked.

She had devoted four years to attempting to understand and anticipate the enemy, to applying mathematics to weigh and balance opposing forces, to conquering complexity and uncertainty with logic, to piercing what von Clausewitz had called the fog of war and earning her place at this table.

"It is, sir."

* * *

Strongpoint Alvis
6 June 1944, 1015 Hours

Somewhere up ahead, Ratcliff held up his arm and the section halted. Shaux saw Johnston go forward to talk to Ratcliff and then return.

"We've reached Alvis," Johnston told Shaux. "Take a look and see if you think it can be attacked by rockets."

Shaux crawled forward to where Ratcliff and Catesby had set up a Bren gun. From this position, it was impossible to see anything useful. Alvis was set in a grassy knoll, perhaps five feet higher than they were, and all he could see were rolls of barbed wire and the top of a Tobruk turret. He pulled out the photo reconnaissance snapshot Cathcart had given him.

It did not look as if rockets would be much use against these bunkers and trenches. The trenches were zigzagged to reduce blast, and the bunkers had closed concrete roofs. Bombs falling vertically would be more effective than rockets hitting at a flat angle, but bombing was too inaccurate and could well hit Johnston's section or other British forces coming up from the beach.

"Very well, sir," Johnston said when Shaux told him, and Shaux suspected that Johnston's opinion of the RAF's ability to contribute to the invasion must be falling steadily. "We'll see if they want us to bypass Alvis or take it. If necessary, we'll do it the old-fashioned way."

Cathcart arrived ten minutes later.

"Brigade wants us to take Alvis. They're concerned if we bypass it, the enemy can continue to shell the beach. Our armor will be here in five minutes."

That was an important decision, Shaux thought. Every minute they spent taking Alvis was a minute less they could advance towards Caen, and a minute more for the enemy to deploy its Panzers unmolested.

The armor, as it rumbled forward, consisted of another Crab flail tank, three Shermans, and a Royal Marines Centaur 95 mm howitzer. The Centaur was a Cromwell modified to act as a sort of moving pillbox. It had a brutish appearance with massive slabs of armor welded to its turret as if daring the enemy to try to attack it.

The Crab went first, its flail beating the ground, followed by crouching marines, who were followed in turn by a Sherman ready to provide covering fire. There was no immediate response from Alvis as the attackers climbed the low rise to the outer strands of barbed wire. Perhaps, Shaux thought, they were waiting for more marines and tanks to reveal themselves.

The Crab must be driven by a lucky crew, Shaux thought, because it managed to reach the wire without setting off any mines. The marines moved forward and began to cut through the wire by hand; if the Crab attempted to do so, the wire would wrap itself into the flail, and the Crab would be ensnared in a trap.

Now, abruptly, the Alvis defenses opened up. Shaux saw, or thought he saw, a shell strike the sloping front armor of the Sherman and bounce skyward. A Tobruk, just visible at the crest of the rise, opened fire on the exposed commandos with twin 20mm cannons.

"We need to get a PIAT on that Tobruk," Johnston said to Shaux. "Can you do it, sir?"

"Of course," Shaux said.

"Send one of your PIAT gunners, Johnston," Cathcart said. "We don't want to—"

"He doesn't miss, sir," Johnston interrupted him.

Cathcart looked from Johnston to Shaux and back again.

"Very well," he said.

Shaux crept forward, wishing Johnston hadn't said he didn't miss.

* * *

SHAEF Forward, Southwick House
6 June 1944, 1015 Hours

Bramble poked his head around her office door. Eleanor had pled with Fred Morgan to take over "Churchill duty" and she had escaped to her office to catch up on a growing pile of urgent information. She was here to advise Eisenhower, not to provide Churchill with a running commentary.

"Four-Niner Commando has reached Strongpoint Alvis," Bramble said.

That was a long way from the beach, she thought with a sudden chill, almost as far inland as the paratroopers on the River Orne. Alvis wasn't very far from the 21st Panzer Division and—

"Don't worry, ma'am," Bramble said. "He can handle things better than anyone I know."

"Thank you, Mr. Bramble," she managed to say, looking at the photograph of Shaux she kept on her desk. "I know he can."

Of course, she didn't really know if he was still with 49 Commando or not, but that didn't make it easier.

Last year, in the grim period of self-recrimination after she had dumped Johnnie, she had gone to the orphanage in Blackheath where he had grown up. It was supposed to be a pilgrimage seeking redemption, or an admission of guilt, or some such psychological twaddle. The visit was not a success; St. Christopher's had suffered bomb damage, and all the children had been evacuated and dispersed across the home counties as part of Operation Pied Piper back in the early days of the London blitz.

Still, an elderly custodian showed her around. The rooms were worn and shabby, and there was no brightness, no cheer, nothing to suggest fun and laughter. The walls were decorated not with bright pictures but with embroidered religious texts and exaltations of the "God Thou See-est Me" variety. The linoleum in the corridors and hallway had been worn away by children's feet. The overall effect reminded her of Dickens.

The matron's office walls were lined with group photographs of staff and children and rare moments of celebration, such as a visit by the Bishop of Southwark in 1927, according to the inscription. The faces in the group photographs were too grainy and poorly focused for her to find Johnnie, but in one photograph, a small boy stood rigidly to attention in front of a grand lady, offering her a scroll—doubtless a memento of the occasion. The boy seemed not to be afraid or overawed except that he was standing with one foot on the other. Something about the image had caused her to read the inscription: "Lady Alice Scott is presented with a memorial scroll by an orphan, on the occasion of her visit, September 1923."

The boy was unquestionably Johnnie. The tiny scar in the shape of a C on his left cheek was unmistakable. He already had his stoic "I can deal with this" face, she saw, with only his feet betraying his inner turmoil. In September 1923, he would have just turned five. If she and Johnnie ever had children, she thought as she stared at his face, this is what they would look like—perhaps she was looking at both the past and the future.

Johnnie didn't have a name, she saw. He was just "an orphan," as if he were not quite a full member of the human race, an appendage, not abandoned by society but not entirely belonging.

The grand young lady also looked familiar. Of course!—it was Princess Alice, now the Duchess of Gloucester, the titular head of the WAAF.

Johnnie had spent fifteen years in these grim surroundings—no wonder he expected so little of life, and no wonder his shock at loving and being loved. Even after four years of marriage, he still seemed amazed that she would welcome him into her bed.

She asked the caretaker if she could borrow the photograph, promising to return it the next day. She brought it down to Barcroft Hall, where MI6-3b(S) shared quarters with an RAF Air Reconnaissance Interpretation Unit. The ARIU had the finest photographic facilities in the country, and the copy they created put the original to shame.

It now stood on her desk, alongside a photograph of her late father and another of Keith Park pinning her Military Medal on her uniform in 1940. That was only four years ago, but it seemed like four hundred.

TEN

Strongpoint Alvis
6 June 1944, 1030 Hours

"Bull's-eye, sir," Johnston said as a PIAT grenade tore a ragged scar across the side of a Tobruk turret taken from an obsolete French Char B1 tank. It was hard to tell if the damage was permanent, but its machine gun stopped firing, at least for a while.

"If you ever get tired of Spitfires, you might consider a transfer to the Royal Marines, sir," Johnston said. "You'd be a bit on the old side but promising. If you kept your nose clean, you might even make corporal in due course."

"I'll bear that in mind," Shaux chuckled.

The Crab, without its flail rotating, was pushing its way into the barbed wire and then reversing out, dragging sections of the fencing loose. A three-inch mortar crew, with the mortar barrel pointing almost vertically, was attempting to lob 10-pound shells into the nearest trenches, although it was impossible to see the results.

It seemed to Shaux that they were making very slow progress.

"We'll send in the Shermans as soon as we get through the wire," Cathcart said, appearing beside them. "It looks as if we'll have to take the strongpoint piece by piece. This may take a while. I've asked for a Funny, but nothing yet."

The army had developed a number of specialized tanks known as Hobart's Funnies, after their inventor. The Crab was one example, and there were others, particularly armored bulldozers, designed to clear wire and similar obstructions.

Shaux sat down with his back to a stone field wall and lit a cigarette. He had a waterproof tin in his Bergen with another fifty cigarettes, and he wondered if they would last. The latest Typhoon howled overhead; evidently the strongpoint had no antiaircraft flak guns.

So far, he had accomplished nothing, he thought, apart from one or two lucky potshots with the PIAT.

He was beginning to lose faith in the whole AGCS idea, at least for himself; he hadn't realized how little he could see on the ground. He'd be a lot more useful up there with the Tiffies, or in a Mosquito, or even loitering about in a Lysander. From the air, he'd be able to see the exact layout of Alvis and perhaps spot some weaknesses.

When he got back to England, he'd have another shot at persuading the powers-that-be in the Air Ministry to let him try Tsetse Mosquitos armed with Molins guns instead of RP3 rockets against ground targets. It was absurd that he was too old to fly at twenty-five—almost twenty-six. Perhaps he could persuade his old boss, Wilfred Freeman, to intercede on his behalf.

"Another five minutes should do it," Johnston said, assessing the Crab's progress. "We'll go first with the Shermans. You come after them in case we need the PIAT for any other Tobruks."

"Do not, under any circumstances, attempt to engage the enemy directly," Cathcart said. "Your job is to have the PIAT on standby if needed, not to join the assault. You are AGCS, not RM."

"Yes, I understand," Shaux said.

* * *

SHAEF Forward, Southwick House
6 June 1944, 1030 Hours

A US Marine sergeant from the Embassy in Grosvenor Square brought Eleanor a small package.

"This came in the diplomatic bag, ma'am," he said. "It's from Mr. Hopkins in Washington."

Harry Hopkins had summoned her to the American Embassy in London a week ago. He was Roosevelt's most trusted confidant and right-hand man and far more powerful than the vice president. Hopkins and she had worked on Anglo-American alliance matters since 1941 and had developed an almost uncle-niece relationship, particularly since her father had died.

He was, she knew, a source of her current position and influence. Last year, Churchill had moved her under Frederick Lindemann, his friend and scientific advisor, who the Americans disliked intensely. Hopkins had insisted that she be reinstated. If she had the support of Hopkins, and by extension Roosevelt, she could not be ignored. She might be an oddity, an irritant, but the generals on both sides of the Atlantic had no choice but to tolerate her.

She always looked forward to seeing Hopkins, and he never came to England empty-handed—perhaps with a jar of marmalade from Florida, perhaps with delicious dark chocolate from San Francisco.

He was here to assess the final preparations for D-Day and report back to the president. Roosevelt had, at significant political risk, made a massive commitment to the war in Europe while many in Washington had urged him to concentrate on Japan—the country that had actually attacked the United States. If the Normandy invasion went badly, Roosevelt's critics would make sure he took the blame, and there was a presidential election just a few months away in November. Given Roosevelt's obviously declining health, his fourth-term reelection might not be automatic and inevitable, particularly as his opponent would be the youthful and vigorous governor of New York, Thomas Dewey.

Hopkins had been one of the architects of Roosevelt's New Deal in the 1930s. He had become so important to the president that Roosevelt had persuaded him to move into the White House. It was typical of Roosevelt's trust in Hopkins's judgment that the president had sent

Hopkins, a civilian, to assess the plans for Operation Overlord, despite all the briefings that George Marshall and Eisenhower and dozens of other military and naval experts must have given Roosevelt.

Eleanor knew that Hopkins respected facts and figures but that he was, in essence, a man who made decisions "with his gut," as he had once told her. It occurred to her that if Hopkins was unhappy with the preparations and told Roosevelt that the invasion might fail, then Roosevelt might overrule the generals and delay the invasion. It was therefore important that Hopkins's gut be satisfied if D-Day was to proceed as planned.

"I read a summary of the Red Tape analysis of Overlord," he told her. "That, of course, is your mathematical evaluation of our chances of success. It is, as always, thorough and convincing."

"Thank you, sir."

"You feel the invasion must go forward?"

"The entire D-Day venture is risky, sir, by its very nature. But it must be done, and done as a matter of urgency. If we don't liberate northern Europe, Stalin will pretend to, and he will never give it back."

"What are our chances, Eleanor?"

"Better than fifty-fifty and therefore mathematically likely, although by no means certain."

"I want you to set aside mathematics for once, Eleanor. You've been living with this for a year. What does your gut tell you?"

She took a deep breath. She knew her opinion was not decisive, far from it, but she knew he took her seriously, and therefore, by extension, so did Roosevelt.

"My gut tells me we have two ways of winning, sir."

"Two ways?"

"We may defeat the Germans, and the Germans may defeat themselves. My gut tells me both will happen, and therefore we will prevail—by the skin of our teeth, perhaps, but we will prevail nonetheless."

They moved to the embassy's splendidly ration-free dining room.

"Well, Eleanor, if your predictions are right, the war will end sometime next year," Hopkins said, as they sat down.

Eleanor felt close enough to banter with him, something she would never dream of doing with Churchill or any of the senior commanders.

"What do you mean, 'if'?"

"Touché!" Hopkins chuckled.

"Yes, sir, the war will end next year. Hitler simply doesn't have the resources to pursue a two-front war for more than a year. Besides, his generals may not let him fight literally to the death."

"A coup?"

"It's possible. When the Russians reach Germany, there will be rape and pillage on a scale seldom seen in history. Genghis Khan would be envious. Remember that Stalin starved two or three million Ukrainians to death ten years ago, and he might well do even worse to the Germans."

"So, a coup is really possible in your view, Eleanor?"

"Not only possible but also logical, sir. The SS may be fighting for Hitler, but the rest of the armed forces are fighting for Germany. Without Hitler, the top German priority is to surrender to the United States before the Russians reach Germany. Von Rundstedt and Rommel might just do so unilaterally in order to save as much of Germany from the Russians as they can."

"A surrender?"

"A preemptive surrender soon after D-Day, before too much damage is done to our forces or the enemy's. That would allow us to put Patton on the East German frontier facing Marshall Zhukov, the Russian commander. We might also—if we are cleverer than we usually are—disarm the SS but agree to permit the Wehrmacht to remain active, which would put Rommel *and* Patton on the East German frontier. That would certainly stop Zhukov dead in his tracks."

"How do you think of these things, Eleanor?"

"It's my job. I'm paid to."

"What about the war in the Pacific? What about the Japanese?"

"I think the Japanese will fight on indefinitely, although I'm no expert on that. But the Manhattan Project is moving quickly, and that will offer an alternative way of ending the war in the Pacific."

"An atomic bomb?"

"Exactly so, sir, as soon as they can make it work. So, both in Europe and in the Pacific, a year seems a good estimate for an Axis defeat and the end of the war."

"We've been at war for two and a half years—well, five years for you Brits, since 1939," Hopkins said, pushing back his chair at the end of dinner. "It's hard to believe it will end." He offered her a cigarette. "The moment it's over, you and that husband of yours will be able to get back to normal."

He was just chatting idly, she knew, but he had struck a nerve, a secret fear, and she trusted him enough to react without dissembling.

"Normal?" she wondered out loud. "I don't know what normal is. Normal for me is using Red Tape to devise new ways of killing people, and Johnnie's normal is just killing people. That's what we've been doing since 1940. That's what defines us. Killing is our core competency; it's all we know."

"Don't be silly, Eleanor!" Hopkins said. "You know infinitely more than—"

She felt as if an emotional dam had broken, something harsh and ugly.

"Last month I turned twenty-six. I have no home, no babies, no job apart from Red Tape, and no idea what comes next. I should have my doctorate by now, and I haven't even started. So, you may know what normal is, sir, but I don't. When the war is over, I won't know what to do."

"Your husband—"

"He won't know what to do either. Sometimes I think it would be better for us if the war went on forever. We seem to thrive in wartime."

He frowned. "Perhaps it would be better for you, Eleanor, if you stopped feeling sorry for yourself."

"That's not fair—"

"I am dying of cancer," he said, his voice hardening. "Is that the most important thing about me? Is dying of cancer my 'core competency,' as you put it? Do you tell your friends: 'You know, Harry Hopkins is really, really good at dying of cancer. He's been practicing it for years'?"

"Of course I don't—"

She had never seen him angry. She had never heard him mention his illness. How had an idle conversation suddenly turned into an argument?

"You know, Eleanor, for a smart woman, you are really, really dumb. One of my little pleasures in life is—or now I should say, used to be—imagining all the wonderful things you will accomplish in the future . . . But I see I've misjudged you."

"I—"

"When the war is over, you'll be responsible for your own life, your own decisions. Is that what scares you. Eleanor? It's called being a grown-up."

Now she was close to tears.

"I'm ashamed of you," he said.

He stood, shook his head, and left.

Now a week later, she took the package from the marine and opened it immediately. It contained a small box of chocolates and a note that said: "Sorry I lost my temper even though you thoroughly deserved it. HH"

"Any reply, ma'am?"

"Yes, let me get a piece of paper and an envelope."

She thought for a moment and wrote: "I did deserve it. Affectionately, Eleanor."

She sealed the envelope, addressed it to EYES ONLY, Mr. Harry Hopkins, 1600 Pennsylvania Ave, Washington, DC, and handed it to the marine.

"Thank you, Sergeant."

* * *

Strongpoint Alvis
6 June 1944, 1045 Hours

Shaux, on his elbows and knees, crawled up the slight rise to Alvis, following Johnston. Now he was covered in slimy mud instead of wet sand, and he wasn't sure that constituted progress. Granger crawled after him, still carrying the radio on his back and more PIAT ammunition.

Shaux could hear machine-gun fire but could not see from where it was coming. Ahead to his right, a Sherman fired its main gun at maximum deflection, presumably at a casemate or Tobruk on the far side of Alvis, and then shook as someone shot back. Golden fire blossomed on the side of the Sherman's turret, but the Sherman kept moving. Evidently two inches of angled armor plate had been enough to absorb or defect the charge, although the sound inside the tank must have been deafening.

Ahead to his right, a Bren gun was barking. Perhaps the first marines were through the wire and had reached the first trench.

Johnston and his men rose and raced up the hill ahead and threw themselves down again. Shaux followed. Now he was almost on the same ground level as Alvis, but he still couldn't see anything. He started to kneel, but buzzing rounds above his head reminded him to keep his head down. This was not the assault course at Achnacarry in Scotland during a live fire exercise; this was a fight to the death. Now there were thuds in the grass in front of him kicking up plumes of dirt, and he remembered Johnston lecturing them that far more men die from ricochets than from bullets.

A marine crawled across the hill towards him. "Sergeant Johnston says to PIAT a Tobruk at 10 o'clock, sir."

Shaux could see nothing at 10 o'clock. "Show me," he said, and followed the marine.

They inched forward, hugging the ground. The Sherman fired again, the Bren was in action, the enemy was returning fire; Shaux seemed to be surrounded by men who knew what was going on and at whom they were firing, but he could see nothing.

"Over there, sir," the marine said, jerking his head rather than lifting his arm to point. Shaux raised his head, inch by inch, feeling as if he was daring the enemy to blow his head off. Some men carried mirrors and little periscope devices—he'd have to remember that for his next invasion. By craning his neck, he finally managed to see the top of a large bush—no, not a bush, a Tobruk camouflaged with branches, less than fifty yards away. This Tobruk was not an obsolete French tank turret like the others he had seen; this was a Panzer Mark 2 armed with a 20mm cannon and a Spandau machine gun.

Off to the right, two of Johnston's marines rose and ran towards a trench Shaux could not see. The Spandau snapped, and one of the marines fell. Shaux beckoned Granger to bring up the PIAT. Shaux needed to inch forward into more open ground and raise himself high enough to aim the weapon. Fortunately, he had left the gun cocked from the last time he used it; otherwise, he or Granger would have had to stand up to cock its powerful spring.

The Panzer 2 turret had a heavy curved gun mantlet and sloping sides—a PIAT grenade would probably just bounce off at an angle, but the turret was seated on a vertical collar that might be more vulnerable. He loaded the PIAT and inched forward, acutely aware that he was exposing himself more and more.

The Panzer 2 turret began to rotate in his direction. In a second or two, the crew would be able to see him. The Spandau was snapping, but Shaux couldn't see what it was firing at. If he waited any longer, he'd be dead. He raised himself into a kneeling position and fired.

* * *

SHAEF Forward, Southwick House
6 June 1944, 1045 Hours

"I am about to return to London, Air Commandant," Churchill said. "I must brief the cabinet and then the House of Commons. I have given Ike my warmest felicitations on our progress so far. Now, pray tell me, exactly what *is* our progress so far?"

The more she saw of him, the more she thought she understood his mind. First the politician in him congratulated someone for their great accomplishment, and then the pragmatist in him found out what the accomplishment really was.

"The weather is tolerable in the east, at Sword, but marginal in the west at Utah and Ohama. Shipping losses are within the expected range—a combination of mining and rough weather. Enemy naval action is *de minimus*, and the Luftwaffe has yet to appear."

She paused to marshal her thoughts.

"It is now H-hour plus four. The Canadians on Juno Beach are doing well, and our 50th Division is making good progress on Gold Beach. The Americans are encountering very stiff resistance, but they are holding Utah and Omaha, and there's no indication that the enemy are pushing them off. The American 82nd and 101st Airborne had very difficult drops last night, but they are slowly regrouping. Our 6th Airborne is still holding the Orne bridges, and Lord Lovat's commandos are on the way to relieve them. We are making some progress inland from Sword, but we are being held up by fierce resistance from a line of strongpoints a mile or two south of the beaches."

She wondered where Johnnie was. He'd be coordinating air strikes against the strongpoints, back from the front lines and not directly in the fight. For no reason at all, she shivered, and Charlie, always alert to her movements, looked up sharply.

"There is no indication that the enemy can push us off the beaches?"

"The enemy has not deployed the 21st Panzer Division against the beaches, sir. They cannot push us off without doing so, with the 12th SS Panzer and the Panzer Lehr coming in behind them to finish us off. If all three divisions had moved, we would be in real difficulty."

"Why have they not done so, Air Commandant?"

"They are doubtless concerned about our airpower and our naval firepower, sir, which make large, armored formations vulnerable, but I suspect the main reason is that, without Rommel, they have no clear grasp of the overall situation and no clear plan. They're just hoping the Atlantic Wall holds. Every hour strengthens us and makes us harder to dislodge."

"Then we are winning?"

"We are not losing, sir."

"Ah, of course, the Shaux Tautology!"

He smiled and puffed on his cigar.

"We have, so far, overcome many dangers and difficulties? Can that be said?"

Clearly, he was seeking an optimistic version of events, and it was true that many dangers and difficulties had been overcome, although many, many more lay ahead. She guessed he had dictated that phrase into his speech.

"It can, sir."

He beamed.

"Then I shall so report it to the House of Commons."

ELEVEN

Strongpoint Alvis
6 June 1944, 1100 Hours

Shaux's PIAT mortar burst against the Panzer 2 collar. The turret stopped rotating—just before it could bear on Shaux—but the Tobruk did not seem to be seriously damaged. Perhaps he had only succeeded in jamming the turning mechanism.

Shaux lay flat and signaled Granger to reload.

"We've only got a flash-bang left, sir," Granger said.

"That won't do any good," Shaux said. "Go back down and find some armor-piercing ammunition."

Shaux inched his way back down the slight rise in the direction he had last seen Johnston. He found him and the rest of the section crouched behind a stone wall.

"We need more firepower," Johnston told him. "Tommy guns against cannons doesn't work."

Machine-gun fire buzzed over their heads as if to confirm the point. The advance had stalled, at least temporarily. More men and more tanks would be needed, and perhaps heavier artillery, to crack

Alvis open. Caen, Monty's objective for the day, was twelve miles from Sword Beach, and they had only come a mile or two in four hours.

It occurred to Shaux that the enemy might seize this moment to counterattack. There could be a hundred men in Alvis, and perhaps hundreds more within half a mile, who could surely overwhelm the lightly armed marines and South Barts. Perhaps there were Panzers hidden in the dugouts. There was no rule that said that the defenders had to stay behind their fortifications, waiting to be attacked.

Shaux was suddenly exhausted—so exhausted that it was too much effort to worry about being counterattacked, and there was nothing he could do about it anyway. They had been advancing almost nonstop since they landed, and now they could go no further. The constant roaring of artillery and the hammering of smaller guns seemed to be dulling his senses, as if he were a battered boxer staggering on his feet. He lit a cigarette and stared blankly at the sky, too weary to think.

* * *

SHAEF Forward, Southwick House
6 June 1944, 1100 Hours
Eleanor and Bob O'Neill left Southwick House and walked across the muddy grass to the so-called Conference Hut, a grimly utilitarian building containing a single large room and a rickety stage. It was filled with reporters from major British and American newspapers and radio services. The air was thick with tobacco smoke and the voices of the reporters all talking at once. Three SHAEF press relations officers were attempting to herd the reporters into rows of seats.

She and O'Neill reached the stage. The herd finally found seats and fell silent. She didn't want to do this, but Beetle Smith had decided that it was better, from a public relations point of view, to have working members of Eisenhower's staff addressing the press rather than professional liaison officers.

"You'll be more authentic," Smith had said. "The horse's mouth."

"Should I look authentically nervous?"

"Eleanor, you don't know how to look nervous."

Now she cleared her throat, and the reporters readied their notebooks.

"Thank you for your patience," she began. "As you will appreciate, General Eisenhower and his senior staff are very busy, but he has recorded a message, and he will speak to the press the moment his duties permit. In the meantime, he asked General O'Neill of the Eighth Air Force and me to brief you in his absence. My name is Shaux, of the WAAF. As you will also appreciate, we cannot provide you with detailed intelligence that might be useful to the enemy."

The room was silent save for the rustle of pencils on notepads.

"As announced in London by the BBC and in the United States an hour ago, an Allied expeditionary force is landing in northern France. The armies involved are the—"

"Where in northern France?" an American reporter asked.

"Sorry, I cannot say."

"Is it the Pas-de-Calais?"

"I cannot say."

"Well, obviously the enemy knows where we're landing, so why the secrecy?"

"We will give you more details as soon as we possibly can."

"That doesn't make sense unless this is a diversionary raid and the real one is yet to start."

"Please don't interpret the announcement like that," Eleanor said. "Please don't draw conclusions. Just accept that we are not announcing the exact location yet."

The reporter gave up, shaking his head.

Eleanor's stomach knotted. She had no desire to deceive these men, but she knew that the enemy would scrutinize every word they wrote or announced on the radio. The reporter was right: of course, the enemy knew exactly where the landings were taking place. But she had agreed with Strangeways, the mastermind behind the Operation Fortitude deception plan, that fudging answers about the location would help preserve the ruse that Patton was about to launch another invasion, the "real invasion," in the Pas-de-Calais area.

"Divisions from three armies are involved," she continued. "They are drawn from the 1st US Army under General Omah Bradley and the

2nd British Army under General Sir Miles Dempsey, which includes the 3rd Canadian Division under General Rodney Keller."

She decided not to say that these armies constituted the 21st Army Group under Montgomery, although it was true. In part she did it because it was an unnecessary complication to her narrative, and in part, to be honest, she did it out of spite. She thought his role was superfluous—Eisenhower was perfectly capable of speaking to Bradley without Montgomery as an intermediary—and, well, she simply didn't like Montgomery.

"We also carried out airborne landings last night as preliminary steps for this morning's beach landings. These paratroop and glider operations were undertaken by the US 82nd and 101st and the British 1st Airborne."

The reporters were taking copious notes.

"Overall, tens of thousands of men are involved. The USAAF and the RAF are in control of the air and conducting supporting operations. The US and Royal Navies are in control of the Channel. Enemy air and naval response has been minimal."

"Are any French soldiers landing?" another reporter asked.

"Yes, the Green Berets, the Bérets Verts."

"Just the commandos? Is that all?"

"The French 2nd Armored Division, under General Leclerc, is part of General Bradley's US 1st Army."

She hoped the reporters would interpret that to mean they were part of the landings. She had no desire to have to explain why they were not. Out of the corner of her eye, she saw a French reporter raise his hand, but she decided to press on to an easier topic.

"We are also receiving valuable assistance from the brave men and women of the French Résistance," she added.

She was not naïf. She had often shaken her head at newspaper reports she knew were not true, and Whitehall was filled by bureaucrats whose job was to present the war in the most optimistic way possible, just as Joseph Goebbels's Ministry of Propaganda did in the opposite direction. Public morale on both sides depended on the civilian population believing there was a light at the end of the tunnel.

But she had never been directly involved in the process of deciding and manufacturing "facts." In just these few minutes, she had fudged the question of whether this was the only invasion, ducked Montgomery's role, and danced around the exact participation of the French army—all without telling a single lie.

The briefing continued, with O'Neill fielding questions about the American troops and Allied air operations.

"Thank you for your attention," she said as the meeting drew to a close. "There will be another briefing this evening and another tomorrow morning. The press relations officers will give you the details and will also be issuing additional briefing materials throughout the day."

"Just for the record, how do you spell O'Neill and Shaw?" a reporter asked.

"It's O'Neill, I-L-L not A-L," Eleanor answered. "And my name is S-H-A-U-X."

"Really? Shaux?" the reporter persisted. "Are you related to the RAF pilot Johnnie Shaux?"

"He's my husband."

"Is he involved in the invasion? What's he doing?"

This was becoming a bit intrusive, Eleanor thought, but perhaps the man wrote a gossip column in peacetime, and she was on her best behavior.

"Knowing Johnnie, he's probably having a quiet smoke," she said, and the room chuckled.

* * *

Strongpoint Alvis
6 June 1944, 1115 Hours

"Regardez, regardez, voici, voici!" the French civilian insisted, stabbing at the photo reconnaissance snapshot of Alvis with a long, nicotine-stained finger. "Look, look, here, here!"

He had attached himself to Johnston's section as an unofficial guide and observer, and Johnston had not shooed him away.

"What?" Shaux said. *"Quoi?"*

He and the Frenchman struggled through a stilted conversation until Shaux finally understood.

Shaux crawled along behind the stone wall to where Johnston was crouching. The Frenchman followed, still talking.

"The Frenchman says there's a side entrance that was knocked open by the last bombing raid," Shaux told Johnston. "It hasn't been fully repaired. It's this smudge on the photograph. See it, here? It used to be guarded by a pillbox, but that was blown up. The Germans built a temporary wooden barrier. He says there's a slit trench we can use to get inside. He says it won't be manned."

"How does he know?" Johnston asked.

"Comment savez-vous?"

The French burst into a voluble explanation.

"Quoi? Lentement! Slowly!"

"He says the local Résistance was considering a sabotage raid and scouted the place two nights ago."

"Why does he say it'll be unmanned?"

"The only things there are the lavatories. All the men are at their posts."

Johnston crawled away to report to Cathcart. Shaux slumped against the wall and lit his umpteenth cigarette of the morning. He wondered what time it was but lacked the energy to look at his watch. Besides, it didn't really matter anyway. He hadn't slept a wink last night; perhaps he could rest his eyes for a—

"The major says we're to give it a go if you trust the Frog. Do you?"

The Frog, as Johnston called the Frenchman, had been right about the mines, and Shaux could think of no reason why he would lie about the side entrance. There was no evidence he really belonged to the Résistance, but the Résistance didn't carry official membership cards in their wallets.

"I do," Shaux said. *"Comment vous appelez vous?"* he asked the Frenchman. "What's your name?"

"Je m'appele Jean Anjou."

Johnston, decisive as always, organized the assault.

"The major says they're going to try to breach the defenses again using Conger Bangalores and bulldozers. Meanwhile, we'll see if we can get in the side. If we can, we'll signal, and he'll send in reinforcements."

He turned to his men.

"Right. Ratcliff and Lovell first, with the Frog to show the way, then Poynings and Catesby with the Bren. Then the PIAT, then Wyatt last."

Shaux reflected that he and Granger were fully integrated into the section as "the PIAT." The radio, his whole reason for being in France, had been relegated to unnecessary baggage. But he was now part of the fighting force rather than a passenger, and he felt a surge of pride: being "the PIAT" was a big step up from being a Glasgow drunk.

The Frog—Shaux found he was automatically thinking of Anjou in that manner—led them down the hill and through a thicket of bushes until they came to a cart track leading to the side of Alvis. The track ended at a puddle twenty feet across filled with muddy water, presumably a bomb crater, beside a ruined concrete gatehouse.

The pillbox had collapsed into a pile of concrete shards, with twisted reinforcing rods sticking out at odd angles. Beyond it, the entrance to a narrow trench was blocked by a pile of wooden beams and rubble. Johnston and his men pulled down enough that they could scramble over the rest.

The trench was cut into the rising ground that hid the Alvis strongpoint. Ratcliff and Lovell led the way into the trench, followed by Anjou and the rest of the section. The trench was deserted, as Anjou had promised. The sides were buttressed by wooden staves. A low doorway led into a foul-smelling cavern.

A cannon fired directly above their heads; they must be right under one of the gun emplacements. It had that same harsh mechanical hammering as an MG 131. Shaux wondered, still in his hazy, slightly out-of-focus frame of mind, why there were so many Luftwaffe weapons being used by the army. Perhaps the Luftwaffe was running out of aircraft to put their guns in. He must remember to report that to the powers that be.

The trench was cut in zigzag fashion. Ratcliff peered round the next corner and backed away, signaling silence. He drew his fighting knife. An enemy soldier appeared around the corner, and Ratcliff plunged his knife into the man's chest, just as Johnston had taught Shaux in Scotland. The man fell silently at Ratcliff's feet, and Ratcliff stepped over him. The rest of the section followed, each stepping over the soldier. It took only two seconds for a live man to become a dead obstacle, Shaux reflected, as he stepped over him in turn.

A short ladder stood against a muddy wall, perhaps leading up to the MG 131. Johnston climbed the first two steps, craning his neck to see over the top. He stepped down against and pantomimed a machine gunner firing a weapon. Then he pantomimed throwing a grenade up and into the machine-gun emplacement above, and pointed to himself and Ratcliff, who nodded and took a grenade out of a pouch on his webbing. Johnston pulled out his pin, as did Ratcliff. Johnston held up his hand and counted down three-two-one on his fingers, and they both tossed their grenades up and over the side of the trench.

There was a double thunderclap above them as the grenades exploded.

"Come on, lads, up on top," Johnston shouted and disappeared up the ladder.

Shaux waited his turn. He almost fell as he climbed: he needed more than two hands to hold the ladder, the PIAT, and his tommy gun. At the top of the ladder was a sandbagged emplacement with an MG 151—a 20mm cannon, not a machine gun, pointing at the sky with the bodies of its dying gunners sprawled around it.

A machine gun opened fire from somewhere behind Shaux, and the section threw themselves down behind the sandbags. Johnston pulled out a flare pistol and fired a red flare to tell Cathcart they were in position. It was interesting to see that Cathcart and Johnston had decided to use such an obsolete form of communication—clearly, they had little trust in radios, even at short distances, when accurate communication was vital. Well, Shaux thought, the Air Ministry had a Pigeon Section ruled by a Pigeon Policy Committee, no less, which managed the pigeons carried in Lancaster bombers, so perhaps flares weren't as old-fashioned as he had assumed.

"Get that gun ready, Wyatt," Johnston said.

Wyatt struggled unsuccessfully with the MG 151 ammunition loader.

"Here, let me load it," Shaux said. "I've seen this before in a captured Messerschmitt."

"Attention!" Anjou shouted.

One of the enemy gunners—who they had assumed were dead—was attempting to raise his StG 44 assault rifle. Anjou snatched the 44 away, turned it on the gunner, and shot him in the chest.

"My stupid mistake," Johnston said, shaking his head. "I should have checked them immediately."

He turned to Anjou.

"Merci, Frog!"

The ammunition belt was entangled under the dead gunner. Shaux started to pull it out as delicately as he could, but Catesby and Lovell simply picked the gunner up and pushed him over the sandbags like a sack of coal. A distant machine gun spat at them, and they threw themselves down. Shaux unlocked the MG 151 loading mechanism, reinserted the belt correctly, clipped it closed, cocked the weapon, and nodded to Johnston.

"All ready."

"Wyatt, Catesby, go back down to the trench," Johnston said. "Our lads should be along in a minute or two. In the meantime, shoot anyone coming from the opposite direction. Clear?"

"Clear, Sergeant."

"You man the gun, sir," Johnston said to Shaux. "You know how it works."

Shaux could see back down the rise they had come from but very little of the rest of Alvis apart from the tops of Tobruks. The one he had hit with the PIAT seemed to be stuck in the same position. Down the hill, a Funny—a Centaur tank without a turret but with a large bulldozer blade—was pushing through the wire. One Sherman was upside down in the minefield, and two others were exchanging fire with the Alvis Tobruks, with little apparent effect on either side.

He could see a small group of three extremely brave South Barts men in a Bren gun carrier preparing a Conger, a rocket pulling a woven tube that could be fired across a minefield with the tube unrolling behind it. The tube would be pumped full of liquid explosive and blown up, setting off the mines—a weapon so improbable that it made his PIAT seem mundane.

"Qu'est que c'est 'Frog?'"

Anjou had asked Shaux what "Frog" meant as they waited.

"Camarade," Shaux answered, using the word for "friend" or "mate."

"Ah, Frog," Anjou said, smiling and nodding.

"Four-Niner, Four-Niner," Catesby's and Wyatt's voices shouted in the trench below. Reinforcements must be arriving along the trench, and Catesby and Wyatt did not want to get shot by their own side.

Cathcart climbed the ladder and squatted down inside the emplacement.

"What weapon is that?" he asked Shaux.

"It's a Luftwaffe MG 151 20mm cannon," Shaux said.

"Is it any good?"

"It's a very good weapon; it fires HEI high-explosive incendiary rounds. It won't penetrate tank armor, but it'll be good against anything else."

"Very well," Cathcart said. "We're going to work our way through the trenches. You will suppress any enemy movement at ground level. From your vantage point, we'll be clearing the trenches in that direction, to your right, which means that anyone appearing on your left is probably the enemy. Clear?"

"Clear."

Just as Johnston had decided that Shaux was a useful addition to Four-Niner, Cathcart seemed to have decided also.

"Sir," Cathcart added, as had become his fashion.

* * *

SHAEF Forward, Southwick House
6 June 1944, 1115 Hours

Eleanor picked up the telephone and waited until she was connected to Bramble.

"Have they heard anything from Johnnie, do you know?"

No sooner was the question out of her mouth than she regretted it. She was supposed to be coolly assessing the situation on the beaches, trying to make coherent sense out of the chaos of dozens of conflicting reports, not driving herself into a tizzy over Johnnie every five minutes.

"I'll check and telephone you back," Bramble said.

Now she had to stare at the telephone, instead of her reports, until it rang.

"Rhubarb ordered continuous patrols on the road from Alvis southward towards Caen," Bramble said. "Those were his most recent transmissions."

"When was that?"

"Approximately 0930."

"Nothing since then?"

"Nothing, ma'am. I've told 2TAF to telephone me immediately when he comes on the air."

Now she was in exactly the situation she had wanted to avoid: a limbo of uncertainty. Now she would have to deal with the knot in her stomach and a tendency to jump every time the telephone rang. Charlie sensed her mood and stirred under her desk. He looked up at her, decided she didn't need immediate comfort, walked in a tight circle, and collapsed again.

She squared her shoulders, shook her head, and picked up the next report, an update on Plan Green. Starting in the early hours of this morning, the Résistance had been carrying out sabotage operations, often at great personal risk. There were several targets, including electrical facilities and telephone lines, but perhaps the most important job was sabotaging the rail system in order to prevent the enemy from bringing in reinforcements and supplies, particularly heavy armor that could only travel by rail.

The Résistance had been summoned into action by a coded message read over the BBC's French service yesterday evening, a snippet from a hitherto obscure poem that translated into English as "wound my heart with a monotonous languor." The Résistance was disabling steam locomotives and cutting lines. A favored technique was to loosen the joiners between rails but to leave the rails in place so that they looked undamaged. The rails would part when a heavy train crossed the joint, causing a major derailment that could take days to repair.

No railways meant, effectively, no more Panzers reaching Normandy—and that could be the margin of victory. If—

The telephone rang and she snatched at it, but it was only a TIO staffer reporting that the British probe towards Caen had become stalled by fierce enemy resistance at Strongpoint Alvis. Which was worse—to not know Johnnie was all right or to know he wasn't?

TWELVE

Strongpoint Alvis
6 June 1944, 1130 Hours

Men in gray uniforms rose from an unseen trench to Shaux's left and began to run across his field of fire. He fired a short burst, and the enemy threw themselves down. Shaux thought it probably didn't matter if he hit them or not, just as long as they couldn't reach the trenches that Four-Niner was clearing. He could hear the muffled rattle of tommy guns firing over in that direction and the thud of grenades bursting. Somewhere just ahead, but totally unseen, a vicious hand-to-hand fight for control of Alvis was taking place.

One of the gray uniforms popped up and lobbed a Stielhandgranate 43 stick grenade towards the Four-Niner trenches, and Shaux fired a single round. The gray uniform twisted and collapsed. Shaux sometimes had nightmares in which enemy aircraft were transparent, made of glass, and he could see the Luftwaffe pilots and aircrew he was hitting. Now he was on the ground in the midst of the infantry. Here he needed no imagination to understand what his MG 151 rounds were doing. When he was flying, he had thought he understood the horrors of war, but he had only been scratching the surface . . .

Mrs. McKinley, the matron of the orphanage, had had a strong belief in the benefits of bible study, and he had been forced to spend hours committing passages to memory. It was her duty, she explained, to do her best to save the children's souls from eternal damnation—although her attitude suggested she expected to be unsuccessful. After all, if God had good intentions for the children, he wouldn't have made them orphans.

What did the bible say? Before, he had only seen through a glass darkly, or something like that, but now he knew clearly—the shock in the eyes of the man he had stabbed, the outrage on the face of the man who was trying to surrender, the agonized twisting of the back of the man he had just shot.

Shaux saw the Tobruk with the Panzer II turret with the 20mm cannon was back in action, the length of its barrel shortening as it swung round towards him. The MG 151 would be useless against it.

"PIAT, Granger," he called over his shoulder. "Armor-piercing."

Granger handed him the weapon. "AP already loaded, sir,"

The Panzer crew inside their turret had a very restricted view through their openings in the armor, and the turret was pointed slightly away from Shaux. Hopefully they wouldn't see him when he raised his head and upper body above the level of the protective sandbags.

He leaned forward using the top of the sandbags to support his arms. The PIAT had far too strong a kick to attempt to hold it and fire it unsupported. The Panzer turret rotated towards him, like the head of a wolf scenting prey. Shaux looked at it and fired.

The Tobruk fired just as Shaux fired.

Something pushed Shaux in the chest so hard that it knocked him backward, and he found himself lying on his back in the mud. He knew without looking and without feeling—indeed he couldn't move his head, and he couldn't feel a thing—that he had been shot. Now the sound of the gun that had fired at him arrived—the round that hit him traveled twice as fast as the sound—and Shaux could tell from the sharp crack it was the Tobruk's cannon.

Of all the weapons that Shaux had fired since the war began five years ago, the 20mm cannon was his favorite, very reliable and remarkably accurate up to half a mile, and devastating in effect—an executioner's gun. His Mosquito had had four in the nose, each with 150 rounds of ammunition. It was therefore ironic, he thought, that he should be shot by his own weapon of choice. Or perhaps it was fitting rather than ironic; it would be demeaning to be shot by a mere tommy gun or some such lesser weapon.

He had been shot down over Dunkirk back in 1940 and again during the Battle of Britain a few months later. He'd been forced to bail out over France in 1941 with his aircraft on fire. He'd crashed into the Mediterranean Sea in 1942 when his Spitfire's controls were reversed by aeroelasticity in a freak malfunction. He'd almost flown his Mosquito into the sea off the coast of Norway as he took off from HMS *Nonsuch* under fire . . . His aircraft had been shot up on occasions too numerous to remember. and he'd had at least a dozen emergency landings. But in all those years, in all those incidents, he had never once been even grazed by a bullet. It was therefore curious—an unexpected twist of fate—that he had survived scores of such incidents in the air only to be shot finally in his very first morning of combat on the ground.

Johnston's face appeared above him and stared at him in alarm.

"Get a doctor," Johnston mouthed to someone out of Shaux's vision, and Shaux realized that after hearing the 20mm cannon, everything had fallen silent.

At least it was much warmer, thank God. He had been cold and wet ever since he arrived in Normandy, and it was very pleasant to feel warm and dry. The wind seemed to have died away—that would probably explain it. He would have stretched in luxury if he had been capable of stretching.

Another face appeared, staring down at Shaux, its eyes narrowing sharply as it examined Shaux's chest.

"I'm a doctor," the face said silently, mouthing the words. "Not much blood, nothing too serious. Could be a ricochet. You're going to be fine."

The doctor looked away and shook his head at someone else Shaux could not see—Johnston, he assumed. Shaux knew he should get back to the MG 151—that was what Cathcart was relying on him to do, and Four-Niner was fighting for its life—but perhaps he'd better rest a little first.

The doctor must have been right, just a flesh wound, because in a very short while, Shaux found he was able to stand and look around. He saw he was on the bank of a river—not the Orne, the nearest river, surprisingly, but the Styx—and saw a group of people waiting for him on the other side. It was a shallow river, narrower than he had first thought, easy to wade across and pleasantly warm: the transition from life to death was surprising easy.

He knew he had died but had no recollection of how or when; he just knew this was the Styx and this was the entry to the after-life, even though the sky was deep blue and the sun was shining brightly. Everything seemed familiar, as if he had been here before, but that would be absurd—you only die once. No, he realized, it really was familiar; he had often had a recurring dream in which he died and crossed the Styx into the afterlife—except this time this wasn't a dream. This was real.

It was a bit confusing, for a man who didn't believe in an afterlife, to discover there was one after all. So, the bible was right: "For now we see through a glass, darkly, but then face to face." Mrs. McKinley really had had his best interests at heart.

Some young men in the group waiting for him—well, it was more than a group. It was a crowd, a totally silent crowd. They were in fly-ing gear, and Shaux knew that these were airmen he had shot down and killed. With each young man stood his mother and father and his wife or girlfriend, and most of the groups had little children, except the little children were strangely ethereal, and Shaux knew that these were the children the airmen would have sired if Shaux had not killed them. He could see a few Wehrmacht soldiers on the fringes of the crowd—these must be men he had killed earlier today—yes, that was the man he had knifed, he was certain, and the man he had shot as he tried to surrender. Unlike the airmen, they looked ill at ease, glancing about uncertainly, and Shaux guessed they hadn't had time to get used to being dead.

No one said anything; everyone just watched Shaux, and he under-stood they just wanted him to see the lives he had ended, damaged, and denied.

Shaux passed slowly through the crowd, looking wordlessly into every face. He came to a stage set on a grassy knoll above the riverbank.

An elderly man sat at a desk on the stage and beckoned Shaux to come forward. The crowd pressed forward and watched in silent witness.

"Ah, here you are at last," the old man said, picking up an old-fashioned quill pen and preparing to take notes. "Now, please evaluate your life."

The old man—he had bushy eyebrows raised in query—and the crowd waited for his answer.

Johnnie looked back and saw Eleanor and Charlie on the far bank. Eleanor was beckoning to him urgently, and he could see that Charlie was barking furiously, even though he couldn't hear him. Standing with Eleanor and Charlie were three ethereal children, looking at him shyly through their fingers because he was a total stranger. Two of them were little girls who looked exactly like Eleanor, and the third, the youngest, was a boy standing with one foot on the other, determined to be brave. Shaux knew these were the children he and Eleanor would never have.

It was a pity, but there was really nothing he could do about it now, and the old man was waiting for his answer. He turned back to the stage to answer the old man's question, but Mrs. McKinley was unexpectedly standing in front of the desk.

"Well, he wasn't difficult, Your Honor, to be fair," she was saying. "But he was . . . private. I don't know how else to put it. He was very self-contained for a small boy. I always got the feeling he could be hiding something from me—no, not hiding, but not volunteering. He was like a parcel tied up tight with string and sealed with wax, and who knew what was inside, good or bad?"

The old man frowned, pursed his lips, and made a note.

This did not seem to be going well, Shaux thought, and eternity lasts a long time. He shivered, or tried to, but it was too much effort. He was lying on cold, wet grass, staring up at Johnston, and he couldn't move. His chest hurt—hurt a lot.

"Here's a smoke, sir," Johnston said, putting a cigarette between Shaux's lips. "Just lie easy until the stretcher comes. The medics are on the way."

PART TWO

Diver/Market Garden

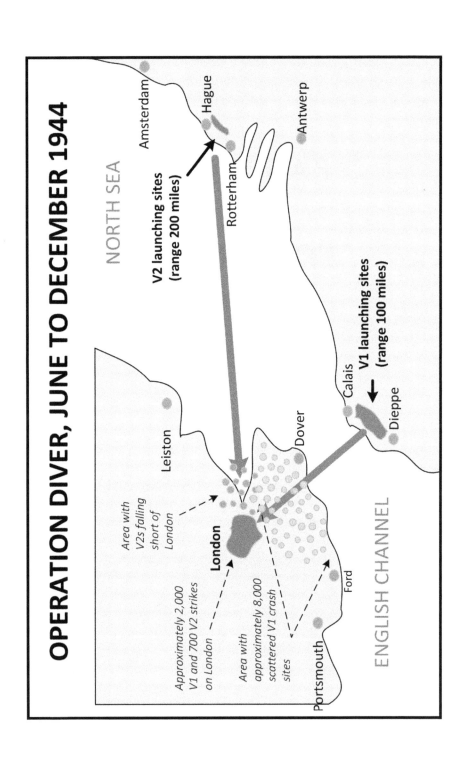

OPERATION DIVER, JUNE TO DECEMBER 1944

NORTH SEA

Amsterdam

Hague

Antwerp

V2 launching sites
(range 200 miles)

Rotterham

V1 launching sites
(range 100 miles)

Calais

Dieppe

Leiston

Dover

Area with
V2s falling
short of
London

London

Approximately 2,000
V1 and 700 V2 strikes
on London

Area with
approximately 8,000
scattered V1 crash
sites

Ford

Portsmouth

ENGLISH CHANNEL

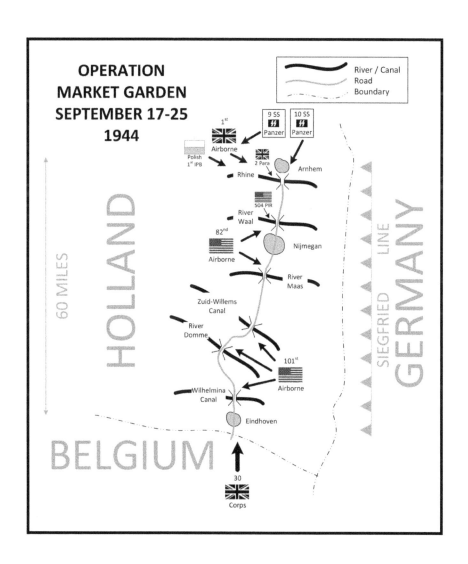

OPERATION
MARKET GARDEN
SEPTEMBER 17-25
1944

River / Canal
Road
Boundary

HOLLAND

60 MILES

BELGIUM

SIEGFRIED LINE

GERMANY

9 SS Panzer
10 SS Panzer

1st Airborne

Polish 1st IPB

2 Para

Arnhem

Rhine

504 PIR

River Waal

82nd Airborne

Nijmegan

River Maas

Zuid-Willems Canal

River Domme

101st Airborne

Wilhelmina Canal

Eindhoven

30 Corps

THIRTEEN

RAF Station Ford, Sussex, England
10 September 1944, 0730 Hours

"Warmer leader, you are cleared for takeoff," a controller's voice said in Shaux's earphones.

"Thank you," Shaux said.

He opened the throttles of his Mosquito's twin Merlin engines.

RAF Ford's main runway headed southwest. He'd cross the coast at Bognor Regis and then swing around to make his way eastward up the Channel to his holding area off the coast south of Hastings.

He permitted himself a big, secret smile beneath his oxygen mask as the Mosquito rose smoothly into the air. This was as close to heaven as he could hope to be—except, of course, with Eleanor. He was flying a Mosquito, now definitely his favorite aircraft. He was miraculously back on Ops, not flying a desk or doing loathsome goodwill tours as a cartoon hero or, indeed, crawling around in the mud with a PIAT in the hope of being useful.

It was now three months since he'd been invalided out of Normandy on D-Day. It had taken almost two months of convalescence to recover from his injuries and another month to convince the powers that be to let him fly again. Wilfred Freeman had arranged for him to return to 645 Squadron, the Mosquito squadron he'd commanded last year. It had been re-crewed and reequipped with Mark 6 Mosquitos since the raid on the U-boat pens at Bodo in Norway and was now part of Operation Diver, the RAF's defense against Hitler's new V1 flying bombs.

He'd gone to Princess Mary's Royal Air Force Hospital in Wendover two weeks ago to receive his official medical release.

"You fractured seven of your ribs," the doctor had said. "They are on your right side. You also severely dislocated your right shoulder."

The doctor was short, youthful, red-haired, and pedantic. He had been in Malta when Shaux and Eleanor were stationed there in 1942, and Eleanor had nicknamed him "the Ginger Runt." He wore a white coat with pockets bulging with complex diagnostic instruments and had large horn-rimmed glasses, perhaps to make himself look older and more authoritative.

"I therefore conclude that you were struck very hard on your right chest by a large blunt object."

He pointed to his right side lest Shaux had difficulties in comprehending spatial concepts. A second and more senior doctor stood behind him, and Shaux saw him roll his eyes.

"You were, as I understand it, under fire from an enemy 20mm cannon, but, as you know, cannon shells are not large, blunt objects. To the contrary, they are smooth and pointed."

He paused to remove his glasses.

"Why, then, did you receive such a blow, one wonders?" Glasses on. "Now, the only thing in front of you, as one understands it, was a projector, infantry, anti-tank mortar launcher, commonly referred to as a PIAT, and you had your shoulder to the PIAT's stock, being in the act of firing the weapon." Glasses off. "I therefore believe a 20mm cannon shell, or a ricochet from a 20mm cannon shell, stuck the PIAT and drove the metal stock, which has inadequate canvas padding, back into your chest."

He pantomimed this theory and paused as if waiting for an acknowledgment of his deductive powers. The senior doctor rolled his eyes again.

"I have examined a PIAT mortar launcher and determined that its stock is physically compatible with your injuries. I have also inquired as to the amount of kinetic energy a 20mm cannon shell would have transferred to the PIAT if it struck the PIAT as I surmise and at a range of fifty yards which, I am told, was the range at which it struck you." Glasses on. "I was assured that the force of a 20mm cannon shell striking a PIAT held against one's shoulder at that range is of sufficient magnitude to cause an injury—injuries, I should say—such as yours."

He paused again, perhaps in self-admiration.

"Had the cannon shell hit you directly, it would, needless to say, have gone straight through your chest, leaving a large and almost certainly fatal exit wound, let alone damage to any organs it might have penetrated in its progress." Glasses off. "I am told the man next to you, your radio operator, was struck directly by a cannon shell and died immediately."

Shaux waited in case the doctor wanted to add something like "Elementary, my dear Watson," or "QED," but he did not.

"Thank you, Doctor," Shaux said finally. "Am I fit to fly?"

"Your ribs were cracked, rather than broken, and therefore you suffered no complications from sharp edges or splinters that could have caused internal lacerations or other damage. Your recovery, in that context, has been full and within the usual six-week convalescence for such an injury to a man of your age and in your physical condition."

Shaux thought the doctor sounded disappointed that his injuries had not been more severe or medically challenging,

"Yes, Doctor, but am I fit to fly?" he asked.

"You are not. You are now twenty-six, and it is RAF policy that you be grounded permanently."

"Surely there are exceptions that—"

"No, there are not," the Ginger Runt said with an air of ultimate authority. "The cumulative mental and emotional stresses of flying operations have been shown to be—"

"Excuse me, if I may, Doctor?" the senior doctor intervened, stepping forward. "As far as your diagnosis is concerned, you are, Group Captain, if I may use a technical medical term, bloody lucky."

Shaux thought he would have been a lot luckier if the cannon had missed completely but did not argue.

"As far as your age is concerned, I received a signal from the Air Ministry, approved by Air Chief Marshall Freeman, voiding the standard age limit."

"That's not—" the junior doctor began, but his colleague cut him off.

"You are therefore discharged from medical care, Group Captain, and passed fit for General Duties (Flying) as specified in RAF regulations. Good luck in 645."

* * *

SHAEF Forward, Versailles, France
10 September 1944, 0715 Hours

"Sir, you asked for my opinion, and I gave it," Eleanor said. "To repeat: I think the Market Garden plan, as currently drafted, has serious deficiencies."

That was the politest way she could think of to describe what she thought of the plan; "recklessly overoptimistic" would have been more honest.

"That's because, with due respect, you're not qualified to judge it," Major General Percival replied. "You have no understanding of airborne operations."

Percival stared at her with hard eyes, perhaps expecting her to wilt. He was on the staff of Lieutenant General "Boy" Browning, the most senior British Airborne commander. They were discussing the newly proposed Operation Market Garden, a plan in which paratroopers would drop into enemy-held territory to capture six important bridges in Holland. The bridges stretched north-south along a sixty-mile stretch of road crossing several strategic rivers and canals.

"Market" referred to an airborne plan to drop the British 1st Airborne Division at Arnhem, sixty miles north of the current Allied front line; the US 82nd Airborne Division at Nijmegen; and the US 101st Airborne Division at Eindhoven. "Garden" referred to a plan for the British 30[3] Corps, led by the Guards Armoured Division, to drive

---

3.   In contemporary military usage, this was XXX Corps in Roman numerals.

north from Belgium through Eindhoven and then Nijmegen and finally to Arnhem to relieve the paratroopers bridge by bridge.

The Allied airborne forces were under the command of Boy Browning, while 30 Corps was commanded by Lieutenant General Brian Horrocks.

Eleanor knew them both. Browning was, in her view, a difficult man who managed to get into arguments with Americans remarkably easily, too easily, which did not bode well for a combined Allied operation. He was married to the novelist Daphne du Maurier, whose work Eleanor greatly admired, and Eleanor had therefore tried hard to like Browning but to no avail.

Brian Horrocks, on the other hand, was one of Eleanor's favorite generals, a no-nonsense soldier who seemed to lack the expansive ego so common among his peers.

"No understanding—none," Percival repeated.

"Then my opinion is of no consequence, and you can safely disregard it, sir."

Percival frowned. "Monty is very set on this plan, and he has Ike's approval," he said.

"He does? Then you don't need my support if Ike's already decided."

"Well, to be exact, Monty is confident he'll get Ike's approval because it's an excellent plan, and that's why it's important that no one at SHAEF muddies the waters."

So that was it: Montgomery and Browning feared she or others would "muddy the waters" by pointing out the problems in the plan.

"It's a British plan, and we're counting on full British support," Percival added, and Eleanor thought it almost sounded like a threat.

She looked out the window and sighed inwardly. The day was wet and dreary, matching her mood. When Johnnie had been wounded on D-Day, she'd been within inches of resigning from SHAEF to devote herself to nursing him back to health. She had spent four years dealing with men like Percival, and it was tempting to say enough is enough and devote herself to being a wife rather than a military analyst, or a strategic shrew, or whatever she had become. Bramble had managed to remain a mathematician and could run Red Tape without her guidance.

But Johnnie's injuries had proven miraculously less perilous than everyone feared, and he had insisted that she stay on the job.

"The only reason you want to nurse me is because it's an excuse to see me naked," Johnnie had said. "Well, the doctors say we'll be out of luck for five or six weeks until these ribs heal. In the meantime, if Ike wants you, you should stay in SHAEF."

Eisenhower had been planning to move to France at the earliest possible moment, taking only a skeleton staff with him. Eleanor suspected that he feared Patton and Montgomery would slip their leashes if he was not literally looking over their shoulders. Patton had been released from the fictitious FUSAG and given command of the real American Third Army; he and Montgomery had resumed their fierce rivalry. Indeed, so fierce was their rivalry that perhaps Ike feared they'd start fighting each other instead of Rommel.

She had been shocked when Ike asked her to join him. SHAEF had now ballooned into a vast organization more than sixteen thousand people strong, split between Bushey Park in London and an inner core of a thousand or so at SHAEF Forward in Southwick House. Ike wanted an even smaller SHAEF "Very Forward" in Normandy consisting of a handful of intelligence and communications officers, with two companies of US Rangers to keep him safe. Beetle Smith would have the all-important role of gatekeeper. Fred Morgan, Beetle's trusted deputy, would herd the remaining 15,900 denizens of SHAEF.

SHAEF "Very Forward" had followed the front lines when the Allies broke out of Normandy and was now housed in regal luxury in Versailles just outside Paris. Johnnie had recovered on schedule and was now back to operational flying. Doubtless, despite his protestations, flying against V1s was hideously dangerous, but at least V1s didn't shoot back.

"Market Garden is the most imaginative use of airborne power ever conceived," Percival said, bringing her back to the dreary present.

"Doubtless, sir," she said, determined to be polite. "Isn't sixty miles a long way?"

"Not in an aircraft," Percival snapped. "Just a few minutes; this is an airborne operation."

She guessed he had almost added "you foolish girl," or some such but had managed to stop himself. She should have opted for seeing Johnnie naked, she thought.

"I was referring to 30 Corps, sir," she said. "They are in earthbound tanks and lorries rather than aircraft, are they not?"

* * *

RAF Station Ford, Sussex, England
10 September 1944, 0730 Hours

Shaux was based at RAF Ford on the south coast of England near Littlehampton. Ford had a shabby, secondhand sort of feel about it, and it was often described as an annex to its grander neighbor, Fighter Command Sector Station RAF Tangmere, home of Douglas Bader's legendary Tangmere Wing. It was said that Ford had to make do with whatever Tangmere had too much of or had already broken. But Shaux liked humble, out-of-the-way places; his favorite airfield was the dilapidated emergency field along the coast at Oldchurch in Kent, where he had spent most of the Battle of Britain.

He turned eastward at five thousand feet—angels zero-five in RAF vernacular—and headed up the Channel with the holiday beaches of the south coast of England below his left wing.

Warrant Officer 1st Class Baxter sat beside him. He had been 645's radar expert last year, but he had since been to Flying School and now wore a navigator's wing on his uniform. He had, he told Shaux, declined becoming an officer, and Shaux thoroughly concurred. As a pilot officer, he would have been dust beneath the feet of almost all commissioned aircrew, whereas a WO/1 was unofficially ranked somewhere up there with Sir Charles Portal, the head of the RAF. Besides, WO/1s earned more money than P/Os.

They reached their holding point off Eastbourne, and Shaux set them into a lazy circular holding pattern.

"Warmer leader on hold," he said into the radio.

"Warmer leader holding," the Diver controller confirmed.

Ingrained habit caused Shaux to search the sky around him for enemy aircraft, even though he knew that very few Luftwaffe aircraft dared to fly above the Channel anymore, but he had been jumped far too often not to remember how quickly an empty sky could fill with Messerschmitt 109s or Focke-Wulf 190s.

In the meantime, ninety-nine percent of Operation Diver was involved in waiting.

Diver was the RAF's strategy to intercept and destroy incoming V1 flying bombs. V1s were small, fast, pilotless Luftwaffe aircraft with a one-ton bomb in the front and fuel tanks in the back, propelled by a tubular jet engine attached to the top of the fuselage. They had first appeared over southern England a week after D-Day.

The engine was a pulse jet that fired forty times a second, creating a very loud buzzing sound. V1s were popularly known as "doodlebugs" or "buzz bombs." They were launched from catapults in France and flew across the Channel and into England at heights up to 3,000 feet. The pilotless V1s were controlled by servomechanisms, one of which timed their flight. After enough time had elapsed for the V1 to reach London, the timer shut off the engine, and the V1 plunged to earth and exploded.

Shaux hated them. Even though they were inanimate, they seemed to possess the malevolence of a barracuda. On the other hand, Shaux was forced to admire the brilliance of the engineering involved; nothing like this had ever been accomplished before.

V1s were fast, flying at speeds up to 400 miles per hour. As they approached London, they used up their fuel, thereby reducing their weight, and therefore flew progressively faster. Very few Allied aircraft were quick enough to shoot them down, but the magical Mosquito was one of them. Relays of interceptors waited mid-Channel, as Shaux was doing now, for an incoming V1 to be detected by radar, triggering a high-speed pursuit before the V1 could reach London.

Many patrols ended in tedium, when the enemy launched no V1s and Diver aircraft waited in vain. On occasion, the enemy launched V1s in packs, trying—sometimes successfully—to create pandemonium. Shaux never knew if this was to be a day of futile waiting, circling endlessly above the Channel, trying to remain alert, or—

"Warmer leader, we have trade for you," the voice in Shaux's earphones announced. "Incoming E/A over Dover in two minutes."

"Dover in two minutes," Shaux confirmed.

Now the chase would begin.

* * *

SHAEF Forward, Versailles, France
10 September 1944, 0730 Hours

"It's the most imaginative use of airborne power ever conceived," Percival said again.

It was certainly the most ambitious plan, Eleanor thought. Thirty thousand troops would be flown into enemy-occupied Holland over two days. About half would land by parachute and half by glider.

The plan required close to two thousand transport aircraft and three thousand gliders—astonishing numbers. Many of the aircraft involved were Douglas C47s, known as "Gooney birds" to the Americans and "Dakotas" to the British. The C47s would carry paratroopers to their dropping points and would also tow large, unpowered gliders. The gliders—British Horsas and American Wacos—were made of plywood and could carry almost thirty troops or light vehicles such as jeeps. When they reached the target areas, the gliders would release their tow ropes and glide down to land in open fields and pastures.

The ground forces of 30 Corps, meanwhile, would race sixty miles northward and reach Arnhem in three or four days.

Nothing on this scale had ever been attempted. Previous Allied airborne operations in Sicily, Italy, and Normandy had been very difficult and only marginally effective, but now Montgomery and Browning wanted to attempt something much bigger.

"It's time for the Airborne to show what it can do," Percival said.

So that was another underlying factor, she thought. Airborne operations were extremely expensive and diverted resources away from ground-based units to the point that some questioned the investment. Since D-Day, there had been numerous proposals for airborne operations to leapfrog German front lines, but none had come to fruition. Now Browning wanted a dramatic victory to justify his Airborne Division.

"The Jerries are on their heels," Percival continued. "No resistance; it's time to knock them for six."

It was true that the German forces had an estimated four hundred thousand men killed, wounded, or taken prisoner in the three months since D-Day, but Eleanor, whose primary job at SHAEF was to understand the enemy, did not think they had been defeated. Von Rundstedt was using eastern Holland to rest and reinforce some of his battered forces: the Dutch underground had reported that the 9th and 10th SS Panzer Divisions were in eastern Holland on the planned line of 30 Corps' advance. Eleanor was certain that just because the SS Panzer Divisions were battered didn't mean that they wouldn't fight like furies.

"It'll be a victory under British leadership."

The plot continued to thicken, Eleanor thought. There was intense daily competition for supplies between Bradley and Patton commanding the American armies and Montgomery commanding the British and Canadian, particularly competition for fuel, which had to be brought all the way from Normandy.

The American 12th Army Group had made dramatic progress in the south and were ready to cross the Rhine. The British 21st Army Group had gone north into Belgium and were still some distance from the Rhine, and, once they entered Germany, they'd be facing the very heavily defended Siegfried Line and the Ruhr valley. Eisenhower had instructed Monty to slow down his advance until the fuel supply problem could be solved. Montgomery was therefore in danger of being outshone by Bradley and Patton.

The Allied supply lines were ruinously long. The Allies had failed to secure any major ports east of Normandy as they drove up through France and into Belgium. The combination of Résistance sabotage and RAF and USAAF bombing had been so successful that there was, in effect, no rail traffic in France at all. Consequently, everything the advancing armies needed had to be trucked four hundred miles, with horrible inefficiency, because it took five gallons of truck fuel to transport one gallon of fuel for a tank at the front lines.

Several major French highways had been designated as one-way only and devoted to endless convoys of trucks. The American operation nicknamed "the Red Ball Express" was, in Eleanor's opinion, just another example of the dominant industrial power and effectiveness of the United States, with up to six thousand trucks moving up to twelve thousand tons of supplies every single day—an operation that hadn't even been planned six weeks ago.

If Hitler had had American Jimmy trucks and American truck drivers when he invaded Russia, Eleanor thought, he'd have won the war in 1941.

Eisenhower favored a balanced strategy against the Germans, a "broad front," as he put it. In practical terms, this meant dividing fuel between Montgomery and Bradley. However, if Eisenhower thought Montgomery was in danger of getting stuck in Belgium, he might just give priority to the US Third Army and let Patton race for Berlin.

But, if Montgomery could suddenly advance north as far as Arnhem in three or four days, he would have skirted the Ruhr valley and the Siegfried Line and be perfectly positioned to turn east and make a dash across the Rhine into Germany. Then he'd get the lion's share of the fuel and, doubtless just as important in Montgomery's mind, the lion's share of the newspaper headlines.

"Imagine what this could mean," Percival urged her. "Look at the big picture."

"I'm trying to," she said.

"Perhaps you lack imagination."

Oh dear, Eleanor thought. He was one of those generals who thought they could get their way by running roughshod over a mere female staff officer.

"With respect, General, I do not," Eleanor said. "I can imagine a broad variety of ways in which this plan could fail, in whole or in part. To make it as painless for you as possible, I will list them in a memorandum that you can ignore at your leisure."

FOURTEEN

RAF Station Ford, Sussex, England
10 September 1944, 0830 Hours

"Single E/A incoming over Church Hougham, three minutes, angels oh-two," the Diver controller said.

"Bandit overhead Church Hougham," Shaux replied.

RAF ground staff protocol referred to radar blips as E/As, for "enemy aircraft," whereas aircrews called them bandits. The USAAF, just to be different, called E/As "bogies." Church Hougham, he knew, was a tiny village between Folkestone and Dover, high above the white cliffs of Dover.

Shaux opened the throttles, and the two Merlin engines pulled the Mosquito up to a speed of 400 miles per hour. Shaux had never ridden a horse, but he imagined that opening the throttles was the equivalent of saying "giddy up"—or whatever jockeys say—to a racehorse and giving it its head. Folksteone was only thirty miles away; at this speed, they were covering a mile about every seven seconds, and they'd get there with time to spare.

He resettled himself in his seat and flexed his hands—his right on the control column and his left on the throttles—in a habitual gesture to counter the adrenaline that he knew was flooding his system and trying to tighten everything up.

Shaux had had backward-facing Monica radar installed in this Mosquito—an idea of Baxter's. Monicas had been invented to warn Lancasters on bombing missions over Germany if they had enemy night fighters on their tails, but the idea had been a mistake: the Luftwaffe night fighters used their Flensberg radars to detect the Monicas, which therefore acted as beacons.

Shaux's strategy was to fly above the V1 and let it catch up to him and then descend to its level using the extra speed of their descent to overtake it. That meant that they couldn't see the V1, which was behind and below their tail, until it overtook them. Baxter fiddled with the Monica until he received a signal.

"Bandit at five o'clock at a thousand yards and closing," Baxter said, sounding no more excited than if he had commented on the weather. They were now flying north towards Church Hougham with the V1 behind and below them, a little to their right.

"Bandit at five hundred yards and closing. Still five o'clock."

Shaux nudged the throttles further open.

"Bandit at one hundred yards and closing."

Now the V1 was passing underneath them. Shaux searched downward past the left wing, and Baxter stared down on the other side. They were crossing the English coast above the fabled white cliffs of Dover, but this was not a moment to enjoy the view.

"Bandit in sight at one o'clock," Baxter said.

Shaux eased the Mosquito into a shallow dive. The V1 appeared ahead of them slightly to the right, a small aircraft with stubby wings and, strapped to its upper body, the long tube of its jet engine snorting smoke and fire. The heart of the exhaust flame seemed to contain a string of brilliant golden diamonds created by the pulsing mechanism.

"Bandit in sight," Shaux informed Diver control.

The south coast of England was bristling with antiaircraft batteries that also shot down V1s. Shaux hoped Diver control would warn the nearest ack-ack batteries not to shoot at this particular V1 lest they hit the Mosquito instead.

"Bandit is gaining on us," Baxter said.

If Shaux descended too quickly, they'd overtake it; if he descended too shallowly, it would get away.

There were two ways to destroy a V1. One was to shoot it down, which meant flying into the shrapnel and wreckage of the V1 as it disintegrated or even into an explosion if the payload itself detonated.

The Mosquito had four cannons and four machine guns packed into its nose, a critical advantage for precision gunnery. Single-engine fighters had their guns in their wings, and the guns had to be trained so that they converged on the target at a given range, typically three hundred yards. The Mosquito's guns fired straight forward along its axis, and the pilot sat directly behind the guns, making accuracy much easier.

At 400 miles per hour, the aircraft was travelling approximately 200 yards per second. If he hit the V1 and it exploded, he'd arrive at the heart of the explosion a second or two later—in general, not a good idea.

The other way to destroy a V1 was to fly beside it, wingtip to wingtip, so closely that turbulence created by the Mosquito's wing would upset the flow of air over the V1's wing, causing it to begin to roll. The V1's inclinometer servos would detect the roll and try to correct it to keep the V1 straight and level, but if the Mosquito pilot judged correctly, he could flip the V1 over on its back before the servos could adjust, and the V1 would fall into an uncorrectable dive.

"We'll try to tip it," Shaux said to Baxter. "If that doesn't work, we'll back off and shoot it down."

"S'pose," Baxter said. His studied indifference—Shaux knew it was a pose to cover his tension as they went into action—reminded Shaux of Flight Sergeant Cranmer, who had advanced less than fifty feet up Sword Beach before his death. Cranmer had risked his life to provide a radio, and he hadn't even turned it on.

Shaux had sometimes wondered if God treated all arrivals in heaven equally, or whether men who had died pointlessly got fewer benefits—or, perhaps, extra benefits in compensation for the futility of their endings.

Shaux adjusted the rate of descent, and the Mosquito closed the gap. As they came closer, Shaux thought how different this was from combat with a normal, crewed aircraft. Whereas a Heinkel or a Junkers rear gunner would be shooting at them by now, the V1 was unaware of, and indifferent to, their presence. And without the need to carry people and all the equipment people need to stay alive in the air, the V1 was remarkably small, with a wingspan of just eighteen feet, yet carrying the same payload as a bomber with a fifty-foot wingspan and a crew of four.

Shaux brought them down until they were just to the right of the V1 and just behind it, close to its fiery exhaust.

"Warmer leader, engaging bandit," Shaux told Diver control. "Doodle-ho."

"Doodle-ho" was his own version of Fighter Command's traditional talismanic "tallyho," used to announce a pilot was starting to attack.

"Thirty feet," Baxter said, estimating their distance behind the V1's wing.

Both they and the V1 were bouncing a little in the inevitable thermal turbulence as they crossed the coast from sea to land above Dover.

"Twenty feet."

Now the Mosquito's nose was level with the V1's tail and its flaming exhaust pipe. The thunderous buzzing of the V1's pulse jet was even louder than the howling of the Mosquito's Merlin engines. The Mosquito's wingspan was almost three times as wide as the V1's. Shaux was less than thirty feet from the V1's barracuda body.

"Ten feet."

If the V1 hit the slightest shear—the slightest sideways push—in the air currents, the V1 could hit the Mosquito before the V1's servos could correct. Or, if the Mosquito was suddenly pushed sideways towards the V1 before Shaux could correct it . . . Shaux had four years of practice at holding high-performance aircraft straight and level in the ever-turbulent air; the V1 had the finest automated reflexes German engineering could devise . . . This was truly a case of man versus machine. Which had the finer reflexes?

"Up a bit," Baxter said. He was half out of his seat, looking down past Shaux's head as their left wing crept up next to the V1's right wing.

"Two feet closer."

The wings swam together. The V1 thundered on indifferently.

"Two more feet."

Now the wings were overlapping, with the V1's wing a foot above the Mosquito's. Shaux felt the slightest tremor as the V1 rocked, just a little, and its wing touched the Mosquito's.

Shaux tried to imagine the complexity of the airflows. The leading edges of the wings of both aircraft were smashing into the relatively calm air ahead of them at 400 miles per hour, creating two powerful overlapping bow waves containing many tons of force, many tons of lift and drag, like two racing powerboats running side by side through calm waters creating two overlapping, clashing wave patterns. Each wing would normally let the air flow smoothly over and under itself, but the air was being roiled into a thousand tiny maelstroms, like a thousand invisible bumps in a road creating friction and drag instead of lift . . .

The Mosquito was far larger and more stable than the V1, with much more mass to drive forward through the fickle air and absorb the instability, and, unlike the V1's servos, the Mosquito's pilot knew what was going on. Shaux nudged the Mosquito a little more. Now fully half the V1's stubby right wing was overlapped. The flow over and under the V1's wing must be severely distorted as it battled the turbulence the Mosquito's larger wing was generating. Surely—

The V1 rocked abruptly down left and then down right, again slapping the Mosquito's wingtip as it did so, like a wet dog with big ears shaking its head. And then it went fully down left until it was flying with its left wing pointing at the earth as its inanimate servos tried to calculate, quite literally, which way was up. The servos made a poor decision, and the V1 abruptly plunged earthward.

"A trifle close that time," Shaux said. "We've never actually hit one before. What do you think, Bax?"

"S'pose."

"Doodle down," Shaux told the Diver controller.

* * *

10 Downing Street, London, SW1
12 September 1944, 1200 Hours

"I understand you are opposed to Market Garden, Air Commandant?" Churchill rumbled.

Eleanor had been summoned to fly back to England at short notice to see him at No. 10 Downing Street, and now she felt as if she had walked into a trap. Churchill sat in the center of the long table in the cabinet room flanked by Sir Alan Brooke and Percival. Brooke was Britain's top soldier, chief of the Imperial general staff, Montgomery's superior officer and strongest supporter. Percival had doubtless been pressing Churchill in favor of large-scale airborne operations and questioning Eleanor's competence.

Montgomery, or Browning, or both, must have been lobbying Churchill to support the Market Garden plan in the hope that Churchill would back it with Eisenhower.

She was pleased to see that Edward Bridges, the cabinet secretary, was also there. She thought he was the most sensible person in Whitehall and was, at least on paper, her own boss.

"The current plan has weaknesses, sir," she said. "Hopefully they will be corrected."

"What you describe as weaknesses are, in military terms, calculated risks," Percival responded.

"Perhaps so, sir, but in objective terms, they are uncalculated risks. For example, the road north—"

"Nonsense," Percival interrupted, but Eleanor had not flown to London just to be talked down.

"It is not wide enough or strong enough to accommodate the amount of 30 Corps traffic it must bear. There will be traffic jams stretching for miles. There are no alternative parallel roads running south to north to relieve the pressure, and the countryside beside the road is too wet to sustain large movements of armor. If—"

"That's not—"

"If it is necessary to bring up supplies or equipment from the rear—bailey bridges to span rivers, for example—all the other vehicles will have to stop and park on the verges. The verges will collapse under the weight of armor."

"That's not—"

"There is a comparable road from Cambridge to Ely, sir," Eleanor said. "Put a thousand lorries on that road and see how long it takes for the last one to get there. It's seventeen miles. If your plan is realistic, if it is a 'calculated risk,' to use your phrase, the last lorry will reach Ely in less than one hour. Will you arrange such a test?"

"There isn't time for practices of dubious value."

"I didn't think there would be. That is why, sir, in both objective and military terms, these are *uncalculated* risks."

Percival looked as if he had just sustained a blow to his midriff.

"Do you have an alternative, Eleanor?" Alan Brooke interceded, perhaps to give Percival time to regroup.

Eleanor knew Brooke well. They shared a mutual but unspoken view that Churchill was a magnificent, indispensable war leader—and simultaneously that he was the greatest menace to the orderly conduct of the war.

"I have three, sir. One is to focus on reopening Antwerp and clearing the Scheldt, which will shorten our supply lines by three hundred miles and improve our fuel efficiency sixfold."

"That's been evaluated and given lower priority," Percival said. "We'll let the Canadians take care of that in due course."

In Eleanor's opinion, the Canadian army was probably the most efficient Allied army in Europe, having consistently outperformed expectations on D-Day and ever since. Percival, however, was implying they were in some way a lesser breed, she thought, suitable only for lower priorities, merely cannon fodder from the far-flung Empire. She saw no value, however, in debating the point in front of Churchill and simply added it to her growing list of reasons she didn't like Percival.

"Second, if we pursue Market Garden, we should do it in stages. Drop the 101st north of Eindhoven and let 30 Corps relieve them. Then, when those bridges are secure, drop the 82nd at Nijmegen and let 30 Corps reach them. Then drop the 1st Airborne at Arnhem when 30 Corps is already in Nijmegen. A drop a day, as it were. Don't drop the 82nd and the 1st so far ahead until we can be sure to reach them."

"That would signal our intentions to the enemy," Percival objected.

"Whereas dropping the 82nd in the enemy's midst at Nijmegen and the 1st at Arnhem does not? It will never occur to the enemy that we will try to reach them?"

"What is your third alternative?" Brooke intervened again.

"If our intention is to get north of the Ruhr and the Siegfried Line, we only need to reach Nijmegen. It's far enough north to turn the flank. We don't need to go all the way to Arnhem."

"But that would make it an American operation," Percival said. "There'd be no role for the British 1st Airborne and . . ."

He fell silent, but it was clear he had intended to say there'd be no justification for Browning being in charge.

Brooke, she knew, had been bitterly disappointed that the top SHAEF job had gone to Eisenhower and not himself, and he was one of many British generals who thought Churchill was too subservient to the Americans. Brooke had had the supremely good professional fortune to be at the top of his career just when the greatest conflict in European history broke out, and he had the supreme frustration of being stuck in London pushing paper while watching an American with no previous battlefield experience leading the Allied armies on the European battlefield.

Perhaps in secret retaliation, he had done his best to insert British officers into the Allied command structure whenever he could, even if these added unnecessary extra layers. Browning's current command of an overwhelmingly American airborne operation was a good example.

"Market Garden is a British plan under British command," Brooke said. He laid both palms flat on the table to indicate the matter was closed. "Our 1st Airborne will be the tip of the spear at Arnhem. Boy Browning will be in command, with the American 82nd and 101st also reporting to him. That is final."

He turned to Churchill, sitting beside him, as if daring Churchill to overrule him.

"So be it," Churchill murmured, and Eleanor thought she saw him give the slightest shrug. Did he agree with Brooke or was he simply tiring of the endless bickering back and forth between the American and British generals?

Percival beamed in triumph. "It will be, Prime Minister, I promise you, an opportunity to display the pinnacle of modern warfare—the most advanced technologies and the most advanced tactics."

Eleanor groaned inwardly. She glanced at Bridges, who shook his head, signaling her to let it go.

She and Bridges left the room together.

"This will not end well, sir," she said. "Lives will be lost. SS Panzer Divisions do not just surrender without a fight."

"Let us hope this is one of the rare occasions upon which you are wrong, Eleanor."

"Let us hope, sir."

FIFTEEN

Shaux was summoned to a meeting at Hillingdon House in RAF Uxbridge. He felt almost as a devout pilgrim might feel stepping onto hallowed ground: this had once been 11 Group headquarters during the Battle of Britain. Steps led downwards beneath the grounds to the Operations Room from which Keith Park had directed Britain's Spitfires and Hurricanes against the Luftwaffe during those desperate days; in one of these tiny, shabby offices Eleanor had created the first version of her Red Tape model.

It had been only four years ago, but to Shaux it seemed like forty. He'd been so young, so naïf, fresh out of college and fresh out of Spitfire flying school and freshly, completely in love with Eleanor . . .

The purpose of this meeting was to evaluate the effectiveness of Operation Diver against V1 buzz bombs. It was ironic that the meeting should be held here rather than at Ad Astra House, the RAF's HQ in central London, as originally planned: Ad Astra House had been severely damaged by a V1.

There were twenty men at the meeting, and Shaux reflected that it was typical of Whitehall's decision-making processes that only he and Remy Van Lierde, the outstanding Belgian pilot who had shot down more than fifty V1s in his Tempest, were pilots who were actually flying in the campaign.

But, Shaux thought, looking round the room, thank God that Wilfred Freeman was in charge of the proceedings. Freeman, vice chief of air staff and de facto head of all research and development for the RAF, was, in Shaux's opinion, probably the most influential—and wisest—officer in the RAF.

"There are two lights at the end of this particular tunnel, gentlemen," Freeman said. "One is that we are quickly overrunning all the areas for their launch sites in France and Belgium that are close enough to reach London. Therefore, in a month or so, we can expect them to recalibrate and attack us in Europe—presumably focusing on the port of Antwerp once we open it. That will give a welcome respite to the long-suffering population of London."

There was a murmur of assent.

"The other light, gentlemen, is the brilliant work done by the Twenty Committee," Freeman continued. "As a result of their activities, many of the V1s are falling well short of their targets. However, as you will appreciate, I can say nothing more specific on that matter."

Eleanor had told Shaux about the highly secret MI5 Twenty Committee run by John Masterson, an Oxford don. The Twenty Committee masterminded an operation to feed false information to the German Abwehr and other enemy military intelligence services. Enemy spies in England were caught by the Twenty Committee and turned into double agents, sending false information back to their German masters.

It was, Shaux thought, a brilliant conjuring trick. Even the name of the group was tricky: "Twenty" was a play on the Roman numerals XX representing the number twenty, which in turn was a play on the expression "double-cross."

In the case of the V1 campaign, the double agents were reporting that V1s were consistently overshooting London, causing the enemy to adjust the servos to fly shorter distances. This resulted in many V1s failing to reach London and crashing into areas in Kent, Surrey, and

Sussex, which had lower population densities. Shaux knew that this deception was controversial because it saved the lives of Londoners at the expense of deliberately created civilian casualties in towns and villages south of London, but Eleanor had told him Churchill had approved it personally.

Shaux was distracted from his thoughts by hearing Freeman mention his name.

"Needless to say, I must also commend the excellent work done by Shaux's and Van Lierde's chaps, indeed by all the Diver squadrons. Between the interceptors and the Home Guard's flak batteries, we're shooting down about forty percent of the V1s; forty percent are falling short, thanks in large part to Masterton's chaps; and only twenty percent are reaching London."

Shaux ignored the compliment, his mind still on the Twenty Committee. Eleanor had told him that Churchill had asked her opinion, and she had supported the deception.

"I wonder how many children I killed in Kent today?" she had asked one evening as they lay in bed entangled. "I hate logic. I hate mathematics. I used to think logic was elegant, admirable, but now I know it's just cold and heartless. It has no soul."

"Don't be so hard on your—"

"I am a logician." She had interrupted him, almost sobbing. "Therefore, it follows that I have no soul."

* * *

10 Downing Street, London, SW1
12 September 1944, 1300 Hours
Eleanor left No. 10 and decided to walk a little to clear her head, wandering through Scotland Yard to the Embankment, where she stared down moodily into the dirty water of the Thames. London was becoming more dilapidated every time she came here, she thought. There was bomb damage everywhere and no money or people for cleanup or repairs, let alone for rebuilding. If victory came next year, as she expected, England would be exhausted. It would take decades to repair the damage.

Churchill must surely know the Market Garden plan was rash, and yet he was approving it . . . If it succeeded, it might shorten the war by a week or two, but if it failed, it could lengthen the war by months . . . Was Churchill finally getting ground down by the relentless pressures of the war? He was turning seventy in November and—

A loud explosion rang out somewhere to the south of the river, like a sudden clap of thunder on a clear day, and she guessed a V1 doodle-bug had evaded Johnnie and all the other Diver defenses. It seemed such a bitter blow that Hitler should unleash so horrible a new weapon against the people of London when his own defeat seemed increasingly inevitable. The enemy was firing as many as a hundred of these heartless machines every day. The V1 launch sites were being overrun as the Allies moved north and recaptured the French and Belgian coasts, but the end was not yet in sight.

Worse, starting a week ago, on 8 September, the Germans had unleashed a whole new weapon, the V2, a rocket that flew high into the upper atmosphere, almost into space, and descended at super-sonic speed. There was literally no defense against this monstrosity, to the point that Churchill, normally a believer in telling the truth, had decided not to inform the public for fear of causing panic.

So, she thought, Hitler was weakened but still fighting viciously, like a cornered animal. The Stauffenberg plot—the German army's attempt to assassinate Hitler on 20 July—had failed. The Allies had outrun their supply lines and were close to stalling. Although Rommel had been wounded and was off the battlefield, the war was far from over.

Hitler's war machine was like a hydra-headed monster . . . The mythological ancient Greek Hydra was a monster with many heads; if you cut one off, it simply grew another. In a similar manner, the Allies had destroyed the Luftwaffe's bomber force, only to be faced with not one but two revolutionary new weapons, the V1 and the V2.

Hercules used fire to destroy the Hydra, she recalled, as one of his twelve labors, and doubtless Johnnie and the other Diver pilots would eventually slay the fiery-tailed V1s . . .

* * *

2TAF Headquarters, RAF Uxbridge
12 September 1944, 1300 Hours

Freeman asked Shaux to come back to his office when the meeting at 2TAF was over.

"I was talking to Barnes Wallis about your preference for Molins guns over RP3 rockets," Freeman said. It was typical of Freeman that he got straight to the point. "He agrees with you."

Barnes Wallis was the brilliant inventor of several of Bomber Command's most remarkable weapons, include the extraordinary Upkeep and Highball bouncing bombs. Upkeep bombs had knocked down German dams in Guy Gibson's heroic Dambusters Raid last year, and Shaux had used the much smaller Highballs to disable U-boat pens.

"I've therefore arranged for a flight of four Molins-gunned Mark 18 Mosquitos to be attached to your squadron in the next couple of days. They'll give you a chance to prove your point."

"Thank you, sir."

Freeman was not normally a loquacious man, but on this occasion, he seemed positively chatty.

"Barnes is not unduly worried by V1s. In addition to our progress in shooting the damned things down, they have only a limited range, so we'll be able to capture all their remaining launch sites in range of London in the next month or so."

He frowned.

"But then Barnes and I got on to the subject of V2 rockets, and the plot thickened, as they say. Once launched, V2s are unstoppable: we're literally helpless. The damned things shoot up into the outer atmosphere and then plunge back to earth at speeds far greater than the speed of sound. They're invulnerable."

He shook his head.

"Obviously, Bomber Command and the Eighth Air Force bomb the fixed V2 installations—the launch areas and supply centers, etcetera, whenever we find them, and the Peenemünde test site. But the actual V2 rockets drive around on their own launching vehicles, the so-called Meillerwagens."

Meillerwagens, Shaux knew, were long multi-axle road transporters, like overgrown versions of tank transporters. A V2 stood about forty-five feet high when standing in its vertical launch position, and the span of its steering fins was about eleven feet. They weighed an estimated fifteen tons, of which one ton was the explosive warhead. A Meillerwagen transported the rocket by road in a horizontal position and included hoisting gear to raise the weapon into the vertical position for operation. Once the V2 was vertical, it was filled with fuel and launched.

Freeman shook his head.

"Once again, I must admit that the enemy has a host of brilliant scientists and engineers, even if their inventions are put to loathsome purposes," he said. "They're critically short of petrol, for example, so their new Messerschmitt 262 jet fighters run on distilled coal, and the V2s run on distilled potatoes! Remarkable! Ingenious!"

He waited as an orderly entered with tea.

"We are told that the Waffen-SS—Hitler's private army—has taken over the V2 program, so we can expect it to intensify. The Dutch underground is quite good at spotting the Meillerwagens as they move around, and the SS seem to be doing most of their launches against London from around The Hague in Holland."

He stopped to light a cigarette while Shaux waited to see where all this was leading.

"Anyway, to get to the point, Barnes said he'd be looking at the intelligence reports and had an idea."

He paused uncharacteristically for dramatic effect, and Shaux had a sudden foreboding that this was all leading to something fairly hairy.

"Barnes's proposal is that you move the Mark 18s to an RAF station in East Anglia. It's only 120 miles from RAF Leiston in Suffolk to The Hague in Holland, for example. So, to cut a long story short, his idea is that you and your chaps sit at RAF Leiston, waiting for the Dutch underground chaps to spot a Meillerwagen with a V2 getting ready to launch."

Suddenly Shaux realized where this was going.

"We believe it takes about an hour and a half for the enemy to get the rocket set up on its launch stand and fuel it. So, when the Dutch chaps spot one, they'll send us a code, and you'll take off like a bat out of hell, fly across the North Sea, and shoot the damn thing before they have time to finish fueling and launching it."

"Good God!"

"I also talked to Hives at Rolls-Royce," Freeman rushed on. "He suggested he'll skip a generation of Merlin engines and give you the new 130/131 Merlins to put in the Mark 18s. They're still being tested, but he's confident they'll work very well. That'll give you more than 4,000 horsepower, almost as much as a B17 or a Lanc. It should take you less than twenty minutes to get to The Hague. What do you think, Shaux?"

"As I said, sir, 'Good God!'"

This was hairy indeed, he thought. What a wild idea—what a stretch of the imagination! It sounded ridiculous . . . except that Wilfred Freeman, Barnes Wallis, and Ernest Hives—the head of aeroengines at Rolls-Royce—were not only innovative thinkers but also intensely practical men with long records of making wild stretches of the imagination work successfully in the real world.

It would be amazing to put 4,000 horsepower in a Mosquito . . . even with the weight of the Molins gun, he might be able to reach 450 miles per hour in level flight! Running flat out across the North Sea whitecaps would be something else . . . as Bob O'Neill would say, "Holy crap."

"Of course, we're still denying the V2s exist," Freeman continued. "We're claiming that the explosions are caused by gas mains blowing up at random across South London, but the story is wearing a bit thin. The general public isn't stupid, and people are beginning to joke about 'flying gas mains.' Churchill knows he will have to announce the existence of the V2 sooner or later, preferably before Hitler does, but he also wants to announce we shot one down before it took off—that's where you come in."

Shaux made a mental note to ask Bob O'Neill what the next step was beyond "Holy crap"—"Holier crap," perhaps?

* * *

SHAEF Forward, Southwick House
12 September 1944, 1630 Hours

Eleanor sat back at her desk in Southwick House as her last meeting ended. Thank God, she thought, that Ike had taken her with him to France, away from the bureaucratic entrails of SHAEF Forward. She had spent the afternoon groveling before accountants who were not happy with MI6-3b(S)'s expenditures, with personnel officers upset by her propensity to promote *far* too many of her staff *far* too quickly simply because they were doing an excellent job and with procurement officers perturbed by the volume of supplies MI6-3b(S) consumed.

"Please instruct your staff to write on *both* sides of *every* piece of paper they use; they don't seem to realize there's an acute paper shortage, and paper doesn't grow on trees," one waspish quartermaster had tut-tutted.

At last, they were gone. She lay back in her chair and lit a cigarette. It was strange to be sitting in this chair without Charlie under her desk . . . she was certain that the staff in Versailles would be spoiling him outrageously . . . she might have to put him on a diet.

She stared at a pile of reports she had not yet opened, each summarizing an aspect of the war in Europe. Even though she was certain the war would end next year, there were still so many threats.

Why had Churchill acquiesced to Market Garden so easily? Was he indulging his weakness for dramatic expeditions? Did he really think that Monty could bring off an unexpected triumph that would restore British leadership over Allied war strategy? It was as if Churchill was the Trojan King Priam, bringing the wooden horse into his city, against all logic and evidence, crossing his fingers and whispering a wish . . . Was he simply getting old?

The pile of reports awaited her attention. Earlier today, she had thought of Hitler's war machine as a hydra-headed monster. There were still so many heads to chop off, and the Allies, like Hercules, had to chop off and cauterize every single one of them.

She wondered idly if Johnnie was flying or not. She had a Lysander aircraft waiting to take her back to SHAEF in Versailles—such was her lofty rank these days! Upon reflection, it was only a very short hop from here to RAF Ford; she could be there in an hour.

She picked up the telephone and waited until the operator answered.

"Please get me RAF Ford on the telephone, 645 Squadron CO's office," she asked.

"Immediately, ma'am."

Eleanor waited for a minute.

"Shaux speaking," she heard Johnnie say.

"Shaux speaking," she replied.

"El? Is that really you?"

"Are you busy this evening?"

"What? No—"

"Excellent. I'm in Portsmouth, leaving for Ford immediately. My intention is to arrive within the hour and seduce you—not once, not twice, but thrice. I was thinking of Hercules, and my thoughts progressed onward in an entirely logical fashion. I trust you are well rested and in excellent physical condition?"

"Why only thrice? Hercules had twelve labors."

"You know I admire you deeply. I am in your thrall. But I am also a realist, and it'll only be for a couple of hours."

"Prepare to be surprised."

She replaced the telephone, scooped up the files, and left the office. As she passed the telephone switchboard, the operator stared at her, wide-eyed.

SIXTEEN

RAF Leiston, Suffolk
16 September 1944, 1030 Hours

Shaux sat in his Mark 18 Mosquito just off the end of the main runway at RAF Leiston on the east coast of England, just a mile or two from the North Sea.

He had been here a year ago when the airfield was still under construction. Returning from an operation in Holland, he had been forced to make an emergency wheels-up landing and had chosen to land on soft grass rather than on a half-built concrete runway. His aircraft had plowed a long furrow on its way to a final halt just short of an antique steamroller pressed back into wartime service.

The steamroller driver, an elderly civilian in a blue boiler suit, had been furious.

"You nearly bloody hit me, you daft ha'pence! Call yourself a pilot? That was the worst bloody landing ever! The bloody runway's all the way over there; you missed it completely! Are you blind?"

Leiston was now complete, the home base for the three squadrons of the US Eighth Air Force's 357th Fighter Group. More than forty P51D fighters stood dispersed on hard pads around the perimeter track. The

357th's mission was to escort B17 Fortresses and B24 Liberators on their daylight flights to Germany and back, protecting the bombers from Messerschmitt 109s, Focke-Wolfe 190s, and now the amazing new jet-propelled Messerschmitt 262s.

Shaux's detachment of four twin-engined Mark 18s stood on their own disposal pads, looking decidedly out of place. Shortly after they had arrived at Leiston, one of the P51 pilots had wandered over to inspect Shaux's Mosquito.

"I couldn't believe they said you put an anti-tank gun in an airplane, so I had to come and see if it's true," he said.

"Well, it's true," Shaux said.

The pilot crouched down to look under the nose. The muzzle of the 57 mm anti-tank 6-pounder protruded from a fairing beneath the nose.

"Holy crap!" he said, reminding Shaux of Bob O'Neill—perhaps it was a semi-official USAAF expression. "How much ammo do you have?"

"We have a Molins autoloader with twenty-one rounds. That's why we call this weapon a Molins gun."

Shaux opened a loading hatch and the pilot stared in.

"So, you can knock out a tank with this thing?"

"We can penetrate two inches of armor at a quarter of a mile," Shaux said.

"Holy crap!"

They struck up a conversation. The P51 pilot, a young captain, introduced himself as Chuck Yeager. They strolled over to Yeager's P51, which had the name "Glamorous Glen" painted on its nose.

"We're getting married as soon as I get home," Yeager said. "Did you ever fly a P51?"

"Yes, I had the good luck to do so a couple of times."

There were always endless debates among pilots as to which fighter was the best—Spitfires, Tempests, P47s, P51s, and their enemy counterparts—but Shaux had concluded long ago that it all came down to style, almost to attitude: Am I going to dance through this encounter, in which case I want a Spitfire? Or am I going to slug it out, in which case I want a P47?

"It must be a bummer being stuck in a bomber after flying a pursuit fighter," Yeager said. "Still, I guess . . ."

His voice trailed away, and Shaux guessed he had been about to say something about pilots growing too old to fly fighters but had managed to stop himself in time.

"Sir," Yeager added, in deference to Shaux's advancing decrepitude.

"Oh, you get used to it," Shaux murmured.

"There's talk we may escort you. If so, I guess you'll take off, and we'll follow."

"It might be best if you take off first, and we'll follow."

"Why?"

"Because you won't be able to catch up unless we wait for you."

"You must be joking!"

"Want a race?" Shaux asked, chuckling. "Look, you have a Model 1650 Merlin engine in your P51 pulling 1,500 horsepower, and you weigh a little under eight thousand pounds empty. I have two 131 and 132 Model Merlins pulling 4,200 horsepower combined, and I weigh fourteen thousand pounds empty. So do the calculation: you have one horsepower for every five pounds, and I have one horsepower for only three pounds."

"Holy crap!" Yeager said. He looked back and forth between the two aircraft. "Will you give me a ride?"

"No, he will not, Captain," said a voice behind them. "He'll give me one."

Bob O'Neill stood behind them. Yeager froze into attention in the presence of a general while Shaux and O'Neill shook hands.

"Yes, let me take you up, Bob," Shaux said. "You may find this interesting."

They inspected the Molins gun protruding from the lower part of the nose.

"I hear they've also put big guns in B25s in the Pacific," O'Neill said. "There aren't any in Europe, as far as I know. So, you took out the Mossie's usual cannons and replaced them with this single Molins, with the autoloader in what used to be the bomb bay?"

"That's not the only change," Shaux said. "All Mossies have four 30-caliber Browning machine guns in the upper part of the nose, right in front of the pilot's eyes, firing forward straight along the Mossie's axis. That's why Mossies are so easy to aim; you just look at the target and shoot."

He accepted one of O'Neill's Lucky Strike cigarettes and lit it with his prized Zippo.

"Each machine gun fires at 400 rounds per minute and has 250 rounds of ammunition," he continued. "Normally the guns fire simultaneously to deliver as much ordnance into the target as fast as possible—about twenty-five rounds in a second. But we don't want to shoot the target with the Brownings. We just want to aim them at the target. Follow me."

They clambered into the cockpit. Shaux pointed to a row of firing buttons on the control column.

"So, what we've done is to trigger the machine guns to fire individually, one by one, and we've loaded them with tracer only. That means we have about two and a half minutes of tracer. The idea is that the pilot uses bursts of tracer to line up on the target. He switches guns every second or so to avoid overheating. The navigator, sitting in your seat, watches to see the tracer striking the target and then fires the Molins gun using that electrical trigger in front of you when he sees the aim is true."

"The navigator fires the big gun?"

"Yes. As you know, when you first pull the trigger, there's an almost irrepressible tendency to twitch and spoil your aim high. This way, we eliminate twitch."

"Can we fly to a range and practice? Can I fire the Molins? Please? I promise not to twitch. Pretty please?"

* * *

SHAEF Forward, Versailles, France
18 September 1944, 1030 Hours
"The new regent of Belgium is coming this morning, Eleanor," Beetle Smith told her. "Prince Someone or Count Something. He'll get a limited honor guard and ten minutes with Ike, then a tour of the map room, and you take him to lunch. It's your turn for babysitting."

As the Allied armies advanced across Europe and liberated more and more territory, SHAEF was becoming inundated with visitors who wanted their few minutes and their photograph with the supreme commander. A few members of SHAEF Forward staff, Eleanor among them, had been "volunteered" by Beetle Smith to act as the visiting dignitaries' escorts and hosts. The visitors were to feel they were welcome, that they were important, and that their suggestions were appreciated, but they were not to waste a second of Ike's time more than was absolutely necessary.

"What do I tell the regent about Market Garden, sir?" she asked. The operation had finally launched yesterday afternoon.

"Look up the Belgian expression for snafu," Smith said, turning away.

Eleanor sent a message to Bramble to give her half a page on "Prince Someone" and received an answer within the hour—doubtless from the Dragonettes. Prince Charles, the Count of Flanders, was the disgraced King Leopold's younger brother. Leopold had surrendered to the Germans in 1940 and remained in Belgium, while the elected Belgian government had refused to surrender and fled into exile first in France and then in England. The king's actions had created a constitutional crisis because the government had not surrendered, although the king had, and Leopold was now a prisoner in Germany.

Leopold carried the shame of surrendering, whereas the government ministers bore the shame of running away; the ministers were, as ministers do, trying to stick the king with the ignominy of defeat while painting themselves as executing a tactical retreat and bravely soldiering on, albeit from the comfortable safety of England.

Charles, who had been to school in England and graduated from Dartmouth Naval Academy, had spent the war in exile in England under the pseudonym of General du Boc. Now that most of Belgium had been liberated, Charles was to become regent, in effect the acting king; he would become the focal point for national celebrations of their newly won freedom. Meanwhile, the government would decide what to do about Leopold.

Every country in Europe had its own set of similar problems, she knew. France had to extricate itself from the Vichy era; Italy was dealing with its post-Mussolini mess; Austria had virtually disappeared into Germany; the Greeks were one inch away from overthrowing their monarchy in favor of communism . . . postwar Europe would be not only impoverished but seething with divisions and resentments.

It was Eleanor's custom to have Charlie with her on these occasions, if only as a conversational gambit. He wore his full-dress uniform: a blue serge harness emblazoned with the RAF roundel on one side and the SHAEF shoulder badge on the other, with his Royal Engineers badge dangling from his collar. She knew he loved these occasions. He even submitted to being bathed without complaint. He was always on his best behavior when he traded his battered everyday scarf for his full-dress grandeur.

They waited at the top of the stairs of the Grand Trianon Hotel in Versailles, where SHAEF Forward was currently located. as the regent's car drew up.

"Charlie, sit," Eleanor said.

"Oh my god!" Prince Charles said as he climbed the steps to meet them. "It's Charlie, *Le Grand Charles*. I've heard so much about you!" He reached down to rub Charlie's head. "Truly, all Belgium talks about the famous RAF and SHAEF Bouvier de Flandres, and I am delighted to meet you."

"Charlie, paw," Eleanor said, and Charlie lifted his front right leg so that the prince could shake it.

"And you too, of course, madame," he added, straightening up and shaking Eleanor's hand. "I am honored to meet you."

"Welcome to SHAEF, sir," she said.

"I have something for Charlie, if I may, in honor of his services. His first master was a Belgian pilot in the Battle of Britain, and now he is the dog of your famous husband and of yourself in SHAEF."

He reached into his pocket and produced a badge.

"This is the pilot's badge of the Aviation Militaire, the Belgian Air Force. Please accept it on behalf of the Belgian people."

"We are honored, sir," Eleanor managed, searching unsuccessfully for something better to say. "Johnnie will be delighted, I know. He has a high regard for Belgian pilots. He and Remy Van Lierde are part of the campaign to shoot down V1s."

It occurred to her to mention Johnnie's admiration for the members of the Belgian underground who had helped his escape to England when he was a prisoner of war, but she kept silent. She did not know if she could trust Charles to keep his mouth shut until the war was over.

"It is a gift from one Charles of Flanders to another." The prince chuckled. "And now, tell me about Eisenhower. I don't want to say anything wrong. Can I ask about his plans for the liberation of Antwerp, or is that a secret? Can I ask about the rumors of massive paratroop drops in Holland? Will his driver be there? If she is, how should I greet her?"

"You can ask him anything you wish, of course, sir. However, I would caution you he is very busy and may not be able to answer all your questions in full."

She did not know if Kay Summersby would be present, nor did she wish to characterize her position.

She led Prince Charles inside. Eisenhower was charming, as he always was on these occasions, but could give the regent no more than five minutes before Beetle Smith bustled Eisenhower away. Charles took it with good grace.

"If you are royal, you get used to being simultaneously very important and completely superfluous," he said as Eleanor took him into lunch. "Now, can you tell me what is happening in Holland, or is that secret?"

She considered Beetle Smith's earlier advice but decided to be more upbeat.

"Rivers present severe challenges to advancing armies, sir," she said. "Heavily equipped armored divisions and artillery find them particularly difficult to cross. So, naturally, the Germans are blowing up bridges as they retreat, making every river difficult for us to cross. The landscape we are entering in eastern Holland is low-lying and wet and crisscrossed by numerous rivers and canals."

She paused as a waiter offered them an extraordinary Pouilly-Fumé—thank God the French had managed to hide some of their best wine away from their German occupiers.

"So, sir, the idea behind Market Garden is to capture the bridges *before* we get to them by dropping Airborne troops behind enemy lines. Then the armor and infantry fight their way to the bridges we have already secured, and we can cross them immediately and advance very quickly."

"I see. How is it going?"

Eleanor considered quoting the nineteenth-century Prussian General von Moltke, who said, "No plan survives contact with the enemy," but did not.

"It's very early stages, sir," she said instead.

One British battalion had reached the northern end of the bridge over the Rhine at Arnhem but lacked the strength to take it. The rest of the 1st Airborne had dropped several miles to the west and immediately encountered severe opposition and were therefore unable to reach the troops at the bridge. The 82nd near Nijmegen had also dropped in a scattered pattern and had not reached their target bridges.

The 101st at Eindhoven, closest to 30 Corps, had been more successful in capturing their bridges, but 30 Corps still hadn't reached them. The Irish Guards tanks leading 30 Corps had been ambushed as soon as they crossed the border yesterday afternoon and had failed, so far, to advance the 13 miles from the Belgian border to Eindhoven.

"I see," Charles said softly, and she guessed he was fully aware of Von Moltke's dictum but was too polite to say so.

* * *

RAF Leiston, Suffolk
18 September 1944, 1030 Hours
"Warmer leader, we have trade for you," Shaux's headphones announced.

He and Baxter sat in their Mosquito-designated KFJ—King-Fox-Johnnie, in RAF parlance—on their holding pad just off the main runway at Leiston. Each of 645's four Mosquitos took turns at being the duty aircraft, which involved sitting in acute boredom in this position for a three-hour shift, waiting in case a V2 Meillerwagen had been spotted by the Dutch underground.

It took less than two minutes for Shaux and Baxter to start up and begin to roll to the end of the runway.

"You are clear for takeoff."

It took another two minutes for the Mosquito's Merlin engines to propel them into the air. Shaux saw, out of the corner of his eye, that a small knot of spectators had gathered on the control tower balcony, watching the Mosquito with its oversized four-bladed propellers howling down the runway and jumping into the air like an Olympic pole-vaulter. Perhaps Bob O'Neill was among the watchers; Shaux knew that he had still not been passed as fit to fly, much to his chagrin. Perhaps the young pilot Chuck Yeager was there, rethinking if a P51 could outrun a Tsetse Mosquito.

Shaux raised the wheels, adjusted the flaps and the trim—King-Fox-Johnnie had a slight tendency to fly nose-down, probably because of the extra weight of the barrel of the Molins gun—and reset the propeller pitch from takeoff to cruise. Now the propellers were slashing their way through huge volumes of air, dragging the aircraft over the tiny village of Sizewell on the east coast of England and out across the North Sea.

All aircraft vibrate in flight, and Shaux, like all experienced pilots, sensed the vibrations without conscious thought, as if they were part of his nervous system. They told him far more about the condition of the aircraft than all the dials on the instrument panel put together. They told him how the aircraft was *feeling*, and on this morning, King-Fox-Johnnie was feeling fine, quivering with excitement, delighting in being set free from the bounds of earth, exalting in the power of the Merlins, and reveling in the way its silky-smooth fuselage slid through the sky.

Shaux recalled a discussion with an aeronautical engineer in which the engineer had ridiculed the idea of inanimate aircraft having *feelings*—"For God's sake, Shaux, they're just machines"—but Geoffrey De Havilland, in Shaux's view the finest aeronautical engineer in England, had known exactly what he meant.

It was a hundred miles to Holland; at this rate they'd be there in fifteen minutes.

The RAF had just introduced its first jet-engined aircraft, the Gloster Meteor, and the enemy had its new jet-engined Messerschmitt 262. Clearly these aircraft represented the future of aviation. Shaux felt irrationally sorry for King-Fox-Johnnie, brand-new and full of life, roaring across the waves as no aircraft had done before, in many ways the pinnacle of all war-born propeller aircraft, not realizing that it was already obsolete and destined to be left to rot in some weedy field, perhaps just a few months from now, no longer a king of the sky, an apex predator, but just a rotting snack for a variety of fiber-consuming bee-tles and termites.

Baxter was engaged in hand-to-hand combat with a large map of The Hague, Holland's administrative capital on the North Sea. The Dutch underground had transmitted the exact location of a Meillerwagen in a park just to the north of the city.

"Got it," Baxter said finally. "Let's see if we can find an approach."

Hitting a ground target with a Molins gun required an open approach so that they could spot the target and have time to line up and aim before they overshot it. At 130 miles per hour, the slowest they dared to go without risking stalling, they would cover a mile every twenty-five seconds, so Baxter had to find an angle where they could see the erected V2 from a mile away. If the Germans put the Meillerwagen in the middle of a wood, for example, Shaux and Baxter would never be able to spot it early enough to aim. Shaux had been able to attack U-boat pens with Molins guns last year because the lines of fire were across unobstructed open water.

"Twenty miles to go, skipper," Baxter said. "It looks as if there's a north/south approach that might work."

The sea was dark gray-green, the sky was overcast, and the enemy coast ahead—where the enemy coast should be—was a bank of grayish-white.

"It looks a bit foggy, Bax," Shaux said. "Might be clear above a thou-sand feet, but that's much too high for us."

"S'pose," Baxter grunted.

This was their third attempt to attack a V2 while it was fueling on its Meillerwagen, and both their earlier attempts had been aborted because of ground fog. Indeed, it had occurred to Shaux that the enemy preferred launching on foggy days. Fog did not affect their abil-ity to aim the V2 but prevented Allied aircraft from spotting V2s on the ground.

"Well, we'll give it a go," Shaux said. "We're two minutes away. We'll head north on a bearing for Rotterdam and then swing around south over the coast. That should—"

"Bit late for that," Baxter interrupted.

Ahead of them, Shaux saw a brilliant red vertical line emerging from the horizontal line of white fog and climbing up into the sky. The

V2 had launched. They were at least a minute away from being in range, and by that time the V2 would be far above their heads, far above the highest altitude any aircraft had ever flown. Besides, the notion of hitting a V2 sitting stationary on the ground was hairy enough, let alone hitting a V2 in flight.

All Shaux could do was sit back and reluctantly admire the genius of the engineers who had fashioned this monster, and fear for the people in London who would never know what hit them. Perhaps it was time to suggest to Wilfred Freeman that this whole idea was a flight of fancy too far, and the Molins guns should be given targets that didn't fly away.

"Bollocks," Baxter said, putting down his map.

"Bollocks, indeed."

SEVENTEEN

SHAEF Forward, Versailles, France
19 September 1944, 1630 Hours

"We still haven't taken the bridge at Nijmegen," Percival said.

He was here, clearly against his will, to brief Beetle Smith on the latest reports on Market Garden. Eisenhower was away in Granville, a small town near Liege in Belgium and temporarily out of communication; Smith and Eleanor would have to drive to Granville to update him.

In the last few days, she had watched Percival's demeanor change from smug superiority to an unpleasant kind of nervous, defensive wariness, as if he were a boxer battered by blows he could not fend off. She might have felt sorry for him if she hadn't loathed him.

"The 82nd is going to attempt to cross the Waal by boat as soon as the boats arrive." He glanced at Eleanor and glanced away, as if fearing she would say, "I told you so."

This was now the third day of Market Garden. It was clear that the British 1st Airborne at Arnhem and the American 82nd Airborne at Nijmegen had landed far too far from their target bridges, forcing the lightly equipped paratroopers to fight their way through far more heavily armed enemy forces.

At Eindhoven, the southernmost battleground, things were now relatively secure, although last night, a massive Luftwaffe bombing attack had reduced much of the city to ruins, and the streets were choked with debris and destroyed vehicles.

At Nijmegen, the 82nd had finally captured the southern approaches to the road bridge across the Waal, as the Dutch called the Lower Rhine, and 30 Corps had just reached the 82nd.

At Arnhem, the British were completely isolated and were facing two SS armored divisions; 30 Corps would have to cross both the Waal at Nijmegen and the Rhine at Arnhem—assuming the enemy did not blow up the bridges across them—to reach the beleaguered 1st Division.

"They're waiting for the boats to come up from Eindhoven, but . . ." Percival's voice faded away. She knew he could not bring himself to say, "They're stuck in traffic."

Eleanor felt an icy anger. It wasn't that everything was going wrong; it was that everything was going *predictably* wrong.

The single road was grossly inadequate for a full Army Corps. Its flanks were vulnerable to German counterattacks, and much of 30 Corps was now at a standstill, repelling these flank attacks instead of pressing forward towards Arnhem. The enemy forces, which were supposed to be burned-out husks of their former selves, were fighting strongly.

Perhaps the worst error of all, in her mind, which typified all the cumulative ineptitude, was the failure of the British radio communications system. Boy Browning had flown into Nijmegen with a grandiose headquarters staff that required no less than forty gliders to transport, only to discover that the radios didn't work, and therefore his command role was limited to criticizing the American 82nd, the only part of his command he could reach.

In fact, the first message out of Arnhem since the operation began had come just an hour ago, at three o'clock this afternoon—by carrier pigeon. A bird had flown from Arnhem to its nest in England, flying 250 miles in less than six hours, carrying a message describing the severity of the British position.

The battalion at the Arnhem bridge was under intense fire, and its heroic commander, John Frost, was badly wounded. It seemed only a question of time before they'd run out of ammunition and be forced to surrender. A small Polish contingent had flown in today, but again their landing ground was much too far away from the bridge, and they were immediately under attack. Eleanor shuddered; God alone knew what SS troops would do to any Polish paratroopers they captured.

"The boats the 82nd are waiting for are Bailey boats, I believe?" Eleanor asked Percival. Bailey boats were light, collapsible rowboats made of wood and canvas, like oversized canoes.

Percival did not reply.

She could contain her anger no longer.

"Ah, yes, sir," she said. "I recall you told the prime minister that this operation would be the pinnacle of modern warfare, using modern tactics and modern technologies."

"That's not fair! I—"

"You also told me I lacked imagination, sir, and I must admit that you were right. I never imagined that the pinnacle of modern warfare involved carrier pigeons and canvas rowboats!"

"I—"

"Thank you for the briefing, sir. We'll let Ike know."

* * *

RAF Leiston, Suffolk
19 September 1944, 1030 Hours

"Warmer leader, we have trade for you," Shaux's headphones announced.

Shaux tried to feel enthusiastic as he and Baxter hurried through their fastest possible start-up and takeoff routine, but without success. Wilfred Freeman had agreed that the chances of catching and destroying a V2 on the ground were growing slimmer and slimmer, but said he wanted to keep going for a few more days. Churchill, it seemed, was very anxious to announce a success against the "flying gas mains."

Shaux wanted the opportunity to show what a Molins-gunned Mosquito could do against ground targets as an alternative to RP3 rockets, but that couldn't happen if they were stuck in Leiston, twiddling their thumbs and waiting for a V2 Meillerwagen to appear on the streets of The Hague.

This time, at least, the weather forecast for Holland was for a bright sunny day, and hopefully the Dutch underground had spotted a Meillerwagen early enough for King-Fox-Johnnie to get there before it launched.

"The map reference is for a polo ground a little to the north of the city," Baxter said.

Shaux noticed that his map-management skills were improving: he had only unfolded and refolded the map five times, and the result was no longer fully cubic.

"It's called the Polo Club Wassenaar," Baxter said. "Hopefully it will be a wide-open field . . . Yes, it looks like there are open fields running northeast to southwest, towards the city. We'll cross the border just south of Leiden and then swing south onto a bearing of 190 degrees."

King-Fox-Johnnie thundered across the North Sea.

"Enemy coast fifty miles ahead, skipper," Baxter said, staring into a radar scope. "Steer 095 degrees and reduce our height to fifty feet to keep under their radar horizon."

Shaux eased King-Fox-Johnnie down until it seemed they were surfing across the endless lines of North Sea breakers. The lower they descended, the faster their apparent speed. They were crossing about a mile of sea every ten seconds. The ride was far bumpier down there as the surface winds churned and snarled above the wave tops. It would have been an exciting run if they'd had time to enjoy the fun.

"Enemy coast in sight," Shaux said. A long line of sandy beaches appeared, with a dark-green coastal strip beyond them. He eased back on the throttles, and their speed leached away. The turbulence increased as their speed decreased. King-Fox-Johnnie creaked in protest.

They swept over the coast. To their left, in the direction of Leiden, a flak battery fired into the air at random. Perhaps the crew wanted to report they'd aimed at and missed an intruder rather than not firing at all.

"Turn to 190 degrees, skipper."

Shaux stood King-Fox-Johnnie on its right wing, and they swung around to the south until they were flying parallel with the beaches. Now their primary concerns were tall trees or buildings or telephone poles. The ground below them consisted of low-lying coastal dunes covered in scrub; it was unlikely that tall trees would grow here, under the endless battering of North Sea gales, but there are exceptions to all rules, particularly for the unwary.

Baxter fiddled with the mechanism that turned on the Molins autoloader and switched the gun safety off. They always flew with a shell already loaded in the breach, so the gun was ready to fire as soon as he pressed the button.

Shaux ran his thumb over the four makeshift machine-gun buttons on his control column to make sure he knew where they were without looking. He'd fire a quick burst from each gun in succession to keep up a continuous stream of tracer without overheating any one gun, just like the twin-mounted Reibels he'd seen in that Tobruk overlooking Sword Beach.

Now there was a village beneath them.

"Wassenaar," Baxter grunted.

Shaux pulled up a trifle to avoid the church tower. He glimpsed white faces staring up in shock as they thundered overhead, just barely above the rooftops. Life as a civilian in an occupied country was grossly unfair, he thought: first your enemies bombed you and then your allies did.

Now there was flat open ground beneath them, perhaps small vegetable fields.

"The polo grounds should be a mile and a half," Baxter said.

At a ground speed of 150 miles per hour, they were covering a mile every twenty-five seconds. A Mosquito stalled at a speed of 120 miles per hour, and the closer they got down to that speed, the more sluggish King-Fox-Johnnie became. A Mark 18 Mosquito could actually fly below its stalling speed but only in a nose-up attitude. Shaux didn't think consciously about raising the nose to improve their slow flying speed, or the extra weight of the Molins gun barrel making them nose-heavy, or the need to keep the nose down in order to be able to aim at the target when they saw it, or, indeed, any other such consideration.

He had always believed—known—that a pilot was part of an aircraft, not separate from it, so he just felt King-Fox-Johnnie, through the feeling in his feet on the rudder bar and the feel through his fingers on the control column and especially through the vibrations transmitted through his seat to his spine. He knew the aircraft would tell him if it was unhappy.

"Forty seconds," Shaux said.

He hopped King-Fox-Johnnie over an unexpected white church spire rising abruptly amid the vegetables.

"Polo grounds in sight," Baxter said. "There, at one o'clock."

"One o'clock," Shaux said, easing King-Fox-Johnnie to the right.

Another church spire appeared at the far end of the polo fields.

"Another spire, skipper," Baxter warned.

The new spire had a curiously sleek shape, and it seemed to be surrounded by large vehicles, almost as if—

"No, Bax, that's the target. Twenty seconds."

Now the geometry of the rocket was clear. It was sitting on its wide fins, pointing to the heavens like a forty-foot-high bullet. Unlike the ugly V1, Shaux had time to think, the V2 combined form and function to make something elegant—malevolent, certainly, but elegant nonetheless. The V2 reminded Shaux of the illustrations in Jules Verne's novel *From the Earth to the Moon*. Perhaps one day a rocket like that might reach the moon. He felt he was glimpsing the future.

"Fifteen seconds."

Machine-gun rounds were accurate up to eight hundred yards before gravity or the winds dragged them off course. Still, he wanted to make sure they were lined up on the target, even if they were too far away for complete accuracy.

He fired a one-second burst of tracer—six rounds of incandescent white-hot phosphorus—and swung a little to the right. Another burst, from another gun, and a slight nudge back to the left. The guns were mounted just ahead of the instrument panel in front of him, allowing him to see exactly where King-Fox-Johnnie was pointing.

"Tallyho," he said, using Fighter Command's traditional battle cry.

Now his tracer rounds were streaking ahead in white lines, burying themselves into the ground on a line to the V2 ahead of them and now striking it as the distance closed. He wondered what it was like to be one of the Meillerwagen crew, to see the white lines streaking towards them, to hear the waspish buzzing of the rounds in the air and the smacks as tracer struck the Meillerwagen and the sides of the rocket, white-hot shrapnel trying to penetrate the skin to reach the highly combustible rocket fuel.

He was hitting the target, flashes climbing up the V2's flank. It was up to Baxter to decide when to fire the Molins.

BANG.

Baxter fired, the gun roared, King-Fox-Johnnie shook as it absorbed the recoil.

THUNK, THUNK.

Beneath their feet, the Molins autoloader extracted the spent cartridge and loaded another round, but there was no need for a second shot: the V2 had been transformed into a volcano.

They swept over the exploding maelstrom towards the center of The Hague. The skyline was spiked with towers and spires rising far above their height. Shaux opened the throttles and turned sharply, pivoting on their right wing. The Merlins spun up and dragged them back towards the safety of the North Sea, down among the rooftops, belatedly pursued by flak.

Now they were back over the sea, bouncing in the turbulence above the wave tops.

Shaux breathed a long sigh of relief. The Mark 18 had done the job.

"Well, it actually worked, Bax!" Shaux said. "Who'd have thought it?"

"S'pose."

* * *

SHAEF Forward, Versailles, France
20 September 1944, 0630 Hours

Beetle Smith put down the telephone.

"The 504th Parachute Regiment is going to row across the Waal to the northern bank this afternoon and storm the bridge from that end," he told Eleanor. "Then the Grenadier Guards will cross the bridge from the southern end, assuming the enemy does not blow up the bridge in the meantime. Everyone assumes the enemy has wired it with demolition charges."

He shook his head, perhaps in frustration that the entire operation had been reduced to such desperate straits or perhaps at the thought of the hideous danger to the men rowing into enemy fire. Eleanor found she was also shaking her head—for both reasons.

"Those poor guys out there on the river will be sitting ducks—literally," Smith continued. "We'll get air cover to suppress enemy fire from the northern bank, assuming the weather permits, but even so, it's going to be ugly. What a snafu!"

She knew he usually managed to control his temper but, on this occasion, with her as the only witness, he did not hold back.

"Rowboats! Why haven't the Brits brought up DUKWs? Jesus Christ! Horrocks has fifty thousand men in 30 Corps, and Browning has thirty thousand in the Airborne and the Air Force, and the RAF have God knows how many thousand airplanes, and we're reduced to a couple of hundred guys forced to paddle across the fucking river in fucking canoes?"

That summed it up perfectly. Johnnie sometimes said that all warfare had always come down to sharpened sticks and vulnerable flesh, and this was a prime example.

"I know it's bad, sir, but if this works, we'll be only nine miles from the bridge at Arnhem," Eleanor said, trying to raise his mood. "We could be there by midnight."

"Well, let's hope the Brits up there in Arnhem can hold out a little longer," Smith said. "That is, assuming they're still alive."

* * *

RAF Leiston, Suffolk
20 September 1944, 0830 Hours
Shaux answered his telephone and heard Wilfred Freeman's voice.

"This is a bit unusual, Shaux," he said, immediately getting to the point. "It appears that Operation Market Garden in Holland is not going smoothly, and 2TAF, as well as the American Eighth, had been asked to help out with a rhubarb. I happened to hear of it and thought your Mark 18s could be useful. Bit of a change from sitting around, waiting for a V2, I should think?"

"Definitely, sir."

"Good. You should stand by for a briefing from 2TAF."

"Very well, sir. When's the op?"

"This afternoon, I believe. Good luck."

Shaux stared at the phone as he heard Freeman disconnect. This was exactly the sort of opportunity he'd been hoping for to demonstrate the potential of the Molins, but he had not imagined it would happen immediately.

Ten minutes later, the telephone rang again.

"Johnnie? Coningham here." Arthur "Mary" Coningham was the 2TAF AOC.

"Good morning, sir."

"Glad you're joining the party this afternoon. By the way, good rhubarb with that V2."

"Thanks."

"I'll put you through to 2TAF Ops."

The telephone emitted a series of beeps and crackles until the voice of the 2TAF Ops briefing officer replaced Coningham's.

"The American 82nd Airborne is going to row across the Waal, as the Lower Rhine is known, at Nijmegen. It's a wide river with a very strong current, and there are German units, probably including SS Panzers, waiting for them. The 82nd will be using collapsible canvas boats."

"Excuse me," Shaux interrupted. "Did you say 'row'?"

"I did."

"Good God!"

"Exactly. Anyway, our job is to suppress all enemy fire from the northern bank of the river. Our sector will be the mile of bank immediately to the west of the bridge. We're sending a squadron of Typhoons and a squadron of Mustangs, all armed with RP3s. Your Molins guns will be a variation on a theme, as it were. We're also sending an airborne controller, an ABC, to direct traffic."

"Very well."

"In addition, the American 357th will provide escort P51s above you. There's some concern that the Luftwaffe might send their new Messerschmitt 262s to spoil the party."

As soon as the briefing was over, Shaux organized a makeshift training mission using the River Ouse between Lincolnshire and Yorkshire to act as the Waal. The flat landscape and the lazy river were like the landscape near Nijmegen.

"It looks as if we'll have thirty seconds to sight and fire," Shaux told Baxter after several dummy runs across the Ouse. "Fifteen seconds as we fly over the south bank and then fifteen seconds more as we cross the river."

"S'pose."

At 1500 in the afternoon, the 357th escort fighter squadrons took off, and Shaux's Mosquito detachment followed them. The plan was for the P51s to establish standing patrols high above Nijmegen before the 82nd began their river crossing.

Thirty minutes later, Shaux looked down at the Maas—the Meuse in French—and at Graves. One of those bridges down there had been the 82nd's first major target. It seemed so easy, looking down from up here, to capture one of those toy bridges, he thought, but those first few hours of D-Day had taught him that nothing is easy down there and had given him a profound admiration for the men who fight there.

Baxter changed a radio frequency, and Shaux contacted the ABC.

"Hello, Sheepdog, this is Warmer leader. I am overhead Graves at angels zero-five."

"Good afternoon, Warmer leader. Descend to angels zero-two and hold over Graves until needed."

It was a familiar pattern—hurry up and wait: the dragging tedium of waiting to be called, perhaps followed by a few short seconds of frenetic action or perhaps not.

Shaux reviewed the plan with Baxter as they waited.

Thirty seconds was not a long time to locate a target and aim and shoot, but it was all they had. The Royal Navy test pilot Eric "Winkle" Brown was, in Shaux's opinion, the finest pilot he had ever seen. Brown had the ability to get everything done, regardless of how little time he had—he seemed to be able to make time slow down. Perhaps it was his superb craftsmanship, so that he wasted no time on unnecessary actions. Perhaps it was practice and anticipation, so he had no surprises. Perhaps it was his clarity of purpose, so that everything he did was a correct step in the right direction. Perhaps it was a combination of all these things and more.

Shaux wished he had Brown's calm. Over the past twelve months, his hands had developed a nasty habit of cramping up into tight fists, making it difficult to control an aircraft. He had developed an annoying counter-habit of frequently flexing his hands. The Ginger Runt, the RAF doctor who had tried to ground him because of age and "excessive stress," had claimed his hands proved that Shaux was losing his grip, snorting in amusement at his own pun.

What rubbish! Shaux had convinced himself it was just a touch of rheumatism.

"Warmer leader, this is Sheepdog. Target is a Panzer 5 Panther tank at location Green Four, four hundred yards to the left of the bridge. You will follow RP3 Typhoons."

"Panzer tank at location Green Four," Shaux repeated back, while Baxter stabbed his finger at a map to tell Shaux he had found Green Four. Graves was perhaps five miles from Nijmegen, no more, and they were ambling along at just 150 miles per hour.

"With you in three minutes, Sheepdog."

"You are cleared for action after the Tiffies, Warmer."

Shaux nudged King-Fox-Johnnie around towards Nijmegen.

"Once more unto the breach, dear Bax?" Shaux asked. "Ready?"

"S'pose. Steer oh-one-five degrees."

Nijmegen, he saw as they approached it, had been wrecked as the 82nd advanced towards the bridge in the teeth of enemy defenses and counterattacks, transformed from a town into a ruin, with hundreds of years of hard work and artistry destroyed in just a few days.

"Gun on, Bax, and safeties off. Thirty seconds."

The river opened before them as they flew over the town. The all-important bridge seemed undamaged, and its arched design reminded Shaux of the Sydney Harbour bridge.

"Turn left just a hair, skipper," Baxter said.

The far shore was sparkling with enemy gunfire. There must be four or five machine-gun emplacements, Shaux guessed. And there were the 82nd's boats, looking from this angle like a dozen little water beetles with lots of legs, seemingly unmoving in the middle of the river.

"Twenty seconds."

Shaud saw two Typhoons above and ahead of them, diving down and firing their RP3 rockets at the far bank of the river, eight streaks of fire leading to eight orange explosions. An enemy light flak position returned fire. Shaux couldn't tell if either side had hit their targets.

"Panzer!" Baxter snapped, aroused for once above his usual torpor. "Muzzle flash eleven o'clock!"

It was a stroke of luck that the enemy tank—assuming it was the Panzer 5—had fired at that precise moment: they might never have seen it otherwise. But, alas, it was not a stroke of luck for one of the beetles, which flipped over on its back and sank instantly.

"I see it," Shaux said. "Tallyho."

He lined up where he had seen the flash.

A Panzer 5, Shaux knew, was a large, well-armored tank with a 75mm gun. The enemy had christened it a Panther. The front armor was steeply angled; if they didn't hit it correctly, even an armor-piercing shell would just bounce off. As if to prove the point, another Typhoon ahead fired its rockets, and one bounced off the Panzer and streaked up into the sky, as if it were a firework on Guy Fawkes Night.

"I'm aiming at the bottom of the turret, Bax, where it meets the body. Ten seconds."

He fired a short burst of tracer. They had fired enough Molins rounds over the last couple of weeks to perfect their teamwork, but Shaux admitted to himself it was a bit arrogant to specify where to strike the tank instead of hoping to be lucky enough to hit it at all. The last time he'd done something like this was on D-Day morning, and that had not worked out well at all.

"Five seconds."

Shaux fired bursts, walking the incandescent lines of tracer to the target, while Baxter waited until he saw it striking exactly where he wanted.

Baxter fired. The turret flew off the body of the Panzer like a jack-in-a-box, as if it weighed nothing. King-Fox-Johnnie roared over the wreckage.

An eye for an eye, Shaux thought, but a Panther for a beetle seemed inadequate.

EIGHTEEN

Eleanor groaned inwardly. By far, the worst part of her job was being right. It was much worse than being wrong. It was worse than being disdained by senior officers and government officials twice her age, who questioned her intrusion into their cushioned all-male world. It was worse than the leers and bottom pinches from men old enough to be her father, who would never treat their own daughters with such oafish disrespect. It was worse than the constant moral dilemmas—if I recommend this, these people will die; if I recommend that, those people will die instead.

The three Market Garden airborne forces were fighting gallantly, but the planned landing fields for the gliders and parachute drops had been too far from their target bridges. German resistance had proved to be much stronger than expected, particularly in the Arnhem area at the northern tip of the Allied thrust and the furthest from help by 30 Corps coming up from the south.

In addition, as 30 Corps had plowed its way north and the Allied salient grew longer, its lengthening flanks were becoming increasingly vulnerable to enemy counterattacks so that the road was even more clogged by stationary men and vehicles fighting off German assaults.

It had taken 30 Corps four hard days to advance fifty miles up the narrow, traffic-choked road to reach Nijmegen. They were now only seven miles from Arnhem, but the 1st Airborne was in critical condition, suffering very high casualties and running out of ammunition. And, to make the situation even more desperate, the 1st Airborne was still on the north bank of the Rhine with no obvious means of escaping south because the Arnhem bridge was still in enemy hands.

Browning and Percival's plan had been for eight thousand men to reach the bridge and hold it for two days. In fact, only the eight hundred men of 2PARA had reached the bridge, but they had managed, against all odds, to hold the northern end for four days. John Frost, their heroic commander, had been severely injured and taken prisoner by the enemy. The remaining seven thousand men had spent four days desperately fending off the SS Panzer Divisions that were supposed to have been empty shells.

Eleanor was reminded of another battle long ago, back in a half-forgotten war in 1854, when the bizarre ineptitude of senior British officers had sent a brigade of light cavalry charging into a death trap, resulting in a fiasco in which three hundred men were killed or wounded out of six hundred. Sending thirty thousand men sixty miles up a single narrow road through enemy-held territory was as absurd as sending lightly armed mounted cavalry to assault—frontally assault—an artillery battery; it was as absurd as sending seven thousand men—lightly armed paratroopers—without reinforcements or resupplies, to face two armored SS Panzer divisions.

The poet Lord Tennyson had memorialized that long-ago charge of the Light Division. She remembered Tennyson had said the survivors were *shattered and sundered*. Or something like that.

Would a poet record the dogged heroism of John Frost and the eight hundred shattered and sundered men of 2PARA?

The disaster, Eleanor thought, had still not run its full course. There were Polish paratroopers with the British 1st Division, under the command of General Sosabowski. As more information leaked in, and as the British position in Arnhem became ever more dire, Percival started muttering—without any evidence—about poor performance by the Poles, and Eleanor guessed that this was the start of a campaign to blame the disaster on them.

Eleanor had not met Sosabowski, but she knew he had questioned various aspects of the plan, just as she had, thereby incurring Browning's and Percival's hostility. She feared Sosabowski would make a convenient scapegoat.

The poor Poles! They had been crushed by Germany in 1939 and were now about to be "liberated"—in her view, conquered—by Russia. The whole point of the war, back in 1939, had been to defend Poland's independence, but Poland had been divided up and swallowed up by Germany and Russia. The Free Poles who had escaped in 1939 had fought bravely on the Allied side in several theaters, notably in Italy, but they were not considered full partners in the alliance.

There were hideous rumors about barbarities being committed by the Germans in Warsaw . . . there were dark tales that more than twenty thousand Polish officers had vanished in Russia . . . there were even stories, too fantastically horrible to be true, that the entire population of Polish Jewish people had been loaded onto trains—thousands upon thousands of men, women, and children on train after train after train—and taken away no one knew where.

When the war was finally over, would Churchill and Roosevelt insist that Poland should be free, as they had promised, or would they cede it away to Stalin in return for some other quid pro quo?

* * *

RAF Leiston, Suffolk
22 September 1944, 1030 Hours
"I think we're getting better at this, Bax," Shaux said.

They had just succeeded in blasting a Panzerwagen, a half-track armored troop carrier, across a road and into a ditch, where it lay inverted with its tracks still turning. This was their third rhubarb in as many days as 2TAF and the Eighth Air Force suppressed enemy activity north of Nijmegen.

The ABC airborne control system was working well. Today ABC was a B25 Mitchell medium bomber converted into a flying radar station, protected by a flight of P51s lest the Luftwaffe should make a rare attempt to challenge Allied air superiority of Holland. To Shaux's delight, the controller was Bob O'Neill, who had decided to interpret his orders to mean that he was not cleared to pilot an aircraft but was otherwise allowed to fly.

Shaux wished he had been sensible enough to realize that, if he was going to direct airborne attacks on enemy tanks and positions on D-Day, he would be much better off in an aircraft looking down on the battlefield rather than crawling around in the mud with his visibility reduced to the next bush. His only contribution to that battle had been firing a few PIAT potshots at obsolete stationary tank turrets.

The 57mm 6-pounder Molins guns were also working well. They were far more accurate than RP3s, and a Mosquito with twenty rounds in its automatic loading racks could do far more damage than a Typhoon with just two salvos of four RP3 rockets. The rockets, adored by newsreel camera operators, were turning out to be all sound and fury, signifying nothing, as Shakespeare had once said. Eleanor had told him they'd done analyses of the hundreds and hundreds of tanks that 2TAF had claimed to have destroyed with RP3s in Normandy only to discover that the true number was close to zero.

"Warmer leader, this is Sheepdog," O'Neill's voice sounded in Shaux's earphones. "Possible bogies approaching from your three o'clock."

Doubtless one of their guardian escorts, a P51 or a Tempest flying far above them, had spotted unidentified but potentially enemy aircraft approaching from the east. He looked in that direction but could see nothing. Baxter twiddled with his radar controls and shrugged.

"Better check the Monica just in case, Bax," Shaux said, and Baxter adjusted the rear-looking radar.

"Nothing, skipper," he said.

Tracer streaked past them from somewhere behind their tail.

"Jesus Christ!" Baxter yelled. "Bandits at six o'clock closing fast. Where the hell did—"

Two gray forms raced past them at an absurd overtaking speed, firing ahead into the empty sky. They had beautifully aerodynamic bodies and swept-back wings, and they struck him as unusually uncluttered, like barracudas. They were painted in a barracuda-like mottled gray pattern, had twin-engine nacelles, and, Shaux suddenly realized, no propellers—that's why they looked so clean.

"They're 262s!" Shaux said. "Jets! Holy crap!"

He switched to radio transmit.

"Sheepdog, Warmer. Bogies are 262s bearing 360 degrees at angels zero-five."

So, these gray barracudas were the new jet-powered Messerschmitt 262 fighters. The 262 had begun to appear in the skies over Germany and Holland a few months ago, but these were the first Shaux had seen. They represented a third dramatic enemy technological achievement alongside the V1 and V2.

There seemed to be only a few 262s—perhaps the enemy hadn't ramped up its production yet—but those few proved that 262s were far faster than any Allied aircraft. If they started to appear in volume, they might force the Eighth Air Force to reduce its daylight bombing campaign, which would, in turn, enable the Luftwaffe to redirect hundreds of 190s and 109s to challenge Allied air superiority over France, Belgium, and Holland.

Shaux had been, for example, ambling around Dutch airspace seeking targets of opportunity without a care in the world. A flight of 262s would end that very quickly.

"Warmer, reconfirm 262s?"

"They are 262s, affirmative, Sheepdog; too fast to be anything else."

"How fast, Warmer?"

"Holy crap fast, Sheepdog."

* * *

SHAEF Forward, Granville near Liege, Belgium
25 September 1944, 2230 Hours
"I think we can all agree that Market Garden has been a notable success, a notable Airborne victory," Percival said. "Obviously our 1st Airborne got knocked about a bit, but we all knew, and agreed before we started, that this was a risk worth taking."

The latest reports from Arnhem were that the last remnants of the British and Polish troops north of the Rhine had finally run out of ammunition and were surrendering to the enemy.

Now that the situation north of Nijmegen had congealed into an impasse, and the few surviving British and Polish remnants of the 1st Airborne had been evacuated south across the Rhine, the process of assigning credit and blame was in full swing, and the fight had moved from the real world of facts and figures to the world of history books. This was a crucial migration, Eleanor thought: not only reputations were at stake but also promotions, medals, and, on the British side, even knighthoods.

Percival was speaking in a stilted manner, as if he were a schoolboy making an elaborate excuse for not doing his homework, and Eleanor guessed that he had rehearsed this speech. Perhaps this was the first draft of the official British report—perhaps also the first draft of his own memoirs.

"As Boy Browning said before we started, Arnhem was probably 'a bridge too far,' as he eloquently put it, and events have proved him right. Of course, had the Poles been more effective, we might have held on, but let us not cast aspersions among . . . I'm sure they tried their best, even if . . . But no matter: we have the bridges at Nijmegen, and that was always the main target."

So this was to be the official story, Eleanor thought. It turned out not only that Browning had advised against his own plan but also that the failure at Arnhem was all the Poles' fault anyway, even though the Poles had not been flown in until after the battle for the Arnhem bridgehead had already been lost.

"Monty does feel, I must add, that SHAEF could have been more—a lot more—supportive . . . but, no matter."

Ah, Eleanor thought, it was Ike's fault as well. Beetle Smith raised his eyebrows but did not respond.

"Still, 30 Corps is firmly in control in Nijmegen," Percival hurried on. "We're ready to move forward."

The fact that Nijmegen had been taken by the American 82nd Airborne, not by 30 Corps, seemed to have slipped from Percival's analysis. In a similar manner, Eleanor knew there were no plans to push further north; the enemy had done an excellent job of building defenses between Nijmegen and Arnhem. The Airborne divisions were exhausted, and 30 Corps was still trying to secure the flanks of the highway from Eindhoven. The SS Panzer divisions, which Percival had dismissed as on their last legs, had won the battle at Arnhem.

"Any comment, Eleanor?" Beetle Smith asked. On this occasion, she could see he had his temper firmly under control, but hers was not.

"Approximately 10,500 men of the 1st Airborne landed near Arnhem, sir," Eleanor said. "Approximately 1,500 have been killed, and 6,500 were taken prisoner. The remaining 2,500 have been rescued, of whom a third are wounded, leaving just 1,600 out of the original 10,500 capable of fighting. I would say—"

"The weather was against—" Percival began, adding God to the Poles and Eisenhower to the list of those to blame, but Eleanor did not let him interrupt her.

"I would therefore say, sir, that we cannot afford another 'notable Airborne victory,' to borrow your expression."

"That's not fair! I—"

"'Getting knocked about a bit,' as you put it, is a novel description for losing eighty-five percent of one's forces in less than a week."

"There's no need to be—"

She thought of using Tennyson's phrase, "shattered and sundered," but she doubted he would know the allusion.

"Be that as it may, let us move on," she said.

"I agree," Percival said, evidently relieved she was not going to press the point.

"Let us consider the effects on the Dutch people."

"What effects?"

"The Dutch civilian railway workers went on strike, at great personal peril, at our request," Eleanor said. "They succeeded in preventing the enemy from moving reinforcements and ammunition up to the front, doubtless saving many British and American lives at the cost of some of their own."

"I scarcely see how—"

"Now, in retaliation, the enemy has announced that all shipments of food to and within Holland are strictly forbidden. There are already severe shortages in the west of Holland, and winter is coming. There may be famine. People, perhaps many people, will starve to death this winter, or get 'knocked about a bit,' as you might prefer to put it."

"I still don't see—"

"I therefore doubt the Dutch people can afford another notable Airborne victory either."

PART THREE

Unternehmen Wacht am Rhein

(Operation Watch on the Rhine)

The Battle of the Bulge

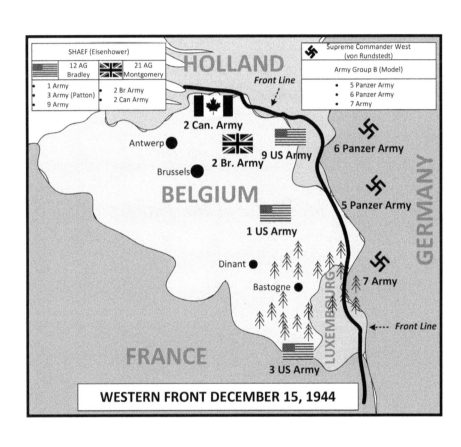

SHAEF (Eisenhower)

12 AG	21 AG
Bradley	Montgomery

- 1 Army
- 3 Army (Patton)
- 9 Army

- 2 Br Army
- 2 Can Army

HOLLAND

Front Line

Supreme Commander West
(von Rundstedt)

Army Group B (Model)

- 5 Panzer Army
- 6 Panzer Army
- 7 Army

2 Can. Army

Antwerp

6 Panzer Army

9 US Army

2 Br. Army

Brussels

GERMANY

BELGIUM

5 Panzer Army

1 US Army

Dinant

Bastogne

7 Army

LUXEMBURG

Front Line

FRANCE

3 US Army

WESTERN FRONT DECEMBER 15, 1944

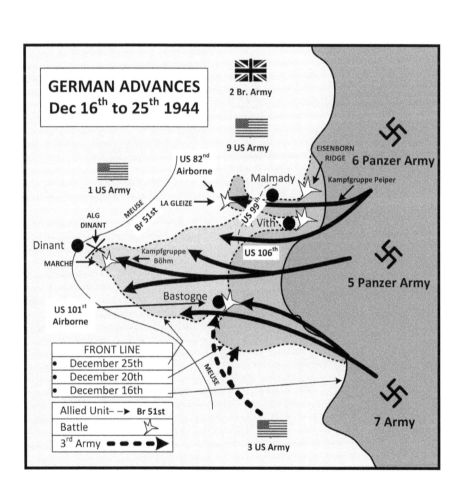

GERMAN ADVANCES
Dec 16th to 25th 1944

2 Br. Army

9 US Army

1 US Army

US 82nd
Airborne

EISENBORN
RIDGE 6 Panzer Army

Malmady

Kampfgruppe Peiper

MEUSE

LA GLEIZE

US 99th

ALG
DINANT

Br 51st

Vith

Dinant

Kampfgruppe
Böhm

US 106th

5 Panzer Army

MARCHE

Bastogne

US 101st
Airborne

FRONT LINE
• December 25th
• December 20th
• December 16th

MEUSE

7 Army

Allied Unit– ➔ Br 51st
Battle
3rd Army ■■■➤

3 US Army

NINETEEN

SHAEF Forward, Charleroi, Belgium
12 December 1944, 0730 Hours

"Monty wants to transfer you to 21st Army Group staff," Percival said. "He has in mind a senior role planning future advances and intelligence analysis."

"Good Lord," Eleanor managed to say. She could not imagine anything more hideous.

"It's a very high honor, a recognition of his respect for your abilities. You will be an inspiration to all the British women who also struggle to make a contribution to the war effort, supporting their menfolk as best they can. What do you say?"

She ignored his insult against women—struggling to support their menfolk, for God's sake!—but strained to be polite.

"That's very flattering, sir, but I have a long list of things I need to do here at SHAEF."

"You'll be based in 21AG Portsmouth, so you'll be close to your husband, which will be a great comfort to you, I'm sure."

So Monty was proposing to send her back to England, where she would be out in the cold, irrelevant and ignored. The pretext was that she was a hapless woman who needed to be close to her husband. She could point out that Johnnie was nowhere near Portsmouth, but never mind.

"He's proposing to transfer you with the rank of chief controller in the ATS—which, I must say, is unheard-of."

The Auxiliary Territorial Service was the women's branch of the army, like the WAAFs with the RAF and the Wrens with the navy. As the war continued, ATS women had become integral to the army's ability to fight, with almost two hundred thousand women serving. The young Princess Elizabeth and Churchill's daughter Mary were both in the ATS. A substantial portion of Britain's air defenses—its antiaircraft batteries, searchlight regiments, and barrage balloon companies—were staffed by ATS women, as were much of the army's communications and transportation infrastructure.

"Your rank will be equivalent to a major general! A major general at your age! And you're only a—"

He stopped abruptly and Eleanor knew he was about to say "only a woman." He adopted a conciliatory tone.

"Look, I know we've had our differences in the past, but let's agree to let bygones be bygones."

"I don't think Ike—"

"It's not Ike's decision," Percival snapped, evidently abandoning conciliation almost as soon as he had started. "You are not an American. You are in His Majesty's service. You will serve the king as his field marshal wishes. I'll tell Montgomery—"

"Absolutely not, sir," she interrupted. "Let's be honest: Monty's simply trying to muzzle me."

"That's an outrageous thing to say!"

"Yes, sadly it is outrageous, sir, but it is still true."

"Monty welcomes suggestions, of course, but once he makes decisions, he expects his staff to accept them. He simply does not want to be second-guessed. Surely that's reasonable?"

"It is," she said.

"Well then, you can see he doesn't want anyone dragging up ancient history or questioning his judgment."

So, she thought, Operation Market Garden, just a couple of months ago, was now ancient history.

"The common soldier's morale, his willingness to fight, depends in large part on his trust in his commander's reputation as a winner. Surely you can see that?"

Ah, she thought, Montgomery was concerned his reputation had taken a knock among the lower ranks—the men who lived with the consequences of his decisions, or died with them.

"I can, sir."

"Then we can agree to the transfer?"

"My department isn't in the armed services, sir," she said. "It's part of the intelligence services, reporting to Edward Bridges, the cabinet secretary. He's the one that has to say yea or nay."

"That's just a technicality. We'll contact Bridges and—"

"I'll send Edward Bridges a note informing him I will resign if I am transferred to 21st Army Group."

"Monty will be very—"

"Surely not, sir. After all, I'm only a woman, as you were about to say."

"I—"

"And now, sir, if you will excuse me, I have menfolk to support, as best I can."

She considered curtseying but decided against it.

Perhaps she had been too short-tempered with Percival, she thought as she walked away. He couldn't help being a pompous snob, and he was merely one of Montgomery's toadies.

Besides, everyone was a little short-tempered these days. The great Allied advance north from Normandy, freeing France and Belgium in a few short months, had run out of steam. Market Garden had proven to be an expensive diversion from the essential task of shortening Allied supply lines that had been stretched to the limit. The Allied armies had had to wait while the Canadians and the Royal Navy cleared the estuary of the Scheldt so that the port of Antwerp could be reopened. That had finally been accomplished—at the cost of many heroic Canadian lives—at the end of November.

As a result, the Allied advance had stalled, and Allied strategic debates had fallen back into feuding between Montgomery and Bradley over priorities for supplies.

Meanwhile, she thought, the enemy was getting a chance to lick its wounds and regroup. At this stage of the war, with the Russian armies bulldozing their way relentlessly from the east, Germany could not possibly win. Instead, the enemy had to create circumstances in which they could negotiate a ceasefire that did not amount to a total surrender.

There were unconfirmed reports that the army might be attempting another plot to assassinate Hitler. Perhaps that plot might have been led by Rommel, who had died—apparently of a heart attack—a month ago. If the German armed forces were able to kill Hitler and seize control of the German government, Roosevelt and Churchill might reconsider their policy of unconditional surrender.

Perhaps the Germans were banking on their new terror weapons, the V1 and the V2, to change the balance of power, but these were not battlefield weapons, and it was very unlikely that the new Messerschmitt jet fighters could overcome the combined strengths of the RAF and the USAAF. Perhaps—God forbid—Nazi scientists had their own version of the Manhattan Project, in which case anything was possible.

The enemy's best possible chance, it seemed Eleanor, was to achieve some stunning blow against Zhukov's Russian armies in the east or against Eisenhower here in the west. Time was very short. It was crucial for Germany's future for it to make peace with, or surrender to, the United States, before Zhukov could reach Germany, because Stalin would never, ever return an inch of territory he occupied.

She shook her head to clear her thoughts. Her job—analyzing Hitler's intentions—was getting more difficult as the months wore on.

Her next briefing was with Ken Strong, head of SHAEF Intelligence, or G2, as it was known. It would be interesting to see what he thought. She and Strong were natural allies. Strong was a British general who also enjoyed Eisenhower's and Beetle Smith's confidence. He, like Eleanor, accepted American leadership in the Alliance. He, like Eleanor, also played a role in diplomacy, having negotiated the surrender of the Italians last year, and he would probably take the lead if the Germans sued for peace.

"I hear Monty's trying to nobble you," Strong greeted her. "He's dispatched young Percy to SHAEF to do the deed."

"No wonder you're in charge of G2. Your spies are everywhere."

"They are. I trust you told him to shove it, Eleanor?"

"I did."

"I'm relieved to hear it."

* * *

2TAF (Forward Deployment Group) Advanced Landing Ground A 192/B 162, Dinant, Belgium
12 December 1944, 0730 Hours

Shaux struggled not to grin. He yawned extravagantly instead. Everything was working out perfectly.

Mary Coningham, the 2TAF AOC, had asked him to take command of all 2TAF squadrons temporarily based in France and Belgium. They'd be formed into a new group, but the paperwork was lagging far behind events, as it usually did. Shaux liked and respected Coningham, who had been born in Australia but grew up in New Zealand—hence his nickname "Mary," a corruption of "Māori." He had fought with distinction in World War I and had led the Desert Air Force during the Battle of El Alamein, when he pioneered close ground support in that titanic battle.

This had endeared him to Montgomery, who had ensured that Coningham was knighted for his efforts and received command of tactical air support for the D-Day landings. But, Eleanor had told Johnnie, Coningham had had the temerity to question Montgomery's tactics after D-Day, causing Montgomery to try—unsuccessfully—to get him dismissed. "Hell hath no fury like a Monty scorned," she had said.

But, beside all that, Shaux was predisposed to like and respect all New Zealanders, having served under the New Zealander Keith Park in the Battle of Britain and the Siege of Malta. Park was, in his opinion, the finest fighter commander alive.

2TAF Forward Deployment squadrons were based on airfields that had recently been occupied by the Luftwaffe. These airfields were known as Advanced Landing Grounds and given numbers, rather than names. Dinant was known as A192 by the Americans and B162 by the RAF. It had been heavily bombed by B-17s before and after D-Day and

had been repaired and made serviceable by American engineers of the
922nd Engineer regiment. These men, Shaux thought, like their RAF
equivalents, were nothing short of miracle workers. They laid a mile-
long stretch of pierced steel planks over the cratered runway in a mere
four days and constructed bombproof revetments for aircraft stands
and maintenance and storage areas. They had bulldozed a variety of
damaged Focke-Wulf 190s and Junkers 88s aside, and now P-51s and
645 Mosquitos stood in their place.

The morning was cold, but he went out for a walk to shake off his
weariness. The best news of all was that Dinant was a mere thirty miles
from Charleroi, which was currently Eisenhower's most forward headquarters, and therefore he was only thirty miles from Eleanor. Each
evening, he made the pilgrimage, and each morning, like this morning,
he yawned his way back to Dinant before dawn broke. It was probably
against RAF regulations but, then again, almost everything was.

His new appointment didn't quite mean that he had been grounded,
but Mary Coningham had made it clear that Shaux was more valuable
on the ground, coordinating 2TAF-FD forces whose composition and
targets changed every day and whose supplies were iffy at best, than he
was wandering around the sky, looking for Panzers to rhubarb.

"You'll be doing a lot of jury-rigging, Johnnie," Coningham had
said, and Shaux had had a blank moment until he remembered that
Coningham was a keen sailor and jury-rigging meant making do with
whatever was available. Someone had suggested that 2TAF-FD be
called the "tramps," and someone else had suggested the "scavengers."
Both names were accurate, he thought.

Shaux's route took him along the airfield perimeter, where the
922nd had pushed the remnants of Luftwaffe aircraft into a tangled
graveyard. It seemed to Shaux that there was something melancholy
about a broken aircraft—a sense of the mighty fallen—even if the broken aircraft had been built and manned by his enemies.

He stopped to inspect the remains of a Focke-Wulf 190. It was
not an elegant aircraft, but it was a triumph of form and function: a
blunt aircraft designed to be a brutally blunt instrument. Its bulbous
nose held a massive forty-one-liter, fourteen-cylinder rotary BMW 801
engine that could generate almost 2,000 horsepower. Its stubby wings
held four Mauser MG 151 cannons—the same weapon he had been

firing in Strongpoint Alvis when he was wounded on the morning of D-Day. The 190 was built to kill other aircraft, and it did it very well.

He remembered the first time he'd seen a 190, back in 1941. It could run rings around his Westland Whirlwind, and he'd been lucky to survive.

He climbed on the wing and stared into the 190's narrow cockpit, but all cockpits look the same: worn, shabby, cramped, and utilitarian. The glamor of aerial combat was entirely in the minds of novelists, newspaper correspondents, and filmmakers.

A tiny sepia photograph was still stuck into one of the side window frames. He pulled it out carefully and looked at the picture of a girl on a beach. The wind was ruffling her clothes, her eyes were screwed up against the sun, and she was laughing at something the photographer had just said. It was just the kind of carefree, anything-goes photograph that everyone takes of every girl on every beach, a casual snapshot into somebody's life. Now it was in the cockpit of a dead aircraft whose pilot was probably dead too. Perhaps the girl was also dead, Shaux thought, and even if she was still alive, she probably wasn't laughing.

For a moment he debated what to do with the photograph, and then he pushed it back down into the window frame, where it shivered in the wind. She wasn't his girl, it wasn't his aircraft, and it was none of his damned business.

He clambered down and resumed his walk. He'd been here in Dinant before, in 1940, as part of the RAF's support for the British Expeditionary Force. The BEF had been crushed by Hitler's blitzkrieg attack on the Low Countries and France. He'd been lucky to escape in his obsolete Defiant fighter before the Panzers arrived.

The Luftwaffe had taken over Dinant and had been here as recently as August, and now it was back in Allied hands. The enemy was still only thirty miles away to the east; perhaps the winds of war would shift in their favor, and Dinant would fall into their hands once more, and Luftwaffe bulldozers would shovel P51s and Mosquitos into the ditch.

He turned back towards the control tower. It was far too cold to wax philosophical.

* * *

SHAEF Forward, Charleroi, Belgium
12 December 1944, 0800 Hours

Eleanor and Kenneth Strong stared at a large map of northwest Europe. A red ribbon zigzagged down the map, held in place by drawing pins, tracing the front line between the Allies and Germans from north to south. No less than eight armies—three American, one British, one Canadian, and three German—faced each other across that ribbon, more than a million men.

Eleanor noted, as she always did, that the Allies were still on the wrong side of the heavily fortified Siegfried Line and the Rhine. Why had Monty insisted on a bridge across the Rhine, so impossibly far away? Why Arnhem and not some easier target?

"It's remarkably quiet, Eleanor," Kenneth Strong said. "Not much activity on either side."

"Perhaps it's the calm before the storm."

"Very possibly. What do you think the enemy is up to?"

"I don't know," Eleanor said, shaking her head. "However, I'm certain they're not just sitting around waited to get crushed by the Russians."

"I agree," Strong said. "Our current intelligence problem is that the enemy doesn't need to use Enigma radio messages anymore, because they're back in Germany using telephones and telegraphs, so our Ultra chaps don't get many transmissions to decode. It's ironic that we advance and they retreat; the better their supply and communications lines get, the worse ours get."

He shook his head.

"And of course, there is no resistance or underground inside Germany, so we no longer have the local civilian population spying on them. All in all, most of our tactical information has dried up."

He offered her a cigarette.

"Let's look at it from Hitler's perspective," she said. "I sometimes wonder if he knows he will not survive the war. Either we'll execute him for war crimes, or his own population will string him up from a lamppost, just like the Italians did to Mussolini."

"Surely he must know he's lost."

"Perhaps," she said. "But perhaps he thinks he's invincible. He's survived the army's plot to assassinate him. So now he has no domestic enemies, and he lives underground in a bombproof bunker. I'm certain he still dreams of a thousand-year Reich. He'll blame all his losses on the failures of his generals. He won't go quietly. I'm sure he'll make one last attempt to pull a rabbit out of a hat, one last miracle against the odds, because he has nothing to lose."

They stared at the map.

"I agree he won't go quietly," Strong said. "From what few scraps of information we have, it seems he is reinforcing and reequipping the 5th and 6th Panzer armies."

He pointed to the map.

"We think they're here, just across the border from Belgium. We think the 5th is in the Aachen area and the 6th is down here near Bitburg. But we can't be sure. And, of course, we don't know if he'll keep them here, facing us, or ship them across Germany to face Zhukov in Poland."

Hitler was being squeezed in a vise between Eisenhower in the west and the Russians in the east, she thought—or, better yet, in a meat grinder. Did Hitler consider Eisenhower or Zhukov to be the greater threat? Would Hitler send these reinforced Panzer armies against whichever army he feared most or against whichever he considered to be the more vulnerable to a sudden counterattack?

"What's your guess, Eleanor? You're pretty good at reading Hitler's mind."

"I wish I was," she said. "But the starting point of any analysis of what he might or might not do is that he's reckless. His entire career is based on a series of wild risks, all the way from the Beer Hall Putsch in 1923 to Barbarossa, the invasion of Russia in 1941. He doesn't let the odds frighten him. He's not rational. That's why so many rational men have underestimated him. It's why he made a fool of Chamberlain before the war and why Stalin left himself wide open to attack in 1941."

"That's true."

"He doesn't attack, he lunges, and at this point in the war, he has little left to lose. My guess is that he'll try another lunge, a lightning counterattack, in the east or in the west. He'll try to catch us with our trousers down."

"East or west, Eleanor?"

"My guess is here, in the west. He doesn't want to have to tell his German subjects that our mongrel boots are trampling the sacred soil of the invulnerable thousand-year Reich."

"I'm sure he doesn't," Strong said. "If you're right, we should be concerned. Omar Bradley is covering a long, long front line all the way from Holland down to Luxembourg. He's stretched a little too thin, in my view. I've told him that he's a bit vulnerable, but he isn't worried. He thinks the enemy is broken."

"What did he say when you warned him?" Eleanor asked.

"He said, 'Let them come.'"

TWENTY

Charlie emitted tiny squeals of pure joy. His stumpy tail wagged so
hard, he couldn't sit still in his seat.

The ground crews had built him a custom seat and bolted it into
the rear compartment of a Miles Master. The Master was the RAF's
principal training aircraft and served as a front-line taxi, because its
rugged construction and short landing and takeoff requirements were
perfect for short hops between war-worn airfields.

Shaux found it the easiest way to travel between ALG airfields.
Belgium's roads—those that were still usable after intensive bombing—were choked with military traffic and slick with ice. Why sit in
a freezing jeep for two hours, crawling along behind an army convoy,
when he could get where he was going in a Master in ten minutes?

Shaux thought of all the hundreds of times Charlie had had to sit
and watch him fly away. Now Charlie could fly too. He sat directly
behind Shaux with his head stretched forward over the rear instrument panel, staring over Shaux's right shoulder with his tongue lolling,

panting with excitement. If he had not been strapped in, he would have been in Shaux's lap.

For four years Charlie had worn Froggie Potter's frayed and tattered white silk scarf. Eleanor had finally sewn the remnants—they could not possibly be thrown away—onto a fine new scarf and added Charlie's new Aviation Militaire pilot's badge. Froggie had died at the height of the Battle of Britain, already a decorated Spitfire pilot, even though he had only just turned eighteen. Sometimes it seemed like a century ago, Shaux thought, a different era, and sometimes it seemed like yesterday.

Those four years since Froggie's death had seen Shaux rise from the duties of a fighter pilot, which, in his mind, came down to the simple formula of kill or be killed, to his present role of trying to turn a haphazard arrangement of a dozen nomadic 2TAF squadrons into a single fighting unit. "Rise," Shaux decided, was not the right word.

2TAF was a hybrid, consisting of squadrons drawn from both Bomber Command and Fighter Command. There were currently twelve squadrons in Shaux's 2TAF FD Group, including B25 Mitchells, Mosquitos, Spitfires, Typhoons, and P51 Mustangs. 2TAF was the only RAF unit to report to Eisenhower in SHAEF rather than to the head of the RAF, Charles Portal.

2TAF tactics were the cumulative result of the lessons learned about close ground-support operations all the way from El Alamein in Egypt to the Falaise Pocket in Normandy. Victory in that massive tank battle had finally allowed the Allies to break out of Normandy weeks after D-Day. Mary Coningham had summarized 2TAF's air support mission into three simple principles: gain and hold air superiority over the battlefield, cut the enemy's supply lines so he is isolated in the battlefield, and then act as aerial artillery attacking the enemy's front lines.

Thus, 2TAF had Spitfires to prevent the Luftwaffe from reaching the front lines. It had Mitchells and Mosquitos to bomb and blast anything moving on the roads and railway lines behind the front lines, and then Typhoons and Mustangs to harry the enemy's front-line positions.

However, one thing that 2TAF tactics could not overcome was the weather. To hit objects on the ground, you need to be able to see them, and when the cloud cover was low and visibility was limited, as it was now, 2TAF could only be a helpless bystander.

Shaux glanced up at the sky. It was ten-tenths overcast, and the forecast for the next week or so was not promising. Whatever the enemy was up to, they wouldn't be spotted from the air.

"All set, sir?" Warrant Officer Jenkins asked, leaning in to make sure Charlie was securely fastened.

Jenkins had been with Shaux ever since the Battle of Britain. He'd been here in Belgium, servicing Shaux's Defiant fighter, even before the Battle of Britain. He'd been there with Charlie the afternoon Froggie Potter had died. He was indispensable as a man who could make ground operations run smoothly, regardless of the difficulties.

"All set, Jenks."

Shaux craned his neck around to check on Charlie, who reached forward an extra inch and yelped in excitement; it was his way of saying he was ready.

"Charlie-ho," Shaux said, and pressed the starter.

* * *

SHAEF Forward, Charleroi, Belgium
14 December 1944, 0800 Hours

"We're very exposed," Eleanor said, stabbing her finger at the map. "Here in the Eifel and Ardennes ranges. Bradley has just two under-strength divisions covering thirty miles."

"Yes, indeed," Strong said. "The terrain is next to impossible, the weather is awful, we don't know what we're facing on the other side."

The Eifel and the Ardennes mountains rose in the southeastern corner of Belgium and Luxembourg. The area was well known for its spectacular natural beauty, with rivers winding through deep valleys amid steep, forested hills. Narrow roads meandered between pictur-esque villages. Now the winter snow had turned the area into a perfect Christmas card.

"We're safe," Percival objected. "The terrain and the weather mean the enemy won't attack. The roads are almost impassable, and the ter-rain is completely impassable. The Germans are not fools. Mind you, if they know the Ardennes are under Bradley's command, they might . . . Well, I'm sure Brad knows what he's doing."

Montgomery had launched yet another campaign to have all the Allied armies report to him, as they had on D-Day, and an important part of his campaign was a steady flow of innuendo questioning Bradley's competence. Eleanor had concluded that Montgomery was keeping Percival at SHAEF primarily to act as an anti-Bradley Greek chorus.

"The enemy is reequipping his Panzer armies somewhere just to our east," Strong said, drawing a circle on the map with his finger. "I'm certain of it. They are somewhere between the 15th Army to the north and the 7th to the south, perhaps here, near Aachen."

"Panzer armies?" Percival asked. "Near Aachen? I doubt it. I doubt it very much."

"The intelligence is sketchy, I admit," Strong said. "However, I think—"

"No, no, no!" Percival cut him off. "That's not my view, or Monty's. The Jerries are licking their wounds. They're down to their last few Panzers. You can take my word for it: the enemy is back on his heels."

"Are you sure, sir?" Eleanor said. "I remember you telling the prime minister the enemy was back on his heels once before."

The more the war went on, the less she was willing to suffer fools gladly, and Percival was an archetypical fool.

"Well—" he began.

"It was just before two SS Panzer divisions destroyed the 1st Airborne at Arnhem, was it not?"

"That's not fair! I—"

The door opened and Beetle Smith entered. Percival suppressed an almost inaudible blasphemy and left abruptly, barely managing to nod to Smith as he passed him.

"Now, Eleanor," Smith said. "Have you been mean to poor Percy again?"

"No more than he deserves," Strong answered for her. "He and Monty don't think the enemy's new armored divisions represent a serious threat."

"Well, to be fair, neither does Brad," Smith said.

"One of those armies includes the LSSAH," Eleanor said, shaking her head. "The Leibstandarte SS Adolf Hitler was originally formed as Adolf Hitler's personal bodyguards. They are Nazis to the core. The LSSAH has several commanders who have a reputation for committing war crimes, including Joachim Peiper."

"The guy who likes to burn down civilian villages?" Smith asked.

"Yes, sir, with the villagers locked inside their houses," Eleanor said, waving her hand across the map. "We don't know if the enemy is going to attack us, or where, or when, but we can't just ignore the risk."

"I know I don't have firm intelligence," Strong said. "We need clear weather to do aerial reconnaissance. But I believe this situation represents a real opportunity for the enemy to strike."

"We should reinforce the line, just in case," Eleanor said. "Bradley needs to bring up more experienced troops."

"Why would the enemy risk an attack rather than just reinforcing their defenses and grinding us down?" Smith asked. "Surely they'd be better off if they reinforce the Siegfried Line, wouldn't they?"

"That's true, sir, but that's probably not what they're thinking," Eleanor said. "They know they're facing total defeat within six months if they simply continue to try to defend the Rhine, regardless of what they do or how hard they resist."

Smith grunted.

"They know they lack the resources to survive," Eleanor continued. "They're facing unconditional surrender—to the Russians as well as us. They are running out of time."

"Exactly," Strong said. "That's why we think they'll try to shake up the balance of power sufficiently to change the outcome of the war."

"What could they possibly do to hurt us enough to make a real difference?" Smith asked, staring at the map. "Since D-Day they've lost half their men, most of their armor, most of their aircraft . . ."

"They could seize this moment to split us in two," Eleanor said. "They could concentrate their remaining forces for a lightning campaign to retake Brussels and Antwerp. Drive a wedge across Belgium that splits us in two. Without Antwerp, our northern forces— Montgomery's British and Canadians and Bradley's 1st and 9th US armies—would be isolated and without supplies. They'd be trapped."

"And here to the south, we might not have enough left to rescue them," Strong said. "We'd be all the way back to depending on supplies from Normandy."

"Even Hitler isn't that crazy," Smith said, shaking his head.

"I wouldn't count on that, sir, if I were you," Eleanor said.

"Are they capable of reaching Antwerp?" Smith asked.

"I don't know, sir," Eleanor said. "But I do know they're capable of trying."

* * *

SHAEF Forward, Versailles, France
15 December 1944, 1800 Hours

Evidently Eisenhower shared Bradley's view that the situation in the Ardennes was not a significant risk because he had decided to return to Versailles to host a diplomatic party.

He gave these parties from time to time, inviting senior officers, diplomats, battlefield heroes, and the occasional king in exile, and Versailles was certainly an excellent place to give them. The SHAEF publicity team used these events to send newsreels and photographs back to America to bolster support for the war effort and to suggest American omnipotence.

Eleanor knew that there was still a significant isolationist camp in the United States and Roosevelt needed to remind the American people that the war in Europe was just as vitally necessary as the war against Japan, despite the hideous cost in blood and treasure. "Total war requires total support," Harry Hopkins had once told her.

She had heard that these diplomatic affairs infuriated de Gaulle because they presented Eisenhower, rather than himself, as the true military commander in France, ensconced amid the royal splendor of Louis XIV's[4] Versailles. Indeed, de Gaulle had forbidden all French officers and officials from attending these "Anglo-Saxon" events.

Perhaps, she thought, that was why Eisenhower gave them here—just to stick it in de Gaulle's Gallic eye.

---

4.   14th

Normally there were very few women at these functions, and Eleanor dreaded them, as inebriated generals and high government functionaries considered her rump—and any other female rumps present—to be targets of opportunity.

Ike made it a habit to have Kay Summersby in attendance, thereby creating an unspoken but acutely awkward evocation of Louis XIV's *maîtresses en titre.*[5] Eleanor had never understood him in this regard; if he wanted a mistress, that was his private business, but why did he have to parade her in public? Eleanor had not met Ike's wife but cringed on Mamie Eisenhower's behalf.

On this occasion, Eisenhower had invited Johnnie to attend, and Johnnie, who hated such events and would normally have made an elaborate excuse not to attend, had seen this as a golden opportunity to spend a weekend in Paris with Eleanor.

She was astonished by the attention he received. She knew he hated every minute of it, but she was nonetheless delighted.

Now that Guy Gibson, the leader of the DamBusters Raid, was sadly dead, just recently killed in a Pathfinder operation in Holland, and Douglas Bader was locked away in the notorious Colditz Castle Stalag POW camp near Dresden, she supposed the RAF was running a bit short of available aces it could parade as heroes du jour, and Johnnie would be more in demand than ever.

She watched him across the room. He was the man she always took for granted; the man she had once tossed away and, to her eternal shame, taken his dog with her; the man whose love she resisted; the man who was as familiar and as comfortable as a well-worn pair of slippers. But here was Jimmy Doolittle—America's greatest flying hero, the man who had led the Tokyo raid and was now the commander of the US Eighth Air Force—in deep conversation with him, and George Patton was patiently waiting his turn. Doolittle was making flying gestures with his hands, and she guessed they were discussing landing techniques. It occurred to her that they had both done the next-to-impossible: they had both flown bombing missions off aircraft carriers in twin-engine aircraft far too big for the carriers.

---

5.   Term used to describe the king's official mistresses.

It was a rare chance to see Johnnie as others did. He was a very shy man, a reluctant hero, and yet he was smiling easily and chatting amiably, dutifully playing the part. Regardless of how well she knew him, she always wondered what lay at his core, his essence.

He had been a working-class orphan, an aircraft mechanic who had somehow transformed himself into an Oxford graduate and then into a successful fighter pilot and then into a natural leader. He didn't lead by yelling, "I'm in charge; follow me," as de Gaulle did, she thought. Johnnie just went, and others followed instinctively.

Perhaps Johnnie was a chameleon with no core or independence, just copying what he saw around him in order to "fit in." But no, of course not: in the end, she always concluded that he had never changed at all: he was still a little boy determined to be brave, standing with one foot on top of the other, doing the best he could, just as he stood in the photograph on her desk.

She saw that Eisenhower and Patton had replaced Doolittle. She would be interested to see what Johnnie thought of Patton—were his boorish ill manners genuine, or a mask? She tipped her drink into a potted palm and glanced round the room. It seemed almost surreal— all these generals and high officials chatting and drinking in these warm, elegant surroundings while, less than a hundred miles away, hundreds of thousands of soldiers were huddled in flimsy canvas tents and trenches and foxholes against the bitter snowy night.

She vaguely remembered that the Duke of Wellington had hosted a grand ball in Brussels on the night before his climatic clash with Napoleon at Waterloo in 1815, the last battle of a seemingly endless and brutal war. Was this party perhaps an encore? If she and Strong were right, and Percival was wrong, then—

A rotund diplomat of unclear origin interrupted her reverie.

"You are far, far too attractive to be on your own," he said, appearing at her elbow, a glass of champagne in hand. "The night is young, and no girl as pretty as you should be left on her own in Paris."

She knew he'd go for her rump in another second and turned so that it was protected by the branches of the palm.

"Well, thank you, sir, that's very kind of you, and I agree completely," she said. "Please tell that to my husband. He's just over there. Come, let me introduce you to him."

* * *

SHAEF Forward, Versailles, France
16 December 1944, 0600 Hours

Eleanor was awakened by insistent knocking on her bedroom door and summoned to a telephone. It was still pitch-black outside, but SHAEF was already humming with activity.

"The enemy has started an artillery barrage all the way from Monschau to Langsur," Strong's voice said. "This may be the start of what we were worried about."

"From Monschau to Langsur?" she repeated, still half asleep, trying to visualize a map of eastern Belgium.

"This could signal a major offensive," he said. "The enemy doesn't have enough ammunition to do this just to shake us up. Can you get back to Charleroi today? Beetle Smith is asking for you."

"I think I can be there in two hours," she said. "I'll fly back with my husband."

"The weather's bad," Strong said. "Don't count on it."

So much for a long, luxurious morning in bed with Johnnie, she thought, as she returned through endless drafty corridors to her room. So much for a romantic weekend in Paris.

Although the front had been quiet over the last few weeks, there were still daily skirmishes and exchanges of artillery fire. However, a barrage along an extended front suggested a large-scale attack rather than a limited tactical assault to straighten out a kink in the front lines between the two sides. Strong was certainly right that Hitler couldn't afford to waste artillery rounds on empty gestures. Bad weather was forecast to continue, grounding the Allied air forces and neutralizing Allied air superiority; 2TAF would be able neither to see the enemy nor attack it.

Perhaps this was the moment Hitler was throwing his dice in one last gamble. Perhaps he had decided to launch his Panzers westward against Bradley rather than transferring them to the eastern front against Zhukov. Perhaps he thought that Zhukov was unbeatable but that Eisenhower and Bradley could crack.

"All hell is breaking loose in the Ardennes, Johnnie," she told him. "Can you fly me back to Charleroi?"

"I can try, if the cloud base is high enough," Shaux said, sitting up and rubbing his eyes. "The forecast for today was pretty bad. You'd better put on every stitch of clothing you possess. It will be really cold in the air."

They drove the short distance to Toussus-le-Noble, a former Luftwaffe airfield now in the hands of the American 9th Air Force and designated A-46. Wrecked Junkers 88s and Messerschmitt 110s lined the perimeter. Eleanor was shocked to realize that the last time she had seen a 110 was back in the Battle of Britain when she had flown in Johnnie's Defiant fighter. Then the 110s had seemed omnipotent and terrifying; now they looked pathetic. It was so long ago, four years, that it seemed like a different, distant war.

Shaux's Miles Master stood on the apron. The ground crew had already started the engine to warm it up.

The control tower staff told Shaux the forecast had not improved.

"There's ten-tenths cloud cover with a thousand-foot base," an American met officer said. "I suggest you wait."

"We can't," Shaux said. "We'll stay low."

"How low?"

"Really low."

"Are you sure?" Eleanor asked. "I do need to get back, but—"

"Piece of cake."

They walked out to the Miles Master.

"Charlie usually yelps as we take off, El," Shaux told her. "I've come to expect it."

TWENTY-ONE

"I'm surprised you were able to get back so quickly, Eleanor," Strong said. "In fact, I'm surprised you were able to get here at all. I thought all flights had been grounded because of the weather."

"You've never met my husband," she said. "What's the situation in the Ardennes? Is it a major attack?"

"I fear so," Strong said. "It's all a bit chaotic so far. There's no definite pattern yet. But it certainly doesn't feel like a tactical probe. The enemy's artillery barrage started at 0530 hours and lasted about ninety minutes. I don't think they did it for fun."

He stabbed his finger at the map.

"We're beginning to get reports of armored attacks in this area," he said. "Here, in the Hürtgen Forest, where the Americans just captured the Wahlerscheid crossroads, the place they call Heartbreak Crossroads."

The Battle of Heartbreak Crossroads, she knew, had been a bitter fight by the Americans to capture a key road junction near the Siegfried Line to the north of Krinkelt. The area was strongly defended by a chain of concrete pillboxes armed with heavy machine guns and anti-tank weapons, embedded in the thickly forested hillsides. Endless tangles of barbed wire, miles of trenches and foxholes, and innumerable mines strewn across the slopes and buried in the gullies combined to make the assault even more difficult. And, as if all this was not enough, heavy drifted snow and icy conditions made movement almost impossible.

"They finally captured the road junction?"

"This morning, if they can hold it."

"Who is on the line? Is it still the American 99th?"

"The 99th and the 106th Divisions," Strong said, pointing at the map again. "The 106th has only just arrived at the front, and it's trying to cover twenty miles. You've got the 99th here in Krinkelt, and the 106th to the south of them, here in this area."

"Have we identified the enemy units?"

Strong shrugged. "We don't know. We think the attackers are from the 6th Panzer Army, but we haven't been able to confirm that yet."

The 6th included the notorious Leibstandarte SS Adolf Hitler, Eleanor thought.

Strong shook his head. "We think that the leading tanks are an SS Panzer *Kampfgruppe* led by Joachim Peiper—the so-called Peiper battle group. They're equipped with Tiger 2s."

Panzerkampfwagen 6Bs, known as Tiger 2s, were superheavy tanks with massive, steeply sloping armor. A direct hit from a Sherman would explode uselessly against their seven inches of armor or simply bounce off. They were armed with a huge 88mm anti-tank gun no Allied tank could withstand. If Tigers had an Achilles' heel, it was that they were so big and heavy that bridges and even roads often collapsed under their seventy-ton weight, and their huge Maybach engines gulped up two gallons of fuel every mile.

Hmm, Eleanor thought. It was roughly ninety miles from Aachen to Antwerp, if that was where the enemy was heading, requiring almost two hundred gallons of fuel for each Tiger 2. She was surprised that Hitler had enough petrol for hundreds of tanks and thousands of vehicles to make it all that way; the Allies must have underestimated German fuel reserves. Or, possibly, she and Strong were misreading the enemy's intentions and Antwerp was not the target.

Another Achilles heel might be the Ardennes themselves, she thought. The roads were few and twisty and unsuitable for military convoys. Tanks need open ground to maneuver, and the densely forested hillsides were anything but open. But, as long as the weather stayed bad, the Ardennes were ideal for hiding large numbers of tanks beneath the trees.

"We have no aerial reconnaissance at all," Strong said, as if reading her mind. "We're completely blind. Your husband managed to fly you here from Paris; I don't suppose . . .?"

"I'm afraid not," she said. "I already asked him about it. He said he was reluctant to send his crews to fly over thousand-foot-high mountains at five hundred feet."

"Yes, I suppose not," Strong said. "He has a point."

She shivered, imaging the conditions in the Ardennes. The roads would be narrow, tortuous, and almost impassable. If a vehicle broke down, it would create an immediate traffic jam. Anyone leaving the road would be plunged into waist-deep snowdrifts. Newly arrived soldiers, some fresh from their training camps in America, would be huddled in trenches that were choked with snow. The wind would attack their exposed faces like a whip. Their hands might be too numb to use their weapons. The cold would eat through their clothing and sap their energy. God alone knew what they would have to endure once night fell. Frostbite, she feared, would claim more victims than enemy gunfire.

The shivering soldiers in the forward areas would be able to hear the menacing growling of the Tigers' Maybach tank engines and the clanking and grinding of their tracks. The steep ravines would echo with the sound. The leaden skies would offer no hope of salvation.

Eleanor shivered in sympathy. The deepest level of Dante's hell, she recalled, was cold, not hot.

* * *

SHAEF Forward, Charleroi, Belgium
17 December 1944, 1800 Hours

All the next day, Sunday, Eleanor and Ken Strong struggled to make sense of the reports flooding in from what seemed to be an increasingly chaotic front line. Someone had coined the term "bulge" for the enemy advance as the line bulged westward into the Ardennes. As the short winter day turned into another bitter night, Strong pulled his SHAEF G2 team together to prepare a report for Beetle Smith.

Eleanor's job for Eisenhower, Enemy Intention Assessment, was particularly difficult in these circumstances, and the Red Tape analysts back in Portsmouth had nothing to offer. Perhaps, she thought, she should change the name of her role to Enemy Intentions Blind Guesswork.

Percival, meanwhile, now permanently in SHAEF Forward as Montgomery's 21st Army Group liaison, spent the day issuing sotto voce tut-tut sounds and shaking his head. He was, Eleanor suspected, carefully suppressing glee at the American army's difficulties.

Much, alas, was going wrong.

In the north, the Peiper battle group was grinding forward slowly but relentlessly.

"Up here on the Elsenborn Ridge, the American 99th chaps are fighting like hell," Strong said, pointing just to the north of the enemy's advance. "But as you can see, Peiper's bypassed them to the south and is moving west."

In the center, another Panzer Army, presumably the 5th, was attempting to cross the Our in several places but had not yet done so. They were probably targeting St. Vith, Eleanor thought, and it was only a question of time before they reached it.

To the south, yet another German army, presumably the 7th, had crossed the old front line and was pushing towards Bastogne, en route, perhaps, for Neufchâteau.

By now, there could be no question that the enemy had launched a major attack. The leading enemy Panzer units threatening St. Vith included the excellent 2nd Panzer Division and the Panzer Lehr. These units, with the LSSAH, were the best of Hitler's remaining forces.

The weather remained awful, with dense cloud cover preventing any reconnaissance flights or air-ground support operations. So poor were the conditions that Johnnie had left his Dinant ALF and come to Charleroi for a conference with Mary Coningham, the 2TAF AOC.

Eleanor stared at a large map of the Ardennes. A man on a ladder was sticking in markers denoting the latest known position of both sides' units. He was constantly readjusting the enemy positions from right to left—from east to west—to reflect German advances and American retreats. The line was "bulging" as she watched.

If the Germans managed to break out of the Ardennes, Eleanor thought, and if they were able to cross the Meuse, then they would reach flatter, more open ground, and they might be able to punch a hole through the remaining American reserves and push forward towards Antwerp—if Antwerp was their target.

Beetle Smith burst into the conference room. "We're getting reports that the enemy is executing POWs!" he shouted.

Eleanor had never seen him so distraught.

"What?" Percival said. "Are you sure?"

"You're goddamned right I'm sure!" Smith barked. "I just talked to our guys in Malmedy. Those Kraut bastards are lining our guys up and shooting them!"

"What? Where?" Eleanor asked, turning to the map.

"The Baugnez crossroads just south of Malmedy."

Joachim Peiper—assuming Peiper was leading the enemy attack— had a record of atrocities, Eleanor knew. He had killed civilians and POWs in Poland and Ukraine. As a true Nazi, he would believe that anyone who wasn't of pure Aryan blood—whatever that was supposed to mean—would be a lesser breed. Indeed, a major objective of Hitler's invasion of Russia in 1941 had been to kill large numbers of Slavs and Jews, simply because they were Slavs and Jews, so that Aryans could take over their lands—the policy of "lebensraum" or "living space." Millions had died, mostly by deliberate starvation.

But killing American POWs was different, she thought, unless Peiper believed that the people of the United States, a land of immigrants, were some sort of inferior mongrel race.

She found the Baugnez crossroads on the map. If Peiper was there, he was moving south rather than west towards Antwerp. She wondered if—

"Your chaps surrendered?" Percival asked.

Eleanor thought she detected just the smallest hint of disdain in his voice, as if to suggest the American troops had given up without a fight.

"Yes, just like thousands of your guys surrendered at Arnhem," Smith snapped back. "It happens when you're outnumbered and out-gunned. Have you ever been on the battlefield, or have you always stayed safely behind the lines?"

Percival recoiled.

"It seems a field artillery observer unit ran into a column of Tiger tanks at the Baugnez crossroads" Smith continued. "Our guys were in trucks with rifles, and the enemy was in tanks with 75mm guns."

Percival seemed to consider a reply but did not.

"The Krauts took our guys prisoner and directed them, about a hundred of them, into a field, and then just mowed them down in cold blood."

"I just can't believe—" Strong began.

"A few of the guys escaped and reached our lines at Malmedy," Smith continued.

"Are we sure it wasn't a misunderstanding?" Strong asked.

"No, it was deliberate," Smith said. "The bastards went around shooting the wounded in the head to finish them off."

Assuming the reports were accurate, Eleanor thought, this would not be the only tragedy. Rules of engagement were fragile and easily shattered. It takes only one man, frightened or impatient or confused, to break them. Prisoners are troublesome and require personnel, time, and resources to feed, clothe, house, and care for them. Dead enemies do not. To a man like Peiper, in a massive Tiger tank and doubtless with a schedule to keep, it would be an easy decision. Even Johnnie, the most reluctant killer she knew, shied away from discussing some encounters during his few hours in Normandy on D-Day.

If the enemy had adopted a "take no prisoners" standard, at some point some Allied unit would seek vengeance, and the bloody battle-field would grow bloodier yet.

* * *

SHAEF Forward, Charleroi, Belgium
18 December 1944, 1800 Hours

"Poor old Brad," Percival murmured. "What dashed bad luck!"

Eleanor saw that his eyes were gleaming with delight.

"What exactly happened, do we know?" he asked. "Arrested by his own chaps, as I understand it, of all things?"

"The enemy has infiltrated English-speaking commando units behind our lines," Strong said. "They're dressed as military police in GI uniforms, and they're driving stolen jeeps. They're causing havoc by misdirecting traffic."

"There are also reports that they are trying to kidnap or kill senior Allied officers," Eleanor added. "The Americans have responded by posting real MPs at every road junction to question every American unit to make sure they are indeed American."

"Unfortunately, an MP stopped Bradley and didn't believe he was American," Strong continued. "The MP thought Chicago was the capital of Illinois. Brad was arrested."

"Oh, deary, deary me," Percival said, his eyes gleaming. "That is indeed unfortunate. Poor old Brad. He has so much else to worry about."

Percival was clearly reveling in Bradley's discomfiture.

Bradley's HQ was in Luxembourg, far to the south of the fighting. As the Germans advanced westward through the Ardennes, he was being cut off from the 1st and 9th Armies to the center and north of the German attack. Patton's Third Army was to the south of the German attack but was too far away to be helpful. Bradley's command, she thought, was being cut in two.

Reserves were being rushed in but might arrive too late. The 82nd Airborne was on its way to Spa on the northern flank to block Peiper's battle group, and the 101st Airborne was racing to Bastogne on the southern flank. Two British divisions were moving to reinforce the Meuse river crossings in the center should the enemy break through.

"We don't know how many of these enemy commandos there are," Strong said. "Of course, under the rules of war, dressing in American uniforms makes them spies, and spies can be shot."

Eleanor was not sure it was as straightforward as that, but let it pass.

"We have a report that this commando operation is being led by Otto Skorzeny," she said. "He's the SS colonel who rescued Mussolini last year. He's exactly the sort of man who might try to assassinate our top generals."

"I think all senior officers should take precautions," Percival said. "If the enemy is trying some sort of coup . . . Please excuse me."

He hurried from the room.

"Let's start a rumor that Percival has replaced Ike." Strong chuckled. "Perhaps Skorzeny will hear it and assassinate him."

"That's a bit too complicated," Eleanor said. "Let's just assassinate him ourselves."

Strong offered Eleanor a cigarette.

"On a more serious note, do you think Brad is on top of this situation?" he asked.

The attack had started on Saturday; this was now Monday. Brad had been out of touch with his two northern armies for almost two days, and his third, Patton's Third Army, was not involved in the fight. Brad was almost a bystander.

He had dismissed the threat of a sudden enemy attack until it became a reality. "Let them come," he had said. He had allocated too few troops to defend the Ardennes, and those he had allocated were inexperienced. He had suffered the humiliation of being arrested by his own men, the kind of blow to his professional reputation that could dog him for years.

This was a moment calling for inspired leadership, a moment when the entire front was teetering on the edge of disaster.

"I wish I could say yes," she murmured.

* * *

SHAEF Forward, Verdun, France
19 December 1944, 1500 Hours

On Tuesday, the fourth day of the attack, Eisenhower called a conference of his senior commanders in Verdun, halfway between Paris and Luxembourg. Eleanor drove down from Charleroi.

Her route had led her past endless graveyards holding the remains of the three hundred thousand soldiers of both sides who had died here in 1916 in the First World War. Her mind boggled at the enormity of the slaughter in what had been a ridiculously trivial cause. And before that, thousands more had died in the War of 1870. Now hundreds of thousands more men were dying in this war . . . Europeans were clearly prone to slaughter each other every thirty or forty years in a sort of recurring collective lemming-like madness . . . "Will we never learn?" she wondered.

"What, ma'am?" her driver asked, and she realized she'd spoken aloud.

The conference seemed out of balance to Eleanor. Looking around the table, she saw that neither Courtney Hodges, the 1st US Army commander, nor Bill Simpson, commanding the 9th Army, were present, yet they were the commanders of the two armies doing the fighting.

Montgomery had not appeared, nor had he sent Miles Dempsey of the British 2nd Army.

Events had cast Ike and Bradley, it seemed to Eleanor, in the roles of observers rather than commanding generals, and Patton was a bystander. Indeed, most of the attendees were staff officers, like herself and Percival, who could analyze the unfolding disaster but do nothing about it. Never had she felt less useful.

Ike was not his usual urbane self. He opened the meeting by attempting to lighten the atmosphere, claiming this was an opportunity, not a crisis. No one agreed. A strained silence ensued, broken by Ken Strong entering the room.

"I'm afraid we've just received some bad news," he announced. "Two regiments of the American 106th have been surrounded at Schönberg near St. Vith. They've surrendered."

Bradley looked haggard. Patton sat with his shoulders hunched, glowering, and seeming to Eleanor like a volcano ready to explode.

"Can St. Vith still hold?" Eisenhower asked.

"I'm afraid I doubt it," Strong replied.

If St. Vith fell, the whole center of the battlefield would be open to the enemy, Eleanor thought. Bradley's command was indeed being cut in two.

"How many men surrendered?" Percival asked.

"We're estimating seven thousand," Strong replied.

No one spoke, and Eleanor was certain that Percival had asked the question just to make Bradley's life even more miserable. It was another blow to Brad's reputation, she feared. Seven thousand! She wondered if the American army had ever suffered such a loss, and if—

"Seven—" Percival began, but Eleanor was determined not to let him gloat.

"The good news is that our flanks are holding, at least for the time being," she jumped in. "The 99th on the Elsenborn Ridge to the north, and the 10th Armored Division to the south in front of Bastogne, are under pressure but holding. Both are doing spectacularly well."

She stared at Percival, daring him to say something negative. She saw him consider it, but he said nothing. She saw Patton looking at her as if he was surprised that she was offering support.

"The 82nd Airborne is now in place to the north, and the 101st has arrived at Bastogne," she added. "They're too lightly armed to turn Panzers back, of course, but I'm certain they'll slow them down."

"We need to put more resources into Bastogne," Eisenhower said, as if eager to move past the surrender. "I don't know how long they can hold out."

"We don't have anyone close enough to get there in time," Bradley said. He spoke slowly, and Eleanor heard defeat in his voice. "I'm afraid they're on their own."

"I can move three divisions starting in two days," Patton growled. "I can be in Bastogne six days from now."

The volcano has rumbled, she thought.

"Don't be ridiculous, George," Bradley snapped. "The Third Army is lined up north to south, facing east. You are proposing to turn it round in two days and line it up to attack northwest?"

"You're goddamned right I am, Brad."

"And then march a hundred miles in four days?"

"Goddamned right."

"And then go straight into battle?"

"Isn't that the whole goddamned point?"

The conference dragged on. No one seemed willing to believe Patton's plan. To be fair, Eleanor thought, it was reasonable to think his plan was merely his usual bluster. On the other hand, no one had an alternative. She was struck by the vivid contrast between Patton's willingness to take action and Bradley's pessimism, while Eisenhower seemed to waver between the two.

Finally, Eisenhower turned to Eleanor.

"What are the enemy's long-term intentions, Eleanor? If they take St. Vith and Bastogne?"

"I think they're going for broke, sir. I think they'll go for the Meuse and then for Antwerp. They wouldn't be taking this amount of risk if they didn't have a huge prize in mind."

"Why did they go now?"

"The weather favors them, sir, and they estimated our center would be vulnerable. They saw the weakness and moved before we saw it ourselves."

She saw Bradley wince.

"What are *their* weaknesses?" Eisenhower asked, perhaps to spare Bradley.

"I'm guessing they expected to be much further ahead than they are. I think a combination of chaotic traffic conditions and shortages of fuel will slow them moving forward. Their supply lines, like ours, must be blocked with traffic jams."

Eisenhower seemed unimpressed.

"As soon as the weather breaks, they'll be vulnerable," she continued. "And the further they advance, the more fuel they'll need."

"What about George's plan?" Bradley asked.

She was sitting across from Patton and resisted the impulse to turn to glance at him. She knew without looking that he had fixed her with a baleful stare.

"It's essential we move fast, sir," she said. "In the north, we have the 51st filling in behind the 82nd, but in the south, we're wide open behind the 101st."

"Yes, but what about his plan?" Bradley insisted.

"I'm not competent to judge from a military perspective, of course, but from a strategic point of view, it's essential that we get to Bastogne as fast as possible. We cannot let it fall."

"So?" Eisenhower asked.

"Speed is of the essence, sir, and General Patton is the fastest general we have."

"Well, thank you, ma'am," Patton said, and she saw him sketch a bow. "At least someone notices."

TWENTY-TWO

SHAEF Forward, Verdun, France
19 December 1944, 1900 Hours

It was bitterly cold. The ground was covered in frozen slush, and the wind was whipping at her greatcoat. Her car was nowhere to be seen. Patton emerged from the building. His car, a vast Packard Clipper, stood waiting. The driver opened the rear door for him, and Eleanor felt a gust of warmth. The hard-charging no-nonsense tough-guy Patton had a heater in his car!

"Let me give you a ride back to your quarters, Mrs. Shaux," he said, and climbed in ahead of her.

He was, she noted, in the category of men who chose not to acknowledge that she had a military rank. Although she'd often talked to him in meetings and conferences, she had never been alone with him.

Patton's bull terrier was sitting on the seat.

"Charlie, lie down," Eleanor said, and Charlie lay down flat on the floor of the car. The last thing she wanted was a confrontation between the two dogs.

"I must confess I have never understood exactly what you do, or why," Patton said as the car began to move. "I must also warn you I don't care."

He flashed her the sort of smile that Eleanor supposed the wolf flashed at Little Red Riding Hood.

"I count things, sir."

That was the answer she had once given to Stalin, and she saw no reason to change it.

"You count things? Such as?"

"Such as it takes five Sherman tanks to kill a Panzer. When a tank platoon commander encounters a Tiger, he would say: 'Do I have the tactical advantage? Can I see a way to win?' I would ask him: 'How many tanks do you have?'"

"That's a pile of piss-soaked bullcrap!" Patton snapped, as if she had just insulted his armored divisions. "Five Shermans? How would you pretend to know a pissant thing like that?"

"By counting the number of Shermans we've lost since Normandy, sir, and how many Panzer 4, Panther, and Tiger wrecks we've seen."

"So, you understand armored warfare better than a goddamned tank officer?"

"Oh no, sir, not at all," she said.

She recalled something that President Theodore Roosevelt had written. "It's not the critic that counts . . . the credit belongs to the man who is actually in the arena, whose face is marred by dust and sweat and blood."

Patton stared at her.

"You're quoting that son of a bitch bull moose Teddy Roosevelt at me? Teddy Roosevelt? I am astonished!"

He seemed genuinely surprised, and she was genuinely surprised he had recognized the allusion.

"That's because you neither understand what I do, sir, nor care."

He stared at her in silence, as if shocked by her temerity, and then looked away. Well, now I've done it, she thought. Montgomery hates me, Bradley hates me, and now Patton will too. Kay Summersby hates me, so Eisenhower probably does, just to stay in her good graces. Why had she gone into her smarty-pants mode with Patton? She remembered her mother's warnings against being a "little miss know-it-all," but it was too late for that now.

The car bounced and rattled through icy potholes. She only had to survive another few minutes of his company, she thought.

"I stand corrected," he said, breaking the silence. "Why were you demanding we move so quickly?"

"Because we're in a race, sir."

"A race against the weather?"

"We're in a race to get to Berlin before the Russians do, sir, and we're losing it," she said. "The Russians will never return one square inch of territory they capture. Europe will become a confederation of Soviet satellites. Russia will milk them dry. Whatever remains of Western Europe in our hands will have to stay armed to the teeth to defend against them."

"We're not losing the race! My Third Army is moving like lightning! You said I was fast, and no army has ever moved faster. Goddammit, only six months ago, we were still in Normandy!"

"The Russians are besieging Budapest, sir—goodbye, Hungary! They are on the Vistula—goodbye, Poland! They have the Ukraine and Rumania in their pocket."

"That doesn't mean we won't get there first," he roared. "If Ike and Brad just give me what I need, we'll—"

"The Vistula is three hundred and fifty miles from Berlin. Bastogne is four hundred and seventy miles from Berlin. Do the calculation, sir. They have a hundred-and-twenty-mile start on us, and we're still going round and round in circles on the wrong side of the Rhine, facing a breakout we have not yet stopped."

He was silent for a moment.

"That's Monty's fault. The bastard screwed up in Normandy. He snafued up in Arnhem. That sock full of shit can't fight his way out of a piss-soaked paper bag. It's amazing to me that the son of a bitch ever beat Rommel in the desert."

She wondered—as she sometimes had before—if he really talked like this or whether it was a calculated display he put on to project a crude sort of boorish soldierly virility.

"Rommel was in Germany for the first three days of the battle of El Alamein, sir. Georg Stumme, a well-known idiot, was in command.

By the time Rommel got back to Egypt, it was already too late for the Afrika Korps."

"I didn't know that."

"I didn't think you did, sir," she shot back before she could stop herself.

The car stopped at Eleanor's quarters.

"This has been most illuminating, Air Commodore," he said.

He had used the incorrect rank but at least he had acknowledged that she had a rank, she thought, and that was progress. The driver opened the door for her.

"Thank you for the lift, sir," she said.

"We're going for Bastogne from Echternach," he said. "Three divisions marching almost a hundred miles in the dead of winter, crotch-deep in snow, colder than the Ice Queen's back passage, straight through five goddamned Kraut divisions, with icicles dangling from our testicles. It's almost impossible—Ike and Brad think I'm a crazy son of a bitch. But I'll show them!"

The wolfish grin reappeared.

"What do you say, Air Commander?" he asked. "Can I do it?"

Patton, she knew, believed in reincarnation and that throughout history he had been reborn as a soldier—and, knowing his ego, doubtless he'd been a victorious general. She'd heard he'd even written a poem about it.

In Roman times, a victorious general was given a triumphant march through Rome, showered with gifts and glory and adoration as if he were a god. As his chariot passed through the cheering crowds, a slave would whisper in his ear, "Memento mori." "Remember you are mortal."

"What do you say, goddammit?" Patton repeated. He grinned his wolfish grin, reveling in the prospect of action, exulting in the prospect of proving Ike and Brad wrong, delighting in his own prowess. She grinned back.

"Memento mori, sir."

* * *

SHAEF Forward, Charleroi, Belgium
20 December 1944, 1000 Hours

The following morning, Eleanor returned to Charleroi. As soon as she entered SHAEF, she was summoned to see Beetle Smith.

"I've been on the phone with Ike all morning," he said without preamble. "He has a decision to make."

"Yes, sir?"

"George Patton is busy preparing his next miracle," Smith said. "He doesn't need—or want or would accept—any supervision. Meanwhile, in the north, Courtney Hodges with the 1st US Army and Bill Simpson with the 9th are fighting like hell, but there's no overall plan for the northern flank of the bulge. It's a series of individual firefights wherever the enemy appears. We're driving reinforcements up to the front and sending them straight into battle. Deployments are haphazard, to say the least—fingers in the dike. This battle is being commanded by captains and majors."

She thought that, given the competence of many of the generals she had met, putting captains and majors in charge was a good idea. But she knew the Americans were fighting for their lives in an increasingly disorganized battlefield, bedeviled by chaotic supply lines, sketchy intelligence, poor communications, and horrific weather.

"Yes, I know," she said. "So, Ike is planning to send Brad up there to sort it out and leave Patton to his own devices?"

"No, Eleanor. Ike is considering transferring command of the 1st and 9th US Armies to Montgomery."

"Good God!" It was the only thing she could think of saying.

"Exactly."

Of course, merging the two American armies into Montgomery's 21st Army Group made perfect sense, she thought. Stabilizing that front called for a painstakingly developed, integrated plan using all available American, British, and Canadian resources, combined with a degree of stubbornness to carry it out, and Montgomery was both painstaking and stubborn.

But, she thought, it would be a massive blow to Bradley's ego and a massive boost to Montgomery's. A quarter of a million Americans would be placed under Monty's command while Brad would be reduced to a cipher. Whether it was true or not, it would appear that Ike had lost faith in Brad and was asking Monty to bail him out.

"Well, Eleanor, what do you think?"

"I see the logic, sir," she said, as neutrally as she could.

"Come on, Eleanor. Don't be coy! Tell me what you think."

"I think Ike should make it very clear that this is strictly a temporary change until the front is stabilized."

"Yes, but it makes sense?" he asked.

"Yes, Monty is good at that sort of overall front-wide organization. He won't be panicked into rash moves."

"Poor old Brad," Smith murmured, and picked up the telephone.

She left his office and returned to her own. Strong appeared almost immediately.

"Bastogne has been isolated, cut off," he said. "The enemy has surrounded the 101st Airborne. Now it's a siege, not a defense. Let's hope Patton can perform his miracle and get there in time—we can't afford another surrender."

She remembered Patton's wolfish smile and his lust for the fight, his excitement at the opportunity to march a hundred piss-soaked miles with icicles hanging from his goddamned balls, crotch-deep in shit—or some such, for the prospect of proving he could do what no one else thought possible.

"Oh, Patton will get there," she said, surprised by her own conviction. "You can count on it."

"Why are you so sure?"

"He's spent two thousand years preparing for this moment," she said, and questioned, just for a fraction of a second, if there really might be such a thing as reincarnation. "He's ready."

Strong looked as if he was wondering if the strain of the crisis was getting too much for her, and she escaped by taking Charlie for a walk. She saw Percival approaching and turned the other way, pretending she hadn't seen him, but he called her name.

"Have you heard the news?" he said, smiling slyly. "Ike's had to ask Monty to take charge."

"That's not—" she began.

"You made a poor career decision, sticking with the Yanks," he interrupted her, his smile broadening. "You'll have to learn how to pick winners instead of losers. You could have been with us. It's a question of which side you're on."

He turned away and turned back.

"And, just to be clear, Monty has no need of your services whatsoever."

* * *

2TAF (FD Group) ALG Dinant, Belgium
21 December 1944, 0730 Hours

"Let's see what we can see," Shaux said to Jenkins.

He and all 2TAF (FD) had been sitting, twiddling their thumbs for almost a week as the enemy rolled implacably westward and a comprehensive combination of mist, fog, and low clouds hid the battlefield from view. The Allies had literally hundreds of aircraft sitting idly on the ground while Panzers drove through the Ardennes with impunity. The meteorologists said that the clouds would clear eventually, but "eventually" covered a span of time from a couple of hours to a couple of weeks. The weather was being driven by a high-pressure system over the Atlantic, they said, bringing in excessive moisture. A competing system bringing much colder, dryer air was supposed to be arriving from Russia "at any time soon," breaking up the perpetual overcast.

Shaux had therefore decided to take a Lysander up and see how far he could get while flying above the fog and below the cloud base. It might be hairy, but he was tired of doing nothing, and he refused to send some other pilot into harm's way. Besides, the alternative was to sit in his office doing paperwork. Jenkins had volunteered to fly with him.

"As long as the clouds are higher than the trees, we should be okay, Jenks."

"Then fly where the short trees are," Jenkins replied.

"Piece of cake."

The Allies desperately needed aerial reconnaissance, to see not only the battlefront but also the roads carrying supplies and reinforcements all the way from Germany. The Allies also needed clear skies to drop supplies to the troops on the front line and attack any enemy tanks and vehicles they could find.

The news had been uniformly bad, and this morning's addition to the lengthening chain of disappointments was that Bastogne had been surrounded by the enemy. The American 101st Airborne, which had arrived there just days ago, was fighting for its life.

Bastogne was only thirty-five miles from Dinant, he reflected, a mere two or three hours for a Panzer. He and Jenkins had been through this before back in 1940, when German Panzers had rolled across France in unstoppable waves. As the enemy advanced, the French army retreated, and as it did, the forward RAF squadrons still in France had also retreated as the French abandoned airfield after airfield.

"Remember Arras, Jenks?" he asked.

"I do," Jenkins replied without elaboration.

Arras had been their last airfield before they were forced back to England. They'd escaped by the skin of their teeth, taking off in Shaux's Defiant as the first Panzers rolled through the airfield's main gates.

The news about Bastogne made a scouting sortie essential. Perhaps the promised cold front might be beginning to break up overcast skies. A Lysander was the perfect aircraft for this kind of operation, Shaux thought. It could take off in less than a thousand feet and fly at a mere 60 miles per hour. ALG Dinant lay amid farmland on a plateau a little to the east of Dinant in the direction of Celles. Bastogne was directly to the southwest.

"We'll fly at five hundred feet on a bearing of 135 degrees, Jenks," Shaux said. "The relief map says there aren't any hills higher than that."

"Except where there are," Jenkins said, examining the map closely.

"Well, that's true, but they have short trees."

* * *

SHAEF Forward, Charleroi, Belgium
22 December 1944, 1000 Hours
"'Nuts!'" Beetle Smith said.

"I beg your pardon, sir?" Eleanor asked.

"The Germans demanded that McAuliffe surrender Bastogne," Smith said. "They gave him two hours to reply. McAuliffe replied with the single word 'Nuts!'"

McAuliffe was the commander of the American 101st Airborne, a man of exceptional courage and leadership who had also fought at Eindhoven in Operation Market Garden.

"We just got his report." Smith chuckled. "Apparently the Germans didn't understand his answer, and it had to be explained to them."

She stared at the map. If Bastogne fell, the whole southern flank of the bulge could crack open, and the Germans could break through Allied lines. No less than seven roads met at Bastogne, making it the most important strategic hub in the southern Ardennes. Patton was on the way, but he was still far to the south and days away.

"How long can McAuliffe hang on?" she asked.

"Not much longer unless we can resupply him from the air," Smith said. "He's running out of food and ammo. He's got almost no medical supplies left and not enough medics. We've got C47s sitting loaded up and ready to go, waiting for the moment the weather lifts."

"Yes, and 2TAF can bring a lot of firepower to the fight," she said. "They're only ten minutes from Bastogne."

Johnnie and his pilots were flying test flights almost every hour towards Bastogne, searching for a break in the clouds and fog, so far without success.

"If only the weather would break," she said.

"George Patton's got that covered, too," Smith said, shaking his head in disbelief. "He ordered his chaplain to write a weather prayer. Apparently, George feels that the good Lord is not doing enough for the Allied cause."

He stared up at the map.

"In the meantime, Monty, in his wisdom, ordered a retreat from St. Vith," he said, his voice hardening. "The enemy has occupied it. That's opened up a big hole in the center. Seems to me a lot of good men died for nothing over the last few days."

"The situation in St. Vith was untenable," Eleanor said. She had no desire to defend Montgomery, but the US 7th Armored Division had been badly outnumbered and ground down by the enemy's Panzers.

"So is the situation in Bastogne," Smith growled. "But we're still there. Perhaps McAuliffe is too dumb to know when to give up. Perhaps he lacks Monty's superior—albeit gutless—strategic wisdom."

Oh dear, Eleanor thought. Since Eisenhower's decision to transfer command of the American armies to Montgomery, every decision would be subject to question. She assumed Monty had decided to pull the Americans back to a more defensible position, thereby saving American lives, but it could also be interpreted as his lack of faith in the ability or willingness of the 7th to fight on.

The ancient Greek orator Demosthenes coined the earliest forerunner of the modern expression "He who fights and runs away lives to fight another day," she thought, but the line between prudence and cowardice had, for more than two thousand years, been a very fine one, and subject to bitter dispute.

TWENTY-THREE

2TAF (FD Group) ALG Dinant, Belgium
23 December 1944, 0400 Hours
"The weather's clearing," Mary Coningham's voice said on the telephone.

Shaux glanced at his watch to verify that it was really four o'clock in the morning.

"We're forming an ABC task force with the Americans," Coningham said. "Bob O'Neill will be the joint forces Sheepdog."

"Very well, sir," Shaux said, suppressing a yawn. He lit a cigarette to wake himself up; it was extraordinary how bad the first cigarette of the day always tasted.

"You'll take Typhoons and your Molins Mosquitos for ground-attack rhubarbs," Coningham continued. "You'll take Spits up top at angels two-zero in case the Luftwaffe decides to come up too. The Eighth Air Force is providing low-level B25s and P47s, and P51 cover up top. You'll probably see some C47 Dakotas dropping supplies as well, so there'll be quite a lot of traffic out this morning."

"Very well."

"You'll be operating in a box from Bastogne northeast to St. Vith and then twenty miles east of that back as far as Bitburg. The objective is to take out every single vehicle the enemy has. We want to isolate their front lines and starve them to death."

"Very well."

"Needless to say, this is all assuming the weather's actually clearing. Good luck, Johnnie."

"Thanks."

He heard Coningham disconnect and dragged himself out of bed, searching for his warmest flying gear. An airman entered his room and handed him a cup of scalding tea. His second cigarette tasted no better than the first.

ALG Dinant came reluctantly to life. Although it was still pitch-black, the ground crews were out servicing the aircraft, rearming and refueling them. It was a testament to their professionalism that they were doing the job at a temperature below freezing and in the dark. If the wheel of fortune had clanked just a notch or two differently, Shaux reflected, he'd be out there among them.

The cold night air was filled with the sounds of engines starting under protest, coughing and backfiring until their cold, viscous lubricating oil warmed up enough and their engines spluttered into life. The Tiffies had massive twenty-four-cylinder Napier Sabre engines that were notoriously reluctant to start, even on a hot summer's afternoon, let alone in this predawn chill.

He looked up but saw no stars—the weather might be clearing somewhere but not yet here. He imagined what it must be like for those GIs trapped in Bastogne, trying to stay warm in foxholes dug in the snow. He remembered how cold he had felt lying on Queen Red beach; this must be infinitely worse. The sky was lightening in the east. It would be Christmas in two days; he had never felt less festive.

Baxter appeared, swaddled in a vast overcoat and carrying an assortment of maps. He wore a large fur hat; Shaux wondered if perhaps he'd break into one of those high-kicking Russian folk dances to warm himself up.

They walked over to King-Fox-Johnnie, whose Merlins were throbbing steadily, in contrast to the Tiffies' snorting Napier Sabres.

They took off heading westward towards Charleroi, away from the Ardennes. As he flew over SHAEF, he wondered if Eleanor was taking Charlie out for his morning walk. As they gained height, the sun rose above the horizon at their altitude, even though the ground was still in shadow. He hadn't seen the sun for more than a week. Shaux swung around to head southeast back towards Bastogne. There were patches of fog down below, but most of the ground was clearly visible. Searching the sky above his head, he saw a squadron of American P51s headed in the direction of St. Vith. This would be a day for the Allies to strike back, at least from the air.

Bob O'Neill's voice filled his headphones. He must be up in his B25 already, somewhere over the Ardennes, directing traffic.

"This is Sheepdog calling Warmer leader."

"Warmer leader," Shaux replied.

"I grovel humbly before you, Lord Rhubarb," O'Neill said.

"I deign to recognize your pitiful existence, Mickey Mouse."

Rank has its privileges, Shaux thought. No other pilots over Belgium would dare disregard radio discipline in such a flagrant manner.

"Warmer leader, patrol east to location Johnnie One-Zero," O'Neill said, reverting to business.

"Johnnie One-Zero." Shaux confirmed.

"Map grid J-10 is Bitburg across the German border," Baxter said. "We'll fly overhead Bastogne and then due east."

Now the fun begins, Shaux thought, settling in his seat. He throttled back to 150 miles per hour and nosed down to a thousand feet. The narrow roads connecting the villages in the Ardennes snaked through the valleys, playing hide-and-seek beneath the trees. They'd have no chance of spotting enemy traffic if they flew any higher or any faster.

Shaux relied on Baxter to look down and spot any targets on the ground while he searched the horizons for any Luftwaffe fighters that might be up this morning. There were P51s and Spitfires far above them in the glare, and the Luftwaffe might be a shadow of its former strength, but Fw 190s were still as good as any Allied aircraft in the air, and the new Me 262s might well be better.

The brilliant sunshine above and the gleaming snow below were in shocking contrast to the dreary gray-on-gray gloom of the last ten days.

They reached Bitburg and turned back.

"Traffic below," Baxter said after a few minutes. "There's a convoy crossing that bridge. Those are horses and carts!" Baxter said as they made a second run. "There are at least five or six carts."

Eleanor, Shaux knew, believed that the war would be won by the Allies because the Allies had American GMC two-and-a-half-ton Jimmy trucks—tens of thousands of them—to haul their supplies, while Hitler's armies still relied predominantly on horse-drawn transportation.

"If they made fewer tanks and more lorries, they'd win a lot more battles," she had said. "They're still stuck in the nineteenth century. Germany is chronically short of oil; perhaps they still use horses because they run on hay."

He never doubted her on such matters.

"I'll swing around to give us a clear shot," Shaux said. "Switch on the Molins."

"You're not going to shoot horses, are you, skipper?" Baxter asked.

Shaux had touched a raw nerve many aircrews had in common. It was ironic, he thought, that men who would kill their fellow men without compunction squirmed away from killing animals.

"Sorry, Bax. We'll be doing them a favor, putting them out of their misery. Imagine what they're going through down there, struggling with the snow and ice in the freezing winds."

"S'pose," Baxter said, but did not seem convinced.

The road, covered in snow and ice, ran through a heavily forested valley. It emerged from the trees and ran straight for a hundred yards before it climbed over a steep humpbacked bridge. A team of four horses pulling a cart was struggling up the far side of the approach to the bridge, while a line of teams and wagons waited behind them for their turn. Drivers and handlers were at the horses' heads.

Eleanor would doubtless point out that Napoleon—or Julius Caesar, for that matter—would feel at home down there.

He could see four hundred yards of road: at 150 miles per hour, they'd cover that in about six seconds. Theoretically, the Molins loader could load and fire four shots in that time.

"I'll start firing tracer while we're still over the trees," Shaux said. "Start firing the gun as soon as we bear on the bridge."

The men down there must be feeling some combination of fear and hopelessness, Shaux thought, as he turned to begin his attack. There was nothing they could do to move the carts before Shaux struck. Even if Baxter missed the cart itself and hit the road or the bridge, shrapnel and ricochets would shred everything nearby.

King-Fox-Johnnie was now skimming the treetops. Shaux flicked off the tracer safety switch on the control column and opened fire. A line of yellow tracer stretched out before them like a searchlight until it cut through the canopy of trees. As the distance closed, the tracer reached the open road, ran up to the bridge and reached the leading cart. Men scattered, flinging themselves into the snowy ditches. A horse reared up as its chest was pierced by two ounces of white-hot phosphorus moving at twice the speed of sound.

Baxter pressed the Molins trigger. The cart on the bridge disintegrated. The gun fired again, and the second cart exploded in an expanding balloon of fire that engulfed the first three carts, their teams of horses, and their handlers. Now King-Fox-Johnnie was over the convoy with the trees on the far side of the valley rushing towards them, and Shaux pulled up sharply as the ground rose steeply ahead of them.

"Turn right to a bearing of 270 degrees, skipper, towards St. Vith," Baxter said mournfully, presumably in sympathy for the horses.

Upon reflection, Shaux thought, Baxter was right. It seemed a bit unfair to shoot horses with 57mm armor-piercing anti-tank ammunition, but all's fair in love and war, or so they said.

* * *

SHAEF Forward, Charleroi, Belgium
24 December 1944, 1000 Hours
"The 5th Panzer Army is still advancing, slowly but surely," Ken Strong said, waving his arm at the big map on the wall. "It's now thirty miles west of Bastogne. They've taken Rochefort, which is only two miles from ALG Dinant."

"That's a bit too close for comfort, don't you think?" Beetle Smith asked. "I hope Coningham pulls those guys out while there's still time."

"So do I," Eleanor said.

She meant it as a joke, of course, but all sorts of things go wrong in battle all the time, without any warning, and it was easy for lightly armed men to get trapped by sudden enemy maneuvers. Johnnie and his 2TAF squadrons at ALG Dinant were directly in line with the approaching juggernaut. The 5th Panzer Army had no SS monsters like Peiper, as far as she knew, but there were still too many stories of the enemy shooting prisoners . . .

"Do we know who their leading units are?"

"Yes, we do, sir," she said. "They are the *Kampfgruppe Böhm* with about 30 Panther tanks, Panzer Mark 5s, followed by the *Kampfgruppe Cochenhausen*, which is a mechanized infantry regiment with half-tracks and another dozen or so Panthers."

"This is going to be very close," Strong said. "We've got reserves coming up, British and American, but we don't know if they'll be enough to stop them."

"I think it all depends on how much fuel they've got," Eleanor said. "The enemy has been moving surprisingly slowly over the last three or four days, starting and stopping. It's not as if we've been able to stop them; I wonder if they keep running out of fuel and having to stop to wait to be filled up again."

"Let us hope you're right," Smith said. "They're getting far too close to the Meuse; Monty's doing lots of organizing and shuffling but very little fighting, as far as I can make out; and George Patton is still a couple of days from Bastogne."

As if to emphasize Smith's point, an officer on a ladder stuck a German swastika into the map at Rochefort. It seemed to overshadow the British flag at ALG Dinant.

"At least George's weather prayer worked," Smith said. "God must like him even though nobody else does."

Eleanor had heard that Patton had given a medal to the chaplain who wrote the prayer.

The phone rang, and Smith reached to pick it up.

"Oh, and Eleanor, one other thing," he said. "Ike wants a conference in Beauraing this afternoon."

"Beauraing?"

"Brad's set up a forward command post there. It's halfway between here and where Patton is, so it's as good as anywhere. I'll see you there."

* * *

2 TAF (FD Group) ALG Dinant, Belgium
24 December 1944, 1400 Hours

It was Christmas Eve. Shaux remembered that when he was a child, he had walked out on Blackheath on Christmas Eve and searched the night sky for bands of angels blowing golden trumpets and singing tidings of comfort and joy. He had seen and heard no angels—in fact it was cloudy and drizzling. He still remembered his disappointment. It was the first time he began to doubt the existence of God.

This Christmas Eve, he thought, the Americans in Bastogne would be searching the night skies not for angels but for Ju 88s; the Luftwaffe had bombed Bastogne every night since that American general had said "Nuts."

Units from the British 29th Armoured Brigade had arrived at ALG Dinant this morning. Comet tanks—new and improved versions of Cromwell and Centaur tanks—belonging to the 23rd Hussars were parked along the eastern perimeter. It was the clearest sign he had seen so far that the Allies might be losing this battle; someone had decided that ALG Dinant needed to be defended from a potential ground assault.

He'd heard distant artillery fire for two days now, and today it seemed less distant. This evening, the sky lit up from time to time with muzzle flashes to the east.

Mary Coningham wanted ALG Dinant kept open as long as possible and said he expected the Allied line to hold, but Shaux had told Jenkins to keep all the aircraft ready for immediate takeoff, day and night, and to have enough lorries fueled and ready to evacuate all the ground crews if necessary. It was hard enough to start Tiffies in the best of times, and he didn't want the ground crews struggling with them as Panzers came bursting through the perimeter fencing. Eleanor suspected that the enemy was short of fuel, so Shaux had also ordered explosive charges to be positioned in the fuel dump, just in case.

This was starting to feel like Arras all over again, he thought. At least Eleanor was another thirty miles further west, safe in Charleroi.

He glanced up at the night sky; there was a flash of artillery fire but still no angels.

* * *

12th USAG Forward Command Post, Beauraing, Belgium
24 December 1944, 2000 Hours

Night had already fallen when Eleanor left the conference. The guards told her to drive back through the village until she reached the shell of a ruined church and then she should turn left. The 12th USAG senior officer's quarters were in a requisitioned chateau a little beyond the church just at the end of the village.

"It's just five minutes, ma'am," the guards told her. "The Rangers'll be there."

The night was bitterly cold. Charlie jumped into the back seat of her jeep. She decided to make do with just her greatcoat and wrapped the blanket around him. The jeep started reluctantly—the cold had turned the engine oil into glue—and crept forward, lurching through slushy potholes and over stray pieces of debris. She was still not quite used to driving American vehicles, sitting on the wrong side with the gear lever on her right. Almost all the buildings she passed were damaged; the war was turning Europe into an endless pile of rubble. It seemed that the price of victory was ruin.

The jeep had a canvas roof but no sides, and the wind was ruthless. Her hands were starting to go numb despite her sheepskin gloves. The night was pitch-black, and the hooded headlights were ridiculously feeble. Charlie, huddled in the blanket on the back seat, was invisible.

This ruin looked as if it had once been a church, and there was a narrow road just beyond it; the wind was too cold to dillydally. She turned left. The ruined houses ended, and she was in wooded country. The road became narrower with fewer vehicle tracks. Had she passed the chateau by mistake? She'd go a little further and then turn around if she had missed it.

She saw a dark shape ahead. Thank God—it must be one of the Rangers standing guard at the chateau gates. The soldier was waving a light, and she brought the jeep to a sliding stop in front of him. He advanced to the jeep and bent down on the passenger side to shine his light on her.

"My name is Shaux," she told him. "SHAEF staff."

"Was ist das?" he asked. *"Wer bist du?"* "What is this? Who are you?"

He leaned further forward. She saw he had a black uniform with silver lightning badges on his lapels.

"Wer bist du?" he asked again.

"Oh, Jesus," she said silently. The man was an SS grenadier. "Oh, sweet Jesus."

He moved the light a little, and she saw it glinting on a pistol in his other hand.

"Hände hoch!" "Hands up."

He raised the pistol. She saw it was shaking. Perhaps he was trembling in nervous excitement or perhaps he was shivering with cold. He might pull the trigger for either reason.

"Amerikanisch?" "American?"

He sounded as shocked as she was. Neither of them could quite believe she had been so profoundly stupid, so utterly reckless, as to drive into an enemy outpost. The light quivered again, and she caught a glimpse of his face. He couldn't be more than sixteen, a child in a man's uniform, alone and frightened, not knowing what to do next.

"Amerikanisch!" he called back over his shoulder. *"Schnell! Schnell!"* "American! Quick! Quick!"

He turned back to her, the shaking pistol inches from her face.

"Hände hoch!" he said again, his voice hardening to a growl and the pistol pointing at her head. *"Hände hoch!"*

She was about to be shot in the face by a youth with pimples.

Charlie lunged from the back seat. His jaws clamped around the arm holding the gun.

The soldier screamed and hit Charlie with his light. Charlie shook his head, worrying the man's arm as if he were worrying a bone. The man screamed again and dropped the light. The pistol fired, and Eleanor felt the bullet almost grazing her cheek. Shouts came from the darkness behind the soldier.

She jerked the gear stick into reverse and pressed down on the gas pedal.

The man slipped half under the jeep, almost pulling Charlie after him.

The jeep stopped, stuck on something, perhaps on the man's leg. She pushed the stick into a forward gear, and the jeep jerked but was still stuck. Now the man was screaming without stopping, long, high-pitched shrieks of agony and despair, jammed half under the jeep and with his wrist in Charlie's viselike jaws. She jerked the stick back into reverse.

"Charlie, let go," she said.

Charlie let go. The jeep shot backward, the front tire bumping over the shrieking soldier.

She stayed in reverse, backing up the slippery lane. As she retreated, she could see a dark shape lying in the road and figures running towards him. She could still hear his screams, or perhaps they were her own. She had no lights pointing backward, but she dared not risk turning around in the narrow lane. In fact, she'd better turn off the headlights so that the SS guards couldn't see her. She might slip in the slush and fall into a ditch but dared not stop. God alone knew what the SS soldiers would do to her—and to Charlie—if they caught her.

She stayed in reverse for an eternity, following an erratic serpentine backward path. There was just enough moonlight to keep her on the road. She was fairly confident she wasn't screaming, but she wouldn't bet on it. After an eternity, she was back among the ruined houses and able to turn around in a driveway. She drove forward blindly, with no plan in mind except to get as far away from the SS as possible.

Now there were new lights ahead of her, and she jerked to a halt in front of a Sherman tank.

"Hey, what do we have here?" an American voice said.

Again a light flashed in her face.

"Steady, Charlie," she said.

"You steal this jeep, mademoiselle?"

"Charlie, stay. It's all right."

"You got ID?"

"Charlie, stay."

"What do you mean, 'Charlie?' Why are you calling me Charlie?"

"Please don't come closer, sir. And please don't make any sudden movements. It's very important. My dog is concerned you might attack me."

"You got a dog? What dog?"

The light swung round to Charlie. He had a black glove in his mouth. Now she knew she screamed.

TWENTY-FOUR

2TAF (FD Group) ALG Dinant, Belgium
25 December 1944, 0800 Hours

Shaux hung up the telephone and stared at it.

Winston Churchill, he recalled, had described the fighter pilots who fought the Battle of Britain as "undaunted by odds, unwearied in their constant challenge and mortal danger." Shaux had been twenty-two when he'd listened to that speech in 1940; now he was twenty-six. Four years of "constant challenge and mortal danger" later, Churchill would need to think again; Shaux might not feel particularly daunted, but he felt utterly weary.

He'd had few close friends. He could count them on the fingers of one hand . . . Froggie, Diggers, Pete, Otto—fewer than the fingers of one hand. He remembered someone at Oxford claiming that you could understand your own character if you knew the characteristics your friends had in common. If all your friends were studious, for example, you were likely to be studious yourself, and so on—a sort of "birds of a feather" idea. He had dismissed the notion at the time, for the simple reason that he had no friends.

Now, years later, Shaux reflected that the largest denominator his friends all had in common was that they were dead.

And the voice on the telephone had just told him that Bob O'Neill, who would undoubtedly have become a lifelong friend, was also dead, so Shaux now had a grand total of five dead friends. Bob had been flying Sheepdog duty in a B25, as he had been since the weather lifted, directing rhubarbs against enemy forces, when he'd been jumped by a flight of the new Messerschmitt 262 jet fighters. Bob's B25 had gone straight down, in flames, and there'd been no parachutes. The Sheepdog B25 was supposed to have a dedicated flight of P51s to defend it, but apparently the 262s had simply been too fast.

This was Christmas morning, Shaux thought, and this was his Christmas present. He had been right, all those years ago on Blackheath, to doubt God's existence. The seventeenth-century philosopher Thomas Hobbes had summed up life very well: it was "solitary, poor, nasty, brutish, and short." In the nineteenth century, Charles Darwin had put the whole thing on an exact scientific basis: the fit survived and the rest got eaten. There was no need for a God to preside over a food chain, however elaborate. A food chain sorts itself out.

He looked out the window. It was another clear day—in fact it was a beautiful snowy Christmas morning. He was scheduled to fly at 1000 hours, the same kind of rhubarb operation as yesterday and the day before yesterday. It would be exactly the same, except Sheepdog's voice on the radio would be the voice of a stranger, and probably no one would take note of it, for there can be no room for sentiment in a profession with a casualty rate in excess of fifty percent.

An artillery shell exploded in the direction of Rochefort, but he had become used to near-misses.

He just had time to write to Bob's fiancée before getting ready to fly. What would he say? "Merry Christmas. Guess what? I have a special surprise for you!" He took out his pen, hoping it had run out of ink, but it hadn't. Better get it over with, he thought.

* * *

12th AG Forward CP, Beauraing, Belgium
25 December 1944, 0900 Hours
"Jesus, Eleanor, what the hell did you do?" Eisenhower demanded. "How come you're driving around by yourself at night, for Christ's sake?"

"I wasn't alone, sir. I had Charlie."

"Yes, so I heard. Thank God!" he said.

He stooped out of habit to pat Charlie on the head but seemed to change his mind at the last second and drew his hand back quickly. Eleanor had decided not to tell anyone what had happened—especially not Johnnie—but rumors seemed to be circulating.

Eisenhower turned to Kay Summersby instead.

"Please arrange for Eleanor to have a general officer's SHAEF car and a driver at all times."

Kay Summersby nodded, and it seemed to Eleanor that Summersby was not pleased.

"Thank you, sir, but that really won't be necessary," Eleanor said. "I'll be—"

"No more going out alone—that's an order," Eisenhower interrupted. "I can't afford to lose you. God alone knows what might have happened to you."

"Yes, sir."

Yes, she could tell that Summersby was definitely not pleased. And why had Eisenhower pulled his hand back?

"Merry Christmas, by the way, Eleanor," he said.

"And to you, sir."

* * *

2TAF (FD Group) ALG Dinant, Belgium
25 December 1944, 1000 Hours
The life of an RAF pilot, Shaux had always thought, consisted of one hundred percent waiting. On days of intense fighting, that changed to ninety-nine percent waiting and one percent action. There was an old recruiting poster in the last war that attempted to shame men into volunteering for the armed services. It showed a little girl seated on her father's knee, asking him, "What did *you* do in the war, Daddy?" If

Shaux was ever asked that question by a putative future daughter, he knew he would be able to answer, with a sense of righteous patriotic pride, "I waited."

This morning was no exception to the rule. After waiting in a holding pattern high over Dinant for almost an hour, the 645 Tsetse Flight was summoned to Bastogne.

The roads leading in and out of the town were littered with wrecked vehicles, the railway lines were pockmarked with bomb craters, and Bastogne itself was still burning from last might's bombing. It all looked quiet down there, but he knew it was anything but. The German 5th Panzer Army had the American 101st Airborne surrounded in Bastogne, starved of food and ammunition, subject to constant bombardment and probing attacks; the German 7th Army was driving westward across northern Luxembourg to secure the 5th Panzer Army's southern flank before Patton's American Third Army could reach Bastogne; and Patton was marching northwest across central Luxembourg to beat the 7th Army to Bastogne.

Three armies were engaged down there, although he couldn't see them. In olden days, soldiers wore bright uniforms as badges of courage, as if to say, "Look at me." Now armies, like chameleons, tried to sink into their surroundings. On a map in SHAEF, the armies would be clearly shown with brightly colored arrows and flags; here there was nothing but snow and treetops.

Tens of thousands of men were either locked in battle or maneuvering hard for decisive advantage, and tens of thousands more were struggling to resupply them with fuel and ammunition.

Shaux's job, as he saw it, was not so much to kill the enemy as to force them to keep their heads down, to stop them moving or attacking until Patton could reach Bastogne. The enemy called ground-attack aircraft like the Tsetses "Jagdbombers," or Jabos for short, meaning "hunter bombers." Captured enemy soldiers reported that P47 and Typhoon Jabos, carrying 500-pound bombs and 60-pound rockets, were widely feared; now word would be spreading of Tsetse Jabos arriving above the battlefield bearing quick-firing armor-piercing anti-tank guns, like modern-day Jupiters hurling thunderbolts.

Shaux could see no aircraft other than his own in flight, but he knew the air above the Ardennes was crowded with dozens of aircraft as both sides took advantage of the clear weather. The aerial battle was taking place at two levels, almost as two separate battles; high above him at angels two-zero, P51s and Spitfires were attempting to deny Luftwaffe fighters access to the Ardennes, and all the way down here, the Jabos were hunting above the treetops.

Hitler had stirred up a hornets' nest above the Ardennes, just as he had set in motion a vast convulsion on the ground.

Shaux was well aware he had no defensive weapons. Even the four machine guns ahead of him in the nose, which normally gave Mosquitos an effective defense, were loaded with aiming tracer instead of live rounds. Things would get hairy very quickly if the P51s and Spitfires up above happened to let a flight of Fw 190s or Me 262s get past them.

"Enemy tanks reported east of Bastogne," Sheepdog's voice broke in, ending 645's wait. "Warmer, contact ABC Bravo."

ABC Bravo was a 101st Airborne officer responsible for directing air-ground support. Baxter switched the dedicated ABC radio transceiver to the Bravo frequency. Shaux looked down and saw they were overhead the little village of Sainte-Ode, three miles west of Bastogne.

"Bravo, this is Warmer," Shaux said. "Warmer is inbound Bastogne from the west, arriving one minute. Four aircraft line astern."

If ABC Bravo didn't warn his GI comrades defending Bastogne that 645 was arriving, 645 would be fired at from all directions as it flew across the town at one hundred feet.

"Message received," Bravo's voice crackled through the static. "Target is due east one thousand yards."

King-Fox-Charlie reached the town, which lay beneath a pall of smoke. Shaux guessed Bravo was in one of those ruined buildings down there on the eastern outskirts. It might once have been a pretty village, Shaux thought, but now it had become an elaborate mosaic of bomb craters and shell holes punctuated by the broken walls of roofless buildings. The drifting snow was doing its best to hide the damage but had not yet succeeded. It had taken hundreds of years to build Bastogne and just three days to destroy it.

Somewhere down there, the 101st commanding general had responded to the demand that he surrender by replying, "Nuts." That seemed to summarize the American soldier's spirit, Shaux thought, undaunted by the odds against them. Churchill would approve wholeheartedly.

"Thirty seconds, Bax," Shaux said.

The chances of being able to spot enemy vehicles on their first pass were slim. They'd have to circle around, and—

"Targets ahead," Baxter yelled.

Three or four Panzers had been foolish enough to expose themselves by crossing an open field, creating trails in the fresh snow like giant arrows pointing the way. They were almost across the field, their tracks kicking up clouds of snow, nearing the shelter of a stand of trees on the far side.

"I see them," Shaux said.

Shaux opened fire with tracer immediately, scarcely believing their luck, tweaking the control column until the stream of tracer reached the leading tank. Baxter fired, and the turret flew off the Panzer as King-Fox-Johnnie flashed over it. The chances of hitting it the first time must have been a million to one, Shaux thought. Bravo must think he was a brilliant sharpshooter, and the legend of the Jabos would gain another chapter.

"That proves it's far better to be lucky than good, Bax," Shaux said.

"S'pose."

"Home run," Bravo shouted through the static. "Thank you, Warmer."

"Merry Christmas, Bravo."

* * *

12th AG Forward CP, Beauraing, Belgium
26 December 1944, 1800 Hours

"George, you did it!" Eisenhower said. "Just in time, before their 7th Army got there."

Eisenhower had organized an impromptu Christmas gathering in his quarters. McAuliffe had reported at 1640 that the leading tanks of Patton's 4th Armored Division had reached the 101st Airborne's outer defensive lines. The siege of Bastogne had been broken; the stubborn policy of "nuts" had been vindicated.

"Was there ever a goddamned doubt?" Patton growled, clearly delighting in proving his doubters wrong.

"Thank God the weather changed," Bradley said. He seemed to be implying that it was the change in the weather, rather than Patton's generalship, that had made the difference.

"I did thank God, Brad, as a matter of fact," Patton said. "On my knees in the goddamned snow."

He's exactly like a little boy, Eleanor thought, crowing in triumph.

"McAuliffe's guys were magnificent," Patton continued. "They fought like tigers. Someone called them the 'Battered Bastards of Bastogne,' and that describes them perfectly."

He turned to Eleanor.

"The air support was excellent," he said. "McAuliffe told me your husband knocked the turret clean off a Panther tank with one shot, Eleanor; said it was the damnedest thing he's ever seen."

Eleanor noted that she had been advanced from "Air Commander" to "Eleanor," and that Kay Summersby had noted it also.

"My goodness!" Kay Summersby exclaimed. "A lucky shot!"

"A lucky shot?" she asked, unable, for once, to bite her tongue. "My husband has spent five years firing many different weapons at many different targets in many different situations. In that time, yes, I suppose he must have learned how to be lucky. I'm sure you're right, Kay."

"Yes," Beetle Smith said. "It's curious how that works."

Eleanor berated herself for letting her feelings get the better of her, but she would not permit Summersby to demean Johnnie, even if only by implication.

"Any news from further north?" Patton asked. "What's Monty been up to?"

"Balancing out his forces," Beetle Smith said. "Bringing up reinforce—"

"Sweet goddamned nothing, huh?"

"Now, George, be nice!" Eisenhower chuckled. "Peiper's stopped in front of the 82nd at La Gleize. Hardly moving. Eleanor's guessing he's run out of gas."

"Certainly petrol, sir, and probably ammunition," Eleanor said.

"So, the mighty SS Kampfgruppe Peiper has been stopped?" Patton asked. "And what about the mighty Panzer Lehr spearhead at Marche?"

"Same thing, sir, it seems," Eleanor said. "Perhaps they're out of gas figuratively as well as literally. And now that you've relieved Bastogne, it will make it much harder for them to advance any further forward— or to retreat, for that matter."

"Here's to you, George," Eisenhower said, raising his glass. "You did it!"

"Was there ever any goddamned doubt?" Patton asked again. He spread his arms, pantomiming disbelief.

"Well, Eleanor had no doubt you'd do it," Beetle Smith said. "She was your strongest advocate."

Patton turned to her and raised his glass. *"Mortalis sum,"* he said, with the slightest bow.

"What?" Kay Summersby asked. "What is that?"

"Ask Eleanor," Patton said. "She understands me."

"It's Latin," Eleanor said. "It means, 'I am mortal.'"

"But what does that mean?" Kay Summersby asked.

"An excellent question, Kay," Patton answered. "I've been asking myself that same goddamned question for more than two thousand goddamned years."

TWENTY-FIVE

10 Downing Street, London, SW1
27 December 1944, 1200 Hours
"Well, Air Commandant, will the Americans recover from their current plight?" Churchill asked.

Eleanor paused to consider her answer.

Churchill had been pressing Eisenhower to let him fly to SHAEF to receive a personal briefing on the situation in the Ardennes. Such a briefing would include Montgomery, who would doubtless use the occasion to advance his own version of events and urge the permanent transfer of all Bradley's armies to Montgomery's command, resulting in an ugly confrontation between Bradley and Montgomery, and perhaps even a diplomatic crisis between Churchill and Roosevelt.

Eisenhower had evaded Churchill—at least for a while—by pleading he was too busy but would send Eleanor to Downing Street in his stead. "She knows as much as I do and is much more pleasant to talk to," he had put in a handwritten note to Churchill.

Eleanor had not been in No. 10 Downing Street for three months and was struck by how dowdy and run down it seemed. She noticed a film of dust covering the dining table when they sat down for lunch. Churchill, on the other hand, did not seem the least diminished.

"Well?"

"Oh, yes, sir, they will," she answered. "The tide has already turned. It is becoming evident that the Wehrmacht's frontline forces do not have adequate fuel supplies and cannot move, and they lack fuel to transport whatever fuel they may have in reserve. They are abandoning their tanks and retreating on foot. It may take a few weeks, but the bulge in the line will be eliminated."

"Field Marshal Montgomery tells me the same thing," Churchill said. "However, he says that his superior strategies will defeat the Germans rather than their lack of fuel."

He raised his eyebrows in question, but she thought it best not to respond.

"Air Commandant, you are employed by His Majesty's government to provide advice and counsel. Pray do so."

He had left her no choice but to be direct.

"General Bradley left the Ardennes inadequately defended," she said, deciding not to gild the lily. "He rejected the intelligence that the enemy was planning an attack, and he couldn't regain the initiative in the days following the German attack. He was wrongfooted. It was clear to General Eisenhower that the defense of the northern flank needed to be organized as a joint effort involving all available forces, and Montgomery was there, on the spot, whereas Bradley was a hundred miles away. Bradley and Patton organized the southern flank."

"The American surrendered in some numbers near St. Vith and became trapped at Bastogne," Churchill rumbled. "The portents are not encouraging."

He seemed to be trying to build a case in support of Montgomery. She would not help him.

"The German army included the 2nd Panzer Division armed with Tiger 2 tanks to the north and the Panzer Lehr to the south. The American forces were outnumbered and outgunned. The portents, as I read them, sir, are that overwhelmed American men fought bravely for as long as they could in hideously difficult conditions, in the middle of a blinding snowstorm, and that General Patton staged a brilliant and successful counterattack."

"Do you favor leaving the northern American armies in Montgomery's hands?" Churchill asked.

"If the implication is that Field Marshal Montgomery can do a better job of managing them than Eisenhower can, then the answer is absolutely not."

Churchill frowned as if this was not the answer he wanted.

"With due respect, sir, that is not an important consideration," she said. "What is important is that the strategic balance is shifting. This German attack in the Ardennes has taken the pressure off the Russians. Soon they will attack Germany in force. They are already a hundred miles closer to Berlin than we are, and we still haven't crossed the Rhine or outflanked the Siegfried Line. That is what is important."

A steward brought brown-colored soup, but she was not hungry.

"When the Russians mount their next major assault, the enemy will be forced to transfer resources from the Ardennes to the eastern front, sir," she said. "That will be our chance."

Churchill attacked his soup with gusto. She pressed on.

"It's essential that we—the combined American and British armies—get as far into Germany as we can, as soon as we can, in order to prevent at least some of it from becoming the Soviet Socialist Republic of Germany. It's too late to save Poland and Hungary, and it's almost certainly too late for eastern Germany, but at least we can try to occupy the rest."

Churchill accepted a second helping of soup.

"General Patton is the general who moves fastest, sir," she said. "We need to move as fast as possible, and so we should therefore throw our support behind him."

At last Churchill was finished and set down his spoon with a sigh.

"I fear that victory will be a bitter pill to swallow," he said, shaking his head. "I fear few people here in England understand that, and thus the shock of realization will make it yet more bitter."

Now he seemed diminished. He has fought his whole life to keep Britain a great world power, she thought, and now he realizes he has failed. America and Russia will be the winners of this war, and Britain, exhausted and drained dry, will be left in ruins, half starved and three-quarters bankrupt. Poor old man, she thought, sitting at his dusty table, shaking his head. His great triumph would be a hollow victory.

Then he seemed to rally his spirits.

"Steward, pray tell me, is there any more soup?"

* * *

2TAF (FD Group) ALG Dinant, Belgium
28 December 1944, 1000 Hours

"Would you mind signing these other forms as well, sir?" the FD Group quartermaster asked Shaux. "I'd like to avoid any more requisition snafus if we can."

Shaux sighed. Reality had caught up with the front line. The FD Group ALGs now had ack-ack batteries, radar warning systems, maintenance workshops, hospitals, chapels, messes, recreation halls, visiting ENSA music hall acts, and all the other facilities and amenities of RAF stations, including the administrators who provided the full spectrum of RAF bureaucracy.

He knew he wasn't being fair. The administrators performed daily miracles in keeping the FD squadrons fully supplied and ready to fly, even though the airfields were still defended by Comet tanks against the possibility of another surprise enemy attack.

He was sighing, he knew, because he was now in the ranks of administrators himself. His flying days were almost over. Every time he climbed into King-Fox-Johnnie, he was breaking RAF age regulations. Each rhubarb might be his last. Soon, some callow teenager would claim King-Fox-Johnnie as his own.

The quartermaster tucked the signed requisitions into a folder and took out another.

"Now, sir, let us move on to the group expense accounts," he said. "I'm afraid they are significantly past due."

* * *

SHAEF Forward, Charleroi, Belgium
28 December 1944, 1000 Hours

Eleanor clicked her tongue to Charlie, and they took a companionable walk. It was sleeting, and she knew he would get more and more muddy, but he loved walking so much—well, not really walking but picking their way around slushy potholes. She'd have to hose him down when they got back. She'd towel him as best she could, but he'd still be damp when he stretched out next to her in bed tonight. But taking walks with Charlie, in companionable silence, was exactly the sort of peacetime thing that kept her sane. Besides, she had to admit that he was much cleaner than she was; as a woman alone in a war zone, bathing was a rare luxury.

A convoy of American ambulances growled past them, bearing wounded from the front. Their faces were so young, she thought as she glimpsed them through the windows, so innocent, yet filled with shock and pain. She asked herself for the thousandth time why these young men were fighting. What cause justified their wounds?

Churchill saw this war as an existential clash between good and evil, she thought, between lightness and darkness, between civilization and chaos—and, of course, the English were the best judges of what was good and civilized and should therefore be in charge. Stalin saw the war as an opportunity to extend his wise and generous rule over the peoples of Western Europe, whether they wished it or not. He had an extensive secret police force to ensure their gratitude.

She saw the war as the first act of a new era in which America would bestride the world like a colossus—soon to be a colossus with an atomic bomb. The Romans and others had created power out of organization and order; Hitler and many others had created power out of terror and oppression. Now the Americans had created power out of freedom.

When she had first met Churchill, he was the leader of the free world—the non-fascist world, she corrected herself. Stalin and Roosevelt sat on the sidelines. Now, four years later, Roosevelt and Stalin wrote the rules and dictated the terms, and Churchill followed in their wake.

Johnnie, she knew, saw this as a war between machines as much as a war between men. Whoever had the best engineers and factory managers creating the best and most numerous machines would win. The war wasn't between Berlin and Washington but between Stuttgart and Detroit, between men like the German rocket scientist Wernher Von Braun and the British bomb designer Barnes Wallis, between men like Willy Messerschmitt and Geoffrey de Havilland.

The generals who populated SHAEF were professional military men for whom this war was a dream come true, a brilliant burst of sunshine after decades of dull gray peace. They had been transported from the tedium of the barracks square, with peacetime promotions inching up with agonizing slowness, into the wildly intoxicating field of battle, with real reputations to be won and real enemies to slay and medals and honors and memoirs in their futures.

But why were all these young GIs fighting? Why would a farm boy from Nebraska risk his life in Normandy? If the Allies won—or even if they lost, for that matter—he'd just go back to being a farm boy in Nebraska. The war had no positive side for him, just the real possibility of injury or death.

Young Englishmen from the backstreets of the east end of London, or the rows of back-to-back houses in Manchester, had nothing to gain. Their lives would be as hard after the war as they had been before it, and perhaps harder.

Why was she fighting, come to think of it? Certainly not out of patriotism or duty. Partly, she was ashamed to admit, she was fighting out of excitement, out of being able to request a Lysander to fly her hither and yon; out of the opportunity to attend a meeting at the White House or No. 10 Downing Street, or being telephoned by Churchill or Eisenhower; or even, as the war wore on, out of pushing back at the arrogant men who surrounded her in SHAEF.

The convoy of ambulances ground to a halt, and the men who could do so climbed down to stretch and smoke. They were still children, she thought, looking into their faces; they made her, at the ripe old age of twenty-six, feel ancient.

A GI with one arm and one eye whistled to Charlie, who glanced up at her for permission to go.

"Charlie, go," she said, and he trotted over.

The GI bent over and ruffled Charlie's ears. "I have a dog back in North Bend, ma'am," he said. "Big and black, just like yours."

"What's his name?" she asked, not knowing what else to say.

"Just 'Dog.' That's all, ma'am. That's enough for us. He's waiting, sure enough."

She had an image of a dog sitting on a farmhouse porch, staring towards a road, waiting, waiting, month in and month out, in the chill of winter and the heat of summer, eyes fixed on the road, never losing faith that the GI would return.

"I'm sure he is," she murmured. "I am certain of it."

"Yes, ma'am, me too. He'll still be glad to see me."

Oh God, she thought, he's worried that people—his family, his friends—would see his injuries rather than him.

He rubbed Charlie's head once more. "Why can't people be like dogs, ma'am?"

"Good question."

* * *

2TAF (FD Group) ALG Dinant, Belgium
29 December 1944, 1000 Hours

"Once more unto the breach, dear Bax, once more," Shaux said as King-Fox-Johnnie lifted smoothly from ALG Dinant's temporary runway.

"S'pose," Baxter responded.

The battle had taken on a different feeling, Shaux thought, as they climbed to their holding altitude. The enemy was unquestionably in retreat. The Panzer Lehr, who had occupied Marche-en-Fammene, just an artillery shot from ALG Dinant, were pulling back in disarray. The Comet tanks of the 23rd Hussars, which had been guarding ALG Dinant, were moving eastward in pursuit.

The road from Marche to La Roche was strewn with abandoned tanks, half-tracks, and lorries—American wrecks from earlier, before Christmas, when the Lehr swept in, and now the carcasses of enemy vehicles as the Panzer tide receded. Dozens of wars had been fought over the centuries in this area between France and Germany, and no doubt dozens of tides of men had swept back and forth, flooding in and ebbing out, as the fortunes of war shifted. Only the dead remained.

Eleanor, back from meetings in London, was more certain than ever that the war would be over in six months. For the first time that he could remember, she had not returned with praise for Churchill. She seemed to be losing interest in moving to America and warming to the idea of starting afresh in Australia.

"Unidentified aircraft at angels one-one, bearing oh-nine-oh," a crisp WAAF's voice announced in Shaux's earphones. ALG Dinant now had its own GL Mk 3 mobile antiaircraft radar station housed in a variety of lorries and trailers, operated by WAAFs attached to the RAF Regiment.

"Estimated range twelve miles," the voice added.

If the radar blip was a 190, Shaux calculated, it would be here in approximately two minutes. The best place for King-Fox-Johnnie was on the deck, where he might be able to play cat and mouse just above the treetops. Up here, at angels zero-five, he had no chance.

"We'll go down to the cellar, Bax," he said and throttled back. King-Fox-Johnnie began to descend. "Watch out for bandits at three o'clock."

"Item-Fox-Fox negative," the WAAF voice informed them.

This was phonetic code for IFF, which, in turn, stood for Identification Friend or Foe. The incoming radar blip was not responding to an automatic radio challenge and was therefore almost certainly a bandit.

"Bollocks!" Baxter shouted. "Jesus Christ!"

Three aircraft in a vic formation crossed just above them from right to left. They were much too big and much too fast to be 190s—these were 262s. They had swept wings and mottled gray camouflage. They had engines hung below each wing and no propellers. They had long, smooth noses like barracuda or shark noses. Like barracudas and sharks, these were top predators.

The 262s angled around to circle behind King-Fox-Johnnie's tail, showing their profiles as they banked, with their swept-back wings looking like rocket ships in a science fiction comic book. The propeller-driven King-Fox-Johnnie was fast, one of the fastest aircraft in the air, pulled through the air by 4,000 horsepower generated by its two Rolls-Royce masterpieces, but the jet-propelled 262 was much, much faster.

Shaux opened the throttles, and the revs spun up.

"This could get a little hairy, Bax," he said.

TWENTY-SIX

SHAEF Forward, Charleroi, Belgium
29 December 1944, 1000 Hours

Eleanor escaped outside and took Charlie for a walk. It occurred to her that she was doing so more often as the war dragged on, day after day, as if SHAEF had become a snare in which she was trapped.

The chilly, wet afternoon was a sharp contrast to the smoke-filled crowded fug inside. Walking Charlie was always a slow process because he was well acquainted with every single person at SHAEF Forward and was obliged, out of politeness, to spend a little time with everyone they encountered.

She wondered if Charlie remembered the night she had driven into that SS outpost and prayed that he didn't.

Red Tape predicted the war in Europe would end within six months. Even if Eisenhower's armies remained stuck on the wrong side of the Rhine, the Russian army would fight, rape, and loot its way across Germany before summer. Then what? She would suddenly be out of the circles of high politics and military strategy, and Johnnie would be out of the RAF. What would they do then? The question was becoming very real as the war reached its climax. She recalled her argument with Harry Hopkins and was determined to be ready to seize the opportunity.

Johnnie had often mentioned Australia, and Sydney in particular . . . she had always wanted to go to Princeton in America, to work with von Neumann on probability and strategic game theory, or something like that, but that dream had lost its allure; she was afraid that any future work might be subverted into some military process, just as Red Tape had become an Allied strategic planning tool . . . perhaps she should go to Sydney to pursue his dream instead of hers . . . she knew someone at the University of New South Wales, and she was certain she could wangle a teaching job.

Johnnie had talked about starting a little company doing aircraft maintenance and perhaps some contract flying . . . she still had all that money George, her first husband, had left her, more than enough to finance something like that, she'd imagine . . . she'd looked at a map of Sydney, and the University of New South Wales was quite close to Kingsford Smith Airfield on the banks of Botany Bay, so they could both be home for supper.

England was in its last throes, she feared, or at least the England conjured up by "Rule Britannia." The cumulative cost of two world wars and the dead hand of Whitehall bureaucracy meant that Britain was destined for mediocracy at best and—more likely—a long period of less than gracious decline. Everything was timeworn and weary and bombed to hell and back. England would not be "this precious stone set in a silver sea," in Shakespeare's words, but merely a sooty little island on the outskirts of Europe where it rained a lot, and the British Empire would soon escape from Britain's enfeebled grasp.

Poor old Churchill! The empire he had fought to preserve would soon fall.

Poor old England! After almost six years of warfare, it was too exhausted to be victorious. What was that other quotation from Shakespeare's Richard II? Oh, yes:

That England that was wont to conquer others
Hath made a shameful conquest of itself.

Exactly so, she thought.

Australia, on the other hand, was young and vigorous, a land of opportunity. If—no, when, not if—she and Johnnie had children, where would it be best for them to grow up? Beneath England's perpetually damp and dreary skies or Australia's endless sunshine? Besides, as a bonus, if she lived in Australia, she'd never have to see her mother or her sisters again—in fact, never seeing her family was reason enough to emigrate as soon as possible.

Perhaps she could finally find peace of mind if she and Johnnie started over in a new country, a new beginning . . . Against all odds, he would have survived years in the forefront of the battle and the healing process could begin . . . She had no civilian clothes, nor did he . . . After living in uniform for over five years, she couldn't even remember the kinds of clothes she liked . . . She vaguely remembered Johnnie had adored a blue dress of hers.

It was now the end of 1944. She estimated that the Manhattan Project would produce results in less than a year, and then the war would end almost immediately, regardless of whether the campaigns against Germany in Europe, and against Japan in the Pacific, went well or not. One atomic bomb on a small German city like Dresden, for example, or a similar city in Japan, would be enough to compel surrender. The war would end with either a bang or a whimper, to quote T. S. Eliot, she didn't know which, but end it surely would. Actually, she thought, the war would end with a bang *and* a whimper.

Regardless, she and Johnnie could be on the other side of the world in Sydney in six months or so from now, as far away from the ruins of Europe as one could get . . . This time next year, she could be pregnant . . . she'd certainly try . . . She'd write to her friend at the University of New South Wales this evening and get the ball rolling . . . And she needed to find out if there were any female Bouviers in Australia—it was best to think ahead.

* * *

2 TAF (FD Group) ALG Dinant, Belgium
29 December 1944, 1300 Hours

Shaux watched as two of the 262s overtook them, appearing from beneath King-Fox-Johnnie's nose and streaking ahead, close enough and fast enough that King-Fox-Johnnie was buffeted by their wake. The third 262 must still be behind his tail. He was not surprised that the first two had missed him. They were probably inexperienced pilots unable to hold an aircraft straight and level at such a high speed, or perhaps the design of the 262 was so new, it was still unstable. God forbid what might happen if they put Adolph Galland in one of those things.

It was shocking to be overtaken by an aircraft travelling at 100 miles per hour faster than himself, particularly as he was already doing 400 miles per hour. Doubtless Bob O'Neill would say, "Holy crap," except Bob was unable to say anything anymore. Perhaps he'd said "Holy crap" as his B25 fell from the sky in flames.

Shaux knew he was looking at the future, galloping away ahead of him. Poor old King-Fox-Johnnie was already an anachronism. Perhaps, after five years of warfare, Shaux was too. Where was the third 262? Perhaps the backward-facing Monica radar could see it.

"Is there anything on the Monica, Bax?"

"Just a mo', skipper."

"That third 262 must be somewhere back there."

Tracer flashed past them from somewhere behind their tail, as if the 262 pilot had heard Shaux and was answering his question. Shaux yanked the control column back. The 262 had to be—

He must be asleep. He was back in that dream again, the dream in which he had died and was crossing into the underworld. Everyone has recurring dreams, they say, in which the brain works out its hopes and fears. The Ginger Runt had lectured him on unconscious stresses, or stresses on his unconscious, or some such rigamarole. Perhaps the 262s had triggered some sort of unconscious anxiety, or something—he'd never had much patience for psychological stuff. Were the 262s simply a new addition to the dream?

Anyway, he'd reached the part of the dream when the old man was questioning him, with the crowd gathered round listening, the part when Shaux always woke up.

"Please summarize your life," the old man said again. "I need your response to the question."

Perhaps the underworld was filled with pedantic bureaucrats with forms, and every form must be filled out exactly. Perhaps the underworld was not a place of fire and devils with pitchforks as it had always been depicted, but a Kafkaesque government ministry peopled with bureaucrats asking questions for unfathomable purposes, and one spent eternity completing forms and trying in vain to satisfy the bureaucrats' demands.

"Well?" the old man asked, quill pen posed. There was a hint of impatience in his voice—like the 262s, this seemed a new nuance to the dream, enhancing its realism. Was it normal for one's subconscious to embellish recurring dreams?

The dream always ended here, leaving the old man's question unanswered, giving the dream an unfinished, uncertain feel, but Shaux was always glad it did end now because he awoke before he had to answer the old man's question.

"Well?" the old man asked again—the dream had definitely never lasted as long as this.

"Well?"

Shaux searched for an answer, but nothing came immediately to mind.

AUTHOR'S NOTES

As the great Prussian general Helmuth von Moltke (1800–1891) said, "No plan survives first contact with the enemy." In writing this story, I realized that I was writing about four plans that did not succeed or fell well short of expectations.

Of course, Overlord, the invasion of Normandy, was the beginning of the Allied victory over Germany in Western Europe, so in that sense it succeeded, but it took over two months to accomplish what had been planned for the first two days. Caen, just twelve miles from Sword Beach, and Montgomery's target for D-Day itself, was not captured until mid-July, after six weeks of bruising battle.

Market Garden in the following September was, I'm afraid, simply an overly ambitious plan poorly executed. Despite their best efforts, 30 Corps was unable to reach Arnhem in time to relieve the 1st Airborne, who suffered a casualty rate—killed, wounded, or captured—of eighty percent.

The V1 and V2 assaults were technological triumphs for Germany but were, from a strategic viewpoint, too little too late.

The Battle of the Bulge was, from the German perspective, a long shot born out of desperation, without realistic chances of succeeding. Hitler simply did not have enough resources to counter the three simultaneous assaults on Germany from Eisenhower's armies in the west, Zhukov's armies in the east, and the Allied air forces from above.

Nothing in these assessments detracts from heroism of the young men on the front lines in these various battles, the hard work and dedication of countless thousands of civilian workers, the extraordinary ingenuity of the engineers on both sides, and the bravery and stoicism of the civilian populations trapped in these massive battlegrounds.

Five years before these events, my fictitious Eleanor had postulated "The Shaux Tautology," which states that the key to winning is not to lose. In each of these real campaigns, the Allies were damaged but avoided losing and were able to recover, whereas each campaign stripped German forces of vital resources they were never able to recoup.

As always, I hope I have treated real characters with respect for their actual opinions and contemporaneous descriptions of their personalities.

Overlord

D-Day took place on 6 June 1944. While the fighting is well illustrated in movies such as *The Longest Day* and *Saving Private Ryan*, I think the vast logistical operation is just as impressive, even if less cinematic. The thousands of ships in precise order . . . the ingenuity of sinkable yet refloatable artificial harbors . . . swimming tanks . . . tens of thousands of cold, hungry, sometimes wounded men needing to be fed, housed, clothed, and cared for . . .

The timeline I followed for the first few hours of D-Day is approximately correct, and the various forces and weapons I mention were really there, with the following exceptions. There was no 49 Commando, and there was no South Barts. (The highest number British commando unit was 48 Commando, and the "South Barts" is a fictitious battalion honoring the real South Lancs.)

I created a fictitious village of Collmanville in Normandy between the real Hermanville and Colleville, and I based the fictitious strongpoint Alvis on the real strongpoint, Hillman, which held up the British advance for several hours and is one of the principal reasons the British were unable to reach Caen on the first day—and, as events unfolded, for another six weeks.

Eleanor and her MI6-3b(S) team and Bob O'Neill of the US Eighth Air Force are the only fictional characters in SHAEF. I don't know if there were any dogs at SHAEF Forward, but Patton's dog, Willy, was real.

Market Garden

Operation Market Garden, also popularly known as the campaign in the book and movie *A Bridge Too Far*, began on 17 September 1944, approximately three months after D-Day, and ended on 25 September. The objective was to establish a long south/north salient into German-held territory, culminating with the capture of a bridge over the Upper Rhine at Arnhem. This was to be the northern point of a pincer movement—with Montgomery's British and Canadian armies to the north and Bradley's American armies to the south—to bypass the Siegfried Line and encircle the Ruhr valley and then race across northern Germany to Berlin.

The plan was audacious: airborne troops would drop into points along a long strip of enemy-held land and capture bridges along a sixty-mile line, while an armored force drove up from the south to relieve the airborne forces one by one. It was the largest attempt of the war to capture territory using airborne troops.

If the plan had been successful, it would have saved weeks of hard fighting to cross the major rivers between Belgium and northern Holland. The principal weakness of the plan was that it required the Guards Armoured Division to drive up a single narrow road with marshy ground on both sides. As it turned out, the road was too congested to maintain the original schedule. Although several bridges were captured and most of the airborne troops successfully relieved, the ultimate goal, the bridge across the Rhine at Arnhem, was not captured.

The following graphic describes the major events; 30 Corps failed to reach Arnhem, where the British 1st Airborne (with the Polish 1st Independent Parachute Brigade) took terrible casualties, and Arnhem was not liberated until several months later, even though it was only seven miles from Nijmegen.

Day	30 Corps	Eindhoven	Nijmegen	Arnhem
17 Sept.	Initial advance ambushed; advances seven miles but fails to reach Eindhoven.	101st lands successfully and captures four of five target bridges.	82nd lands scattered and captures one bridge but not the main Nijmegen bridge.	1st lands scattered; a small group reaches northern end of bridge but cannot capture it.
18 Sept.	30 Corps reaches Eindhoven at noon.	The Germans recapture and destroy one bridge, which has to be replaced by a Bailey bridge.	Germany counterattacks; day ends indecisively.	Remainder push towards bridge but encounter heavy SS opposition; cannot reach bridge.
19 Sept.	30 Corps reaches Nijmegen but cannot advance as the bridge is still in enemy hands.	German counterattacks are beaten back. At night, the Luftwaffe bombs the city, causing widespread damage.	30 Corps reaches Nijmegen, but the bridge remains in enemy hands. Boats needed to cross the river are stuck in traffic.	Very heavy German counterattacks; no Allied progress. Small Polish detachment lands but far from bridge.
20 Sept.	30 Corps tanks finally cross the bridge at Nijmegen at the end of the day.		82nd crosses the Waal under heavy fire in collapsable rowboats, with high losses. The bridge is finally in 30's hands.	Very heavy attacks force the British at the bridge to accept a truce while their wounded are taken into captivity.

21 Sept.	30 Corps suffers counterattacks all along its single road, preventing it from advancing to Arnhem.		Intense counterattacks prevent 30 Corps from advancing to Arnhem.	The remaining 1st Airborne forces face fierce counterattacks. The remaining Polish troops are dropped in but are under immediate intense fire.
22 Sept.				Attempts to link up the Polish and British units fail under intense fire.
23/24 Sept.	Sporadic fighting continues; 30 Corps still unable to advance.			The British and Polish positions weaken under intense fire.
25 Sept.				The British and Polish north of the Rhine withdraw, having suffered eighty percent losses to casualties and capture.

26/28 Sept.	The situation stabilizes along the road. The Allies control the bridges as far as Nijmegen but have failed to take Arnhem. Arnhem was not liberated until seven months later in April 1945.			

Eisenhower was lukewarm towards the plan, but Montgomery argued with him vehemently to get the plan approved.

There are several references in the literature to Montgomery telling Eisenhower that his "broad front plan" was "nothing but balls, sheer balls, rubbish." And Eisenhower put his hand on Montgomery's knee, telling him: "Steady, Monty, you can't speak to me like that. I'm your boss." I'm not sure if they are accurate.

The prohibition of food supplies imposed by the Germans as punishment for the railway strike resulted in the "Dutch Famine" or "Hunger Winter" of 1944/45 in which an estimated twenty-two thousand Dutch civilians starved to death.

I do know that Prince Bernhard of the Netherlands said, "My country can never again afford the luxury of another Montgomery success." I stole the phrase and gave it to Eleanor.

Percival is the only fictious character in this part of the story; 645 is a fictitious squadron.

Diver

The V1 was a testimony to German engineering prowess, and the fact that the Germans had two more revolutionary technologies—the V2 and the Me 262—being developed to fruition in parallel makes it even more remarkable. Thus, in 1944, the Germans deployed the world's first fully operational cruise missile, the first fully operational ballistic missile, and the first fully operational jet aircraft in a matter of weeks of each other, under the extremely difficult conditions of massive Allied bombing attacks against Germany's industrial centers.

The V1 was a cruise missile launched by a steam catapult up an inclined ramp. It then flew at a speed of 350 to 400 miles per hour (it got faster as it burned up fuel) at two thousand feet with a range of up to 150 miles.

The weapon was terrifying in that its pulse jet, firing sixty times per second, made a very loud buzzing noise as it was flying—it was known as a "buzz bomb" and a "doodlebug." When it reached its planned target, the engine would shut off, and people below waited in the ensuing silence to see where it would hit and explode.

(My mother considered V1s more frightening than the much larger, more destructive V2s, which were ballistic missiles, because she could hear V1s coming, but V2s, travelling far faster than the speed of sound, exploded first and were then followed by the noise of their descent. Thus, if you could hear a V2, you had already survived it.)

RAF countermeasures were known as Operation Diver. RAF Tempests and Mosquitos were by far the most successful V1 interceptors, shooting down 638 and 623 V1s respectively. Spitfire 14s and P51 Mustangs were also fast enough to catch V1s, and each shot down half that number.

Some V1s were also shot down by P47s with their Double Wasp engines cranked up to an amazing 2,800 horsepower.

Almost ten thousand V1s were fired at England between 13 June and 15 October 1944, of which some two thousand reached London.

The V2 was the world's first successful ballistic missile, taking off vertically and rising into the upper atmosphere before plunging back to its target. It had a range of approximately two hundred miles and carried a one-ton warhead. Once launched, it was unstoppable.

Approximately five thousand V2s were built, with much of their manufacture completed by slave labor. Approximately three thousand were fired, half against London and half against Antwerp after it had been liberated.

The V2 was designed by Wernher Von Braun, who surrendered to the Americans at the end of the war and moved to America, where he led the early American rocket program for both military and civilian uses, culminating in the NASA Saturn V rocket that powered the Apollo moon program. Controversy surrounds him as he was a member of both the Nazi party and the SS yet escaped any legal judgment.

The RAF's tactics against V1s were historically accurate as I described them, but the use of Tsetse Mosquitos to destroy V2s is entirely fictitious—the Molins-gunned Mosquitos existed but were never employed in this fashion.

Battle of the Bulge

Operation Watch on the Rhine, *Unternehmen Wacht am Rhein*, was the last major German initiative on the Western Front. At the end of 1944, the battlefront ran approximately north and south along the German border with Belgium and Holland. Both sides were exhausted from six months of intensive combat. The Allies had stretched their supply lines to the limit, and the Germans were attempting to absorb the loss of four hundred thousand men.

The German plan called for a surprise assault against the center of the Allied lines, bursting through to the port of Antwerp. If successful, the Allied armies would be split in two and without supplies. Such a dramatic reversal of fortune might even force the Allies to accept a ceasefire.

As with Market Garden, by coincidence, the battle is best seen as three components.

Date	North	Center	South
December / Weather	6th Panzer Army	5th Panzer Army	7th Army

16 Heavy snow, low visibility	*Kampfgruppe* (Battle Group) Peiper leads the German attack in the north, with the objective of breaking through to the Meuse and reaching Antwerp.	The 5th Panzer Army attacks towards St. Vith and Bastogne.	7th Army attacks through Luxemburg to secure and establish the German left (southern) flank.
17 Heavy snow, low visibility	Peiper encounters strong US resistance at the Eisenborn Ridge and cannot advance northwest; commits Malmont massacre.	Schoenberg falls.	7th Army makes limited progress.
18 Heavy snow, low visibility	Pieper reaches as far west as Stavelot and La Gleize.	Otto Skorzeny launches covert operations.	7th Army makes limited progress.
19 Heavy snow, low visibility	Peiper runs out of gas, and 82nd Airborne arrives at La Gleize, blocking advancement.	Surrender of seven thousand men; the British 106th Division reinforces the Meuse.	101st reach Bastogne; 7th Army makes limited progress.
20 Heavy snow, low visibility	Montgomery is given command of US 1st and 9th Armies.	Montgomery is given command of US 1st and 9th Armies.	7th Army finally reaches Bastogne, which is cut off.
21 Heavy snow, low visibility	Peiper is forced to retreat.	St. Vith falls.	Patton sets off to relieve Bastogne; 7th Army continues west towards Meuse.

22 Heavy snow, low visibility	Retreat continues.	5th Panzer Army bypasses Bastogne and continues west.	McAuliffe refuses to surrender, replying "Nuts."
23 Russian High-pressure system clears the clouds and fog	Northern attack is effectively defeated as Peiper completes withdrawal.	Clear weather permits Allied air strikes against enemy tanks and supply columns.	Clear weather permits Allied air strikes against enemy tanks and supply columns. Supplies, ammunition, and medical team dropped into Bastogne.
24 Clear and cold		Air strikes continue for the next several days.	Air strikes continue for the next several days.
25 Clear and cold		5th Panzer reaches Marche, just short of Diant on the Meuse.	
26 Clear and cold		Allies counterattack, cutting off the 2nd Panzer.	Patton's Third Army reaches Bastogne.
27 Clear and cold		Counterattacks continue; the 5th Panzer supplies are exhausted.	7th Army halts for lack of supplies.
28/29 Clear and cold		Counterattacks and retreats continue.	Counterattacks and retreats continue.

The Battle of the Bulge continued until the end of January, another month of intense fighting after this book ends on 29 December 1944. The front lines were essentially returned to the same positions they had occupied before the battle began. Each side suffered approximately eighty thousand casualties.

Montgomery retained command of the US 1st Army until 17 January 1945, and the US 9th Army on 4 April. His contemporary public statements implied that he'd had to rescue the Americans and were highly controversial. He gave the impression that British and

American troops were equally involved, even though there were thirty GIs in the battle for every one British soldier.

Churchill, on the other hand, told the House of Commons that "the United States troops have done almost all the fighting . . . Care must be taken in telling our proud tale not to claim for the British army an undue share of what is undoubtedly the greatest American battle of the war and will, I believe, be regarded as an ever-famous American victory."

The descriptions of 2TAF and the ALG airfields are based on facts; however, the 2TAF FD Group and ALG Dinant are fictitious.

Additional Notes

As always, I have tried to stay within the context of real historical events, as seen through the eyes of my protagonists Eleanor and Johnnie Shaux (and their dog, Charlie.) I have noted portions of the story without a historical basis; any other deviations are my unwitting errors, for which I apologize. Also as always, when I have given fictitious dialogue to real people, I hope I have reflected their opinions, as best I know them, and have done so respectfully.

People and Organizations	
Allied forces	There were three principal Allied army groups in northern Europe in 1944 under Eisenhower's command: the US 12th Army Group under Omar Bradley, the US 6th Army Group under Jacob Devers (coming up from the south through Vichy France), and the British/Canadian 21st Army Group under Bernard Montgomery. Bradley's command included four US armies, including George Patton's 3rd Army, while Montgomery's 21st Army Group included the British 2nd Army and the Canadian First Army. Parts of Bradley's command were transferred to Montgomery's command in December, as I described. The orders of battle shifted as the campaign evolved and included several units from other countries, including most notably French and Polish contingents. The 2nd Tactical Air Force (2TAF) also reported to Eisenhower rather than the RAF.
German forces	German forces were organized under *Oberbefehlshaber West* (OB West), commanded by Gerd von Rundstedt. Order of battle changed constantly, but in general included: Army Group B under Rommel during D-Day and subsequently under Walter Model during Market Garden and the Battle of the Bulge. It included the 7th and 15th Armies, with the 6th SS Panzer Army added in December 1944. Panzer Group West consisting of the 5th Panzer Army. OB West suffered approximately five hundred thousand casualties in the six months this book covers.

French forces	There were several different Free French forces following the fall of France in 1940, surviving in France's African and Middle Eastern colonies. By far, the most successful were: The 1st Free French Brigade, which, under the command of Marie-Pierre Kœnig, fought a brilliant defensive battle against the Afrika Korps in Libya in 1942 (where Susan Travers rescued her man).
	The Free French "L Force" under Philipe Leclerc, which fought in Tunisia and was subsequently reconstituted as the French 2nd Armoured Division, fighting in Normandy under Omar Bradley and permitted by Eisenhower to be the first troops to "officially" liberate Paris.
	The various components of the Résistance which, in 1944, was unified under Kœnig's command as the French Forces of the Interior, known as the FFI. The most important contribution of the Résistance on D-Day itself was a very successful campaign to sabotage the railway system in Normandy, preventing the German army from bringing supplies and reinforcements.
	We should also mention Philippe Kieffer's small but brilliant Fusiliers Marins (Marine Commando) unit, the only French forces to land on the first morning of D-Day.
Omar Bradley	Omar Bradley was in command of the American armies in Western Europe in 1944 and 1945, the 12th US Army Group. He lacked the flamboyant style of Patton, and that is perhaps why Eisenhower chose him as his de facto second-in-command—to act as a buffer so that Eisenhower did not have to contend with Patton's ego on a daily basis. Bradley was also often in contention with Montgomery, who was constantly seeking priority treatment for the 21st Army Group over Bradley's 12th Army Group.
	Bradley was known as "the GI general" for his plainspoken style. After the war, he became the first chairman of the joint chiefs of staff.

Arthur Coningham	Mary Coningham, an Australian brought up in New Zealand, was a successful fighter pilot who rose to command 2TAF. He is considered the principal architect of the RAF's air-ground support strategy. Originally a favorite of Montgomery's, he had the temerity to criticize Montgomery's decisions in Europe, causing Montgomery to attempt—unsuccessfully—to get Coningham dismissed.
Winston Churchill	Churchill needs no introduction. Although he claimed to be "the father of D-Day," it was he who had favored extensive Allied campaigns in the Mediterranean in 1942 and 1943 and was therefore arguably the person who delayed D-Day by a year, with uncalculatable consequences. By this stage of the war, his influence over events was fading in comparison to Stalin's and Roosevelt's. I know he was at SHAEF on D-Day, but I do not know if he was at SHAEF Main in London or SHAEF Forward in Portsmouth (where I placed him). I should mention that he was almost seventy, overate, overdrank, and was prone to periods of acute depression—just the attributes Eleanor slyly told him Friedrich Dollmann suffered from! One of his favorite pastimes was bricklaying.
Dwight D. Eisenhower	Although he had no prior battlefield commands, Eisenhower was given overall command of American forces in North Africa in 1942 and appointed as Supreme Allied commander in the Mediterranean in 1943 and then SHAEF in 1944. His primary task was to keep the balance between the contending demands of the British and American armies for priority in supplies. As the Allies moved closer to Germany, their supply lines grew longer and more expensive. Indeed, it took five gallons of fuel to haul one gallon of fuel from Normandy to the Rhine. He made the decision to transfer command of some US forces to Montgomery during the Battle of the Bulge, a decision that Montgomery exploited. He did indeed say, as he says to my fictitious Eleanor, "plans are worthless, but planning is essential." After the war, he became the first NATO commander in chief and president in 1953.

Charles de Gaulle	De Gaulle was, before all things, a patriot. The abject collapse of the French army in 1940 and the humiliations of Vichy France were profoundly painful to him. The fact that he was completely dependent upon the Americans and the British—*"les Anglo-Saxons"* as he called them—added salt to the wound. This is, I think, why he was so adamant that France should be freed and ruled by the French and that he was the appropriate ruler—to free France not only from the Nazis but also from the Anglo-Saxons. He managed to outmaneuver both the Anglo-Saxons and the French communists to establish himself as the de facto leader of France following the liberation of Paris in August 1944. Such was his animosity towards the United States that he refused to meet with the dying Roosevelt in 1945. He was president of the Provisional Government of France from 1944 to 1946 and president of France from 1959 to 1969. Having insisted on being treated as one of the great powers and being a founding member of NATO, he withdrew from NATO in 1967.
Charles of Flanders	Charles was King Leopold's younger brother and served as regent of Belgium from 1944 to 1950 while Leopold was in disgrace, accused of collaboration with the enemy. The meeting I describe is fictitious.
Harry Hopkins	Harry Hopkins was Roosevelt's closest advisor and confidant from the New Deal period in the early 1930s until Roosevelt's death in 1945. He acted as Roosevelt's personal emissary to Churchill. He suffered from stomach cancer and its aftereffects throughout the war and died in 1946.
Philippe Kieffer	Kieffer was a founder of the Free French Navy's marine commandos and rose to command 1er Bataillon de Fusiliers Marins Commandos, known informally as Les Bérets Verts (the Green Berets). He personally led the famous attack on the Riva Bella Casino on D-Day and was one of the first Frenchmen to enter Paris when it was liberated.

Marie-Pierre Kœnig	Kœnig was a French general who fought with distinction in the Middle East and at the Battle of Bir Hakeim, where his 3,700 troops successfully resisted 37,000 soldiers of the Afrika Korps. He subsequently represented de Gaulle at SHAEF (due to de Gaulle's poisonous relationship with the British and Americans). He was placed in command of the French Forces of the Interior in June 1944, a conglomerate of all Résistance and Maquis forces.
Bernard Montgomery	I fear I have not painted Britain's most successful general in a very favorable light, but my portrait does reflect what his contemporaries thought of him. He was spiky and cantankerous, fiercely competitive, and chafed under Eisenhower's command. He was often criticized for excessive caution, which makes his rash endorsement of Operation Market Garden even more extraordinary.
Frederick Morgan	Frederick Morgan was a British general who was the original COSSAC when the Allied supreme command structure was first established and was responsible for the early Overlord planning. Eisenhower gave the COSSAC job to Beetle Smith when he was appointed Supreme Commander. Morgan was offered a field command but chose to stay as Deputy COSSAC. He was highly regarded by the Americans and had the thankless task of trying to reason with Montgomery.
George Patton	Patton took no part in D-Day, having been sidelined for slapping a soldier suffering from PTSD and used as window dressing for the fictitious USFAG. He took no part in Operation Market Garden. He was subsequently given command of the US Third Army, under Omar Bradley, and performed brilliantly, racing across France. In the Battle of the Bulge, he marched north from Luxemburg and successfully relieved the 101st Airborne in Bastogne. He was killed in a car accident in Germany shortly after the war ended. Patton was a complex character. He laced his words with profanities and believed in incarnation, as I have presented him.

Erwin Rommel	Erwin Rommel was a brilliant battlefield commander. In France in 1940, he raced to the English Channel, outflanking the British BEF and leaving it isolated in Dunkirk. Although he was defeated in North Africa, it should be remembered that he almost succeeded in taking Egypt and was starved of supplies by the survival of the British island of Malta (as I describe in *A Slender Thread*). Hitler admired Rommel but never gave him full control of the battlefield. Had Rommel had full control of the Panzer divisions in 1944, he might well have succeeded in throwing the Allies back into the English Channel. Rommel was seriously wounded on 17 July and took no further command. He was associated with the 20 July plot against Hitler, although not a prime mover; as a courtesy, Hitler allowed him to commit suicide on 14 October rather than face death by hanging and even gave him a state funeral.
SHAEF	The Supreme Headquarters Allied Expeditionary Forces had two locations, SHAEF Main located in Bushy Park in southwest London, and SHAEF Forward located in Portsmouth. SHAEF Forward was Eisenhower's immediate command center and moved with him, while SHAEF Main was the central staff and administrative organization. Both moved to Versailles, France, in September 1944, by which time SHAEF had ten thousand American and six thousand British staff. Eisenhower also used a number of temporary HQs as the battlefront moved. SHAEF Very Forward is fictitious, although it is true that Eisenhower had two companies of Rangers as a bodyguard.
Walter Bedell Smith	Known as Beetle Smith, he served as Eisenhower's chief of staff to the Supreme Allied Commander—COSSAC—from 1942 to 1945. During the war, he was frequently called upon to manage disputes between the senior Allied commanders, who were constantly competing for resources, particularly Patton and Montgomery. After the war, he held various government positions, including director of the CIA and US ambassador to the Soviet Union.
James Stagg	Stagg was the senior SHAEF Forward meteorologist who persuaded Eisenhower to delay D-Day from 5 to 6 June.

Kay Summersby	Kay Summersby was a British driver assigned to drive Eisenhower beginning in 1942 and became his constant companion, traveling with him. He arranged for her to become an American citizen, promoted her to captain, and awarded her the Bronze Star. She is generally assumed to have been his mistress, although the matter is hotly debated.
Kenneth Strong	Ken Strong was a British general who served as Eisenhower's head of Intelligence (G2) at SHAEF. Like my fictitious Eleanor, Strong warned of dangerous Panzer formations ahead of both Market Garden and the Battle of the Bulge but was ignored, first by Montgomery and then by Bradley.
Susan Travers	Susan Travers was a British driver who was a member of the French Foreign Legion. Early in the war, she drove doctors; subsequently she drove General Marie-Pierre Kœnig, with whom she had an affair. Her awards included the Croix de Guerre, the Legion d'Honneur, and the Medaille Militaire. She published her autobiography when she was ninety-one, having waited until all her contemporaries were dead.
Remy Van Lierde	Remy Van Lierde was a Belgian pilot who flew with the RAF. He first served in the noted 609 Squadron, which was manned entirely by non-British nationals. He is remembered principally for his courage and success against V1 rockets, shooting down over forty in his Hawker Tempest aircraft.
Gerd von Rundstedt	Von Rundstedt was Germany's most senior soldier before the war, retiring in 1938 at age sixty-four. He was recalled when war broke out. His subsequent career alternated between successes and dismissals when Hitler would blame him for a defeat but then reappoint him. He was in command of OB West during D-Day, dismissed, and reappointed for Market Garden and the Battle of the Bulge.
Chuck Yeager	Chuck Yeager was a young P51 pilot in 1944. After the war, he became one of the United States's most important test pilots. He became the first man to officially break the sound barrier in 1947, flying the famous Bell X1. He did marry Glennis, and they had four children.

David Strangeways	Strangeways was the principal architect of the various deception plans designed to deceive the Germans over D-Day, notably Operation Fortitude.
William of Orange	William of Orange was a real British carrier pigeon who flew from Arnhem to his home in England, carrying a message. He retired and lived at least another 10 years.
Dogs	George Patton had a bull terrier named Willie who outlived Patton and died in 1955 at the ripe old age of thirteen. He wore his own official GI dog tag. Bernard Montgomery had two puppies who traveled with him: a fox terrier named Hitler and a Cavalier Spaniel named Rommel. We can assume they were the only members of the Allied Expeditionary Force that did not dislike him. It is often said that Hitler hated Bouviers and ordered them killed, because he had once been bitten by one in World War I, but I have found no evidence that this is true. What is true is that German soldiers routinely shot dogs in occupied countries, and the Bouvier population of Belgium was decimated.
Weapons, Aircraft and Technology	
Advanced Landing Grounds (ALG)	ALGs were created and operated as I describe. However, my ALG in Dinant is fictitious.
Centaur/Comet	The Centaur was a derivative of the British Cromwell medium tank, powered by an American rather than a Rolls-Royce engine. The Centaurs saw limited service but were used on D-Day by the Royal Marines Armoured Support Group armed with a 95mm howitzer, the first time the lightly armed commandos had armor of their own. The Comet was an enhanced version introduced just before the end of the war.
Focke-Wulf Fw 190	The 190 was one of the Luftwaffe's duo of highly successful air superiority fighters, along with the Messerschmitt 109. It was competitive with its Allied adversaries until the end of the war and caused great damage to the USAAF's daylight B17 and B24 bomber fleets. Over twenty thousand were built.

Messerschmitt 262	The 262 was the first jet fighter to enter combat in World War II. Although it had limited effect because it was introduced so late in the war and in small numbers, it demonstrated that the era of propeller-driven fighters was drawing to a close. The characteristics I give it are accurate.
Mosquito	I wrote extensively about the Mosquito in the previous book in this series, *Trial and Tribulation*. Powered by two Merlin engines and constructed primarily from plywood, this aircraft was arguably the most versatile of all Allied aircraft and certainly one of the fastest. Mosquitos were as fast as Tempests and able to catch V1 rockets, shooting down over six hundred. Tsetse Mosquitos carrying the 57mm Molins gun were developed as anti-submarine weapons and saw limited action. I do not know of any instances in which Tsetses were used in the general ground-support role I have given them in this book, and certainly not for destroying V2 rockets on the ground.
P51 Mustang	The Merlin-powered North American P51 Mustang was a highly successful air superiority, long-range escort, and air-ground support fighter. It excelled in all these roles, but its most important accomplishment was, in my view, as a long-range escort fighter escorting B-17s and B-24s into German airspace. These missions forced the Luftwaffe to focus its resources on defending Germany, allowing the Allies to establish air superiority over France, Belgium, and Holland, which was an absolutely necessary prerequisite of the D-Day invasion. Indeed, it is fair to say that D-Day would not have been possible without the sacrifices of the P51 and B17 pilots.
Panzer IV to VI	The Panzer 4 was the principal German tank available on D-Day, with some Panzer 5 Panthers also available and a few Panzer 6 Tigers. The principal practical difference between these tanks was the increasing amount of armor they carried and therefore their survivability, offset by their decreasing maneuverability and increasing cost to produce. Fourteen thousand Panzer 4s and 5s were built; in comparison, the United States built fifty thousand Shermans.

PIAT	The Projector, Infantry, Anti-Tank was a British handheld spigot mortar, firing a 2-pound shaped charge projectile with an accurate range of 100 yards and capable of penetrating four inches of armor. Although clunky in appearance and use, it was highly effective: during the Normandy campaign PIATs knocked out more Panzers than RP3 rockets from aircraft.
RP3 Rocket	The RP3 was an air-to-ground rocket with a 60-pound warhead and a solid fuel propellant. First introduced in 1942, RP3-armed Typhoons were the RAF's principal air-ground support weapons. On D-Day, 2TAF had seven Typhoon (RP) and two Mustang (RP) squadrons available. Although many hundreds of Panzers were claimed during the campaign, particularly in the Falaise Pocket, only seventeen tanks were found to have been knocked out by RP3s.
Sherman DD	The Sherman DD (Duplex Drive) tank was an amphibious version of the Sherman with twin boat propellers driven off the rear idlers and high, inflatable waterproof canvas sides that rose six feet, higher than the turret. DD Shermans were the first tanks on all the D-Day beaches, launched from their landing craft a mile offshore and swimming to land. British tanks lacked DD technology and had to be landed directly on the beach. Much has been written comparing Shermans unfavorably to Panzers, but suffice it to say D-Day would not have been possible without them.
Stützpunkts/ Wilderstandnests	Wilderstandnests—nests of resistance—were defensive positions in the Atlantic Wall. Large or heavily fortified Wilderstandnests were known as Stützpunkts or strongpoints. They were numbered; thus, for example, the Riva Bella Casino captured by the French commandos was Wn 18. Hillman was Wn 17. I gave my imaginary Alvis the number Wn 06, which, as far as I know, was not allocated in real life. In real history, it took the Suffolks, with support from the 13th/18th Hussars, eight hours to overrun Hillman, and this delay is considered one of the primary reasons the British failed to reach Caen on D-Day.

Tempest	The Hawker Tempest was an advanced version of the Typhoon (see notes below). Produced in only limited numbers, it was the fastest fighter available capable of catching V1 rockets and is credited with shooting down 638 between August and October 1944, out of a total of approximately ten thousand V1s launched.
Thompson submachine gun	The M1A1 Thompson submachine gun was widely used by special service forces in World War II. It was a simplified and therefore more robust version of the M1928 "Chicago Typewriter" beloved by gangster movie fans. It had a straight 30-round magazine rather than the classic but failure-prone 100-round circular drum magazine. Contrary to the biases expressed by my fictional characters, it had an effective range of 150 yards. Bugsy Capone was Johnnie's conflating the gangsters Al Capone and Bugsy Siegel.
Typhoon	The Hawker Typhoon was the RAF's principal air-ground support fighter in the later stages of the war in Europe, often armed with eight RP3 rockets (see nearby notes.) The Typhoon was fast and strong, but its huge H-block twenty-four-cylinder Napier Saber engine was rushed into production too soon and proved to be problematic throughout its life.

ABOUT THE AUTHOR

John Rhodes is the award-winning author of the Second World War Breaking Point series, and of the Thomas Ford cozy detective series. Rhodes graduated from Cambridge University with an MA in History. His focus on World War II stems from his earliest memories—he grew up in London where, he says, the shells of bombed-out buildings "served as our adventure playgrounds." He is currently working on the next book in the Breaking Point series, and he blogs regularly at johnrhodesbooks.com.

Milton Keynes UK
Ingram Content Group UK Ltd.
UKHW040628111224
3594UKWH00019B/61